HIND....

Liz Harrison

For Margaret & Alan
With much love

Liz Harrison x

Published by Liz Harrison

ISBN 978 0 9928457 0 4

For Dad

And then she got bored and turned into a fish

HINDSIGHT

Prologue

I waved helplessly at the beach as my mouth filled with water and I went under again.

They hadn't seen me.

I fought back to the surface, coughing up and spitting out the foul sea. Gasping, kicking, clawing, trying to scream.

They didn't know I was here.

I could still hear the hollow music of the calliope jangling over from the fair, faint and distorted by the breeze.

It had been daddy's idea to come to the seaside for the day. The fun things were always daddy's idea. He had woken me at six thirty, singing Summer Holiday and dancing around my room in a huge red sombrero. He'd sung tunelessly along to the radio all the way from the house, whistling or telling jokes when he didn't know the words and winding the window down to enjoy a smoke when he didn't know the song at all.

The sickly sweet smell of seafood and doughnuts had made my tummy rumble as we wandered along the busy seafront. People had bustled in and out of the gift shops; trying on sunglasses, jangling novelty key rings and chuckling at cheeky postcards while children in swimsuits ran after their parents, bright buckets and spades rattling and banging against their sand stained legs.

I'd spotted a pair of glittery pink jelly shoes in the picture window of Johnsons Gifts and Souvenirs and begged daddy to buy them for me. After consulting his wallet he'd checked with mummy and then nodded, taking my hand and leading me into the cool shop. The glitter had sparkled in the hot sun and I'd imagined I was a princess. I'd hummed a song out of Cinderella but couldn't remember the words so I'd just kept singing that I was a princess.

Mummy told me to stop it.

At the fair they'd let me go on all the rides I wanted except the ones I wasn't tall enough for. Mummy had kept saying I was too little and I'd kept reminding her that I was nearly five and would be going to big school in two weeks. We had hotdogs and daddy laughed because I got red sauce all over my face and then all over the fluffy pink cloud of candyfloss that he'd bought for me.

By the time we left the fair to find a place on the beach where it was quiet enough for mummy to read and daddy to make a start on his crossword my feet had been throbbing and the shoes had started to bite. It was like having my feet inside two cheese graters. I'd wanted to put my pumps back on but mummy would have shouted so I'd shuffled along, trying to bend my feet as little as possible to stop them digging into my flesh. I'd sat in the warm sand and carefully removed the shoes. Long watery blisters had inflated along the sides of my feet. I'd winced. Poorlies always hurt more when you see them.

Mummy had called for me not to go out too far and I'd promised that I wouldn't. The sea had been deliciously cool. Dying waves had licked at the puffy flesh of my feet as sand squished pleasantly between my toes. Oh yes, today had been glorious.

But the candyfloss and the hot dogs didn't matter anymore. All that mattered was the water. It was all around me and I couldn't swim. As the endless struggle made me ache, the water started to feel thick like glue. Mummy and daddy looked like tiny dolls on the beach and every time I tried to scream for them my throat was flooded with horrible salty water.

I hadn't meant to go out this far. It had been those stupid shoes again. One of them had ended up in the water, bobbing past me as I paddled, and I'd known that if one of them got lost in the sea mummy would be mad. I'd followed it deeper and deeper and by the time I'd decided to go back and let them shout at me because I was on my tiptoes and getting frightened, it had been too late. I was going under for longer and longer now and knew that soon I wasn't going to come back up. I was so tired.

Miniature daddy's head appeared from behind his newspaper and then he stood up, looking around frantically. His eyes finally found me and he ran into the water. I could hear mummy screaming as pages from the newspaper fluttered past her but I couldn't make out the words.

I wrestled with the water, thrashing with my aching legs, tilting my face towards the bright sky as it became more difficult to keep afloat, waiting for daddy to come and rescue me. The salt was burning my eyes and my lungs felt like they would burst.

Then his arms were around me, safe and strong. I threw my arms around his neck and began to sob as I wrapped myself around him. I can't remember ever feeling safer than I did when I was in my daddy's arms.

'What are you doing all the way out here, Jess?' daddy asked.

'My shoe went in the sea,' I sobbed.

He told me to hold on tight and swam back towards the beach. When the water was shallow enough he scooped me up and carried me back to mummy.

'I'm sorry,' I said over and over again after throwing up a thin string of seawater and bile. Mummy started to shout at me and then at daddy and I sobbed harder than ever. I told her about the shoe and she shouted about that as well. I didn't know if she was pleased or not that I hadn't just floated away forever. Eventually she went back to her book. Daddy said nothing. He just held me to his chest, swaying and crying, glad that we were both safe.

'I love you, daddy,' I whispered.

Part One

1

My dad died when I was thirty years old.

I can't remember ever feeling so empty. Every hope I had died with him. Every part of me that felt I belonged somewhere in the world disappeared with his last breath. I felt scared and I felt lost and I felt cheated and it was only after he'd gone that I realised he was all I had. He'd always been there and I'd assumed that he always would be. It's not like he was old or anything.

When I walked through the door of our small living room with the shopping, when I saw him like that, his ashen face filled with fear as he gasped painfully for air; for the first time in years I wanted my mum. She had died when I was ten. Car. Too fast. Black ice.

When I called the ambulance his face was white. No, white's the wrong word. White has weight and texture. Dad's complexion had neither. The fifty two year old man I had to position carefully on the sofa to stop him choking on his own tongue, feeling his bones in my hand because his arms were so thin, looked seventy. Bright blue eyes that I'd inherited bulged in his head as they frantically searched the room, seeing things that weren't there. He spoke to invisible people, asked for things that I couldn't find. He called for my mother twice. Then he looked up at me with a childlike expression of wonder as if he couldn't understand why I was upset. His hand made a clumsy attempt to stroke my hair. 'Ess,' he managed, his voice thick with whatever had done this to him, and tears fell hopelessly over my cheeks.

The ambulance arrived quickly and rushed him into A&E. He'd blacked out at the house and they'd kept talking to him, trying to keep him conscious, trying to keep him alive. They did everything they could for over twelve hours. But they couldn't save him.

My dad, the dad I knew, was a big strong man with a red Santa Claus face and a modest beer belly. Over a period of time I hadn't measured he'd lost a lot of weight and the red face had faded to grey along with his beautiful thick black hair. It had all happened so slowly that I suppose I hadn't really noticed. Maybe I'd just thought that he was growing into middle age. I can't remember now.

After an operation to try to stem the internal bleeding they moved him up to intensive care and hooked him up to machines that would temporarily keep him alive. It was only then that I was allowed to see him.

All I could see was his head. His frail and damaged body was hidden, wrapped in a cocoon of white blankets. Machines beeped and hummed around him and a corrugated tube the width of a drainpipe ran from a large machine on the floor into the bottom of his bed. FOR USE IN RECOVERY ROOM ONLY was printed ironically on the side. Dad would have laughed at that.

It was like seeing a stranger. My brain told me it was my dad but somehow it wasn't. He looked too sick, too fragile. Only that morning we'd been watching a Queen tour DVD and he'd minced around the living room impersonating Freddie Mercury. He'd clutched his hip with one hand and held the TV remote to his mouth with the other as he sang. The only thing in his mouth now was a pipe that might have been feeding him oxygen. Blood had dried on his bottom lip and around his nostrils. But his eyes were the worst. I assumed they would be closed. They always are on TV.

Two small squares of hard transparent plastic had been placed over his eyes, forcing the blood from their lids and squashing their long lashes against his cheek. His head was resting on its side and the square over his left eye had slipped onto the blood spotted pillow. The eye was half open, the way it looked sometimes when he'd had too much to drink. But it wasn't shiny anymore. It was dull, like he was already dead. I looked into that eye for a long time and it didn't blink once. It just stayed open, staring into a room that he couldn't see. My heart ached with resignation and I felt sick to the stomach as I took it all in.

I put a gentle hand against his cheek. It was warm, but it didn't react to my

8

touch. The doctors had said that after the operation they hadn't had to sedate him, he'd slipped into a coma he'd never recover from. I kissed his forehead and slowly removed my shaking hand from his cheek. Then I sat down in a hard backed plastic chair to watch him die.

Fumbling beneath the blankets for his hand, I found another pipe threaded between his middle and third finger. I didn't want to know where it went. It didn't matter anymore. My fingers closed around his as the oxygen was reduced and his heartbeat began to fall slowly; 107, 106, 107, 106, 105, 106. When it got down to 74 the doctor turned a dial and it went straight back up to 90. I thought that maybe dad was trying to fight it, that he wouldn't leave me. Then it began to fall again. Once it got to 38 it fell more rapidly and I held his hand so tight, as if that would stop it from happening.

I was scared that his muscles would spasm, that he might suddenly grip my hand. You hear about stuff like that happening all the time. But he didn't. There was no drama, no sudden movement, no waking up and living through it. He was just another man dying in a hospital bed surrounded by machines.

His heartbeat fell to 0, jumped to 15, fell back to 0 and that was it. Just like that it was all over.

2

I could smell him on my clothes as I left the hospital, something between urine and new pennies, the high yellow smell of dying, putrid and heavy. Squinting in the early morning sunlight I stepped out into the cool and hazy dawn of a day that my dad would never see. Walking through the almost empty streets towards the bus station it felt like a horrible dream. I'd been awake for so long that nothing felt real anymore. I'd get home and open the door and dad would be in his chair attacking the crossword just like every other day.

He'd damaged his spine when I'd been eighteen. It had been my fault. I'd been angry and thinking about getting some gig tickets for the following night instead of thinking about how dangerous it would be to leave my shoes on the stairs where dad could fall over them. For a while he hadn't been able to walk at all. For the rest of his life he hadn't been able to stand up straight and he couldn't walk for long periods of time. So I'd forgotten my plans for uni and stayed at home to look after him. We'd sit up until the early hours of the morning; drinking, watching TV, talking about everything and nothing. I know it sounds weird and a lot of people probably don't think that rattling around a house all day with your dad is any kind of life, but I'd been happy enough. I didn't understand how detached we were from everything else because it never felt like that.

I stopped suddenly at a low brick wall, sitting down before I fell down. Didn't that make me responsible for this? At the hospital I'd been told that he'd had emphysema and jaundice and had been bleeding internally. How the hell had I missed all that? Alcoholic liver disease. That was something else he'd had. Something that had, more than likely, caused the emphysema, the jaundice and the internal bleeding. That made me responsible. I'd been the one drinking with him, buying another bottle of cider when we ran out. But to die of it? Wasn't that something that only happened to hopeless, bearded men that sat on

10

park benches with a bottle of cheap vodka clutched in their dirty, shaking hands?

He'd been fifty two but had the organs of an old man. Rotting from the inside out, hiding the blood he must have been coughing up for god only knew how long. My dad must have known that he was dying and he'd never said a word.

I took a deep breath before I got up and started to walk again. Without him I had nobody. The only living family I had were my maternal grandparents. They ran a pub in Yorkshire and I used to spend the summer holidays with them after mum died but they asked me not to go there one summer, I don't remember why, then dad had had an argument with grandma Jean and we hadn't spoken to them since. The only person I ever really spoke to was the woman that usually served me at the Co-Op and I couldn't remember her name.

I took the first bus to the estate and made my way to our house with only dark thoughts of blood and death for company. My head hurt with them. I stopped at the space where our gate had once hung an unknown time ago and stood, looking across our messy patch of garden at the house. I couldn't go inside. I looked up at his bedroom window, at the nicotine stained net curtain that he'd been threatening to wash but never gotten round to.

'I'll do it tomorrow, Jessica. My back's playing up and I think I need to rest it today.' I'd always smiled at his excuses. A smile that I couldn't help even though I was trying to look stern. That smile was something else I'd inherited from the man who now occupied a long metal drawer in the hospital morgue.

I wondered where my dad was now, what he'd seen after he died. Did anyone come to collect him? Did he know I'd been there at the end? Questions that would go forever unanswered. I knew there was at least fifteen pounds of his money in the house. What would I do with it? With his shoes? His toothbrush? His clothes? At the moment the most important question was where could I go? The only person I'd ever been close to apart from dad was

11

Scott and I thought that maybe he wouldn't want to see me.

I knew he wouldn't want to see me.

Scott Jordan hated me.

I couldn't blame him, I suppose. He'd been the only real boyfriend I'd ever had and I'd dumped him for my dad. He'd asked me to marry him, I'd said I couldn't leave dad to look after himself, we'd both shouted, I'd left. End of story. That had been almost eight years ago and we hadn't spoken since. But I couldn't go inside and he was the only person I could think of.

I sighed as I headed for his parents house. His now. His parents had emigrated to Spain and Scott had stayed there alone. Or so I'd heard.

What the hell was I going to say?

I probably wouldn't get the chance to say anything. He'd probably just slam the door in my face.

I stopped outside his house. The black iron gate was still intact, recently repainted. I pushed it open and walked down the narrow path to the new front door. He probably didn't even live here anymore. I knocked and waited, finger brushing my hair in an effort to look somewhere near presentable, and then I knocked again. Any minute now some ninety year old stranger would answer the door and I'd be lost. I'd try to explain what I was doing knocking on the door before seven on a Sunday morning, the stranger would take one look at me and phone the police.

The reality was worse. A Scott Jordan I'd obviously woken up opened the door and I winced. When he saw me on the doorstep his sleepy expression changed to something between suspicion and disbelief. He stood in the doorway with his mouth open, waiting for an explanation while I shuffled uncomfortably from foot to foot.

'Can I come in please?' I asked feebly.

Scott looked up and down the street and then back at me. He folded his arms over his chest, an old habit that said he was well outside of his comfort zone, and shook his head.

'You're still mad at me?' I frowned. 'Scott, it's been eight years.'

'It's early.' His voice was full of sleep. His hair was shorter.

'But I've got nowhere else to go,' I tried to explain.

'You look like shit.'

I rolled my eyes. 'Well, you're still as charming as ever.'

'Why are you here?'

I ran the last few hours over in my head and blinked back tears.

He yawned. 'Look, Jess, I don't know why you're here and I really couldn't care less. It's early and I want to go back to bed. If you want to talk, come back in another eight years and we'll see how I feel then.'

'Please, Scott. I can't go home.' I hated how desperate I sounded.

'Why not?' he asked. 'Did you finally kill the bastard?'

My mouth fell open and tears stung my eyes before they rolled helplessly over my face. I turned to leave.

'Jess?'

'Forget it,' I called back.

I heard him coming after me, his bare feet slapping against the concrete path, then he was pulling me back. His eyes searched mine and I was relieved to see in them something that could be concern.

'Jess, what happened?'

I tried to talk, couldn't, and instead burst into fresh tears, gasping for breath. His arms encircled my exhausted body and I let him hold me, my arms dangling, my head lolling against his shoulder. He led me into the house and closed the door.

'Sit down, I'll get you a coffee.'

I sat down heavily on the huge cream sofa. 'I don't want any coffee.'

'Did you and your dad have a fight?' he asked. 'Because I really don't think I'm the best person to talk to if you did.'

13

'We didn't have a fight.' My throat felt tight and sore.

'Why would you come here after what happened the last time we spoke?' he asked as he sat beside me

I looked at my lap, remembering the argument, the tears, slamming the door on my way out.

'I didn't know where else to go.'

'What happened?'

'He died, Scott.'

Silence filled the room and I felt sorry for him. He couldn't possibly know what to say.

'I, I'm so sorry,' he stammered. 'When?'

He was struggling to stop himself from folding his arms over his chest again. This was about a million miles outside of his comfort zone.

'A couple of hours ago.' Crying again. 'I'm sorry, Scott. I just couldn't go back into that house.'

'Sure you don't want a drink?'

I nodded. 'I just need somewhere to sleep.'

He left the room and I looked around. The furniture and carpets were new and it had also been decorated recently. The walls were an unbroken buttery shade of yellow and fresh gloss shone along the skirting boards. Scott came back with a blanket and a pillow. 'You can crash down here if you like,' he offered. 'We can talk later.'

He turned to leave and I searched frantically for something to say, tired of being alone with my tedious brain churning the last twenty four hours over and over.

'What have you been doing for the last eight years?' I asked quickly.

'Get some sleep and we'll talk later,' he replied, making his way to the stairs.

'I've been doing more or less the same as I always did,' I tried to joke.

'Surely you must have some gossip for me?'

He turned towards me and smiled. It was a smile I'd had seen a thousand times before, something familiar in the new Twilight Zone that was my life.

'Maybe I should start with Joanne Howard.'

Joanne Howard. I hadn't heard the name in years. 'Joanne Howard the psychopath?'

'Joanne Howard my wife.'

'Oh.' My eyes went back to my lap.

'You should try to get some sleep.'

'Yeah,' I agreed numbly. *Joanne Howard?*

I didn't dream and only slept for a couple of hours. When I woke up I could smell the unmistakable aroma of the great British fry up coming from the kitchen. My stomach growled as I went to the kitchen door and looked in at him. Once upon a time he'd been mine and a selfish part of me wished that he'd just waited until today. How easy it would be to just stay here with him.

He smiled when he saw me. 'I hope you're hungry.'

'You didn't have to,' I replied, pleased that he had.

'It's your favourite. I know I can't cook it quite how you like it but I'll do my best to burn it in the right places.'

I laughed. Dad had been a terrible cook. He'd always burnt whatever he'd tried to make so I'd done most of the cooking and he had been responsible for cleaning duties. That's why we'd lived on microwave meals and the house had always been a mess. Har de har har.

'So, how is Joanne?' I asked purely to make conversation, hoping he'd fill me in on some flesh eating disease she'd contracted.

'Okay,' he called back over the noise of sizzling meat. 'You're lucky, she's with her parents.'

'Why?'

'They're moving. She's giving them a hand.'

'Why didn't you go?' Maybe there'd been an argument.

'You know I can't do heavy lifting because of my shoulder.'

My heart sank. No disease, no argument. I was something from the past and I had no place here now.

He plated up the food and we went back to the living room. I should have spotted the wedding photos. Scott looked proud and happy. Joanne looked smug. I hated her. She'd always wanted Scott, must have sharpened her claws as soon as she'd heard we were over.

'When did you marry her?'

'Last summer.'

'Congratulations.' The word left a sour taste in my mouth.

'Thanks.'

I ate quickly, barely tasting the food. The last time I'd eaten was at breakfast yesterday and I was ravenous.

'Would you like a shower?' he asked while I mopped up grease with a slice of fried bread.

I nodded. 'A shower would be good.'

'Well, you know where it is.' He picked up the plates and went back to the kitchen. 'Towels are in the airing cupboard.'

The hall and staircase had been decorated too. I ran dirty fingers over embossed wallpaper thick with large pink flowers before I went into the bathroom and turned on the shower as I undressed. This room was deep blue with stencilled goldfish swimming nowhere fast around the walls. Their toothbrushes stood side by side in a plastic cup on the windowsill beside a hairbrush with her hair entangled in the bristles. Her deodorant. Her razor.

I stepped into the shower, tilting my head back and closing my eyes against the water as my thoughts went back to dad. He'd had three heart attacks before he'd died. The first had been strange. His face had twisted and he had reached up, curling his arms over his head in silent slow motion. His agony had been

16

obvious, but there had been nothing I could do about it.

The second had been like something out of a horror film. He had tried to sit up but had been too weak to move properly. Blood had spewed from his mouth and nose, so much of it, warm and bright, staining the blankets, running over his face and chest. I'd been asked to leave and ushered away when I'd discovered that my feet wouldn't move and I couldn't take my eyes away from the monster on the bed.

After I'd showered, using their soap and shampoo, I dried with their towels. I used her deodorant, which smelled like flowers; big pink ones no doubt. I didn't clean my teeth.

The sound of the television floated up from downstairs as I looked curiously across the landing at Scott's room. If I was quick he'd never know. I hurried to the door and pushed it open slowly. I'd been in here so many times before. The first time we'd made love had been in this room, slow and quiet so we wouldn't wake his parents, the only sound his breath in my ear.

Now it was the same hideous pink as the stairs and smelled of lavender. This had to be Joanne. Scott would never have decorated like this. There was a new bed, new curtains, photos of them in places I'd never been, Scott wearing clothes I'd never seen him in before. The dresser was home to her make up, her jewellery, blister packs of her birth control pills. Bile rose in my throat. The thought of them together in bed repulsed me.

If I died right now nobody would mourn me. Nobody would miss me because to most of the world I'd never existed in the first place.

'I thought you were taking a while.'

I gasped and spun around to see Scott standing behind me at the door.

'I, I was just, I didn't mean any harm.' Struggling for words again. 'I just wanted . . . I was being nosy,' I surrendered.

He managed a small smile. 'Changed since you were last here.'

I nodded, looking distastefully at the collection of pottery cats in the

17

windowsill. 'I'm going to ring my grandparents,' I said. 'They live near York, maybe they'll let me stay with them for a few days.'

I took out my phone as we went back downstairs, finding the number for my own grandparents via Google. An unfamiliar female voice answered, cutting short the second ring. 'Good morning, The Unicorn?'

I was silent for a moment. Then I leaned against the wall at the bottom of the stairs and spoke cautiously. 'Hi, er, is Jean or Don around please?'

It was the woman's turn to be silent.

'Hello?' I ventured.

'Do you mean Jean and Don Baker?'

'Yes,' I replied.

'They left here a good four years ago,' she said. 'Retired down to Cornwall.'

'Oh.' I said, ignoring Scott who wasn't trying to hide the fact that he was listening to every word. 'I don't suppose you've got an address or a phone number for them?'

'I haven't, I'm sorry.'

'What about Geoff Carpenter?' I asked. 'Would he know?'

More silence. 'I'm sorry,' the woman said. 'Geoff died last year. He had a stroke.'

My brain stopped working and I could only listen to the static silence between us as I struggled to think of something else to ask. Scott took the phone, exchanged a few words with the unfamiliar woman, and then he hung up.

'I don't know what to do,' I murmured. 'I need to go back to the house. It's all got to be sorted out but . . .' I trailed off, I didn't want to stay here but the thought of going back there, moving things from where dad had left them, that was worse.

'I can come with you if you like,' Scott offered.

I nodded dumbly. Maybe I'd be okay if he was with me. Joanne would be back tonight and Scott wouldn't be allowed anywhere near me for the rest of his life. She hated me almost as much as I despised her. Bitch.

I started to play with the radio as Scott drove towards the house, trying to distract myself. I remembered a boy at school, Dean, who had said that when his parents argued he used to shut himself in his room and play with the radio, replacing the angry sounds downstairs with something, anything, that wasn't his crying mother or violent father.

When we arrived I had to force myself out of Scott's car and towards the house, slowing as I approached the door, unsure of myself. I didn't think I could do it. A comforting hand stroked my shoulder and I managed to lift the impossibly heavy key to the lock but when the door swung open I could smell him again and I sat down hard on the doorstep with my back to the house, holding my head in my hands.

'I can't do it.'

Scott sat beside me and put his arm around my shoulders. 'Maybe you should leave this for a while,' he said.

'Seeing as I've got so many alternatives,' I replied sarcastically. I wanted to take it back as soon as I'd said it.

'I can go in first if it helps,' he offered softly and I was grateful.

I nodded and followed him into the eerie quiet of the house, closing the door behind us. I could smell dad everywhere as we went through to the living room and I looked around, taking in how much was his. His coat was draped over the back of his chair, his slippers lay under the old gas fire and his tobacco tin sat untouched on the coffee table.

'Are you alright?'

I nodded but I didn't dare look at him. 'It's just strange,' I explained. 'Everything's exactly where he left it and if I don't move it it'll stay there forever. What am I supposed to do with it all?'

'Whatever you want to,' he replied. 'We'll sort it between us.'

19

I knew he was trying to comfort me but all I kept wondering was how he really felt about outliving my dad. I knew it wasn't fair but I thought that maybe he'd enjoy throwing dad's stuff out.

I picked up dad's coat. Searching the pockets I found seventeen forty five in crumpled notes and change, painkillers, a handful of old bus tickets.

'What do you want me to do?' Scott asked, bringing my thoughts away from blood and hospitals. His stuff was everywhere and all of it had to go somewhere.

'There are bin liners under the sink,' I said robotically. 'We'll start in here.'

3

Scott ordered pizza around five. I hadn't felt hungry but I polished off my half with vigour. We had a break for half an hour and sat together on the sofa, talking about old times. He even mentioned a few funny things dad had done, laughing genuinely at the memories.

The first time I'd introduced Scott to dad it had been tense. Scott had been the first boy I'd ever introduced as my boyfriend and he'd been desperate to impress while dad had been trying to judge whether or not the scrawny teenager was deserving of his only daughter. When I'd asked dad what he thought he'd said Scott was 'alright I suppose'.

The end of their brief friendship had come the next day. I had been in my room when the phone rang.

'Jess?' dad had called up the stairs. 'Snot's on the phone.'

I'd been mortified that Scott might have heard. Dad had handed the phone over innocently and gone back to his crossword.

'Hi, babe,' I'd said brightly, praying that he'd been afflicted with temporary deafness.

'Did your dad just call me Snot?' he'd asked. The seriousness in his voice would have made me laugh if I hadn't been so embarrassed.

'I don't think so,' I'd replied, glancing over at dad who'd looked like a child feigning innocence even when they're caught holding the felt tip that scrawled the bad word on the wall.

Scott had invited me out for the afternoon. We'd agreed to meet at three, he'd sound the horn when he arrived, no need to come into the house.

Replacing the receiver I'd gone through to the living room. 'Why did you do that?'

Dad had shrugged. 'Thought it might make you laugh.'

'Calling my boyfriend Snot?' If I'd been honest I would have admitted that I couldn't say the word without fighting back a smile.

'Well he gets up my nose,' he'd replied seriously.

I'd managed to get back to my room before the laughter escaped. Whether or not dad had known that I'd thought it was funny I didn't know. But the name had stuck and Dad had never called him Scott again after that day.

When all the pizza was gone Scott rang Joanne to let her know that he probably wouldn't be home when she got back. He didn't get the chance to say much after he mentioned my name and I took the pizza box outside to the wheelie bin while they argued, feeling the chill air of late autumn against my skin as daylight faded.

After he hung up we went to dad's bedroom. My head throbbed and my heart ached and I felt so drained. It's strange. When people die everything has sentimental value, everything is precious because there will never be anything new. What there is now is all there will ever be to show for a whole lifetime. The dog ends in the ashtray were suddenly precious to me because he'd held them in his hands, they had touched his lips.

Scott went in first and I followed hesitantly. The whole room smelled of him. This was his space. This had been where he'd slept and woken up, where he'd dreamed and dressed. I sat on the bed, picking up his pillow, smelling him like he was in the room with me as I pressed it to my face. It could have been him sitting beside me and telling me it was okay to cry.

When dad's parents had died I'd been twelve. He'd held me so tight that his fingers had pinched into my ribs as he told me that if I wanted to cry that was okay but it was okay if I didn't cry as well because everyone was different. But this time it wasn't dad. Dad would never hold me again. And I did cry. I cried until I thought that my eyes would bleed.

I couldn't just throw his things away. I sat quietly with almost everything, just for a few moments, before I let them disappear forever. We put his clothes in a black bag. All except the only suit he'd owned which he would wear to his funeral. When I pulled the duvet off the bed I froze, my breath caught in my sore throat. There was a large dark bloodstain on the sheet near his pillow. Scott looked at me for an explanation but I could only stare blankly at the place where he'd coughed it up and hidden it like an animal burying its' shit. I dropped the duvet, quickly pulled off the sheet, trying to ignore the stiff maroon spots that had soaked through to the mattress, and stuffed it into a bag with his pyjamas, his alarm clock and his ashtray. Nothing was going to charity. I didn't want people to be walking around in this dead mans clothes or waking up to his alarm when his own time had expired.

It took two hours to clean the small room because I kept stopping and telling Scott stories that were already taking on the painful tone of nostalgia.

'What are these?' Scott asked as he held up three splintered wooden balls, looking confused. I laughed long and hard.

We'd gone to the fair once when I'd been eight or nine and I remembered being so excited. Loud music blared from huge speakers, the smell of frying food and sugar made my belly rumble, people laughed and screamed and men hollered, 'Only two seats left,' 'Scream if you want to go faster.' Bright lights illuminated the ecstatic faces of teenagers as they swung higher and higher on the rides that I hadn't been big enough for.

'Come on, roll up, three balls for a pound!' The man at the coconut shy practically threw himself in front of dad. 'Only a pound,' he roared, thrusting the balls out in front of him.

'Three?' dad asked. 'And you only want a pound?'

I watched with interest as dad pulled a pound out of his pocket. Mum was looking at a big fluffy tiger hanging at the back of the rickety stall.

Passing the man his money, dad took the balls. 'Bargain,' he commented as he strolled off towards the waltzer, leaving the man slack mouthed and speechless behind him. Mum scuttled after him, dragging me behind her. Later, dad would make lots of jokes about how his balls were too big to get in his pockets and how heavy they were.

'Keep,' I said quietly.

Scott sat on the stripped bed and yawned. 'Come and stay with us for a couple of days.'

I shook my head. 'Joanne wont have me anywhere near your house and you know it.'

'You can't stay here on your own, Jess,' he protested. 'Just for a few days until you feel...' his voice faded to nothing.

What? I thought. *Better?* I was glad he'd realised how stupid he sounded before he'd finished.

'There's really no need.'

'There's every need. Joanne'll understand.'

I raised an eyebrow at him and he went to the phone without another word. She immediately proved me right. He explained the situation to her four times and raised his voice twice. I went to the kitchen and poured myself a pint of cheap cider, what dad had always called chemicals and alcohol. Hadn't stopped him drinking it though, had it? Joanne was reacting exactly as I would in her position. There was silence for a while then Scott returned red faced to the sofa.

'She was fine.'

I laughed so hard that I almost choked on my drink and he laughed too. We sat up until the early hours talking about the last eight years. Scott was teaching maths like he'd said he would, Joanne was working for some insurance company in town. I didn't really listen to that part.

'I waited a long time, hoping you'd come back,' he said. 'I just thought you might want to know that it was a long time before me and Joanne got together.'

I didn't. I didn't want to talk about that.

'I suppose I'd better get some sleep.' He said it purely to fill the silence. 'I've got to be up for work in the morning.'

'Thanks again for today.'

I went to bed, leaving him to finish his drink and let himself out. I cried as quietly as I could until sleep came, dark and dreamless.

4

I woke up at eleven thirty and stretched, feeling marginally better than I had when I'd woken up at Scott's yesterday, more refreshed. But right away the space in my life that only dad could fill gaped.

'Jess, do you want the bathroom before I park my breakfast?'

He'd called variations of the same theme into my room every morning for the past ten years after I complained that I couldn't clean my teeth in a room that smelled like whatever he'd just dumped into the toilet had crawled up his backside and died a while ago.

I wanted to walk down the stairs and see his familiar figure hunched over the crossword, listening to Radio 2 with his reading glasses perched on the end of his nose like an old headmistress. Resigning myself to the fact that that wasn't going to happen I pulled on underwear and wandered downstairs. If I wanted clean clothes I'd have to iron.

I stopped dead at the bottom of the stairs, listening to the noises I could hear from behind the living room door. I'd heard about other houses on the estate getting broken into after people died, scavengers looking for anything of value, but it didn't normally happen when someone was still living in the house.

I'm going to be murdered in underwear that doesn't even match, I thought stupidly.

I could only stand and watch with wide unblinking eyes, struggling with my bladder as the living room door opened. I knew it would let go as soon as I saw them; doped up strangers with knives. I was going to die in a white bra and purple pants and I'd take my last breath as I lay in a puddle of my own piss and blood.

Scott cried out when he saw me. Luckily my bladder didn't let go and I let out a hard sigh instead. I hadn't realised I'd been holding my breath.

'You said you were going to work,' I shouted, more scared than angry.

'I called in sick,' he explained.

'You scared the shit out of me.'

He gave me a look that said he'd experienced much the same thing. 'You want to put some clothes on.'

I walked past him into the kitchen and fumbled through the ironing basket. 'They need ironing.'

'You put a coat on or something and I'll do it.'

He was looking everywhere but in my direction. His cheeks were flushed and he was tugging uncomfortably at the bottom of his shirt. Another Scott Jordan anxiety trait that I'd somehow forgotten existed.

I handed him a pair of jeans and a tee shirt and went back to the hall for a coat.

'Do you want any breakfast?' he asked.

'I don't think there's much in,' I called as I put on my heavy winter coat and went back to the kitchen. He was frowning as he examined the sparse contents of the fridge. 'Told you.'

Dads last meal had been sausage and mash with onion gravy. We had half an onion left, a few eggs and mushrooms, cheese and a quarter pint of milk. Half a loaf of bread sat on the worktop. Scott checked the empty freezer.

'How do you live like this?' he asked.

'Fine,' I replied defensively.

'Jesus Christ, Jess, this is horrendous. There's more mould in the fridge than food. You can't enjoy living like this.'

'Well this was my first choice, Scott, so I suppose that says a lot for you, doesn't it?' I regretted the words as soon as they left my mouth. 'I'll make breakfast,' I added quietly.

The shopping I'd bought yesterday had been a couple of microwave joint things for Sunday dinner but they'd been thawing out on the living room floor since… since then. They'd ended up in the bin.

Scott found the iron and plugged it in silently, laying the jeans out on the worktop.

'Omelette?' I asked. He didn't reply. 'I'm sorry.' It was almost a whisper.

'You're upset. I understand.'

'I didn't mean to shout at you.'

No reply.

I busied myself with breakfast until he passed me my clothes and I put them on silently while he sat down and turned on the TV, flicking through the channels until he settled on an old episode of Open All Hours. I put the kettle on and took dad's old address book from a drawer beneath the microwave. I'd have to phone all the people he used to work with, his old friends, the council and the funeral parlour. But I wanted my omelette and a mug of coffee first. As I served breakfast I noticed countless stains on the table, coffee rings that we'd never bothered to clean up. Well, it wasn't like we'd been expecting company.

I curled up in the chair behind the living room door, his chair, and began to eat. Scott ate without offering a word of thanks, taking a long swallow of coffee when he had finished. His face crumpled with disgust but he noticed me looking at him and attempted a careful smile. I suppose after the fridge comment he was scared of what I'd say if he questioned the quality of our 47p Best Café. I put down my fork and pressed the back of my hand against a smile. He glanced at me from the corner of his eye and put the mug back onto the table. I picked up my own, drinking deeply, and his mouth curved downwards as if he could taste the bitter liquid himself.

'Mmm!' I exclaimed dramatically. 'Nothing like a hot mug of cats piss to get the day started.' I rubbed my belly enthusiastically as a grin split his face.

'That's got to be the worst coffee in the world,' he agreed cautiously.

'Dad made it better than me,' I replied.

'It certainly couldn't get any worse.'

28

After we'd cleared away the breakfast pots I rang the names in dad's address book. I didn't think I actually knew any of these people and they probably didn't even remember my dad. It was horrible. They didn't know what to say to me, I didn't know what to say to them. I just explained what had happened, promised to be in touch with the date of the funeral and accepted their sympathetic words. The answer phones were the worst but Scott kept giving me the thumbs up and flashing smiles of reassurance.

'You're doing fine,' he said as he brought me my third mug of Gold Blend that he'd fetched from the supermarket. I smiled, sick of talking. I was putting off picking up the death certificate.

'If you want to go today, I'll take you,' Scott said. He knew me better than anyone. Well, anyone that was still alive.

'I don't know if I can.'

'If we go today at least you wont be on your own,' he said as we sat together on the sofa. 'You might struggle if you have to go on your own.'

I had to agree. At the moment I was numb. The tears had dried up, the emotions were on hold. Being handed a piece of paper confirming that my dad was indeed dead, deceased, dinner for the worms, I didn't know how that would affect me. And I thought that Scott was right. I'd need help.

'Okay,' I said quietly.

5

I told the middle aged receptionist that I had come to collect my dads death certificate and while I struggled not to choke on the words, she didn't even flinch. She'd heard it before. Happened all the time. She phoned somebody and told me to take a seat. Scott put an arm around my shoulders, trying to comfort me as we sat down.

'It'll be okay,' he said. 'I'm here, Jess.'

I nodded but couldn't meet his eyes. It wasn't that I didn't appreciate him being there, he just wasn't dad. Dad was never coming back and how long would it be before Scott had to go back to the life I had disrupted? Soon I would be alone and the thought of it scared the hell out of me.

'Miss Morgan?' I looked up at the smartly dressed woman and nodded dumbly. 'Would you like to come with me please?'

I stood up, swaying on my feet. Scott put a supportive arm around my waist and led me after her into a quiet room that looked much like the ones I'd sat in, hour after restless hour, waiting to hear how my dad was doing and hoping that soon I'd be able to take him home. Scott sat with me on a pale blue sofa and the woman sat in a large yellow chair on the other side of the small room offering me a big friendly smile. I ignored it. I'd seen that before as well.

'My name is Sandra Thompson. I'm a consultant here at Medway. Were you related to Mr Morgan?'

'I'm his daughter.' I stared vacantly at the floor. 'This is Scott. He's my friend.'

She nodded. Sandra Thompson understood perfectly. 'Now, unfortunately we can't release the certificate until our coroner, Dr Murray, has signed it.'

Here we go. More bad news.

'Now, because your father died in the early hours of Sunday morning,'

Sandra Thompson continued, 'Dr Murray wasn't on duty. He's not due back until this evening.'

I knew that I was new to the whole death procedure but surely you couldn't be expected to die between nine and five Monday to Friday.

'So it's not ready,' I said flatly. 'Couldn't anybody have let me know?'

Sandra Thompson flashed the all knowing, all understanding smile again and apologised. 'If you give the coroners office a call first thing tomorrow morning it should be ready for your collection.' She handed me a piece of paper with the coroners office telephone number printed neatly in blue ink.

'Okay,' I said resignedly, getting up to leave. 'I'll ring tomorrow. Thank you.'

Scott put his arm around me again and led me outside. I felt tired and dizzy.

'Do you want to sit down?'

I could only nod as I sat down hard on the floor beside the entrance to the hospital.

'Are you alright?'

I didn't answer. Everything had a dreamy quality to it. The colours of the world were sharp and bright like a cartoon and I felt lost, detached. I wasn't here. I was watching this from the outside. Scott sat down as I watched people going in and out of the hospital, looking at me with curiosity or distaste. I didn't care what they thought. My dad was dead, I missed him, and I couldn't do a thing about it.

'His stomach was bleeding,' I said to nobody in particular. 'They couldn't stop it. Everything just decided to stop working.'

'Is she okay?' A tall man stood over us. He was holding the gloved hand of a small girl who peeped out at me from behind her father's legs as if I were a dangerous animal.

'She'll be fine,' Scott replied.

'Does she need a doctor, daddy?' the girl asked.

31

'I'm not sure, darling.'

I stared at Darling. She held on to Daddy's hand tightly; he would protect her. He was her dad and he wouldn't ever let anyone hurt her.

'He'll tell you he's fine,' I mumbled. 'He'll tell you that you're worrying about nothing and then he'll go to bed and he'll bleed and he'll hide it. And you wont know that your daddy's dying until you can't do a fucking thing about it.'

Darling's eyes grew wide as she shrunk back behind Daddy.

'Jess, you're scaring her,' Scott said as he pulled me to my feet, trying to drag me in the direction of the car park.

As Daddy pulled Darling inside the hospital tears exploded from my eyes and the strength drained from my legs. I would have slithered bonelessly to the floor if Scott hadn't held onto me, and then another strong arm clutched at my back. I looked up to see a man in his mid thirties looking back at me with a concerned, somehow familiar, face.

'Is she okay?'

'Her dad died,' Scott explained. 'She's upset.'

'I know you,' I said quietly. The man didn't hear.

'Wow,' he said. 'Look, I've got a friend, he's a bereavement counsellor. He could probably help. He's on his lunch break at the moment. I can find him if you want.'

'If you could just help me get her to the car,' Scott said.

The man with the familiar face nodded and lifted me into his arms. As he carried me to the car I linked my hands at the back of his neck and stared into his calm, concerned eyes. His arms were safe and strong and I could have stayed in them for a long time. As he set me down Scott bundled me into the passenger seat.

'Thank you.'

The man smiled down at me. 'Sure you'll be okay from here?'

'Yes,' Scott said before I could reply. 'Thanks again for helping me out.'

'No problem.' The man offered me one last sympathetic smile before he walked away.

'I know him,' I said, considering calling him back. I didn't want him to leave.

'Really?' Scott was stretching the seatbelt over my chest. 'Who is he?'

I thought for a few seconds before admitting that I didn't know. Maybe he just looked like someone I knew or had one of those faces that lots of people think that they've seen before. But he'd made me feel so *safe*.

Scott knelt beside me and took my hands in his own. 'Just try to calm down,' he soothed.

'I can't do this, Scott,' I sniffed. The panic was back and I was starting to shake. 'He was everything to me and now he's gone and…'

'Jess, there's a whole world outside that house.'

'I don't care,' I sulked. 'I want my dad.'

6

Scott followed me into the house and I filled two glasses with cider, handing one to him.

'I'm driving,' he said.

'Don't drink it then,' I replied.

He took the glass and almost emptied it. I refilled it for him and we went to the sofa. Looking at him as he sat beside me it was hard not to just reach out and lay my hand over his. Memories of his kiss, his touch, his smell, all lost. Everything was gone. Nothing was mine.

'Do you remember when we went camping?' Scott asked with a smile.

Burgers cooked on a disposable barbeque lit only by the headlights of his Peugeot; the frigid 4am air forcing us into the car where we could bathe in the warmth of the heater on the dashboard. I nodded.

Scott took another long drink from his glass and smiled again. Some part of him felt the same as I did, wanted to be back there. There was something safe about looking at the past. If the memories were good you laughed and relived them. If the memories were bad you shrugged and said that part of your life was gone, that it had made you stronger or smarter and that you wouldn't be the person you were now without that bad experience. And you'd wonder how things might have been different if you'd known then what you knew now.

'I sold the tent,' Scott said as he set his empty glass down on the coffee table.

'But you loved that tent!'

He nodded. 'I just hated camping.'

We both laughed and it was almost like nothing had changed. Scott and I were together, my dad was alive and all was well. A glance at the empty chair in the corner proved otherwise and the laughter died on my lips.

'Shall we have another drink?' Scott asked.

I looked at my glass. It was still half full. 'You help yourself,' I replied. 'But she's going to kill you.'

'She doesn't scare me,' he said as he picked up his glass and went to the kitchen. He was a bad liar.

I looked over at the empty chair again, wishing it was my dad I could hear pouring a fresh drink and muttering under his breath as foam swelled and spilled over the rim of the glass. I was starting to regret throwing his stuff out so early. I would have liked a few days just to . . . to what?

'Why don't you stay with us tonight?' Scott asked as he sat down. I threw him a look that said the reason I wouldn't stay with them tonight was obvious. He put his drink down and slid an arm around my shoulders.

'You shouldn't be on your own.'

I closed my eyes. Whether it was the familiar smell of him or how his arm felt around me I neither knew nor cared. What I did know was that he was here now and I didn't ever want him to leave. As if he could hear my thoughts he gave my shoulder a gentle squeeze and kissed my temple.

'She wouldn't let me stay even if I did come to yours,' I said. 'I'll be fine. I just got a bit overwhelmed at the hospital.'

He pulled me closer to him and I laid my head against his chest. 'You broke down,' he replied. 'If it hadn't been for that bloke I'd never have got you back to the car.' He started to rub my neck and I closed my eyes again, feeling drowsy and drained.

'Do you remember the day we went to the lake?' he asked. 'The day it rained?'

The temperature of the room seemed to rise substantially as his lips brushed against the nape of my neck. I could only nod.

'I still think about that day,' he continued. 'It always makes me smile.'

I didn't want to go down this road. I felt hot and confused and uncomfortable, but I couldn't bring myself to break the embrace. 'Let me keep

35

you safe, Jess.'

I took his arm from around my shoulders and shook my head. 'I think that you should think about what you're doing,' I said softly.

He only looked at me sadly. 'I should have waited for you.'

'Until dad died, you mean?'

'No.' He raised his hands defensively. 'I didn't mean it like that. I meant,' he paused and then dropped his hands into his lap. 'Whatever I say's going to sound wrong.'

'It's been a long couple of days. You just need some proper rest.'

The silence that followed was heavy and uncomfortable. Scott tugged at the bottom of his shirt and refused to look at me.

I took a long drink before I touched his shoulder gently. 'I do appreciate what you've done for me.'

'I should have married you,' he said, finally looking back up at me.

I could only stare back at him. That he'd been feeling the same as me could only be a bad thing. I wasn't deluded enough to believe that a happy reunion between us was anything more than a fantasy. We couldn't jump into his car, drive off into the sunset and live happily ever after. I had a funeral to arrange, he had Joanne and as much as I despised her and hated the fact that of all the arms to fall into after we split up he had chosen hers, he was still her husband.

He took both of my hands, stroking them gently with his thumbs as his eyes filmed with tears. I watched helplessly as he battled his own thoughts.

'I wanted to be with you,' he sniffed. 'And when I saw you at my door I thought that you'd changed your mind, that you'd been thinking about it for all this time and you'd changed your mind.' I tried to pull my hands away but he held on tight. 'My god this sounds awful,' he continued as he shook his head. 'I do love Joanne. I wouldn't have married her if I didn't. She's just,' he sighed and I wondered whether to interrupt him. I decided against it, mainly because I had nothing to say, and waited for him to finish. 'She's not you, Jess.'

36

His hand touched my knee and I began to feel uncomfortable all over again. The worst part was that I wanted him. I wanted him to stay with me and watch TV, I wanted us to eat together, I wanted him to take me to bed and hold me while I slept. I wanted to wake up with him in the morning and I never wanted to let him go.

'I'm not going to pretend that I haven't thought about it,' I started carefully. My throat was dry again but I didn't dare move to take a drink. 'I loved you and you know that but, well, things have changed, Scott. You're married to someone else.'

I stood up and headed for the kitchen. I didn't want anything in particular, but putting some distance between us seemed like a good idea. He followed quickly.

'You're saying that if I wasn't you'd want us to go back to how we were?' he asked slowly.

'But you are and I can't change that,' I said irritably.

He touched my cheek and smiled. 'I love you, Jess.'

'Go home, Scott,' I replied sadly.

'It's you that I want to be with. You do know that.'

The only thing that I knew was that I was exhausted. I looked at the floor as he put his arms around me, his hands gently stroking my back as his lips pressed against my throat.

'We can't,' I said feebly. 'Please go home.'

'Please, Jess.'

I pushed myself out of the embrace and shook my head at him. 'You're married, Scott,' I cried. 'To *her!*'

'Can't we just…'

'What?' I was backing away from him. Soon I'd hit the fridge and then I'd be trapped. 'Pretend?'

His face was red and angry. Scott wasn't used to not getting what he wanted.

For a second I hated him for being so fucking selfish.

'My dad is dead, Scott,' I said. 'My head is all over the place. The last thing I need is this getting any more complicated than it already is.'

'What I've done the last couple of days has meant nothing to you,' he replied. The words cut deep.

'Go home, Scott,' I said slowly. 'Go home to your wife.'

He left without looking back, slamming the door behind him.

7

Once the silence of the house became unbearable I dragged a bottle of cider from the fridge and took it into the living room. I gulped down what Scott had left and wondered how long what remained in the bottle would last. Flopping down on the sofa I gripped my temples with the fingers of one hand. My head was starting to ache and I began to wonder if the bottom of the bottle would come before the headache or whether sleep would conquer both. I drained the glass, refilled it and then lay down, closing my eyes and hoping for sleep but my head was beginning to throb as if my brain had outgrown my skull and was trying to get out through the hollows of my temples. I got up again, which seemed to send my brain swishing around inside my head and I paused, holding onto the arm of the sofa until the dizziness passed. There were painkillers on top of the fridge. I picked up my glass, taking it to the kitchen and setting it down on the worktop. The feeling of dizziness refused to leave and I stared out of the kitchen window for a moment, trying to focus. I didn't see the unused shed or the long yellow washing line tied between two weary looking apple trees. The grey November sky had brightened to the beautiful blue of August. I saw the lake, the woods, the picnicking families.

Blinking hard, I dragged myself away from the past.

Painkillers.

On top of the fridge.

I took the small white bottle from between the iron and a box of matches, listening to the pills rattle inside as I opened it. The painkillers were as cheap as the coffee and they must have been there for years. No doubt sugar coated pills didn't taste as bitter, but medicine's supposed to taste nasty, that's how they make sure that you only take it when you really need to. Dad's voice of eternal reason.

Turning back to the worktop I shook the bottle. Six white pills fell into my palm. Dad had drank himself to death but he'd always had water with pills. Whether he'd had seven or eight ciders beforehand and would have more after, he'd always swallowed his pills with water. I shrugged. So I was taking mine with cider. So what? So I was looking at the six pills in my hand and wondering how many more there were in the bottle. Big deal. Maybe I'd take all of them and wash them down with bleach. Who cares? All I wanted was for my headache to go away. And to forget the lake. I put four of the pills back into the bottle, tossed the remaining pair into my mouth and gulped down the full glass of cider, clenching my teeth for a long moment against the urge to throw up.

'*Fuck you, Scott!*' I screamed into the empty house. I threw the bottle across the room, scattering pills over the floor and worktops. Shaking, I stumbled back to the sofa and sloshed more cider into the glass. Was this it? For the rest of my life would it just be me sitting here on my own feeling sorry for myself? I drank all that I had poured in three long gulps, almost threw up, and dropped the glass, watching as it rolled around the side of the sofa. Now I felt sick as well. Cold sweat stood out on my forehead and I began to shiver as I lay down and closed my eyes again, seeing the lake and the woods and the picnicking families. And Scott.

'We made love in the rain,' I mumbled.

It had been a scorching hot day. The perfect day for a picnic. We'd gone out to the lake with a cool box filled with sandwiches, snacks and a bottle of wine. We'd rowed on the lake and walked through the lush woodland that surrounded it before sitting down in the grass to eat. Children had laughed in the fragrant warmth of the day as they ran around the lake, playing games while their mothers shouted that they mustn't go too close to the water.

We had ham and cheese sandwiches, a bag of Kettle Chips and a couple of apple pies which we washed down with the sweet wine while an occasional breeze whispered over us, cooling our faces.

If anyone had noticed that dark storm clouds were gathering, heavy and pregnant with rain as afternoon became evening, they didn't show it. A few families remained scattered around the waters edge, laughing and chattering and throwing Frisbees. Then the heavens opened and gave birth to a hard, dramatic downpour. As warm summer rain bounced off the lake and saturated the sun baked earth around us the remaining families quickly decided that today's adventure was over and hurried back towards the car park, herding their children and calling their dogs. Scott and I threw what remained of our picnic back into the cool box and stood up to leave.

'It might only be a shower,' Scott said hopefully and I laughed. His tee shirt was already plastered to his chest and his hair was dripping. 'It'd be a shame to end the day here just because of a bit of rain.'

If the truth were told, I don't think he wanted to take me back to dad.

'A shower?' I asked. 'I don't think so.'

He picked up the cool box and took my hand. 'Come on, we'll shelter in the woods for a while.'

Laughing, we ran deep into the woodland, halting beneath a high canopy of oaks, both of us breathless, listening to the steady patter of rain on the leaves overhead.

'If there's any lightning we'll fry,' I panted.

Setting down the cool box he held my waist and planted a soft kiss on my lips. I felt the rain sliding over our flesh as we undressed each other and lay back on our wet clothes. And I loved him more that day than I did at any other time. I think I could probably say the same for him. It had been perfect. We had been perfect.

Afterwards we'd laughed at the dirt and leaves that were stuck to our wet clothes and hair. I'd felt so lucky to have Scott. Before him there had been others, but none worth remembering.

When I'd been fifteen a boy called Dean Meakin, the boy who turned up the radio to drown out the cries of his battered mother, had dumped me because I wouldn't let him put his 'joystick' in my mouth. That was what he'd called it. Idiot. He told everyone at school that I was frigid so I told everyone at school that it was because it looked like he hadn't washed it for a month and it smelled funny, even though I hadn't actually seen it. Dean hadn't had a girlfriend for a long time after that.

I dozed for a while. Half dreaming, half remembering, wishing that I could have five minutes with my dad to say goodbye properly. Didn't I deserve that much? Thirty years together and all of a sudden it's over. No final I love you, nothing. Just here one minute and gone the next.

And now this was it. This was my forever. I wouldn't need a voice anymore. I'd probably never speak to anyone again apart from the woman at the Co-Op whose name still eluded me.

The knock at the door shocked me awake. It had been a long time since anyone had knocked at our door. *My* door. There was no *our* anything anymore. I sat up quickly, wincing at the pain inside my head as the knock came again. I got up and went down the hall on legs that were still dozing. When I opened the door I was almost knocked to the floor as Scott strode past me into the living room. I followed him, opening my mouth to say something, closing it again as my brain pulled a blank on what that something was.

'I wanted to apologise for earlier,' he said. He was short of breath and his hands were shaking. 'I was out of order and I'm really sorry.'

'Accepted,' I replied cautiously.

'Am I okay to sit down?'

I nodded. I didn't want him to see the NeuroHelp littered kitchen.

'I went home,' he said. 'I've spent the last few hours just thinking about what I said and, and I'm really sorry for putting you in that position. You've got about a million things on your mind and I wasn't helping.' He ran a hand over his face. 'I just don't want to lose you again, Jess.'

I sat beside him. 'Where does she think you are?'

'She got home, changed and went out again. She's gone to some club or another with some people from work. She's pissed off.'

'I'm sorry.'

'I wasn't going to come back but I didn't see the point of us both sitting on our own.' He looked at his shaking hands and clamped them firmly between his knees.

'Coffee?' I asked.

'Please.'

As I waited for the kettle to boil I collected up all the painkillers I could find and put the bottle back on top of the fridge. When I took the coffee through to the living room he didn't look any better. Another uncomfortable silence filled the room. I had nothing to say and Scott seemed to be deep in thought. I could hear the occasional car passing the house, the muted drip of the cold tap with the dodgy washer as I sat beside him and sipped my coffee, waiting nervously for him to speak.

'We both know that we shouldn't be apart.' His voice was low and thick with emotion. 'I know that all those feelings haven't just gone away. Not for either of us.'

The only thing worse than wanting him was knowing that he knew that I wanted him. I couldn't reply.

He touched my shoulder with his fingertips and then leaned over, kissing my cheek. His lips brushed briefly against mine and I wanted him so badly. 'Take me upstairs, Jess.'

I shook my head painfully. 'I can't, Scott. I want to. I just, I can't.'

'I'm going to leave her.'

My stomach lurched. Leave her? It was exactly what I'd wanted but leaving a wife isn't like dumping the girl you've been screwing around with for the last two weeks. 'You're serious?' I asked.

43

'After the funeral,' he said. 'Once that's sorted out, I swear.'

He kissed my mouth and I put my arms around him. I wouldn't have to be alone. I'd have him by my side and everything would be okay.

'It's you that I want to be with,' he said as he kissed me again.

I smiled up at him. 'I love you so much.'

He took my hand in his as he returned the smile. 'Take me upstairs.'

8

'I'm sorry, Jess, I've really got to go,' Scott said as he sat down on the bed and rested his head on my stomach. 'It feels so wrong to leave you.'

I ran my hand absently through his hair. It was past ten o clock. We'd talked, even laughed, and held each other, all the stuff that we used to do when we were together. And now I could stop thinking about that in the past tense because we were going to be together again, we would be happy. Joanne wouldn't like it and I had no doubt that she would make it as difficult as possible for us, but she couldn't stop us being together.

He buttoned his shirt and I sat up, holding him.

'I'll ring you in the morning,' he said before he kissed my forehead softly. I watched him leave and then rolled myself up in the duvet, closing my eyes against the silence of the house and for the first time since my fathers death I was asleep in seconds.

'Hello, Jess.'

I opened my eyes to see him sitting on the bed to my right. He was stroking my hair. I smiled. I knew he wouldn't be able to stay away for long.

'Hi, dad.'

He smiled back at me and ran a cold finger over my cheek. 'I didn't mean to wake you. You looked so peaceful. I haven't watched you sleep since you were little.'

'It's late, dad.'

'I know, sweetheart. I'm sorry. But I've got something to show you.' He grinned, flashing a full set of nicotine rusted teeth.

I opened my mouth to speak but he put a skeletal finger to my lips. 'Let me show you,' he whispered.

He picked something up from the floor and placed it on the bed. My mouth fell open and I watched in horror as blood drained from Joanne Howard's severed head, spreading over the bed like a plague. Her eyes were missing and her mouth was a frozen O of surprise. Her purple tongue was swollen against the roof of her mouth. I felt bile rise in my stomach as I looked at her blue lips and bruised cheeks and clamped my hands over my mouth.

'Dad, I, I don't…'

'Shh,' he soothed. 'You don't have to thank me.'

Joanne's head rolled and came to rest on her left cheek as dad let go of her blood matted blonde hair. Unable to look at it anymore I pulled the duvet up over my head, closing my eyes, begging dad to let me sleep, promising that we would talk in the morning.

And now I could only hear the sound of my own breathing.

I opened my eyes and inched the duvet down to my nose to look at the room.

No head.

No dad.

Just moonlight spilling over the bed.

Just a dream, Jess, all just a dream.

I took a couple of deep, steadying breaths before rolling over and burying my face in the pillow Scott had lain on only hours ago. I could still smell him there, the familiar scent that belonged only to him. It calmed me. I wished that he hadn't had to go.

I needed a drink. My mouth was dry and my tongue felt thick and gummy. Standing up, I took dads coat from the pile of his stuff underneath the window and pulled it on against the chill of the house. I wandered out onto the landing and flicked on the light, squinting against the sudden brightness as I stretched, yawned and went downstairs, unable to completely shake the feeling that dad was still around somewhere, waiting for that chat I'd promised him.

I stopped dead on the last step. I could smell cigarette smoke. My cold fingers began to shake as I slowly leaned over the banister and looked into the deep darkness of the living room where I could see the small orange glow of a burning cigarette. My breath caught in my throat and I held it, not daring to move or breathe or blink. As my eyes adjusted to the darkness I could see him sitting motionless on the sofa, staring out of the window with his back to me. A cigarette was pinched between two fingers of his right hand. I could hear my heart beating and wondered if he could too. Any second now that shape would move. It would stand and come towards me or the head would turn and I would see his face and then I would scream and the scream would drive away any lingering illusion of sanity that I was clinging to.

I edged slowly towards the front door, my eyes never leaving the living room. Pulling at the door handle I begged for it to open, hoped that Scott hadn't locked it on his way out. He hadn't. Cold air swept over my feet and I ran, screaming into the night, automatically heading for Scott's, refusing to look back for fear of seeing dad's face pressed against the window, watching me with dead eyes.

The asphalt tore at my feet and tears streamed from my eyes as I sprinted across the estate towards Dukes Court. The houses were all in darkness and a cold wind blew ghostly moans through the trees as I ran to the door and knocked urgently. Looking around I saw cars observing me emotionlessly from their driveways as the wind continued to play a phantom chorus through the last leaves of autumn. I knocked again and the hall light flashed on.

'Thank god,' I breathed.

Scott unlocked the door and opened it as wide as the security chain would allow. 'Jess? What the hell's going on?'

'Scott, who is it?' Joanne's voice floated down from the top of the stairs.

'Please let me in,' I croaked.

'Jess, we need to do this another time.' I could hear panic in his voice.

'What? Scott, please let me in.'

47

He must have seen the fear in my eyes because he closed the door and I heard the light clanking of the chain being released before he opened it again. Joanne was standing behind him now with contempt in her eyes. I could imagine her smiling happily while she tore out my throat but it did nothing to remove the fear of what was waiting for me at home. I stepped into the house, curling my toes gratefully into the soft carpet. Scott led me into the living room and I sat, shaking, on the sofa.

'You're bleeding all over my carpets,' Joanne said sourly. I looked at my feet. The soles were cut and freckled with grit.

'I'm sorry.'

'Get her a dressing gown, Joanne.'

Joanne left the room obediently and Scott sat beside me. 'Why are you here?' he asked.

'He's in the house,' I said. In my mind I could see dad, motionless on the sofa, all in black and white apart from the orange glow of his cigarette.

'Someone broke in?'

I shook my head. 'Dad. He's in the house.' Saying it to someone else, I realised how stupid it sounded.

'Jess,' he was speaking to me as if I were a child, 'your dad's dead.'

'It wouldn't have bothered me so much if he wasn't,' I shot back.

'It must have been a bad dream.'

'No,' I protested. 'It was after that.'

Joanne returned with a dressing gown which she threw at me from across the room. It was pink.

'Thank you.'

Scott went over to her and she took hold of his hands. 'Jess, are you sure you weren't dreaming?' he asked.

'Yes!' I told them I'd had a bad dream but left out the part about Joanne's head. I told them I was thirsty and had smelled cigarette smoke and he was

48

sitting on the sofa. They were both looking at me as if I'd lost my mind.

'It could have been a burglar,' Joanne said.

'How many burglars do you know that sit smoking roll up while you run screaming down the street?'

Joanne bit her bottom lip. 'I'm going back to bed.'

'Can you get her a blanket?' Scott asked.

She threw him a bemused look. 'She's not staying.'

'She's got nowhere else to go,' Scott explained. 'Just tonight, I promise.'

Joanne got up from the armchair and Scott and I looked at each other silently as she climbed the stairs. A blanket was thrown back down before she slammed the bedroom door behind her. Scott fetched the blanket with a sigh and I settled down on the sofa.

'Night, Jess,' he said stiffly before he went back upstairs.

Joanne started shouting as soon as the bedroom door clicked shut and I buried my face in a throw cushion to try and block her out but it was useless. It didn't matter anyway, I knew I wouldn't sleep. I spent the next two hours tossing and turning, tired but restless. Every time I closed my eyes I saw dad on the sofa, whispers of smoke hanging in the air around him, and every time I opened my eyes I saw Joanne's house, the pink carpet now faded in the milky moonlight. I turned over again to face the fireplace.

I blinked hard, suddenly feeling wide awake. *I can't be seeing this.*

The wedding photo which had stood, proudly mocking me from the mahogany mantelpiece, hung weightlessly in the air above the fireplace. As I watched open mouthed it rotated slowly, floating higher and higher until it was more than six feet above the floor, dancing from side to side, moving towards me. My skin crawled, seeming to shrink, as I found myself able to watch but unable to move and now it was within my reach; Scott and Joanne rocking back and forth, smiling in glossy eight by ten. I reached out, my trembling fingers almost touching it before it was rudely snatched away, floating high above the table in the middle of the room.

'Dad, stop it,' I whispered. 'You're scaring me.'

As if I'd been heard the picture fell to the floor and the sound of shattering glass filled the room for only a second before my scream took its place. Scott and Joanne landed, grinning up at me through the sharp teeth of broken glass. I watched, helpless, as a long shard rose up, swinging back towards the mantelpiece. I could hear it digging and scraping through the varnish, deep into the wood and I started to shake as adrenaline flooded my body, willing me to move. But I could only stare helplessly at the fireplace.

Then the glass lay still.

I crept over as quietly as I could, stepping carefully over the glittering glass on the floor. As I caught sight of the words scratched into the mahogany I groaned.

LOVE YOU

Joanne caught me as my legs failed. She dropped me into an armchair and looked around.

'What the hell?' she cried as she glared at me. I pulled my knees up to my chest and hugged them. My whole body was shaking. 'Why'd you do this?'

'Dad,' I managed.

She called for Scott and I heard him coming quickly down the stairs, looking tired and dishevelled. His eyes surveyed the room and then his arms were around me and I thought that maybe this was it. He was going to tell her now. But he couldn't. I couldn't handle that now. We had to do that later.

'Well that says it all,' Joanne cried dramatically. 'I don't even have to ask.' I could only stare at her blankly. 'Have you got anything to say to me?' she roared. I shook my head and she slapped me hard across the face. My head snapped back and my cheek began to tingle. I only offered her the same blank stare. Scott shouted for her to calm down.

'Calm down?' she screamed. 'Have you seen what she did to the fireplace?'

Oh god, she thinks I did it.

'It was dad,' I tried to explain, feeling like the kid in that film; *Drop Dead Fred did it.*

'Don't give me that shit. What's going on?'

Neither of us spoke.

'I want you out, Jessica,' Joanne said shakily.

'Joanne, she's…'

'She's not welcome here.'

'Please, Joanne, just…'

'Out!' she screamed.

'Calm down.' Now he was holding her.

Joanne's eyes pleaded with him. 'I want her to leave. Now.'

'She doesn't have anywhere to go.'

'Not my problem.'

'Joanne, please. You can't.'

She pushed him away. 'I am,' she said defiantly.

Scott looked over at me. He didn't know what to do. I couldn't help.

'I don't know exactly what's been going on for the last couple of days but it ends now.' Joanne folded her arms over her chest. 'Make your choice, Scott. Her or me.'

I braced myself. Now he had to tell her. I thought that the chance of us staying here any longer was slim and hated the idea of going back to the house. But Scott would be with me. We'd be okay.

'I'm sorry, Jess, but you'll have to go home.' He was looking at the floor. 'We'll talk tomorrow.'

'No,' Joanne said. 'She goes and that's the end of it.'

He looked at her as he placed his hands on his hips. 'Joanne, this isn't fair.'

For a moment our eyes locked and I was sure that he was going to tell her. I stood up and held my hand out to him but he stepped backwards, put his hands on Joanne's shoulders and looked at the hideous carpet. 'I'm sorry, Jess,' he said quietly.

It hurt more than the slap and I wanted to throw up.

'That's it then,' Joanne cried triumphantly. 'Get out.'

Scott's eyes remained on the floor as I slid out of her dressing gown. There was nothing left to say or do. I went silently to the door, stepping out into the first mellow light of the day.

The headlight eyes of the cars accused me blindly as I walked slowly through the estate towards the fields, oblivious to the people walking the streets. A man in his fifties asked if I was alright and an old woman shouted that I should be ashamed of myself. I didn't answer them. They were just voices floating into a dream, disembodied and unimportant.

The soft grass felt luxurious after the roads. I could see my breath as it plumed from lips that felt unnaturally dry. I could hardly feel my feet.

And then there it was, twinkling in the early morning sunlight like a long silver lane in a fairy tale. I smiled. I was going to be okay. He was behind me now. I could feel his cool breath on the back of my neck as he urged me forward and I couldn't feel the cold anymore, couldn't hear the sounds of the world coming to life. I felt nothing.

The Swanmore River stretched out before me, the answer to a question I hadn't even known how to ask, sparkling like diamonds beneath a cold sun. I looked back over my shoulder. There was nobody there.

I dipped a toe in the water, trying to imagine how it would feel to have my whole body held in its dirty, unforgiving embrace. *Cold*, I concluded and had to smile. *Well done, Jess. What a deduction!* The smile faded.

I sat in the wet grass and dangled my legs in the water. Colder than the air. A bone biting cold that was indistinguishable from fire. But after a while, once you got used to it, it felt warm.

I cast one more fleeting glance around me before I pushed myself calmly into the water and closed my eyes.

Elaine. The woman at the Co-Op, her name's Elaine.

And I had been right.

It was cold.

9

I stood at the bus stop feeling cold and stupid. Dad's coat was drying on my back and I prayed that nobody would see my like this.

I thought about the house. I didn't want to go back there but it was light now. Dead dads don't come out in the daytime, do they? And when it got dark I could just switch on all the lights and maybe that would keep him away. If there was enough money in the meter. I imagined the house being plunged into darkness while I sat alone, his voice coming out of the shadows, that orange light bobbing as he paced the living room like he used to when he was thinking hard about twenty one down.

Well, there we go, thinking time over, here comes the bus. I pulled at the bottom of the coat, trying to stretch it down over my thighs as the doors opened with a smooth *whoosh* and the driver looked down at me, puzzled. Looking down I understood why. Dirty, bloody feet, bomber jacket that barely covered my backside and dark sopping wet hair. I wouldn't be winning any fashion awards today.

'I, I don't have any money,' I said stupidly.

He smiled serenely and beckoned me forward with a plump forefinger. As I boarded he leaned over and slid a hand into one of the coats pockets, pulling out a slip of paper, a bus ticket. He examined it and nodded.

'Standard two way ticket,' he said as he tucked it away somewhere. 'Enjoy your return trip, Miss Morgan.'

As I opened my mouth to speak he waved me away so I took a seat halfway down the crowded bus next to an old man in a brown suit and green bow tie while other passengers looked at me with distaste. I couldn't blame them, but I tried to ignore them. At the end of the day I'd been born wearing less.

'Mummy?' Across the aisle, a blonde boy of four or five was tugging at his mothers sleeve.

'What?' she asked.

'Why is she on our bus? She shouldn't be on our bus.'

The boy's mother looked over at me and his eyes followed. 'You shouldn't be on our bus,' he said.

'It's called public transport because anyone can use it,' I replied indignantly. The boy hid his face against his mother's side and she frowned at me.

I turned to the old man, who was also frowning at me. As soon as our eyes met he turned away from me to look out of the window. I followed his gaze and a new wave of fear swept over me. This wasn't the fear of seeing your dead dad smoking contentedly in the living room two days after he died or the fear that you had nobody in the world to turn to, although it was similar to the latter. It was the fear of being lost. I didn't know the places we were passing. It was all much too green to be the estate or anywhere near it. On the wrong bus. Suited my luck at the moment.

'Where are we?' I asked.

The old man chuckled as if I'd cracked a mildly amusing joke but he didn't answer me so I sat back in my seat, looking out at the fields. Apart from the obvious problem of being on the wrong bus, something else wasn't quite right.

'Mummy, I don't want her on our bus, it's not right,' The boy whined.

'Don't be so rude,' his mother hissed. 'She'll be gone soon.'

It came to me. The beautiful landscape was all there was. There were no people, no animals or birds, no traffic either in front or behind us, nothing coming from the other direction.

'Where are all the people?' I asked nobody in particular.

'Your stop, Miss Morgan,' the driver called as he brought the bus to a smooth halt in the middle of nowhere. I didn't want to get off the bus but everyone was looking at me with that same *the sooner she gets off this bus the better* look. As I looked around their eyes went back to the windows, refusing to meet my confused gaze.

I got up and walked down the aisle. 'I don't know where this is,' I explained to the driver. 'I think...'

'Your stop, Miss Morgan,' he repeated.

This had to be a dream. I must have bashed my head and been washed up somewhere. This couldn't be real. But, real or not, I felt uncomfortable leaving the bus and stepped out into the clear day with reluctance. I could feel the sun on my face. The day was warm.

I turned back to the driver to ask where I was but he wasn't looking at me anymore and neither were any of the passengers. They were looking at something else, something behind me, something that was breathing warm air onto the back of my neck. I froze, willing my feet to stop shuffling me round to look at whatever horror was in store for me now.

'I missed you so much.'

A scream bubbled in my throat as I looked into his bright, smiling face and I turned back towards the bus, I'd get off at the next stop, but it was already rolling silently away. I shook my head, looking apprehensively back at dad. This was my insanity. Had to be. He looked different. He was healthy. His cheeks were ruddy and his hair had regressed to the sleek black I remembered from my childhood. He moved towards me with open arms and I stumbled backwards, almost tripping over my own bare feet.

'You're dead,' I said as if he may have forgotten. 'You can't be here, you're dead. You died. Didn't you?' I was beginning to doubt myself, struggling to remember what was real.

He looked puzzled. 'You know what happened, sweetheart,' he replied softly. 'You were there.'

'But this,' I couldn't say anymore and began to cry instead. He put his arms around me and the confusion seemed to matter less and less. In his familiar embrace I felt real again and I could have stayed like that forever.

'I love you, dad.'

56

'Love you too, sweetheart.'

I grudgingly allowed him to break the embrace and take my hand, leading me to the other side of the road where a tall white building seemed to have appeared from nowhere.

Definitely lost it, Jess.

'I'm so glad you're here,' he said. 'But how you got here,' he looked down at me with pity, 'it was painful to watch, sweetheart.'

It was then that realisation dawned, black and heavy. I hadn't bashed my head and been washed up somewhere. Somewhere a million miles away I was floating in the dark water, or lying alone, a washed up corpse by the side of the river. But I felt so good, so alive. Realisation, however, was swiftly replaced by the burning fear and anger I had felt since dad's death.

'Painful?' I cried as I snatched my hand away. 'You haven't got a clue!'

I had to postpone telling him off because he was ignoring me. He had opened one of the huge white doors and stepped inside the building. I followed him closely, looking around the vast space we now occupied. A wide staircase stood in the centre of the white floor, which invariably matched the ceiling and walls. A few people wandered around in silver pyjamas or robes. Some paused as they passed us, looking at me with the same disapproval as the people on the bus.

'Why are they looking at me like that?' I asked as I turned to dad who now looked quietly handsome in his own pair of silver pyjamas. I looked down at myself and saw that the coat had been replaced with a long robe, although mine was orange.

'All of the people here were taken by disease,' he explained. 'Cancer, heart disease.'

'Alcoholic liver disease,' I interjected.

He looked half ashamed. 'But you took your own life,' he continued and it was my turn to look shamefaced. 'You shouldn't be here.'

'So how come I am?'

'I wanted to see you,' he replied simply. 'And, well, she'll explain the rest.'

'Who?'

He didn't reply.

'Dad, you do know that if it wasn't for you I'd still be alive?' He started towards the staircase and I followed hurriedly. 'You were in the living room. You were at Scott's.' We were climbing the staircase now. 'Joanne thought it was me that smashed the picture you know. So well done, I did this because of you. And just because it took a few years for you to drink yourself to death it doesn't make it any less of a suicide.'

He seized my wrist painfully, his blue eyes now cold. 'Enough.'

I followed him silently to the top of the stairs.

'I've done what I can, Jess.' He was dragging me down a long white corridor now. Numbered doors lined it like sentinels. 'But I don't know what decision she's going to make.'

'Dad,' I pleaded.

He ignored me. 'I know that a lot of this is my fault and that's what I told her. I think she agreed with me. Here we are.'

He pushed open one of the doors and pulled me inside. A large woman sat behind an empty desk. Her hair, pinned up neatly at the back of her head, was as white as the rest of the building. A deep purple robe skimmed over her heaving bosom. To me she looked around three hundred years old, but her eyes were clear and young.

'Jessica Morgan.' Her voice was like a soft and soothing song. 'Take a seat.' She flicked through a slim white file as I sat. 'I've heard a lot about you.' She looked at dad as she said this. 'When a person decides to take their own life, what usually happens is this.' She spoke quickly as if getting to the end of this part of her day would make her feel a whole lot better. 'Your soul is despatched to the relevant department and then sent from there into the first available human body to begin again.' She closed the file and slid it into a drawer behind her without leaving her chair. 'As you may already know, Miss Morgan, this is not your department. Truth is, after your dad had been to see me, I spoke to the relevant personnel and we thought that I should be the one to handle this.'

'She's been here for a long time,' dad said.

'Mr Morgan, I believe that you have had ample time to say all that you wanted to.'

Dad apologised and the old woman turned back to me. I didn't like her very much. 'Your father appealed both to me and the head of your department. He's quite the negotiator, he promises to be quite an asset to us in the future.'

I smiled. Dad had been a union rep when he'd worked. A very good union rep. But to think that while I'd been swallowing dirty river water he'd been talking a couple of old women out of throwing me straight back out there was somewhat unsettling.

'So,' the woman continued in her singsong voice, 'we had a discussion and we made a decision.'

'I don't like how you make me sound like a stationary budget rather than a person,' I said quietly.

She continued as if she hadn't heard me. 'We decided to give you a second chance. You wont get put into the first new body that comes along to start again. You will begin your own life again. Quite literally we are giving you the chance of a lifetime. Your lifetime. Everything will be exactly the same as it was before, but you will be equipped to make more informed decisions this time around.'

'You're saying that I made bad choices?' I asked. 'I'm being given another chance because I messed up somewhere?'

'You will go back with whatever knowledge you had at the time of your death and should be able to recollect our little conversation today.'

Conversation? I thought a conversation was a two way thing?

'Do I make myself clear?'

I nodded dumbly, my eyes never leaving hers.

'Now go,' she said. 'Your bus will be along shortly.'

My head buzzed with questions. 'But what. . .'

'Jess, she's finished.' Dad was pulling at the back of the chair as if he meant to pull it out from under me. 'Now, get yourself on that bus and think yourself lucky.'

'Will you be there?' I asked him.

'Everything will be as it was,' the woman said firmly. 'Were you not listening?'

Dad put an arm around my shoulders and led me back out into the corridor, pausing briefly to thank the old lady with the attitude problem. It was cooler out here.

'I'll have to do it all over again?' I asked.

'You heard the lady,' he replied. 'I think they made the right decision.'

'But I don't want to,' I whined.

'Jess, sweetheart, you spent your whole life looking after me instead of you. When you made your decisions you made them for both of us, never for yourself.'

'So did you.'

He smiled. 'I'm supposed to put you first, I'm your dad. You need to go out there and do what's best for you. Not what's best for me or for anyone else. Go and live your life, Jess.'

I jogged down the stairs, following him to the big double doors before pulling him back roughly by the sleeve.

'Dad, I'm scared.'

He enveloped me in his arms and kissed my forehead. 'Think of the advantages, Jess,' he said. 'You know what's coming. You'll know everything that you died with.' He kissed my cheek. 'Safe journey, sweetheart.'

60

He pushed me gently outside and closed the door. I was alone again on the silent, empty street. I tried the door to the big white building but it wouldn't budge. I shouted for dad and then cringed at the sound of my own voice as it boomed through the eerie silence. The bus was on its way. I could see it coming, slowly and smoothly along the perfectly level and unmarked black road. I gave up on the door and went to the side of the road, feeling anxious as it pulled up and the doors opened. I sighed, looking back at the big white building, wondering if dad felt as lost and alone and unwanted as I did.

'I haven't got all day, Miss Morgan,' the driver called. This man was thin and blonde with a small round scar above his right eye. The rest of the bus was empty.

'I can't even die properly,' I mumbled to myself.

I took the first seat I came to and looked out of the window at the unfamiliar landscape of wherever I was, trying to think of one single advantage to living my life again. It was such a strange concept.

I remembered my GCSE results although I'd never been to school. I'd loved – and hated – Scott Jordan but I'd never met him. I'd killed myself although I hadn't been born yet.

I closed my eyes and wished for the nightmare to end.

Part Two

1

Sheila Morgan sat in the quiet of the doctor's waiting room watching her daughter spin the brightly coloured beads of an abacus with her small four year old hands. The walls were painted an inoffensive magnolia and were broken only by two long windows that looked out on the miserable March afternoon. Hard rain fell from the dirty sky and spattered against them. She shivered involuntarily.

'You're worrying again.'

Sheila was startled by Karen's small voice as it broke the tomblike silence. Looking down she saw that she was wringing her hands as she always did when she worried. She untangled them like reluctant lovers and set them carefully on her knees. Karen offered her a sympathetic smile. They both knew what this was doing to her. Sheila looked worn and much older than her twenty three years. She hadn't had a decent nights sleep since her daughters birth. Jessica woke her parents night after restless night, wailing into the deep darkness of the witching hours. She said that when she slept she saw her daddy dying in a hospital bed.

After sitting with Jessica until she fell back into her haunted sleep, reassuring her that it was just a bad dream, Sheila would lie with her husband and let him hold her as she wept. He passed it off as an anxiety dream. Soon Jessica would be going to school and she wouldn't be with them all of the time. That was all the dream was about. She'd grow out of it.

But Jessica hadn't grown out of it. She had only grown into a different 'anxiety dream'. It had woken her for the first time last week. Paul had said that it was much the same as the first, but Sheila had never believed that the first dream was childish anxiety and she didn't believe that this dream was either.

Jessica said that the phone had been ringing. Her dad had spoken to someone for a couple of minutes, his voice mutating from the soft tone that had soothed Jessica back to sleep on so many occasions to unwritten notes of agony. Then she'd heard hoarse, anguished sobs that were eventually replaced by moans and gasps and then, finally, silence. This was when she dared to venture down the stairs. Foil decorations hung from the ceiling and an artificial Christmas tree stood in the far corner beside the television. There were no gifts beneath its sparkling branches. Christmas Day had been and gone. The gas fire was on high and Paul Morgan was watching the flames from the sofa as if hypnotised by them.

'Why are you crying, dad?'

In this dream she didn't call him daddy because she wasn't little anymore. She was older. The swell of her developing breasts pushed gently against her thin sweater. He looked up, his face melting into hopeless pity for her and his harsh cries began again as he opened his arms and she went to him.

This was when Jessica had screamed herself awake, just like she had with the first dream. Paul had told her that her mother had been killed in a car accident on her way home from shopping with Karen. Skidded on black ice straight into the path on an oncoming lorry. Death had been instantaneous. Karen had been taken to hospital with a broken leg and collarbone.

This dream gnawed at Sheila's mind, growing like a cancer until it seemed that she thought of nothing else. The main reason for this was that Jessica hadn't described it as a dream. Instead of saying *I dreamed* she said *I saw*. After she had finished explaining, Jessica had sat quietly in her mothers lap, observing her pitifully.

Sheila was here today because she wanted something that would put her out at ten every night and let her sleep until six the next morning without hearing her daughters screams. She didn't want to know about the dreams; couldn't bear to hear anymore.

The way Jessica had looked at her had reminded Sheila of a day last

September when Paul had put Countdown on and Jessica had looked at the television with a puzzled look on her small face. Paul had asked her what she was thinking.

'I thought Richard Whiteley was dead, daddy,' she had said. 'Oh no,' shaking her head as if she'd made an elementary mistake. 'Ignore me. Not yet.'

The same feeling of dread had embraced her then, making the air seem too thick to breathe properly. How could a four year old even know who Richard Whiteley was? How could a four year old speak in such articulate, adult sentences? Jessica just knew things and, like knowing when Richard Whiteley was going to die, Sheila was becoming more and more convinced that her daughter had accurately foreseen her death in that horrible dream.

Jessica had never had normal dreams – not even nice dreams. She never flew over turreted castles inhabited by green pixies or saw a noble prince riding towards her on a silver unicorn. No, not Jessica. Jessica saw death and hurt and woke herself up screaming for someone called Scott Jordan.

She watched her daughter push the beads back and forth with a mixture of love and fear as a young woman with short hair that was a shade of blonde you could only get out of a bottle entered the room with a boy around Jessica's age. She sat beside Sheila, temporarily breaking her train of thought. The boy went straight for the toys.

'Hello, Dean.' Jessica welcomed him like an old friend, her voice the only sound in the silent room.

Dean frowned. 'How do you know my name?'

Jess shrugged and continued to slide red beads from one side of the abacus to the other. 'Dirty dick Dean,' she said to nobody in particular. Sheila's hand went to her mouth, partially covering the colour that was rising in her cheeks. Dean's mother sat open mouthed.

'Jessica, come here please,' Sheila said, nakedly aware that everybody in the waiting room was looking at her. Jessica left the abacus and plodded over

67

obediently as Deans mother watched her with cold eyes. Sheila lifted Jess into her lap.

'Where did you learn that word?' she asked, cringing at how loud her voice sounded in the quiet of the room.

'That's his name,' Jess replied as she looked over at Dean. He had claimed her abacus and was shaking it, making the beads rattle noisily.

'Jessica, we don't use naughty words, do we?'

Jess shook her head slowly.

'And that's a naughty word.'

'But it's his name,' Jess insisted.

'I'm so sorry,' Sheila spoke to Dean's mother quietly.

The woman shrugged. 'Kids pick up the strangest things.'

You have no idea, Sheila thought, but she said nothing. After the Richard Whiteley incident Jessica had beaten her dad at Countdown by four points. A four year old who had never gone to school had somehow seen the word *perceive* inside a jumble of letters. Paul had been convinced that she was a child prodigy. They played chess, they watched Countdown, he'd even taken her to a neighbour who taught piano and sat her down in front of a thick book of Beethoven's sonata's, asking her to play.

'I can't read music, daddy,' Jess had giggled. But she had understood what the symbols were, that they weren't a foreign language or just pictures.

'Maybe chess and word games are the same as the other stuff,' Sheila had suggested. 'She just knows how to play chess and rearrange letters.'

'You can't just know how to play chess,' Paul had said. 'It takes time to learn how to play well.'

'Paul, you set the pieces up and she made her move. You didn't explain anything to her.'

'I beat her though.'

'She's four years old.'

'Sheila Morgan, please.' The robotic voice came from the intercom on the wall. She ran a tired hand over her face and offered Dean's mother another apology before sweeping Jess into her arms and leaving the room as quickly as possible.

Karen ran a hand through her blonde hair as she sighed and the bangles on her wrist jangled prettily. Sheila had been so outgoing – the life and soul of whatever party she happened to be crashing that weekend. Now she was quiet and withdrawn. The last time she had been to a party was New Years Eve and she had left well before midnight, slinking out unnoticed with her husband.

Two years ago Sheila had been seeing Colin Mayers behind Paul's back. He'd been the latest in a string of affairs, but the only one that Paul had found out about. Sheila had gotten an infection and passed it on to him. Of course, being the devoted husband that he was, Paul had forgiven her.

Sheila had been faithful to her husband for eight months after that; until she and Karen had kissed for the first time. It was one of the rare occasions when Sheila had actually been drunk before she invited someone into her bed and Karen had expected it to be exactly what Sheila had told her husband that her relationship with Colin had been. A one time 'Let's never speak of it again' thing. But that hadn't happened. And Paul didn't suspect a thing. He was too concerned with what Jessica was doing – that was probably the one thing Karen thought the kid had going for her.

She had seen a film once called The Omen and the kid in that film reminded her of Jessica. Strange things happened when Jessica was around. This morning she had known someone's name. Tomorrow she might tell someone that their dog was going to die. The first time she had ever visited Sheila at home Jessica had looked at her with frightened eyes.

'You're Karen Howard,' she had said.

Karen had nodded. Sheila had told her about Jess but actually seeing it for herself had been unnerving.

'You're Joanne's sister.'

Karen knew Sheila was waiting for the day when Jessica would tell her that she knew about what they were doing behind Paul's back. That was why Sheila had tried to end their relationship so many times. Thankfully, she had always come back.

Jessica just wasn't a normal child. She didn't play with the toys her parents bought for her, she wasn't constantly fighting for attention and she was happy to sit alone in her room and read or draw for hours. Two weeks ago Sheila had found her making a cup of coffee. She had boiled the kettle and been standing on a chair pouring water into a mug when Sheila had walked in on her. When Sheila had told her off, Jess hadn't got a clue what she'd done wrong.

'She'd put coffee and sugar in the mug,' Sheila had told her. 'She knew exactly what she was doing.'

Karen walked home with them after Sheila had seen the doctor. Thankfully the rain had stopped. Jessica walked in front of them, her head down and her hands in her pockets. She was frightened. Frightened of everything. Mummy might think that knowing people she'd never met before was scary, but that was nothing. And Jess was sure that she *had* met them before, she just couldn't remember where. Mummy was scared of the dreams as well but Jess didn't think that they were dreams. She never felt like she was dreaming, she felt like she was obtaining important information.

Mummy was going to die in a car crash. A lady Jess didn't know was going to hold daddy's hand while he died in a hospital. Then there was Scott. She didn't know where the information came from, but she knew that it had something to do with a lady that was very old.

'Are you coming round later?' Karen asked. 'Mum and dad are taking Joanne to her ballet class in about in hour.'

Sheila nodded. 'I just need to speak to Paul about what happened today.'

Karen touched the small of Sheila's back and she flinched away, looking at

Jess.

'Are you alright, Sheila?' she asked.

'Not really,' she sighed. 'She's my little girl, Karen. I'm responsible for her. It was me all those people were looking at when she called that little boy, well, what she did, not her.'

'You're not a bad mum, Sheila,' Karen reassured. 'She's just a really difficult kid.'

'And who's fault is that?'

'It's nobody's fault. You should probably get a doctor to have a look at her. A head doctor who could sort out the dreams and stuff.'

Sheila laughed wretchedly. 'You think Paul would let a doctor anywhere near her?' She shook her head in response to her own question. 'No, he thinks he can handle this all by himself.'

'Then let him,' Karen said. 'Tell him he either lets a doctor look at her or you're not having anything else to do with it.'

'I'm her mother, Karen, I can't do that.'

'Why not? It's making you ill. Is Paul happy for this to kill you as long as nobody finds out he's got a daughter that sees the future?'

'It's not seeing the future, it's just dreams.' But Sheila didn't sound sure.

'What about that woman who lives next door to you?' Karen asked. 'Jess told us that she was going to have a baby girl and she was going to call her Rose, after her Grandmother. And what happened?'

'Stop it,' Sheila said bitterly.

'Well my sister's the same age as her and she doesn't ask for books or videos for Christmas, especially books that don't exist. And what the fuck are DVD's? She asks for toys and games like every other normal kid.'

'Look, forget tonight,' Sheila said as they approached the house. Paul was just pulling up outside and Jess ran to him. 'I'll ring you tomorrow.'

'Sheila?'

71

Sheila was walking away from her. She met her husband and kissed his cheek. Karen watched as she followed him into the house without looking back.

'I just wanted to curl up and die Paul, I really did,' Sheila said as they went into the kitchen to start dinner. Jess had gone upstairs to draw.

'Have you tried talking to her about it?'

'She doesn't listen to me,' she said as she put sausages under the grill. 'She doesn't think she's doing anything wrong.'

'Well it's not like she's drawing on the walls or throwing things around.'

'Please talk to her, Paul,' she begged. 'She listens to you.'

He kissed her briefly. 'Okay, I'll talk to her,' he agreed. He climbed the stairs and went to Jess's room, pausing to put on his best stern face before he opened the door.

'Jess, I need to talk to you, sweetheart,' he said as he sat on the bed. She looked up from her drawing of a group of red people playing football in front of purple trees. What looked like a pond was drawn near the bottom of the paper. He patted the bed and she sat beside him. 'Why did you call that boy a rude name at the doctors today?' he asked calmly.

'Because that's what people call him.'

'And how do you know that?'

'Because it's true.'

'And how do you know that it's true?'

The girl shrugged. 'Because my brain told me.'

Paul ran a tired hand over his face. 'Well, next time your brain tells you something like that, you keep it to yourself because it upsets people. Especially mummy.'

She nodded. 'But sometimes I can't help it, it just comes out.'

'Okay,' he said as he scratched his head. 'Well, when you can help it, you don't say anything when mummy's around. You can come and tell me though if you want to.'

'Okay, daddy.'

'I mean it, Jess,' he said sternly. 'Stop scaring your mother.'

Jess went back to her drawing as he left but her hand paused, hovering over the paper. She had started to add a boy and a girl to her picture, but now she was stuck. She couldn't remember what the boy's face was supposed to look like.

2

Sheila dressed slowly, listening to the silence of the house. They could be back any second.

That had been far too risky. They had to be more careful. She looked down at the rumpled sheet and quickly stretched out the corners, tucking them back into place before she picked up a pillow and inhaled deeply, checking for Karen's scent. She didn't think that it was there. She picked up the rest of the covers from the floor and carefully made the bed, sure that something would give her away. Karen should have told her that they couldn't do it here. She should have warned her that once it was over the panic and paranoia would set in. But Karen was only out for herself, wasn't she? Just like the others. She didn't care what happened before or after as long as she got what she wanted in between.

She sighed and smoothed down the duvet. It wasn't fair to blame Karen. Karen was single. It wasn't her that was doing anything wrong. Sheila stood at the bottom of the bed with her hands on her hips and looked it over. Nothing seemed to be out of place. Even if Paul came home and said he could smell someone on the sheets, which she was sure - almost sure - that he wouldn't, she would tell him that it was Karen. She would tell him that she hadn't felt well and had come up here for a lie down.

She looked at the clock on the wall. Any second now. They could have come back before now. Fifteen minutes ago they had been frantically searching the room for Karen's bra. Baby pink lace that Karen knew was Sheila's favourite. How it had gotten behind the dresser was anyone's guess. But sometimes passion takes over and it stops you from thinking straight. She hadn't been thinking about what would have happened if her husband and four year old daughter had suddenly arrived home and found mummy begging Karen to do it harder – *harder!* She didn't think ten minutes ahead. Sheila lived in the here and the now. And the only person Sheila Morgan truly cared about was Sheila Morgan.

If she found herself with her back against the wall, or the mattress in this case, she would come at you with her claws out and her teeth bared. She would blame the whole world before she accepted any responsibility for her actions. It was Paul's fault for giving every ounce of his attention to their sideshow of a daughter. It was Karen's fault for, well, for whatever excuse she could think of at the time.

'Still only eight years old inside that thick skull of yours,' her mother used to say. And there was some truth in that. She didn't think about Paul catching her with Karen because she didn't believe that it would ever happen. Inside her head she was still a child, invincible and untouchable and impulsive. She had proposed to Paul after less than a week of knowing him and had become pregnant because then he couldn't leave her. Absolute madness when she looked back at it now, but at the time it had seemed completely rational.

Then there were the affairs. She made her mind up that she wanted something and she went out and got it. When Paul had found out about Colin Mayers because of the infection, she had buried the blade of a kitchen knife in her own leg so that he wouldn't leave her. The doctors had said that she had been lucky not to sever any major arteries and sent her to see a shrink. Paul had stood by her side and looked after her as she had known he would. Of course he would. He was her husband, he had to.

'I did it to punish myself,' she had told him. And he'd lapped it up. Poor old Sheila, always the victim and never to blame. She'd been having sex with Colin every Thursday for over five months but of course she only told Paul that it had happened once, when she'd had too much to drink. He'd taken advantage of her. She couldn't even remember it. *But look, Paul, I put a knife in my own leg because I wanted to hurt myself as much as I hurt you and I know that it was a really bad thing that I did.*

75

The knife thing had really hurt though and she had wondered if he would have stayed anyway and she could have avoided the scar. When Karen had asked how she'd got it she had lied; an accident she'd had as a child. And Karen had kissed it and told her that she was beautiful.

And that was all that mattered to Sheila.

Her mother could say whatever she wanted, Sheila didn't care. The old cow only said it to make herself believe that it wasn't her fault anyway. Everyone knows that if a child grows up to be bad or mad or whatever, it's always the parents that people look at. It wasn't her fault that she was like this; it was all down to her mother.

She paused. That was what people thought when they looked at Jessica. They thought it was her fault that Jessica was like that. Society always blames the parents. But it wasn't her fault. Jessica couldn't control it. The look in her eyes every time Sheila told her off said she hadn't got a clue what she'd done wrong. No, Sheila knew it wasn't her fault. But it wasn't Jessica's either. She had pushed her daughter away, all but disowned her because of something she knew the child couldn't do anything about, and then told her husband, who had been so very good to her when she had done nothing but take him for granted, that it was his problem. And Paul, dear sweet Paul, had told her that it was okay, that he would deal with it if it made her life that little bit easier.

She had been a bad mother and a bad wife – not that they needed to know. She could fix it. She could make it better.

She sat down on the bed. This had to stop and it had to stop right now.

3

Jess was forced awake by her dad struggling his way through Summer Holiday, and the almost constant sense of déjà vu that she was learning to ignore passed by nearly unnoticed. She opened her eyes slowly. Daddy was standing at the foot of the bed. He was wearing a huge red sombrero and waving his arms enthusiastically as he sang. She giggled and looked at the clock by the bed. The hands hung at six thirty.

'Come on, sweetheart,' Paul said as he finished the last chorus in a deep, warbling flat note. 'Up and dressed in fifteen minutes. Grandma Morgan's cheese and egg for breakfast,' He danced out of the room and went downstairs. Jess smiled. Mummy hated him cooking grandma Morgan's cheese and egg. The recipe was simple. Take two eggs, a few chunks of cheese about the size you'd put on a stick with a piece of pineapple and throw the lot into a pan. The pan starts to burn – *Et voila!* You have breakfast.

'Morning, Jessica,' Sheila said chirpily as she entered the room in a powder blue dressing gown that was beginning to fray at the cuffs. She pulled clothes haphazardly from Jess's wardrobe and put them beside her on the bed. 'Get dressed, darling. We're going to the seaside. Hurry up.' She pulled the curtains open and left as quickly as she had arrived. Jess clambered out of bed slowly, yawning and rubbing her eyes.

She could hear her dad coming back up the stairs as she took off her pyjamas and started to dress. He poked his head around the door to check that she was up and tutted as he strode across the room.

'How many times do I have to tell her?' he said to himself as he closed the curtains. 'You never open the curtains until you're dressed. Otherwise the nasty men might see you.'

Jess pulled on a plain pink tee shirt and jeans, following Paul downstairs where the smell of burning was thick and acrid. Paul ran into the kitchen to check breakfast as Jess sat on the sofa with Sheila and listened to Billy Joel as the sound of the radio floated in from the kitchen. Paul whistled along.

Then the hiss of cold water hitting the frying pan Paul had used to cremate breakfast filled her ears. Sheila rushed through to see what he was doing.

'Paul, what the hell have you done?' The kitchen was full of smoke.

'Just a spot of breakfast,' he replied.

'I know animals that could cook better than you,' she said. 'How am I ever going to clean that pan?'

'It's only a bit of egg.'

'Witches being burned at the stake didn't smell as bad as that, and I bet they didn't make half as much mess.'

Jess watched as Paul brought her a plate of brown cheese and egg.

'Tell your mum how nice it is,' he said quietly as he handed it to her. She giggled. Paul went back to the kitchen, his sombrero almost knocking a picture of Sheila's parents off the wall.

'Yum, yum, yum,' Jess cried dramatically as she rubbed her stomach. 'This is very nice.' She heard Paul laugh and bet that even mummy had smiled.

'Put the pan in soak,' Sheila said. 'I'll have a go at it when we get back.'

The cheese and egg wasn't particularly tasty, but Jess finished it to get daddy out of trouble. Then it was time to go to the seaside. Paul sang along to the radio all the way there, whistling when he didn't know the words, rolling down the window to enjoy a smoke when he didn't know the song at all.

'What do the donkeys at the seaside get for dinner?' he asked as they finally saw the sea.

'I don't know,' Jess called from the backseat, 'what do the donkeys at the seaside get for dinner?'

'Half an hour, same as everybody else.'

Jess laughed and Sheila groaned.

'Come on, it's a good joke,' Paul protested. Sheila shook her head and looked out of the window.

They arrived at lunch time and headed for the shops on the sea front. Sheila offered to buy Jess a bucket and spade for the beach but she didn't want a bucket and spade. She wanted the pair of glittery shoes she had seen in the window of Johnsons Gifts and Souvenirs. Paul took her hand and led her into the crowded shop. Children in cheap plastic sunglasses with bright yellow sticker suns at the corners of the frames swarmed around the toys and adults turned the postcard carousel, chuckling at the double entendres printed beneath blushing middle aged holiday makers or well endowed blonde girls. Jess froze. A deep feeling of dread turned her stomach. Her feet began to ache and all she could see was water.

'I don't want the shoes, daddy,' she said quietly.

'I thought you liked them?'

'I'll only wear them today and then they'll just go to waste,' she said, grabbing at the first excuse that came to mind. 'They're not the kind of shoes I can wear to school are they?'

Paul dropped to one knee and placed his hands on her shoulders. A tall girl with red pigtails almost tripped over his outstretched leg.

'You've got a wise head on your shoulders, Jessica.' He kissed her forehead and they left the shop.

Jess went on all the rides that she wanted to at the fair. Paul and Sheila waved at her as she went around and around on the little helicopters that lifted you six feet off the ground if you pulled the joystick all the way back. She laughed, enjoying the breeze on her face as she traced monotonous circles above their heads.

After the rides they ate hot dogs and candy floss and walked slowly to the beach. Paul sat down in the sand to make a start on today's Daily Telegraph crossword. Sheila lay back and opened a new Mills and Boon that she had bought at The Pickwick Paperbacks near the fair. Jess looked out to sea. The water glinted silver where the sun hit the restless waves. She shivered in spite of the heat.

'Do you want to go for a paddle?' Sheila asked.

Jess shook her head. 'I'll just stay here with you.'

She lay down and put an arm over her eyes. Her feet hurt and she couldn't breathe. To begin with she would only care that mummy might shout about her losing her shoe, but when the water was all around her that wouldn't seem like such a big deal anymore.

She knew that none of this was going to happen because she wasn't going anywhere near the water. The choking and the kicking was only in her head. She rolled over and held onto Paul. She hadn't seen this before. Not in her dreams or when she was awake. But whatever it was, it was wrong. It was wrong because she wasn't going anywhere near the water.

Cold comprehension made her skin break out in goose bumps. She wasn't going into the water because of what she saw in her head. She hadn't gotten daddy to buy her the shoes because of what she saw in her head. It wasn't because she hadn't wanted to wear the pretty shoes or paddle in the sea. What had stopped her was knowing that the shoes would hurt her feet and in her head her feet hurt when she was struggling to breathe.

She began to cry against Paul's shoulder.

'What's the matter, sweetheart?' he asked.

'Nothing, daddy,' she sniffed.

'Haven't you enjoyed yourself?'

'It's not that. I,' she cupped a hand around his ear, 'I can't say the rest because mummy's here.'

Paul's jaw tensed involuntarily. 'Do you need to tell me now?' he asked. He hoped that she would shake her head but, predictably, she nodded. 'Let's go for a walk on the beach and collect some shells.'

He put his paper down and got up, brushing sand from his shorts. They walked together for a while before she spoke.

'I wanted the shoes,' she said, 'but if I'd had them I think I might have drowned.' Paul was holding his breath. 'When we went into the shop my feet started to ache and I could see water. Nothing else, just water.' She swallowed hard and looked out to sea. Her eyes had a faraway quality, as if she wasn't seeing the water at all. 'Then when I got here my feet started to ache again and I could see you and mummy on the beach looking for me. But I'm not on the beach, daddy, I'm in the water and it's so hard to breathe.'

Tears were running from her eyes and his knees popped unnoticed as he bent to hold her. 'Nothing bad's going to happen, Jess,' he soothed. 'You didn't get the shoes, so nothing can happen can it?'

'But normally when I see things like that I know it's right. It's definitely going to happen.' She looked into Paul's eyes, willing him to understand. 'This time I saw something bad and I changed it.'

Paul's head began to ache and he felt cold despite the warmth of the day. A seagull landed close to where they stood as he held his daughter protectively and closed his eyes. How could she live with these terrible images locked inside her head?

'The bad things aren't just dreams, are they?' he asked.

She shook her head. 'I see people I know all the time but mummy says I don't know them. I know things about them that I shouldn't know but I do because someone told me.'

'Who told you sweetheart?' Paul asked. 'Was it Scott?'

'No, not Scott.'

'Is that how you knew who the little boy at the doctors was?'

She nodded and looked back at her mother, Sheila was deep inside her book.

'Who tells you these things, Jessica?' he asked impatiently. She shied away from the frustration in his voice. 'What you're saying is serious, Jess. Do you understand that? Nobody else see's the things you see or knows the things you

81

know. How do you know that what you're telling me is the truth?'

She glared at him angrily. 'You think I'm lying?' Her voice was enormous for such a small child. Paul looked back over his shoulder but his wife was still reading. 'I don't need to justify myself to you,' she shouted. 'I told you because I thought I could trust you and you think I'm making it up.'

You don't need to justify yourself to me? Where did a four year old learn to speak like that? He was going to ask but Jess was already heading back towards her mother.

4

'You look beautiful.'

Sheila finished plaiting her daughters hair and stood back to look at her. She was wearing a blue and white checked dress with the Filton Primary School logo embroidered over her heart.

'Come on then,' Sheila handed her a pink plastic lunchbox, 'or we'll be late.' She took Jess's hand, telling her to listen to the teachers and be a good girl and don't cause any trouble as they walked to school.

'I wont,' Jess replied.

'And don't…'

'I wont tell them about that,' Jess finished for her as they went through a gate into the playground. Pairs of girls stood opposite each other and slapped their hands together as they chanted. Boys ran around with their hoods on their heads and their coats flying out behind them.

Sheila smiled. 'Good girl.'

She straightened Jess's collar and kissed her cheek. 'Now go and have fun with the other boys and girls.'

Jess stepped apprehensively away from her mother and looked at her watch. Mummy and daddy had bought the watch for her birthday. It had come with a book and a cassette tape that was supposed to help her learn to tell the time. She hadn't really needed the book or the tape. She understood what time was.

'It's like trying to teach your grandma to suck eggs,' Daddy had said when he'd periodically asked her to tell him the time, just to make sure buying it hadn't been a waste of money. Jess hadn't really understood that. It was beyond her why anyone would want to suck eggs, especially if they tasted like the ones daddy cooked.

Still a couple of minutes before the bell would ring and they'd all have to line up outside their classrooms. She looked back for her mother but Sheila had already gone.

Ignoring the déjà vu, Jess walked deeper into the playground, looking for someone that she knew. She decided to keep her mouth shut whenever she could, to ask people's names if they hadn't been at playschool with her and to play the same stupid games every other four year old was playing at break time. She sighed to herself. School was going to be hard work.

Sheila rolled over and sat up, pulling the sheets up to cover her breasts. She took a pack of Lambert and Butler from the bedside table and lit one. Karen shuffled over to lie on Sheila's scarred thigh.

'The house feels so strange without her,' Sheila said. 'If I'm honest I'll admit that I miss her.'

Karen looked up at her. 'Miss her?' she asked. 'You couldn't wait to get rid of her.'

Sheila stroked Karen's hair and passed her the cigarette. 'I know,' she said. She had been waiting impatiently for Jess to start school so that she could get at least some of her freedom back. 'But this morning,' she left the sentence unfinished, smiling proudly at the memory of her daughter looking clean and tidy and pretty on her first day of school. Karen didn't like that smile one bit. 'Oh, Karen, you should have seen her.'

'Sheila, there's something wrong with her,' Karen said with a touch of agitation. She hated to talk about Sheila's family when they were together. It was rude of Sheila to do it in the first place. 'There's something really wrong with her. You've got a daughter with a serious problem and a husband who wont let you take her to a doctor.'

Normally Sheila would agree. Paul had refused to let her find professional help for Jess, scared that Jess would be taken away from them. Once upon a time Sheila had thought that having Jess taken away would have been a blessing but now she hated herself for ever thinking like that. Now she wanted to help, even if it was just to make this alien feeling of guilt go away. It had been sitting heavily in the pit of her stomach for the last few days and she didn't like it. It confused her.

'I'm sorry, Karen, but I think he was right,' she said. 'We can get through this as a family. If I ever felt that Jess was at risk of being, I don't know, damaged, by what was happening, I'd have done something about it. But I don't think being taken away from her parents and analysed by the men in white coats would help her.'

She knew that Jess still talked to Paul about all that stuff and she was grateful that she didn't have to listen to it anymore. But what about Paul? He never complained; not to her anyway. But then why would he? All he was doing was being a good dad and no matter how much Jess scared him he would take it – because she was his daughter and he loved her.

'I've failed as a mother,' she said mournfully.

'That's bullshit,' Karen said. 'You're the one who's been looking after her all day every day, who had to get her ready for school this morning.'

'You make it sound like a chore.'

'Isn't it?' Karen asked as she handed the cigarette back to Sheila.

Their eyes met for a second and then Sheila pushed her way out of the bed, crushing the cigarette out in an ashtray.

'No,' she replied. 'I should be enjoying her, bringing her up properly. Instead I just gave birth to her and handed her to Paul as if that was my part done.'

She pulled on her clothes, her back to Karen's fierce glare.

'What the hell are you trying to say?' She sat up and lit another of Sheila's cigarettes.

Sheila buttoned her shirt and sat on the edge of the bed to pull on her shoes, unable to look at Karen as she said, 'This has to end.'

'What?'

'I'm sorry,' Sheila replied, 'but I can't do this anymore. I risk losing my family every time we do this. I mean, what if Paul found out? What if Jess…' She trailed off, unsure how to finish, but they both knew what she was trying to say. What if Jess just happened to have a dream about this?

'I love you, Sheila.'

'Then you'll understand that this has to stop.'

Karen jumped out of bed and went over to her. 'No,' she said defiantly. 'Actually I don't understand. You can't just leave me.'

'Please, Karen. Don't make this any harder than it is already.'

'Hard?' Karen replied angrily. 'You make it look easy. Like this is what you wanted all along, just to mess me around until you got bored.'

'That's not true.'

'I love you.'

'I need to go back to my family.'

'No.' Karen was shaking her head frantically. 'I'll, I'll tell Paul. I'll tell him everything. Everything, Sheila.'

Sheila refused to back down. If she didn't do this now, while she felt so awful about it, she never would. 'He'll never believe you,' she replied calmly. 'Another man? Maybe. But you? No way.'

'What the hell do you mean by that?'

'A woman, Karen? You honestly think he'd believe I was having sex with a woman?' She picked up her bag and went to the door of Karen's small bedroom. 'You're nowhere near close enough to Paul for him to believe you over me. I'll just deny it and you'll end up looking like an idiot.' Hating the pained look on Karen's face she kissed her once, briefly, on the cheek. 'We don't have to fall out over this,' she said. 'You're still my friend, Karen, I just can't lose my family.'

Karen shook her head, watching with hateful eyes as Sheila left.

5

'Where's my big girl?' Paul called as he hung up his coat.

'She's at your mum's.' Sheila went to her husband and kissed his cheek. 'They wanted to see how she got on at school.'

'How did she get on?'

'Fine.' She sat on the sofa and turned off the TV. 'Paul, I want to talk to you about her. About the stuff she knows.'

Paul sat beside her and looked at their reflection in the dark eye of the television screen. 'I thought it upset you?'

'It does,' Sheila admitted. 'But I'm her mum and I should be as much a part of this as you are.'

She could almost hear the buzz of a million conflicting thoughts run through Paul's head as the colour drained from his face. He looked old, tired. How hadn't she noticed the effect this was having on him? Had she just ignored it?

'Okay,' he said carefully. The last thing he wanted to do was scare her off. She was right, she should be involved. But Sheila had a habit of changing her mind more often than her underwear and he didn't want her to decide that actually she had been right the first time and couldn't be a part of this. 'What do you want to know?' he asked.

She ran a shaking hand through her hair and Paul touched her arm. 'What is it?' she asked. 'Where does it come from?'

'I don't know.' He rubbed his chin, thinking about the things Jess had told him. 'They're like premonitions. She can look at people and tell you what they'll be doing in ten, even twenty years. She just knows.'

Frosty fingers stroked at Sheila's forearms, teasing up cold goose bumps.

'Let me show you something.' Paul offered his hand and she took it hesitantly. He led her upstairs to Jess's room and went to the drawing of the lake, pointing at the two figures beside the puddle of blue crayon.

87

'Look at the girl,' Paul said. 'If you didn't know any better, who would you say it was?'

Sheila looked at the girl in the drawing. Long dark hair fell over her shoulders and two blue dots stared out of her face. 'That's how Jess draws herself,' she said.

'That's what I said,' he was still staring at the picture. 'But she says it's not her. She says it's the lady that's with me at the hospital.'

Sheila looked at him, puzzled.

'I think we're both right,' Paul said. 'They're one and the same.'

He pointed at two squat u's on the girls chest that were obviously meant to be breasts. 'It's just that she's older.'

He went to Jess's bed and sat down, putting his head in his hands. His wife sat with him and put her hands in her lap. 'That's just guessing though, isn't it?' she asked. 'You don't know for sure.'

'It's the best explanation I've got,' he said. 'If you'd heard what I've heard, seen what I've seen...'

'It might just be an overactive imagination,' Sheila suggested, remembering how she had scorned Paul for suggesting that the dream about her car accident had been nothing more than anxiety.

'Do you think it was her overactive imagination that plucked that boys name out of thin air at the doctors?' Paul asked. 'Talk to her Sheila. You talk to her and see if you think what she's saying and what happens are just her imagination.' He wiped his sweating palms over the knees his trousers. 'Because I'm convinced that one day I'm going to be lying in a hospital bed and she's going to be holding my hand and watching me die.'

She looked back at the picture. At the headless boy. 'Who's that?' she asked.

'That's Scott Jordan.' Paul replied. 'The boy she dreams about.'

Sheila looked at the picture and rubbed her cool arms. 'Why hasn't he got a face?' she asked.

'Because she can't remember what he looks like.' Paul uttered a small, nervous laugh. 'She can't remember what someone she's never met looks like.'

'What?' Sheila looked at her husband for an answer she already knew he didn't have. She pulled him to her and held him, trying to offer some comfort.

'I've tried to narrow it down to just one thing,' Paul continued. 'But I can't. It's not just people her age or people that live near to us. She knows big things. National things, international things.'

'International things?' Sheila asked. 'What like?'

'Wars, films, celebrities I've never heard of. TV programmes I've never heard of, bands I've never heard of.'

'Like the Princess Diana thing?'

Paul nodded. A week ago they had discussed something Jess called the Millenium Bug, something that people thought would break all the computers in the world. Jess had enjoyed talking about the turn of the millennium, people burying time capsules in their back gardens, people believing that the world would end at midnight on 31st December 1999. Paul had found it exciting until he'd remembered the reality of what his daughter was saying. She was talking about things that weren't going to happen for more than a decade.

He had asked who Scott was but she didn't know. She knew that he would be nice and then he would be mean but that was all. Broken fragments of knowledge. He'd asked who told her these things, wondering if maybe his little girl had some sort of guardian angel, but she didn't know. It was like she'd just been born with certain pieces of information.

He had worried about her starting school. He knew that his wife had worried too, but he worried for different reasons. It wasn't just premonitions, there were the things she could do physically. She could solve complex maths problems, she could read and write. Not just The Cat Sat on the Mat stuff, big words.

She had cooked a full English breakfast once. Paul had helped her with pans that were too heavy but she had known that you put the sausages under the grill

89

first and fry the eggs last. She even knew how he liked his bacon. She knew what ingredients were needed to make a roast dinner. She watched the news and understood it. She could tune a radio, wire a plug, plait her own hair.

If Sheila had been watching more closely she would have noticed these things. Paul had concluded that his daughter wasn't a genius or a psychic, it was like she was an adult trapped inside a child's body. She didn't watch cartoons or children's programmes. She browsed the newspapers, sometimes pausing to read a whole story, sometimes making a start on the crossword.

'We should go out,' Sheila said with a sudden smile. 'Just me and you, like we used to. We haven't been out in ages. I'm so sorry, Paul. I was scared and I've pushed her away and I've pushed you away too.'

He kissed her forehead. 'I'm scared too,' he replied. 'But we're a family. We'll be fine as long as we've got each other.'

6

Sheila swept down the stairs in a long blue skirt that she had bought last year. She had worn it twice; the last time had been New Years Eve and Paul had told her how beautiful she looked. It had been hanging, unworn, in the wardrobe ever since.

'You need to get ready, Paul,' she said. 'Karen'll be here any minute.'

He stood and embraced her. 'You look great,' he smiled.

Sheila kissed him before going over to the sofa and sitting beside Jess. She stroked her daughter's hair and pulled her onto her lap. 'Tomorrow me and daddy are going to take you somewhere special,' she said.

'Where?' Jess asked excitedly.

'I don't know yet.' Sheila put her arms around Jess as Paul went upstairs to change. 'It's a surprise.'

Jess put her arms around her mother. 'I love you, mummy,' she said.

Sheila pulled her daughter's head to her breast and held her tight. 'I love you too little girl.'

'Hello?' Karen called as she threw open the front door. Sheila took her daughter from her lap and set her down as she stood up. Jess went upstairs to her room.

'Hi, Karen,' she said. 'Thanks for coming.'

Thanks for coming? Karen frowned. It was normally a seductive smile, an over friendly hug. Sheila didn't even seem pleased to see her. It really was over. 'No problem,' she replied flatly.

Sheila went to the kitchen to pour a small glass of wine and Karen followed closely.

'I want to talk to you about the other day,' Karen said.

Sheila put the bottle back in the fridge and took a sip of her wine. 'I haven't changed my mind,' she said. 'I'm sorry.'

91

'Sheila, I want to be with you,' Karen said. 'I can't bear the thought that I'll never touch you again. We'll be careful, we'll see each other less often.' She stopped. Sheila was shaking her head.

'I don't want to never see you again,' Sheila said. 'But I can't keep sneaking around behind their backs. I married Paul. I love Paul, and I love Jessica.'

Karen nodded. 'I know,' she said resignedly. 'You know what Sheila?' She gave her lovers hand a squeeze as her eyes filled with tears. 'I know you love them and I know I love you enough to let you go back to them.'

Sheila frowned, still braced for an argument. 'Really?' she asked cautiously.

'I'll miss you,' Karen sniffed. 'But I just want you to be happy.'

They embraced and Sheila fought the urge to kiss her. 'Thank you,' she said. 'You know, I never felt like I bonded with Jess, but these last few days, it just feels different. Like I've got a second chance.'

She lit a cigarette and blew thin smoke into the air.

Karen nodded. She was still thinking about telling Paul. Sheila couldn't just use her like this. She was giving up what they had, and for what? A snotty nosed four year old freak of a daughter?

'She says the Berlin Wall's going to come down,' Sheila said.

'Really,' Karen replied flatly.

'How does she even know what the Berlin Wall is?' Sheila asked. 'Let alone how important it would be if they ever took it down?'

'School?'

'They don't teach politics to four year olds,' Sheila said as she put the cigarette between her lips and inhaled.

'What time are you planning on being back?' Karen asked, desperate for a change of subject.

'Around midnight.'

'Have a good night,' Karen said as she offered a saccharine smile.

'Thank you,' Sheila replied, smiling back at her.

92

She felt as if a weight had been lifted from her. Everything would be fine now. She was finally acting like an adult. She was putting her husband and her child first and it felt good. When Paul came downstairs she took his arm and called her goodbyes to Karen as they left the house.

7

The sound the rain made as it spattered the hood of her coat made Sheila feel as if she was caught inside a blanket of bubble wrap that hundreds of feet were trampling. Paul pulled her into a small pub and they went upstairs to the bar, bypassing the downstairs family room and taking a seat by the window.

She slid out of her coat while Paul fetched their drinks, watching people scurrying along the streets below her as the rain hammered down hard enough to bounce back off the ground. To Sheila it looked like a coat of television static had been painted over the street, flashing orange and silver in the glare of streetlamps and the fluorescents thrown out from bars and shops. She looked at Paul with sad eyes as he sat down opposite her and put their drinks down.

'I'm sorry I've been such a bitch,' she said quietly.

He looked at her as if she had slapped him. 'What?' he asked. 'Where did that come from?'

She offered him a small, fraught smile. 'I don't deserve you, Paul.'

He nudged her chin with his forefinger and she looked across the table at him. He looked concerned, although she couldn't tell whether it was for her or for himself. 'What's happened, Sheila?' he asked.

She knew what he was thinking and while part of her hated him for it, most of her couldn't blame him. How many people had warned him that if she'd done it once she would do it again?

'Nothing,' she said and then quickly changed her mind. 'Everything.' She drank and then continued. 'After what happened with Colin,' she saw Paul's face tighten at the mention of his name and she knew how much it must hurt him to have that image conjured up again after all this time. 'When we found out that Jessica would be our only child, why would I, her mother for god's sake, why would I abandon her?'

Paul took her hands. 'You haven't abandoned her,' he replied, although all he was thinking was, *Who is he, Sheila?*

'I love you both so much.' She was on the verge of tears. 'But it was like if I didn't talk about it, then it wasn't happening.'

'What wasn't happening?' Even as he spoke he was preparing himself for her confession, feeling ridiculously naïve for believing her when she'd said that it would never happen again and ridiculously stupid for not suspecting a thing.

'Jess,' she said as if it had been obvious. 'I just thought that if I ignored it then I wouldn't have to think about . . .' She looked down at the table and he was pleased that she had. Otherwise she would have seen the stupid grin of relief that spread across his face before he could stop it. Then came the guilt. How could he have thought that she had been cheating again? She wouldn't. Not just because she had been warned that if it happened again he *would* leave and he *would* take Jess with him and she knew that Paul Morgan was a man who kept his promises, but because she was his wife and she loved him and it wasn't fair for him to assume that she was going to confess to an affair every time she said that they needed to talk or that something was on her mind. She had been drunk, it had been a one off thing and it had never happened before or since.

'You don't have to think about that,' Paul soothed as images of his wife driving into a lorry before her world went black made his flesh crawl.

She nodded. 'Yes I do.' She looked at him again with sad eyes. 'I just thought that if I didn't see it or hear what she had to say, if I just ignored that part of her, that it wouldn't be true.' She finished her beer in one go and set the glass down heavily. 'But it's always been at the back of my mind anyway and all I've done is push my little girl away. My god, she must hate me.'

'She doesn't hate you, Sheila,' Paul said. 'She does wonder why her mummy's scared of her though.'

A look of horror crossed her face and tears began to roll silently down her cheeks. 'How did she pick up on that?'

'Kids are far more perceptive than we give them credit for,' Paul shrugged.

Sheila swiped at her wet face and sniffed hard. 'It's like she's older than she is, if that makes any sense.'

Paul nodded that it did. 'Do you want another?'

'Please.'

As Paul went to the bar she turned her gaze to the window. There was a whole world out there and she'd never really been anywhere. She made a mental note to travel more and added it to the ever growing list of things to do before . . . another tear rolled over her hot cheek. She'd have to start writing things down. If she made many more mental notes her brain would explode. She wanted to buy a designer dress, taste caviar, go to Vegas, make things up with her parents, and numerous other things she couldn't remember. Twenty three years had been wasted in the same way that millions of lives are wasted, with the 'I'll do it tomorrow' attitude, the idea that you have your whole life to do something and it's not until you're old and incapable of climbing your own stairs that you realise that you never actually got around to doing anything.

She hadn't spoken to her parents in years. They knew they had a grandchild but they'd never met Jessica. Maybe now was the time. They had been so wrapped up in their high morals that they'd never seen the only child of their only child. All that wasted time because of a stupid disagreement between her dad and Paul. She thought it had been about politics to begin with but couldn't remember, it had all happened so long ago. They had never seen eye to eye after that and Sheila had only ever spoken to them on the phone. Over time the calls had become less frequent until they hadn't come at all.

Paul set the drinks down and sat back at the table. 'What are you thinking about?' he asked.

She turned back to look at him. 'Everything and nothing.'

He put a hand over hers, squeezing it supportively. 'You know you can talk to me, don't you?' he asked.

She gulped at the cool beer . 'It's just a lot to take in, Paul.'

There was so much she wanted to say but her thoughts were muddled. An old couple put their drinks down at a table nearby and she watched as the man pulled out a chair for his wife, pushing it beneath her as she sat down before sitting down himself.

'I'm never going to be old,' she said sadly. 'I'll never get a bus pass or go through the menopause.' She smiled cynically. 'What am I taking about? I'll never even see thirty.'

Paul didn't know what to say. This was worse than talking to Jess about the World Trade Centre. His wife's heart was breaking. Patting her on the head and saying *'there there'* wasn't going to help. He was powerless to do anything but watch as she tried to come to terms with it.

She sipped her drink. 'What's the future like, Paul?' she asked, trying to smile.

'Nothing special,' he replied. 'Those portable phones everyone's been laughing at are really going to catch on. You'll be able to take pictures with them and send notes to each other. There's a thing called the internet where you can go onto a computer and talk to anyone in the world in real time.' He expected her to look sad at the prospect that she would never see these things but she seemed genuinely interested in what he had to say. And he'd been dying to talk to someone about it. 'The Labour Party get back into power, you can get about four million channels on the telly, they make three more Terminator films.'

'You'll always love me wont you, Paul?' she asked.

He took her hands and kissed them. 'Until the day I die.'

They finished their drinks and went outside. Sheila shivered and pulled her coat around her tightly . At least the rain had stopped. 'Another drink?' she asked as they reached a dimly lit bar only yards from the cinema they were supposed to go to. She didn't want to sit in silence. She wanted to talk. Paul nodded and they went inside.

'I want to talk about it but I don't know what to say,' she said as he joined her at the table. 'I can think about it and try to accept it but I can't understand it. I just can't take it in.'

'You always knew it was going to happen,' Paul said. 'You just didn't know when.'

'Thanks,' she replied sarcastically, 'It's not just that, Paul. It's everything. Where does it come from?'

Paul shrugged. 'She doesn't know and I can't work it out.'

They talked honestly and openly, discussing Jess, making plans for the future. Sheila asked questions and Paul told her what he knew. Sometimes she struggled to ask and often he struggled to answer. Eventually last orders were called. Sheila thanked him for listening to her. He didn't reply but took her hand and squeezed it as they strolled out into the night and made their way home.

Karen was lying on the sofa. A cigarette lay smouldering in the ashtray. She sat up quickly when she heard the door open.

'Good night?' she asked brightly.

'Really good.' Sheila's eyes sparkled as she kissed her husband's cheek.

'Where's Jess?' Paul asked.

'Asleep,' Karen replied.

'I think I'll make coffee,' Sheila said as she took off her coat.

Paul went up to check on their daughter and Karen followed Sheila into the kitchen. 'We need to talk,' she said seriously as Sheila filled the kettle, turning to look at her suspiciously.

'About what?' she asked.

'About your daughter asking me why I kiss you when Paul's at work.' She didn't know if Sheila would believe her but it was the only shot she had. Sheila looked at her, unblinking, her face pale. 'I thought I should tell you before she wakes up.'

Sheila looked up at the ceiling. Paul was up there. She could be telling him right now. 'You're making it up,' she said uncertainly.

'What?' Karen asked. 'Don't be stupid, Sheila. I told you, I love you enough to understand that your family's more important to you than I am. I told you that. If that wasn't true I wouldn't be warning you, would I? I'd just let her tell him.' Sheila was silent, trying to make sense of what Karen had just said. She wasn't very bright and this, paired with two or three drinks too many, made it too hard to think about right now. 'Ask her if you don't believe me,' Karen added.

'What the hell did she say?'

Karen put a hand to her mouth, trying hard to suppress a smile and look concerned. 'She said she was going to tell Paul,' she said. 'She knows it's wrong, Sheila. She cried.'

At this Sheila began to weep. Not for her daughter, or for Paul, but for herself. Instead of thinking of how to explain this to her husband she was thinking of excuses. Curiosity; Paul only cared about Jessica; it was only one kiss. Her heart thumped inside her chest as she fingered the necklace at her throat. Think. Think Sheila.

'What the hell am I going to do?' She looked helplessly at Karen.

'The only thing I can think of is telling Paul before she does,' Karen suggested. 'Surely it'll sound better coming from you than his four year old daughter.'

'But he'll leave,' she replied desperately.

Karen shrugged. 'Wont he leave regardless of who tells him?' she asked. 'If it comes from you at least you'll be able to explain.'

'We can deny it,' Sheila said quickly as she began to pace the kitchen, running a shaking hand through her hair.

'And you think he'll believe us over her?' Karen looked doubtful.

'He might.' Sheila leaned against the sink and put her head in her hands. 'Oh god, he wont, will he? You know I told him tonight that I wanted to talk. I meant about Jessica, but I could see it in his eyes that he was waiting for it to be Colin Mayers all over again. I'm finished, Karen.' She looked up, her face pale and frightened.

'I'm here, Sheila,' Karen said softly.

Sheila fled to the bathroom as her bile rose, pinching her mouth closed until she fell to her knees before the toilet and threw up the night's drinks into the bowl. The muscles in her back and stomach contracted violently as she retched over and over again. Then she sat back heavily with her skirt pooled around her legs, dry heaving until it felt as if her throat was on fire. A cool sweat had broken out all over her body.

Paul came across the landing. He knocked on the door and went in. Sheila looked up at him through angry tears.

'What's the matter?' he asked.

She only cried and clutched at the toilet seat. He lifted her and took her into the bedroom, undressing her slowly, putting her to bed like a child. Sheila sobbed, cursing the day she had ever laid eyes on Karen Howard.

'I love you, Paul,' she sobbed.

'I love you too,' he said. 'What's the matter?'

'Nothing,' she replied. 'I'll talk to you tomorrow. I want to go to sleep.'

He looked puzzled and that made her cry harder. He stood up and she turned over so that she wouldn't have to look at him.

Downstairs, Karen smiled to herself.

8

Sheila buried her head under the covers and listened to Paul start the car. She couldn't go out. She'd never be able to look her husband or her daughter in the eye again. Never. She wept softly, hugging herself and pulling her knees up to her chest. When they came back he would know. It would be over, everything would be over.

'So where do you want to go?' Paul asked. Jess shrugged and looked up at her parent's bedroom window as they pulled away, wondering why mummy hadn't come with them. Daddy had said it was a hangover but he'd been lying, she could tell. 'Well, I'll drive and you tell me where to go', he suggested. He hadn't wanted to leave Sheila but Jess was so excited about their mystery trip that he had agreed to take her out. They wouldn't go far, would be back within the hour.

Jess didn't reply and only looked out at the passing streets of the estate. The names were familiar. Jessica Morgan lived in a world where things were rarely new. Everything was always expected and always on time. The houses all seemed to be holding some secret that she already knew but couldn't remember. It was like forgetting a telephone number or the words to a song and it irritated the hell out of her.

Lake Rise, Marjorie Road, Beaufort Street, Ripon Crescent, Dukes Court. She gasped and automatically turned in her seat to look at the other side of the road where the street fell away to fields.

'I want to stop here,' she said.

'We're not even off the estate, sweetheart.'

'Please, daddy.' Her eyes remained on the fields. Paul pulled up by the side of the road and she got out, heading straight for them.

'Do you want to go for a walk in the fields?' he asked as he jogged after her. No reply.

He could hear her breathing. It was strangled and quick in her throat as she ran over a small hill and disappeared from his view. Ghosts of a future past were rattling their chains and screaming themselves to life here. Paul started to run as he realised with horror that she was heading for the water.

As the Swanmore River came into view she gasped again, pausing momentarily, the cold wind blowing her hair out behind her. Paul stopped to look at her. She had changed. Her eyes were wide and alert and Paul hadn't seen eyes like that since he and four of his friends had experimented with acid in high school. Her lips were clamped together in a thin line and her hands were trembling. She continued slowly towards the water, halting at the river's edge. Paul hurried to her and clamped his hand over her shoulders.

'Cold,' she whispered as Paul dragged her away from the water. Their feet tangled, spilling them both backwards into the wet grass. Jess struggled away from him and forced herself to her feet, standing over him and staring into him with those wide eyes.

'Jess, calm down,' he begged. 'Please calm down.'

'Elaine,' she said. 'Her name's Elaine. It's your fault, daddy. Your fault and Joanne's fault and Scott's fault.' Her voice rose in a terrifying crescendo until she was screaming into his face. 'You were smoking and I ran.' Her eyes fixed on him, wide and red rimmed, tears began to spill from them as she continued. 'I ran and she shouted and I, I...'

She threw back her head and pitched a piercing scream at the grey sky. Then she fell back into Paul's arms, chest heaving, eyes closed. He lifted her and staggered back towards the car. After pulling himself inside he placed her in the passenger seat and rested his head against the wheel. He'd never been so scared in his life. What was he supposed to do? She was his daughter and he loved her but this was beyond him. She needed real help, professional help that he couldn't offer.

Jess stirred as he started the engine. He didn't want her to wake up here, he

102

wanted to get her home and calm her down. That was assuming he could calm her down. Maybe she'd gone too far and he wouldn't be able to bring her back. He should have gotten help for her a long time ago.

He drove slowly, scared that she would wake up and start screaming again. He was already shaking and if she screamed he would lose control of the car. His eyes began to leak helpless tears as the streets passed by in a blur. When he pulled up outside the house his stomach turned with dread. Sheila. He had to tell Sheila.

He carried Jess into the house and laid her on the sofa. 'Sheila?' he called. 'Sheila?'

He went to their bedroom but it was empty. 'Sheila?' She wasn't in the bath or in Jess's room. He checked that Jess was still on the sofa and went to the kitchen, walking into the door as he tried to push it open. His nose squashed painfully against his face. Something was behind the door.

'Sheila?' He pushed again with a little more force and he heard something move, something sliding back from behind the door. He pushed harder and the door opened all the way. His feet seemed to take wings as he hurried in and he fell hard on his elbow, letting out a yelp of pain. As he sat up and pulled his injured arm to his chest he noticed the blood.

The floor was a deep and glossy crimson. It was on his clothes, his hands, his shoes, his hair. It was *everywhere.* Crawling around to the back of the door he saw his wife's nightgown. He looked back at the sofa, Jess was still there, he could see her feet poking out at him over the arm.

He knelt up and pulled the door back towards him. His wife lay in her own blood. Half of her face was only spotted with it but the other side was resting in it. A knife which looked cartoonishly oversized lay on the floor and a piece of paper sat on the seat of a kitchen chair. *Sorry* was written in his wife's slanting hand.

The blood was from her throat.

She had cut her own throat.

His wife had cut her own throat.

He felt his balls shrink and try to crawl into his stomach, which seemed to be tumble drying his intestines.

'Sheila,' he managed before spilling his breakfast. He threw up for a long time and when he finished he saw that it was mingling with the blood and was in his wife's hair. A large chunk of partially digested sausage had landed on the back of her hand and that made him throw up again. A long trail of saliva hung from his open mouth, suspended inches above the congealing mess of blood and breakfast. He brushed it away with the back of his hand and slid over to take his wife's hand. Tears blurred his vision. *She's still warm,* he thought. He put her limp hand to his cheek and cried over it.

'Oh darling,' he moaned. 'What...' he couldn't finish. Memories swamped his head. Once upon a time they had been lovers and teenagers. Together they had married and cried and laughed.

Stupidly, he checked her pulse. Nothing. His wife, his lover, his friend, was dead. He sat for a long time without proper thought or intention, just trying to wake up from this terrible dream that his mind must have conjured to torture him.

'Daddy?'

His heart began to pound as he stood up quickly, desperate to shield her from this terrible scene. Then he slid to a halt, almost falling again. *I'm covered in her,* he thought and instead of going to his daughter he closed the door against her.

'I'll just be a minute, sweetheart,' he called shakily, tearing off his clothes and dumping them beside his wife. He went to the washing machine and pulled out yesterday's clothes, hurrying them on as quickly as his shaking and bloody hands would allow. He would have to wash them.

'Daddy?'

Paul wiped his hands on a towel, smearing blood in abstract fingers over the yellow cloth. 'I'm coming,' he called back. 'Are you feeling better?'

Jess said that she was and Paul felt at least a twinge of relief. 'Go upstairs,' he said. 'I'll be up in a minute.'

He waited until he heard her bedroom door close before he hurried to the phone and called the police.

Part Three

1

The Unicorn Inn had stood proud, surrounded by the picturesque Yorkshire countryside, for almost three centuries. Looking out over lush green fields and the dense woodland beyond, tourists and locals alike laughed and chattered as they had since the rule of King William III.

Don and Jean Baker had spent the last ten years building up the pub's reputation for fine home cooked meals and well kept ales. A traditional pub, The Unicorn suited its surroundings, which were beautiful in the full bloom of summer and charming as a Victorian Christmas card during winter. To look at a picture of it you would be forgiven for assuming that it was miles from civilisation when in reality it was only three miles from York itself and very close to other small towns and villages which provided most of their regular custom.

It had been their regular's that had first warned them about the ghosts.

Geoff Carpenter, a retired train driver who could be found perched on the same stool at the same place at the bar at the same time every day, had taken great delight in passing on to them the same information he had given to the last three landlords – that The Unicorn was haunted by more spirits than they had behind the bar. Don and Jean had taken his words with a pinch of salt. They had been in the trade for almost twenty years, they'd heard such stories before. And in ten years, only the odd incident had made them briefly consider how much truth there might be to the rumours. Pubs, especially pubs as old as The Unicorn, which might very probably have played host to Dick Turpin and Guy Fawkes if Geoff was to be believed, always have a tragedy or two to tell and will always be shrouded in the mystery of times and people past.

Everyone locally had heard about Henry Ferns hanging himself in what was now the restaurant – what had then, back when Queen Victoria had only just begun to mourn the passing of her husband, been the stables. It had taken only one tourist a few months back to run screaming before people had decided to come ghost hunting. Always the same questions, always the same fascinated faces and eager eyes.

It had been excellent for business. Takings had gone up and people had started visiting from all over the country. Despite this, Jean missed how it had been before, when she had been able to stand around the bar gossiping with the locals and take the time to prepare proper home cooked meals. Nowadays the names that appeared on the booking list for Sunday lunch were unfamiliar and most of the food was brought in. While she still prided herself on her home made Yorkshire puddings and slow roasted meats, she simply didn't have the time to cook everything in the vast quantities that were required.

Most of the people that came had scared themselves half to death with hearsay before they arrived and the food was secondary anyway. People claimed to feel things, hear things, sense things. It was all part of the game.

Jean and Don had laughed behind their backs to begin with, shaken their heads at them taking it so seriously. More recently it hadn't been quite so funny. People cried, screamed or simply ran whenever they saw whatever it was that was in the restaurant. Talk of an old man with huge staring eyes and a woman in white had circulated, changing like Chinese Whispers as the stories made their rounds. More recently a young boy had been mentioned. There were what the tourists called cold spots and occasionally the kitchen doors would swing open for no apparent reason, but whoever the visitors were they had never shown themselves to the landlord or his wife.

Don looked at his wife. More wrinkles were appearing every day. Neither of them were getting any younger.

'I only know twenty three of the names down for lunch today,' Jean said as her eyes ran over the diary.

'It'll die off,' he offered optimistically. 'They'll find an image of the Virgin Mary in a barrel of Best somewhere and they'll all disappear.'

Jean smiled and wrinkles folded around her mouth and eyes. 'You've been saying that for the last six months.' She closed the diary.

A young couple entered loudly from the car park and Don smiled his friendly landlord smile. He didn't know them.

'Yes, please?'

They asked about Henry when he offered their change. He ran through the story as he had a thousand times before. Henry Ferns had taken his own life after losing the little that remained of what had once been a fortune on cards and dice.

'His little boy saw him do it,' he explained. 'Spent the rest of his life in the nuthouse. As far as I know his wife moved to Somerset and remarried.'

Before Henry there had been accidents, brawls turned bad, whores and highwaymen. But Don was tired of telling the same old stories and ended there. It was enough. The couple ordered another drink and booked for Sunday lunch in four weeks time.

In the kitchen, Jess stared blankly out of the small window. She was feeling it again. A trapped, disconnected feeling like she shouldn't be here. She missed her dad. She wanted to be back in Filton with him but she daren't suggest it and neither would he. Both for the same reason. What if it happened again?

'One beef, one turkey with no carrots, table two,' Fiona yelled. Jess took the plates and backed carefully out of the kitchen. The restaurant was heaving with faces she didn't know.

She hated Sundays.

She made her way through the chattering tables and placed the meals in front of a large man and his wife.

'We ordered a child's beef as well,' Wife said impatiently.

'It's on it's way.' Jess offered a polite smile and hurried back to the kitchen.

'They've got you earning your pocket money today,' Geoff said as she passed the bar. She flashed another smile as she disappeared through the doors.

'Child's beef?' she asked.

Fiona thrust the plate at her and she almost dropped it.

She loathed Sundays when Fiona worked.

Heading back to the table she saw Wife had her arm around her child. 'Child's beef,' she said as she slid the plate onto the table. 'Would you like any sauces or…'

'Can't you see that my son is upset?' Wife snapped.

'Is there a problem?' Jess asked.

'He says there's another little boy watching him.'

Jess looked from Husband to Wife to Child. 'What?'

'From over there.' Wife pointed to a space between two tables on the opposite side of the narrow room. Predictably, the surrounding tables hushed and the silence spread like a plague.

Jess looked over. The people dining at the tables Wife was pointing at were looking at the empty space with wide eyes. 'I don't see anything,' she said.

'Well he does. We'd like another table please.'

Jess cast her eyes over the crowded room and the customers waiting at the bar for someone to finish so that they could sit down.

'There aren't any other tables,' she replied.

Wife folded her arms over her ample bosom. 'Then what do you intend to do about it?'

Jess shrugged. 'There's nothing we can do.'

The child began to cry softly.

'Can I see the manager please?' Wife's lips tensed into a thin line.

'There's nothing we can do,' Jess repeated.

'Manager please.'

Jess turned her back on the table and strode to the bar, uncomfortably aware of the many pairs of eyes on her back.

'Granddad, they reckon the kid can see something,' she said. 'They want a

112

new table.'

Don looked over at the family. 'Have you told them...'

'There's nothing we can do,' she sighed. 'I know.'

Don walked through the silent room to the table and spoke to Wife in no more than a whisper. Jess leaned against the bar and folded her arms.

'They come to see ghosts,' Geoff said. 'If they don't they're disappointed, if they do they want a manager.'

Jess nodded her agreement. Wife was holding her son in her lap as she continued to demand a different table. Husband only looked at the floor. She'd seen it before. Wife would walk out with her son in her arms. Her husband would follow, apologising as he left.

Everyone watched as Don returned to the bar. Wife got up, slung her bag over her shoulder, and snatched at Child's hand. She shuffled past the bar and out into the car park as Husband picked up a Yorkshire pudding and gobbled it hungrily before making his way after them.

'I'm really sorry about that,' he said to Don.

'No harm done.'

'Sorry, love.'

'Okay,' Jess smiled and headed back to clear the table. She took the plates back into the kitchen and looked at the other tickets.

'Why have they been sent back?' Fiona asked.

'They weren't sent back,' Jess replied. 'They said they saw something and left.'

Fiona paused over a tray of spitting roast potatoes. 'It's happening more often,' she said. 'I'll tell you now, Jess, the second I see something, I'm gone.'

Jess ignored her. She was tired, fed up and she had a pile of homework that needed doing before tomorrow.

'The two sponge and custards for table four are going cold,' Fiona nudged her. 'Are you okay?'

113

Jess nodded. 'Just tired.' She picked up the pair of white bowls and went back out into the restaurant.

'I think we should send her upstairs,' Jean said as she watched Jess deliver the desserts.

'Why?' Don asked, passing another stranger her change.

'Because we don't know how it's affecting her.'

'She seems fine to me,' Don said.

'Well, I'm not going to wait until she doesn't seem fine,' Jean replied as she started the glass washer. 'We promised Paul that she'd be okay here.'

Don smirked. It hadn't been a promise, it had been Jean's way of telling Paul that she could look after Jess better than he could.

'This has been going on for a long time,' Don said. 'She hasn't heard or seen anything. I don't even think she believes in all that.'

A scream from the restaurant made them both look up. Geoff looked over at table sixteen. A woman was staring at the chair on the opposite side of the table. Her companion, a lanky man in his mid thirties, was sitting by her side and looking at the same spot.

'Can I help?' Jess asked as she reluctantly approached the table.

The man shrugged. 'I don't know what the matter is.'

Jess looked at the shaking, slack jawed woman. 'Are you alright?' she asked stupidly.

'Don't you see him?' Her voice was barely audible and her eyes never moved from the chair opposite her own.

Jess shook her head as she made her way around the table and laid a hand on the woman's shoulder. She tensed and her knuckles paled as she gripped the edge of the table tightly.

'He's just sitting there staring at me.'

'I don't see anything.'

'He's two feet away from my face.'

'Would you like to go outside for some fresh air?'

'I daren't move,' the woman whispered.

The high smell of urine hit Jess's nose and she felt dull pity for the woman.

'I want to go home.' Tears began to run from her glassy, unblinking eyes.

Jess looked at the man as he put an arm around the woman's waist and lifted her slowly from the chair. She pressed her face against his coat. Don and Jean stood with Geoff, arms around each other.

'The bill?' the man asked as he approached the bar.

Don shook his head. 'Don't worry about it,' he said. 'You didn't touch any of your meal.'

Only Geoff saw the sharp look Jean gave her husband as her hand hovered over the till.

The man made a slight nod of thanks before leaving. Jess looked once more at the empty space before joining her grandparents at the bar.

'That poor woman,' Jean said.

'What did she see?' Geoff asked.

'A man,' Jess replied. 'He was staring at her apparently.'

'That's Henry.'

Jean got herself a coke. 'Why all of a sudden?' she asked nobody in particular.

Geoff turned his huge body on the bar stool. 'It's a mystery.' He finished his pint and gestured for another. 'I thought Abe Hamilton had sorted it all out, but that was more than twenty years ago.'

'Who's Abe Hamilton?' Jean asked as she took his money and placed the drink on the bar. Jess smiled. Her grandmother had played right into Geoff's liver spotted hands. Jess thought that the day someone didn't ask Geoff to share his vast local knowledge, otherwise known simply as gossip, would be the day he'd give up and die.

'He was a strange character,' Geoff said before taking a sip of his beer.

115

'Local bloke. Saw things, felt things, told you stories that gave you nightmares for months.'

Jean pulled her cardigan tight around her skinny body.

'I was here one night,' Geoff continued. 'People had been seeing things for months. Then this Abe turns up. The landlord had asked him to come in, heard about his reputation.'

'What reputation?' Jess asked, cursing herself for doing so immediately afterwards.

'He had a name for himself. Talked to ghosts. Got them to go wherever it was they were supposed to go.' He took a cigar from his breast pocket and lit it, puffing for a few seconds before he went on. 'I thought it was a joke, didn't really believe it. Not until he had a wander round.'

'What happened?' Jess asked, the waiting diners forgotten.

'He wandered round, upstairs and downstairs, then he went into the restaurant and sat at a table. He put his hands down on top of it,' Geoff put a palm flat against the bar to demonstrate. 'Then he closed his eyes. You could have heard a pin drop. So then he starts humming, not a tune just a sound.' He took another drink. 'Then his head snapped over to one side and he grabbed his neck. Me and the landlord ran over and when he took his hand away there were these scratches all down his neck. They were bleeding. Not deep, but bleeding just the same.'

'So he tells us to leave and started humming again. Apparently there was a woman who'd been a prostitute about a hundred years before. So she'd been shagging the landlord and she'd wanted him to leave his wife. He refused, she threatened to tell his wife everything, got this bloke really wound up. He ended up strangling her with his own two hands. Got hanged up at Knavesmire for it.'

Jean finished her drink and poured another. 'Place was crawling with them,' Geoff said. 'If I were you I'd get someone in to sort them out before they all come back.'

Don and Jean exchanged glances. Jess was looking at table sixteen.

'Have you got Mr Hamilton's number?' Don asked.

Geoff laughed. 'He died more than ten years ago,' he said. 'Massive heart attack. Dead before he even knew about it.' He licked at the end of the cigar before wrapping his fleshy lips around it again.

'I bet they cost a fortune,' Jean said.

Geoff shrugged. 'Only one way to find out,' he said. 'His son Russ is in the phone book. Lives on Proctor Road or Proctor Drive or something like that, in Leeds.

Jean frowned dubiously. 'Does he do the same thing?' she asked.

Geoff nodded. 'Far as I know.'

Jean looked at Don for reassurance. 'Worth a shot,' he said. 'Get the place back to normal.' She nodded and went upstairs to find the phone book.

Jess drank what remained of her grandmother's coke and then ran her fingers absently over the cold glass. 'What did Abe do then?' she asked.

'Spoke to them,' Geoff replied. 'Understood them. Showed them a way out.'

'Sounds weird.'

'The unexplained is a very strange thing.'

The unexplained. That could be an interesting discussion with her grandparents. Here they were trying to arrange for a real life ghostbuster to come and sort this out, probably going to spend a fortune, but they hadn't talked about what had happened to her since she'd arrived. Weren't they just two sides of the same dark coin?

'You'd better go and do some work,' Don said. 'People are waiting for their food.'

Jess nodded and went back to the kitchen. Jean reappeared minutes later. 'Thanks Geoff.' It was difficult to distinguish between genuine appreciation and sarcasm.

'What did he say?' Don asked.

'He can be here on Wednesday,' she replied as she poured herself another coke.

2

He was thinking about his wife. He did it every day. Sometimes he smiled, sometimes he cried. Sometimes he did both. Today he was smiling.

He was thinking of the day they had returned from their honeymoon. He thought about it often. They had gone to Paul's parent's house. Sheila had taken the suitcases upstairs and he had made them both coffees. They had been sitting in the kitchen, sipping at their drinks and gazing into each others eyes as the world spun unnoticed around them. He had taken her hand and kissed it softly.

'Don't stop there,' she had purred, and he hadn't.

That had been his wife. And she had been beautiful.

The smile faded a little and he knew that the tears were coming. They had been happy, they had been a team, and then…

Tears fell gently and he knuckled them away. Then she had been lying in her own blood, gone forever, and he still didn't know why. She had made plans, she had wanted to help their daughter and… he didn't want to think about that. That was over now.

Within two weeks he'd lost everything that meant anything to him. His wife was dead and Jess had been taken away to live with Sheila's parents. It had been 'for the best'. It had been too much for her, too much for both of them. He'd spent so much time treating her like an adult that he'd forgotten how fragile a child's mind was. He'd done her more harm than good and she was better off without him.

His decision to stay away from her hadn't been easy but she'd been better since she'd gone to stay with her grandparents. Better apart from the fact that she hadn't spoken a single word for eighteen months after her mother's death. But Jean had said that that was normal and, of course, Jean knew best.

When Don had finally phoned to say that she was talking again, Paul had cried. He'd asked cautiously what she was talking about, scared that she might be babbling about two planes crashing into the World Trade Centre.

'You,' Don had replied simply. 'She wants to see you.'

He hadn't realised how worried he had been until that moment. Relief had washed over him, warm and comforting. She was talking, and she had asked for him.

She had grown and her dark hair had been longer. But she had never looked more like a child. They had sat together, talking and remembering. The faraway look he remembered had touched her eyes a couple of times but she hadn't said anything about her dreams or the stuff that, once upon a time, a million years ago, she claimed that her brain told her, and his heart's conditioned response to hammer wildly whenever he saw it had slowly gone away.

It had been so hard without her. The house had been quiet and he'd felt so useless. He'd tried relationships, failed, and given up. Paul smiled sadly and lit a cigarette.

'Anyone home?' Karen called as she poked her head around the front door.

'I'm in here,' Paul called from the living room. She came through and went to the kitchen as she always did to make coffee before they had a chat. When she brought the mugs through he turned off the TV.

The change in the house no longer surprised her. It wasn't the family house it had once been with ornaments his wife had bought cluttering the windowsill and crayons strewn across the floor. It was the sparsely decorated home of a single man. Only framed photographs hanging from the walls suggested that once he had had a family.

'You look tense,' he said.

'House full of screaming teenagers,' she said, replaying the scene in her head. Joanne and two other girls playing with make up, dotting their eyeballs with mascara while boys laughed as they threw each other into the walls and

120

furniture.

Paul chuckled, wondering if that was what Jess would be like if she came back. Or would it be more of the same? Premonitions and long discussions about a future she seemed to know so much about? She'd never mentioned it, but he'd seen that look in her eyes enough times for it to bother him. He couldn't work out if she was clever enough to try to hide it from him or if it had all just gone away.

'If they carry on I think I'll come and stay with you,' Karen joked.

Her relationship with Paul had been difficult at first. The plan had been to get Sheila to leave him. *She* might not have had the power over Paul to split them up, but Jess had and Sheila had known that. Karen had thought that Sheila would have chosen to come clean rather than have her husband hear about the affair from their daughter. How wrong could a person be?

Guilt had been a powerful motivator and Paul had been so fragile. Helping him hadn't driven the shame away but time had a way of helping it to become that bit easier to live with. Once he and Jess had started speaking again she'd assumed it would only be a matter of time before she came home but there was still no sign of that happening. Paul had said that he wouldn't ask her to come back. He didn't want her to feel like she had to come home just because he wanted her to.

'Well, I wouldn't say no to the company,' Paul replied.

Karen knew how much he missed Jess but would never suggest that he ask her to come back. Karen still feared Jess. What if she took one look at her and just knew that this was all her fault? But Karen was confident that Jess would stay where she was. She had a life in Yorkshire. Her school, her friends, they were all there. And she'd be taking her exams next year.

After Sheila's death Paul had considered moving to be closer to his daughter but had never been able to bring himself to do it. Even though he would sometimes sit alone on the kitchen floor, tracing his fingertips over the spot

121

where his wife had died, leaving would be so much more agonising. This was all he had left of her. If he wanted to sit where his wife's blood had pooled and congealed, he could. He'd rather have that that someone else, a strange family, crying where she'd once cried, lying where their bed had been, carelessly treading over the place where she had fallen every time they cooked a meal.

And his daughter was doing fine without him. Coming back here might only put her right back at square one. He wondered if she knew that she had been right. The Berlin Wall had fallen, the Labour Party were back in power. She always said that she couldn't remember what she'd said as a child but he wasn't sure if he believed her.

If Jess ever wanted to come home, she'd tell him. And he was scared to death that one day she might. As much as he wanted to have his daughter back at home with him, he was terrified that he wouldn't know how to look after her anymore. He thought that he probably hadn't had much of an idea to begin with.

3

Jess threw down the cloth and stomped out from behind the bar.

'It doesn't matter what you say, Jess,' Jean said as she shook her head. 'There's no way on this earth.'

Jess didn't reply, but bashed through the double doors into the kitchen.

Jean rinsed the cloth, wrung it out and wiped down the bar.

'What time's he due?' Geoff asked.

'Any time now,' Don replied. 'And we want her out of the way.'

They all hushed as Jess stormed back out of the kitchen.

'It's for your own good,' Jean tried to reason.

'Everything's been for my own good for the last eleven years,' Jess shouted back.

'We're only thinking of you, dear,' Don said.

'Bollocks.'

Geoff laughed. 'What's the matter, Jess?' he asked. 'You wont be missing much.'

'So what's the problem?' she shot back. 'Be honest, gran, what's the problem?'

'We just, we think it's best that you...'

'Stay locked in my room the whole time he's here,' Jess finished for her. 'I got that bit. I just don't understand why.'

'You know why,' Jean snapped.

'I'm fine. I've been fine for ages.'

'And we want it to stay that way, darling.'

The sound of a car pulling up outside caused them all to look towards the door.

'Sounds like he's here,' Geoff said, casting a sideways glance at Jess. She sat defiantly on a bar stool.

Jean shook her head wearily. 'Please, Jess.' It was more sigh than request.

Jess huffed and puffed as if it took a huge effort to get down from the stool before slinking back into the kitchen as Russ Hamilton entered the bar, looking around as he approached Jean, Don and Geoff.

'I'm looking for Jean Baker,' he said.

'I'm Jean,' she smiled politely. 'You must be Russell.'

'I am,' he replied, offering a hand which she shook limply. 'I'm looking forward to working here.' He turned, looking into the restaurant. 'My dad told me a few stories about this place. I always meant to visit, just to have a look around. It's very nice.'

'Thank you,' Jean said.

'I hope you don't mind but I brought my son along.' He saw Jean's eyes narrow with suspicion and held his hands up defensively. 'Don't worry,' he said. 'An extra body doesn't mean an extra fee. He's here purely for the experience. He's a very intuitive person, I think this experience will be very important to him.'

'Okay,' Jean agreed unsurely. 'Would you like a drink?'

'Just a coke thanks.'

He wandered the length of the bar and back as she poured the drink.

'On the house,' she said. Before he could object she had picked up her cloth and started wiping down the other end of the bar.

Rory Hamilton pushed open the door and strode confidently to the bar with a small black suitcase. Placing it beside a vacant stool he swept back shaggy, dark blonde hair and smiled at Jean, forming beautiful creases in his tanned face. She smiled back at him and put the cloth in the sink. A tall, straight twenty one, he looked around at the large empty restaurant with glittering eyes that darted over the tables, decorative paintings and modest light fittings, although he looked as if he wasn't seeing any of these things.

124

He ordered a coke but didn't wait for it to arrive before he wandered into the restaurant, running his long fingers over the polished surfaces of the tables, stopping occasionally before moving on. Russ smiled to himself as he glanced sideways at the three people at the bar. They watched his son, lips parted, eyes unblinking, waiting, waiting for anything.

This was what his son did. Watching him wander through the restaurant anyone would be forgiven for thinking that he'd been doing jobs like this one since the beginning of time. In fact, this was Rory's first big job. He'd been giving private readings since he was eighteen, against his mothers wishes and only to those who would agree to someone so young performing such an intimate task. Russ hadn't wished this for his son, but he hadn't been able to ignore that Rory had inherited his gift.

Rory stopped when he reached the far end of the room, turned and strode back to the bar. 'Thank you,' he said as he picked up his drink and sipped thoughtfully.

He was nervous. This was very different to what he was used to. Three pairs of eyes watched him expectantly and he nodded. 'At least two,' he said.

Jean put a hand to her throat and looked at her husband.

'Nothing to worry about,' Rory reassured. 'We know what we're doing.'

By 'we' he meant his dad. He was only here to help and to learn. Jean looked at Russ for the first time since Rory had entered the building and he nodded his agreement.

'What do we do?' Jean asked.

'You leave it with us,' Rory replied with a comforting smile.

'I need to open up,' Don said. 'I'll show you to your room and we can talk about this later.'

Rory took another quick drink and picked up his case.

'Hang on,' Jean said. 'Couple of rules while you're here.'

Rory and Russ exchanged a quick glance.

125

'First, you can bring in whatever food and drink you want, long as you only eat it upstairs. If you do want any food from the restaurant you'll be charged the same as any other customer.'

Russ and Rory nodded their agreement.

'Second rule,' Jean continued. 'My granddaughter, Jess. She's fifteen and I think that's far too young to be involved in what it is that you're doing. She lives here with us but I want you to avoid her. You don't discuss what you're doing, or anything else, with her.'

'Okay,' Russ agreed.

'I'm afraid I wouldn't allow you to continue to work here if you involved her at all,' Jean pressed. 'Is that clear?'

'Absolutely, Mrs Baker,' Russ nodded.

'So you're Abe's grandson,' Geoff said. Rory looked him up and down with soft brown eyes before nodding. 'He was a good man.'

'Yes, he was,' Rory agreed.

'How do you,' Jean paused and tugged lightly at her necklace. 'How do you know they're, well, there?' she asked.

'I get a tingling feeling between my shoulder blades,' Rory replied. 'Like when you can feel someone looking at you.'

Jean nodded slowly as if it was all very difficult for her to take in. Don showed them to their room and they changed before going back to the bar to talk to the locals. Geoff began to reel off the stories he had told a hundred times as the bar began to fill. Both men nodded politely although it was obvious they'd heard it all before.

'And then his head…' Rory held up a hand and Geoff closed his mouth with an affronted frown.

The tingling sensation started between his shoulder blades, creeping up to the nape of his neck. He turned to the kitchen to see Jess walk through the double doors and into the restaurant. She took a tiny notebook from her apron

126

and proceeded to take table three's order.

His mouth hung open. 'Who's the waitress?' he asked.

'That's Jess,' Geoff replied flippantly, eager to get back to his stories.

Rory looked at her curiously. She was real, she was alive. Then why…

'That's the granddaughter?' he asked.

'The one we're staying away from,' Russ reminded as he caught the way his son was looking at her.

Rory didn't really hear it. He'd sensed a presence, something supernatural, something long dead. 'Staying away,' he repeated.

'Her mum died when she was very young and she took it really badly,' Geoff said. 'If you've got any sense you'll stay well away.'

'Okay,' Rory lied easily.

He waited for his dad to approach a young couple who Don informed them had heard voices in the restaurant about a month ago and then slid across the bar until he was standing right beside Geoff.

'I'm interested in Jess,' he said quietly.

'Forget it, son,' Geoff said. 'She's too young for you. Only fifteen.'

Although that hadn't been what Rory had meant, he only said, 'She looks older.'

'It's her eyes.' Geoff lit a cigar and pointed it at him. 'They're too old for her head.'

'Poe said they're the windows to the soul.'

'If I were you I'd leave her soul well alone,' Geoff puffed. 'Jean and Don are very protective.'

'Has she ever seen anything?'

'No, she never saw a thing.'

Rory puzzled over her for a second. The question was this; why would Jess, perfectly normal and perfectly alive, give him that feeling? He glanced behind the bar as Jean pulled a pint of Pedigree. What hadn't she told them? Why was she so desperate to keep them away from her granddaughter? *You don't discuss what you're doing, or anything else, with her.* Anything else? First chance he got he was going to find out what Jean had meant by that.

4

Karen looked relieved when she opened the door. 'Thank god,' she said dramatically. 'Come in, please.'

He had been able to hear the noise from halfway down the street. As he stepped inside he could hear girls giggling and boys shouting. Something crashed into the other side of the living room door as he followed Karen through the house.

'We should probably make sure everything's okay in there,' he said.

Karen gave him a look that said she wouldn't go inside that room if her life depended on it.

'Want a coffee?' she asked.

'I'd love a beer if you've got one.'

As they went through the kitchen to the back room, Karen grabbed two cans of Fosters from the fridge.

'I brought that price list you asked for,' Paul said as he took a folded sheet of paper from his coat pocket. 'You can even get the really new models for a decent price.'

'Thanks,' she said as she took it and put it on top of an old stereo without looking at it. 'Mum's been after a new washing machine for ages. If Joanne didn't have so many clothes I reckon it would have lasted another ten years.'

The door opened and a girl stumbled in. She was attached to the pimply face of a boy with dark greasy hair.

'Can I help you?' Karen asked.

They both looked at her, startled. Then the girl began to giggle as she dragged the boy out of the room and closed the door.

'Honestly,' Karen said. 'It's like this every day and it's not even the summer holiday's yet. I've asked for more hours at work but they haven't got any. I swear I'm going to end up killing one of them before much longer.'

'Well, you know you're always welcome at mine,' Paul offered.

That thorny feeling of guilt again. 'Thanks, Paul.'

They both drank and Karen put on the stereo in an attempt to drown out the squeals from the other room.

'What the hell are they doing in there?' Paul asked.

'I don't know and I don't want to,' Karen replied. 'You do know I was meant to be an only child? That Joanne was a mistake because mum forgot to take her pill once? She's spoilt rotten because mum thought about aborting her and she still feels guilty about it.' She tweaked the volume on the stereo but they could still hear squeals from the other room. 'I keep wondering if it's just me. I mean everyone was a kid once, but I'm sure I was never like that.'

'Well, I was fifteen that long ago I can't even remember,' Paul joked.

'Has Jean ever rang you because Jess's playing MTV loud enough to rattle the windows?' she asked.

Paul shook his head. 'Thank god,' he said. 'But I think if Jess did rebel I'd be the last to know.'

'How come?'

Paul took another drink from the cold can and spoke as he started to roll a cigarette. 'Jean's far too proud,' he said. 'Likes to think she's got one over on me.' He spit sealed the cigarette and lit it. 'No, I'm talking out of turn,' he apologised. 'She's done a good job of bringing her up. Her and Don. I should be grateful really.'

'Why did you let her go in the first place?' Karen asked.

'Jean used to do some kind of work or another in mental health,' Paul explained. 'She seemed like a good person to have around for Jess. I was in no fit state to look after a child anyway.'

'Well, thank you very fucking much,' Joanne cried as she threw open the door.

130

'Joanne, how many times do I have to tell you not to use that word?' Karen asked sternly.

'You just made me look like a right idiot,' Joanne said, ignoring her.

'What?' Karen asked. 'I haven't been anywhere near you.'

'Jane and Tommy just said you barged in on them,' Joanne said.

'More like they barged in,' Karen replied. 'We were sitting here and they came in like they were about to do something they really shouldn't be doing at their age.'

Joanne rolled her eyes and put her hands on her hips. 'Get a grip,' she said. 'Stop acting like mum.'

Get a grip. Karen hated it. It was one of Joanne's catchphrases at the moment, along with *whatever* and *way cool*. The new Max Factor mascara was way cool, Robbie Williams was way cool. Karen was not way cool. Karen needed to get a grip.

'Just go back to your youth club, Joanne, and leave me alone.'

Joanne looked at her with disbelief. 'You're acting like this just to make me look bad in front of Scott, aren't you?'

'What?' Karen replied with equal disbelief.

'Scott?' Paul asked.

Karen willed Joanne to close the door and go away but knew that she wouldn't.

'He's way cool,' Joanne said. 'And it's taken me three weeks to get him to even talk to me.'

'Scott Jordan?' Paul asked.

'Do you know him?' Joanne looked excited.

'I've heard of him,' Paul replied.

'Joanne, just go,' Karen said. 'Please.'

'Just leave my friends alone,' she warned as she slammed the door.

'He's real,' Paul said.

Karen had known this for a while now. She'd wanted to talk to Paul about it but it had never seemed like the right time.

'She told me about him a couple of weeks ago,' she confessed as she turned off the stereo. 'I was going to tell you.'

Paul drank deeply. 'Why didn't you?'

She shrugged. 'I didn't know how to.'

They both sat silently, listening to the noise of the kids in the other room. Somewhere on the other side of the wall was the boy with no face. The boy that was nice and then he was mean.

'I'm sorry, Paul.'

'You've got nothing to apologise for,' he said. 'Have you met him?'

Karen nodded slowly. 'Are you thinking about going in there?'

'Thinking about it,' he replied. 'Not sure it's a very good idea though.'

It was times like this when he was pleased that Jess was miles away, safe and guarded from the truth of her premonitions.

'If I were you I'd want to know who he was,' Karen said. 'You've got to be curious.'

'Yeah,' Paul shrugged, 'but I can't just walk into a room full of kids and ask him to raise his hand, can I?'

Karen heard the front door open and quickly crossed the room to look down the hall. 'If you want to get a look at him, now's your chance,' she said.

He went to her without another thought for right or wrong and peered at the group of kids leaving the house.

'You can come round tomorrow after school again if you like.' Joanne was talking to a boy with dark hair.

'Okay,' he replied as he stepped outside.

'See you tomorrow,' she called.

They both went back to their drinks and Paul sat in contemplative silence. He didn't know what he'd expected. O Fortuna to ring in his ears? Horns and a

132

pointed tail? He was just a normal fifteen year old boy.

'I should have told you before,' Karen said apologetically.

He waved a hand at her. It didn't matter. 'He's real,' he said, looking at his tobacco tin. 'Just like everything else.'

Karen looked at the broken man in front of her. It had taken years for him to accept that Jess didn't see the future anymore and he still tried to catch her out every now and again as if he couldn't believe that it had just gone away. He hoped it had, Karen knew that. But when things like this happened it put him back ten years. Whether she still saw the future or not, she had been right. Scott Jordan was just one more example of that.

'You've asked her about him before,' Karen said. 'She can't remember ever mentioning him.'

'But she did mention him.' Paul looked at her with tired eyes. 'When she was four she knew exactly who he was. She even knew about him and Joanne being together.'

'You can't do anything about the past,' Karen replied sympathetically. 'She's fine now. You know it and I know it.'

'You think I should ask her to come home?'

Karen didn't think that at all. Paul was okay. Paul had lost his wife and it hadn't been his fault and Karen had helped him through it because of the guilt. But Jess? She didn't want Jess around all of the time. Just in case.

'I just think you need to let go of what happened with her,' she said. 'It's gone, it's over, forget about it.'

Paul nodded and rolled another cigarette.

5

Jess stood quietly with her back against the trunk of a willow that shaded her from the hot sun, trying to work out what the hell Shakespeare's star-crossed lovers were babbling on about. Thee's, thou's and thy's were making her head hurt and her eyes kept blurring over the words. She'd been able to hear the lunch time rush in her room and thought that being outside in the quiet would make it easier to concentrate. She was quickly learning that wherever she chose to study, Shakespeare was never going to be her friend.

'Oh Romeo, Romeo. Wherefore art thou Romeo?' she said to herself. What did that even mean? She was sure that Mrs Glynn had told them but she couldn't remember. School had never been a problem until now. For some reason when Mrs Glynn had brought out Romeo and Juliet, Jess had been expecting Macbeth.

She closed the book and sat in the grass, looking out over the grounds. There used to be a large pond out here but she had been terrified of it and her granddad had filled it in years ago. Some people were scared of spiders or mice; for Jess it was water. Whenever they had swimming at school she would either purposely forget her kit or tell the teacher that she had her period – for the third week in a row. Bath's and shower's were fine, but a large body of water? Forget it.

She had never told the teachers that she was scared. That would have been worse than having to get into the swimming pool. She was already the poor girl whose mother was dead and whose dad was halfway to the nuthouse. That was enough, thank you.

Sometimes she wondered if her mother's death had been her fault. Why hadn't she seen it? Why had she seen another five years for her? Why did she know useless stuff about people she didn't know but hadn't been able to save her mother's life?

She had been wrong and everyone had paid for it. That was why she had made the decision to pretend that it had all just stopped. It had only ever caused problems so she had ignored it and hoped that it would go away. So far it hadn't. But at least now she didn't have to see the colour drain from her dad's face every time she mentioned something she shouldn't know or that hadn't happened yet. She'd kept her mouth shut for eighteen months, learning how to hide it, scared that if she started to talk she'd slip up. And when she had been ready, she'd asked to speak to her dad.

The first few visits had been difficult. He'd lost a lot of weight and his hair had started to grey prematurely. She hadn't mentioned it but knew that if she ever did he'd say that it was distinguished silver, not grey. It had gotten easier over time. The uncomfortable silences they'd endured when they both thought about her mum but daren't mention her had soon disappeared. They'd talked about Sheila and about what Jess had 'been through'. She'd told him outright that she couldn't really remember any of it and because the seven year old only shrugged when her dad mentioned Scott Jordan or Osama Bin Laden or Kate Middleton, trying to trip her up and failing, he'd started to believe her. They all still treated her like she was a mental patient, but they believed that she was telling the truth.

'Deny thy father and refuse thy name; Or, if thou wilt not, be but sworn my love and I'll no longer be a Capulet.'

Reciting the words didn't help her to understand them. When was she ever going to need to know any Shakespeare anyway? She lay back in the grass. She often came out here to think. Sometimes about her dad, sometimes about whether Lee Carter was looking at her in French or if she was just imagining it. A lot of the time she thought about what she had come to think of as her disability. Like any other disability it didn't matter how much you tried to live a normal life it would always be there and every now and again you would be

135

reminded of that fact.

Her dad had stopped asking questions now but he still tiptoed around her sometimes and Jess knew that even though none of them mentioned it, they were still all waiting for her to have a mental breakdown or something. That was why she wasn't allowed to meet the ghostbuster. People who saw the future should not interact with people who play with tarot cards and Ouija boards.

But she was curious to know how this charlatan was going to convince her gran that he could actually communicate with the dead. She hoped that he would experience something like the old man that had made the woman wet herself on Sunday, but what fun would that be if she wasn't around to see him screaming and running for the door?

'Enough,' she said as she stood up, pacing backwards and forwards as she found the next line. 'But, soft. What light through yonder window breaks?'

Rory watched from the side of the building, making sure that nobody else was around. He'd been watching her for five minutes and the only person she'd spoken to was herself. He'd seen her leave the building fifteen minutes ago and had followed her as quickly as he could without Jean getting suspicious. Now he was here he was trying to work out what he should say to her.

Hi, my name's Rory and when I first saw you I thought you were dead, how weird's that? had been considered and rejected. *I've been watching you talk to yourself for the last five minutes* and *I had a really strange dream about you drowning last night* were also non starters. He had to move in somehow and, as was usual when Rory was clueless, he resorted to what he thought of as his most natural qualities; charm and wit.

She had stopped pacing and was now standing with her back to him, looking out at the fields that ran far into the distance.

'Arise, fair sun, and kill the envious moon, who is already sick and pale with grief that thou, her maid,'

136

'Art far more fair than she.'

Jess squealed as she turned , dropping the book and tripping over her own feet.

'Woah,' Rory caught her by the waist as she fell towards him. She pushed him away and stumbled backwards, leaving the book between them.

'What the fuck are you doing?' she cried angrily.

Rory was starting to think that the dream line didn't seem like such a bad idea now. 'I'm sorry,' he said. 'I didn't mean to scare you.'

'What do you expect when you go sneaking up on people?' She was more embarrassed than angry. How long had he been listening to her talking to herself?

'That's a point to you,' Rory replied. 'I'm sorry, it was stupid.' He bent and picked up her book, looking at the picture of the dramatically dead Elizabethan couple on the cover. She snatched it away from him and took a big step backwards.

'Look, I really am sorry, Jessica, I…'

'How do you know my name?' She clutched the book to her chest. 'Who are you?'

'I'm Rory,' he replied with a big, welcoming smile. 'I'm working for your grandparents.' The smile faded when she didn't return it and he sighed, feeling stupid. 'Look, can we forget the last couple of minutes ever happened please?'

She took another step backwards. 'You're the ghostbuster?' she asked. 'Where's your proton pack?'

'Well, I've never heard that one before,' he replied sarcastically.

Her face tightened. He should have just laughed politely.

'If you know who I am then you know you can't be here talking to me.'

'I'm not really a rules person.'

'Well aren't you the big tough guy?' she scoffed.

He cursed himself again. *Rory, just play the game her way and you might get her to stay where she is.*

'Okay, I'm out here because I thought I'd survey the whole area,' he lied.

Her eyes narrowed. 'You must have spoken to fifty people since you got here,' she said. 'And I know that none of them saw anything out here.'

'Never hurts to check.'

'Cut the bullshit, why are you really here?' She looked briefly at the building, she was just as aware as he was that they could be spotted at any time.

'You know, if I'd spoken to people like that at your age my mum and dad would have given me what for.'

'Yeah, well my mum and dad aren't here.' There was more sorrow than aggression in her voice and she was looking at the ground instead of him. He'd touched a nerve.

'Truthfully,' he said. 'I came out here to talk to you.'

Jess levelled her eyes at the stranger. 'You're not allowed to talk to me.'

He took a step towards her. She folded her arms defensively over her chest but stayed where she was. 'It's not my choice,' he explained. 'I was forced to notice you and I can't ignore that.'

She rolled her eyes. 'Don't give me all that Derek Acorah cobblers.'

'What?'

'Never mind.'

'You don't believe in the supernatural?' he asked. 'After everything people have experienced here?'

'I don't believe in you,' she replied abruptly. 'How much are my grandparents paying you to pretend you can do what you say you can do?'

'You think I'm a conman?' he asked with less outrage than she'd expected. 'Well, I'm not a conman and I'm not getting paid.'

'Yeah, right.'

'Why don't they want me anywhere near you?'

'If they wanted you to know they would have told you.'

138

'I'm asking you.'

'I'm fifteen,' she said. 'They don't think it's appropriate for me to be involved in this type of thing.'

'What do you think?'

She shrugged.

'I think you saw something or something happened,' he guessed, 'and it scared you. A lot. Whatever it is, you need to tell me. The people I've spoken to, none of them gave me the feeling you did when I first saw you.'

'I've got to go,' she said. 'If we get caught I'm going to be in a lot of trouble and you could lose your job. You wont get a penny.'

'Is there anywhere we can go where that isn't a risk?'

She shook her head. 'I don't want to talk to you.'

He pointed at the book. 'Are you reading that because you like Shakespeare or because your teacher told you to?'

'What do you think?'

'If you need any help I was really good at that at school.'

'Bet you liaised with the bard himself.'

'Now that one I haven't heard before,' he smiled. 'No, I just listened hard. People struggle with Shakespeare because of the language but it's not as hard as it looks.'

'Goodbye, Rory.' She turned and started to walk away.

'Well it's an open offer,' he called after her. 'Anytime you want help with it just let me know.'

She stopped and frowned at him. 'What does wherefore mean?'

'Why,' he replied. 'It means why.'

'Why art thou?'

'Why are you.'

'Why are you Romeo?' she asked doubtfully. 'That doesn't make any sense.'

'Why are you Romeo, a Montague, related to the sworn enemy of my family,' he explained quickly. 'It's a difficult start for a relationship if they're not supposed to have anything to do with each other.'

They both smiled at the irony. He took a wary step towards her. She didn't move. 'And we all know how that worked out,' she said.

'I don't like you that much,' he replied with a playful grin.

'Thanks for the offer,' she said as she slid a hand into the back pocket of her jeans. 'But if we got caught, well, it's just not worth the risk.'

He understood. He wouldn't like to get on the wrong side of Jean.

'I could slide notes under your bedroom door,' he joked.

'Do you really see dead people?'

'Sometimes I see them, sometimes I hear them, sometimes I just feel things.'

'Can you prove it?'

'You still think I'm trying to con your grandparents?'

She shrugged.

'I'll make a deal with you,' he said.

Her eyes narrowed. 'What kind of deal?'

'You let me help you with your homework and I'll prove we're not trying to swindle anyone.'

'Doesn't sound like there's much in it for you.'

'I get to spend time with you,' he replied smoothly.

'You talk like a conman.'

'You're fifteen,' he frowned. 'How many conmen do you know?'

'You talk all slimy like a conman.'

'That's not slime, it's charm.'

She laughed. The sound made him smile. 'We could go and sit in the garage,' he suggested, casting another furtive glance at The Unicorn. 'Away from prying eyes.'

'Have you got any idea how inappropriate that sounds?'

Her tone, the words she used, they chilled him. Fifteen years old and she was telling him to cut the bullshit and asking if he could hear how inappropriate he sounded? He managed a cool smile. 'You know I didn't mean it like that.'

'Maybe tomorrow,' she said.

'What's wrong with now?' he asked, reluctant to give her the chance to change her mind.

'I've known you for two minutes,' she replied. 'First you were spying on me and now you're asking me to go into the dark scary garage with you?'

'They've really drilled that stranger danger thing into you haven't they?' She looked at him with distrust and he shrugged. 'I don't know what to say.'

She didn't offer any suggestions.

'Okay,' he said, going to her. She didn't move and he mentally congratulated himself on gaining her trust. 'Sit down.'

'Someone could come out here any second,' she said.

'Either you sit down or we go into the dark scary garage,' he said.

'Or I could just go back inside.'

'Please, Jessie, I only want to help.' He touched her arm and then withdrew his hand as if he'd received an electric shock. 'What the hell was that?' he asked.

'I didn't do anything,' she frowned.

He looked at his hand and then at her. She was looking back at him with wide eyes. 'Are you okay?' she asked stupidly. It was pretty obvious that he was definitely not okay.

His head spun with disjointed thoughts. He was supposed to meet her. He couldn't just walk away and say that if he was supposed to talk to her then she wouldn't have been so damn obstructive. He'd had complicated readings before. The woman with the dead five year old son, the woman who wanted to communicate with her husband except he didn't want to talk to her because he'd always preferred her sister; but this was something else. It was like a

141

lightning bolt filled with anguished screams. An explosion of nonsensical, fragmented information that he struggled to understand.

'Rory?'

He could only stare at her blankly. His brain was still trying to process what he had seen. Flashes of a child, a young woman, a water bloated corpse. He lifted his hand to touch her again but reconsidered and dropped the hand to his side.

'Are you going to let me help you or not?' he asked, trying to regain some composure.

'What's wrong?'

'Nothing.'

She was terrified that he'd seen through the lie she'd managed to keep to herself for eleven years and shouted at him to tell her.

'Who's Sheila?' he asked.

6

Jess let out a slow, relieved sigh and shook her head at him. 'You got that from gran,' she smiled. 'You'll have to do better than that.'

Rory ran both of his hands through his hair, ignoring her and trying to keep hold of the images that were now fading fast. 'Karen,' he said. 'She was. . . '

'Gran,' Jess interrupted, unimpressed.

He looked up at her seriously. 'It's you, Jessie,' he said. 'It's you sitting next to the hospital bed.'

Jess gasped. Would her gran have said anything about that to Rory? Had her dad even told her about that?

'How do you know that?'

'Sheila,' he said firmly. 'She's so sorry but . . .'

'Stop it,' she screamed and pushed him hard. He fell backwards into the grass. 'How the fuck do you do that?'

'I'm sorry,' he spluttered. 'The information came from you.'

She looked at him with wide, frightened eyes. 'Fine, I believe you,' she said. 'Anything else?' She asked because if he knew her secret then she had to convince him that it was nobody else's business.

He shook his head. 'It's gone,' he replied with confusion. 'It's all gone.'

She held out her hand and he took it cautiously, allowing her to help him up. 'Okay,' she said. 'Dark scary garage it is.'

He brushed grass from the seat of his trousers and they walked slowly towards the garage. Whatever had overwhelmed him was gone now.

All it takes is a little charm and intelligence, he thought and congratulated himself on possessing both qualities in abundance.

The garage smelled fusty and unused. He opened one of the heavy wooden doors wide to let in some light and went to the car that he shared with his dad.

143

He sat behind the wheel and she took the passenger seat. The lighting wasn't very good but it would have to do.

He took the book and started to rifle through the pages. 'You know the famous balcony scene never called for a balcony,' he said, pointing at the text. 'Look, it just says that she appears at a window.'

She looked at the book and then back at him. 'Okay, I'm impressed,' she said.

'Just a matter of reading it properly,' he replied modestly.

She shook her head. 'I can read it as much as I want. I'm never going to understand it.'

'Okay,' He lit a cigarette and Jess rolled down her window, 'which bit are you stuck on?'

She fanned through the book from cover to cover. 'Just that part,' she replied. He laughed and she smiled at him. 'I'm sorry,' she said. 'But I really haven't got a clue.'

He took the book from her, undeterred. 'Why are you looking at the balcony scene?' he asked. 'It would probably make more sense to start at the beginning.'

'Because everyone knows the balcony scene,' she replied. 'At least I understand what's happening in this bit.'

'Okay,' he said. 'What is happening in this scene?'

'Romeo and Juliet fall in love but they're not supposed to because their families hate each other. They talk bollocks for ten minutes, kiss each other about a hundred times and then say they'll meet tomorrow.' Rory raised an eyebrow at her. 'That's not right is it?' she guessed quietly.

'They fell in love at the party,' he explained. 'They discuss their feelings, how the feud between their families affects their relationship and then agree to get married tomorrow.'

'That's what I said,' she replied. He laughed and she found herself giggling

144

despite herself. 'You must think I'm such a dunce.'

'Little bit,' he joked and then winked at her.

'So what's really going on?' she asked, looking back at the book.

He bent the spine of the book and held it out so that she could see the text. 'You can see from what they say that how they feel about each other is more important than their family loyalties,' he explained. 'It's intense and passionate and so pure that nothing's going to stop them being together.'

'You can see all that?' Jess asked. 'All I see is lots of words I don't understand.'

Rory pointed at a line halfway down the page. 'Thou art thyself, though not a Montague,' he read. 'She sees him as a person in his own right, not just as a Montague. They both say that they wont be a Capulet or a Montague anymore, renouncing their families before their love for each other. I take thee at thy word. Call me but love, and I'll be new baptised; hence forth I never will be Romeo.'

'So if she swears she loves him he would belong to her and not to his family?' Jess asked.

'You're getting there,' Rory said.

She laughed happily. 'Thank you so much.'

'I can't imagine loving a person so much that I'd rather die than be without them,' he said thoughtfully as he wound down his own window and flicked ash out into the half darkness. Something inside Jess knotted her stomach, spread to her mind, held for a moment and then released.

'Jessie?'

She blinked and turned to him. 'Sorry,' she said. 'I was miles away.'

His kind eyes danced over the pages and she found herself staring at his full lips as he talked her through other parts of the text, describing the characters and the story and explaining the words as if he were expertly trying to teach her to speak a foreign language. After an hour she had made real progress.

'Have I helped you?' he asked.

'Yes,' she replied gratefully, tearing her eyes away from his lips and back to his deep brown eyes. 'Thank you.'

'What happened to you?' he asked casually. Whatever this was it was much deeper than seeing a couple of ghosts.

She took the book from him and closed it, looking at him miserably. 'That's why you agreed to help me, isn't it?' she asked. 'Because you wanted something from me.'

'I just want to help you, Jessie.'

She opened the door and stumbled out of the car. 'Forget it,' she said as she began to walk away.

'Oh, come on,' he said. 'I just wanted to help you.'

She didn't reply.

'Come on, Jessie. Please don't go. I'm sorry.' He jogged after her and she turned, holding an arm out between them.

'One more step,' she warned, 'and I'll tell them that you're bothering me.'

'Please don't be like this,' he pleaded but she turned and he could only watch as she walked away.

He went back to the car, trying to work out what the hell he was going to do as he locked up. Russ was sitting in the restaurant eating a plate of fish and chips when he came back inside.

'Pint of Pedigree please.' Don poured the drink for him and he went to sit with his dad.

'You look tired,' Russ commented. 'Maybe you're not ready for this yet.'

'It's not that,' Rory said.

'Did you get enough sleep?' he asked. 'We didn't go to bed until half three and you were up before me.'

Rory drank but didn't speak.

'What's the matter?'

146

'I can't tell you because you'll shout at me,' Rory replied.

Russ put his knife and fork down and shook his head. 'You went after her, didn't you?' he asked.

'Dad, I wouldn't have done it if I didn't feel like I had to.'

'Has she told Jean?'

'No,' Rory stole a chip and Russ slapped his hand before picking up his cutlery. 'But she doesn't like me very much.'

'Right, well you got away with it this time so now you leave her alone.'

'I touched her arm and I got all this information from her. It wasn't like anything I've felt before.' He looked at his hand as if there would be some residue of the experience lying in his palm. 'I think she might be like us, but scared of it. I think they've all told her to ignore it or forget about it or something.' He ran his hand through his hair and sighed. 'I don't know.'

'Rory, are you listening to me?' Russ asked. 'This is not worth us losing this job over. Your mum was pissed off that I even brought you here so don't go poking your nose in where it's not wanted and get us thrown out.'

'Dad, she…'

'She nothing,' Russ said. 'You leave her alone.'

'If I wasn't meant to have anything to do with her then I wouldn't…'

'Stop it, Rory.' He threw his cutlery down again. 'If she'd come to you for help then I might agree that you had a job to do but she didn't so you just stop chasing her around.'

Rory nodded like a scolded child and took another chip from his dad's plate.

7

It was almost midday. Jess was setting out menus when Rory came downstairs, yawning and running through last nights events in his head. The restaurant seemed quieter now, thank god. If it hadn't been for his dad he wouldn't have been able to control it. There were restless spirits and then there was The Unicorn. This place was in a league of its own.

'Morning,' he called brightly.

Jess looked up briefly and then carried on with her work.

'I said morning,' he called a little louder.

'My granddad's only in the cellar,' she replied as she wiped down a table and put out salt and pepper pots, sliding a menu between them. 'He'll be back up any minute, so you should leave now.'

'I'm just going out for a walk,' he said. 'Do you want to come with me?'

She put down the stack of menus and stood with her hands on her hips. 'When are you going to get it, Rory?' she asked. 'I've got nothing to say to you. Just leave me alone.'

He stepped out from behind the bar but kept his distance. 'I'm not doing this to irritate you,' he said.

'But you *are* irritating me.'

As Don came up the cellar stairs Jess turned her back on him and continued to work her way down the room. Rory opened a newspaper that lay on the bar and pretended to read. Don acknowledged Rory and went whistling into the kitchen.

'You don't have to hide what you are,' Rory said as he closed the newspaper and went to the door. 'And nobody should have asked you to.'

She turned open mouthed and looked at the door as it closed slowly behind him. He could see straight through her. And he wasn't frightened. He didn't want to ignore it or push it away, he wanted to talk about it. Even if he didn't know exactly what it was. If she wanted to discuss what she had kept locked away for so long, now was the time.

Customers began to filter in as Don came back from the kitchen and the day began as it always did, with the sound of friendly chatter and the beeping of the till. She finished laying out the tables and was about to go back upstairs when her dad walked in.

'Hello, sweetheart,' he said as she hugged him and he kissed the top of her head. 'I swear you get taller every time I see you.'

'Are you okay?' she asked.

'I'm fine,' he replied as he released her. 'What about you?'

'Busy.'

'Paul,' Don said. 'What can I get you?'

'Pint of Fosters please,' he said. 'Jess?'

'Coke please.'

Don poured their drinks and they took them over to a table by the corner of the bar.

'What are your plans for the holidays?' Paul asked.

'Working here most of the time,' Jess replied. 'Might as well get hold of as much money as I can before I have to go back to school.'

Paul nodded his approval. 'Only one more year to go,' he said. 'Make it count, sweetheart.'

Jess slumped in her chair. 'You sound like gran.'

'You've been going to school since you were four, you might as well get something out of it for all the time you've put in.'

Jess rolled her eyes. 'I will,' she said. 'Can we change the subject?'

'Your gran said they were getting someone in because they'd had people seeing ghosts,' Paul said a little too quickly.

Jess wasn't surprised.

'Yes,' she replied. 'It got bad last Sunday.'

'How bad?'

She wanted to tell him to stop it but knew exactly what the response would be. He was only looking out for her. Roughly translated that meant that he still saw her as a fragile four year old.

'Two in one day,' she said instead. 'We've never had that before.'

'Did you see anything?'

She clawed the ice out of her drink and dropped it into the ashtray. 'I never see anything.'

'Have you met them?'

She couldn't believe him. Surely he knew that she wasn't stupid enough to think that he hadn't already discussed this with Don and Jean.

'What do you think?' She folded her arms over her chest.

Paul drank before he responded. 'Did they tell you they spoke to me about it?' he asked. She shook her head. 'I thought it would be best to keep you away from them,' he explained. 'I don't want you anywhere near crystal balls and runes and things. They're not toys.'

'Why didn't you speak to me about it, dad?'

'I thought it was best to speak to your grandparents and see how they felt about it.'

'And make a decision behind my back as usual,' Jess concluded. At four years old she'd been treated like an adult, now she was more than ten years older and he was treating her like a child.

'Don't be like that,' Paul said. 'We only want what's best for you.'

'How do any of you know what's best for me?' she asked. 'You never ask me for my opinion.'

'I don't understand why it bothers you so much,' Paul said. 'Why would you want to have anything to do with them anyway?'

'That's not the point.' Jess lowered her voice as a couple sat at the next table. 'You treat me like I'm retarded or something,' she said. 'I do well at

150

school, I hang around with the right people, I work hard, I do everything right and you still treat me like I'm a stupid little kid.'

She watched him patiently as he drank. He was thinking, processing what she'd just said. His face was stormy.

'Your gran used to be a nurse,' he started. It was a line she'd heard innumerable times before.

'That was forever ago,' she said. 'She probably gave electroshock therapy to Jesus Christ.'

'Don't talk like that,' Paul replied. 'Jess, I don't want us to argue. Please.'

She was in the mood for an argument, but she didn't see her dad often enough to waste time fighting with him. Instead she nodded her agreement. 'Love you, dad,' she said.

'Love you too, sweetheart.'

8

Jess stepped out into the warm afternoon with Emily and Anna, giggling with the kind of excitement felt only on the last day of summer term. They stood in the wide asphalt expanse between the front of the school building and the high black iron railings that surrounded it, chattering about how Anna's party tomorrow night was going to be so cool and swapping rumours about who had set off the fire alarm this afternoon.

'I think Lee Carter's going to come tomorrow,' Anna gushed. 'Oh god, I hope he does, that would be so cool.'

'Isn't he going out with Jen?' Emily asked.

Emily shook her head. 'He finished with her last week,' she said. 'He's keeping his summer free just for me.'

'You wish,' Jess grinned.

'I'll give you my signed Robbie poster if I'm wrong,' Anna replied. 'If he doesn't ask me out before September I'll even gift wrap it for you. What do you reckon, Em?'

Emily didn't respond. She was looking through the railings. A devious smile curved her delicate mouth.

'Em?' Anna repeated.

Emily glanced at Anna then went back to staring through the railings.

'Forget Lee Carter,' she said. 'Look at that.'

Three pairs of eyes turned to look at whatever had stopped Emily in her tracks. Anna's widened. Emily noticed this and burst into a fresh bout of schoolgirl giggles. 'I saw him first,' she said as she nudged her friend playfully.

Jess rolled her eyes and the bright smile she wore faded quickly. 'Please tell me you're not serious,' she said in a low voice.

'Jesus, Jess, are you blind?' Anna squeaked.

Rory watched all of this with mild amusement. He couldn't hear the words but he'd seen those looks before. 'Still got it,' he smiled to himself.

'No,' Jess replied, 'but it's Rory.'

'You know him?' Emily asked.

'He works for my grandparents.'

'You have got to invite him to my party.' Anna's eyes never left Rory's face. 'In fact, you should introduce us now.'

Jess looked at her friend. 'I don't really want to talk to him.'

'Please bring him to the party,' Anna clasped her hands under her chin in a dramatic begging gesture.

'I'll see what I can do,' Jess said purely to bring an end to the conversation. 'I've got to go, I'll ring you later.'

She stalked towards Rory with her head down.

'Good day?' he asked brightly as she came out onto the street and started towards home. She didn't reply.

He fell in step beside her. 'I used to love the last day of summer term. Six weeks to yourself, no more early mornings.'

'What do you want, Rory?' She was walking quickly but Rory's long legs kept up easily.

'I want to know why they don't want me talking to you,' he replied simply.

'*I* don't want you talking to me,' she said as she shifted the heavy bag on her shoulder.

'Want me to carry that for you?'

'No, I want you to leave me alone.' She checked the road before crossing onto Gainsborough Avenue. 'You and your dad will both lose your job if gran finds out you're following me around. This is your last warning, Rory. Leave me alone or I'll tell her.' Rory said nothing and she wondered if he'd just chosen to ignore her again. 'Did you hear me?'

He nodded. 'Final warning. Got it.'

'Good.'

'But seeing as we're going the same way I might as well walk with you.'

She stopped, regarding him with those old eyes. Her lips parted as if she were about to speak, then closed again as she turned and continued her journey home.

'Do you want me to tell you a secret?' he asked.

'No.'

'I get this feeling,' he continued anyway. 'Like the feeling you get when someone's watching you, just between my shoulder blades, as if their eyes are heating up my skin.'

'Good for you.'

He smiled. If she was responding then she was listening.

'But I don't get that feeling when I'm being watched,' he said. 'I get it just before I see spirit.'

'Who's Spirit?'

'Spirit,' he replied as if it was self explanatory. 'Dead people. Ghosts.'

No reply.

As much as he wanted to take this slowly, he didn't have long before they would be approaching The Unicorn's long driveway.

'Can you tell me why I got that feeling just before I saw you for the first time?' He hoped that he looked like he was observing her casually. If she noticed he was looking at her intently, looking for the slightest indication that she –

There it was.

Yes, her face said. *Yes, I know, but guess what? I'm not going to tell you.*

'Jessie?'

The look was gone from her face as quickly as it had appeared, but it had been there all the same.

'Because you got it wrong.'

'I've never been wrong.'

She laughed. 'Then I must be dead. Sorry, I forgot.' Something else touched her face then and she slowed momentarily. But it was only the shadow of an expression and she started to hurry through the streets again as soon as it disappeared. 'Sorry to damage your ego, Rory, but I'm alive and well. You got it wrong.'

He had five minutes to get this out. Five minutes at the most, and she was speeding up.

'See, I don't think that I did.' He was trying to speak as quickly as she was walking but he was already getting breathless. 'Everything happens for a reason, Jessie, and I think I got that feeling because it always gets my attention. Getting that feeling made me turn around and there you were. It happened for a reason and I want to know what it is.'

He could hear her breathing heavily. If she went any faster she would be jogging.

'Please talk to me, Jessie.'.

No reply.

'It's obvious that you want to get whatever it is off your chest,' he tried.

No reply.

'Did you see something Jessie? Did something happen to you that they want to keep secret?'

No reply.

'When I was at school, especially when I was little and I didn't understand that other kids didn't see the world like I did, I got called names and my mum tried to tell me that I should pretend it didn't happen because it was important to fit in at school. Children can be very cruel.'

No reply.

But she was walking a little slower.

'My mum tried to make me believe that it wasn't a gift I should share with the world. But it is, Jessie. It's special and it can help people and . . .'

155

'Gift?' she interrupted angrily, thinking of her dad's frightened face every time she had mentioned Scott or Iraq or Tony Blair. Her Gift had quite probably killed her mother and turned her dad into a bag of nerves.

'You see it as a curse?'

'It's . . .' she bit her lip and looked at the pavement.

He grinned and she stopped talking.

'You can't kid a kidder,' he said.

She looked up at him, angry that he had tricked her so easily. He was grinning back at her but his eyes were soft with empathy. She began to walk again, looking only at the ground before her feet.

'Jessie, if you don't want to talk I'm not going to force you,' he said softly. 'Other people might have told you that it's bad or wrong or that it makes you a freak. I know better. I've been there and I think I could help you if you'd just let me try.'

She didn't look up. He'd lost her again.

'Okay, look,' he said resignedly. 'I'm sorry that I've been following you around and I've obviously pissed you off and I'm sorry for that too, but if you're anything like me . . .'

'I'm nothing like you.' She was on the verge of tears.

'You feel alone just like I did,' he replied sympathetically. 'You need someone to talk to, Jessie. I can see that you're stressing about it. I wont make you do anything you don't want to but you should know I'm here if you ever do want to talk about it.' They halted abruptly as they reached the driveway. 'I'll wait here until you're inside,' he said.

She nodded and left him at the low stone wall. He didn't know if he'd managed to get through to her or not. He thought that maybe he hadn't. The man who loved the sound of his own voice had run out of things to say.

She walked slowly, looking back only once. He stood at the end of the driveway, watching her. For the past eleven years the people that knew her

156

best, all the people she loved, had avoided talking about what had happened to her wherever possible. But Rory? He had seen deep inside her and told her exactly how she felt. Alone, an outcast, a freak.

I could help you if you'd just let me try.

It had been better since she'd come here. It had been easier. She still wasn't surprised by the news headlines but she didn't know the people here like she'd known the people in Filton and maybe trying to ignore it was why. Maybe eventually it would stop altogether.

And maybe it wouldn't.

9

She lay in bed, unable to sleep. He was downstairs. He was downstairs right now and if she wanted to talk to him now was her chance. She'd heard their car crunching over the long driveway about twenty minutes ago. Russ must have gone out. Rory was downstairs, on his own, right now.

She was scared, though. What if it was getting better because she was ignoring it? What if Rory couldn't help her? How the hell was she going to talk about it when she'd kept quiet for so long?

She kicked off the covers, her decision made, and went quietly downstairs.

'Is Rory around?'

Russ looked up from the papers in front of him as she stepped out from behind the bar. 'It's two in the morning,' he said. 'Shouldn't you be asleep?'

She shrugged. 'I'm not tired.' Rory had gone out? Perfect. She should just go back upstairs but Russ, against his better judgement, patted the seat of the chair beside him and she went over.

'If your gran comes down you're going to get me into a lot of trouble.'

'She wont.' She picked up his bottle of Bud and took a long drink from it.

'And if she catches you sitting down here drinking with me I'll be in even more trouble.'

'It's not me that's drinking when I'm supposed to be working,' she smiled.

'Touché.'

'So is Rory around?'

'He went to the kebab shop,' Russ replied. 'Should be back soon. What do you want him for?'

'I wish I had your job,' she said. 'Sitting around in the pub all night drinking and eating kebabs.'

'There's a bit more to it than that.'

She took another drink from the bottle and put it back on the table. 'Like

158

what?' she asked.

'You know I can't tell you that.'

She rolled her eyes. 'Oh yeah, you're under strict instructions from mien fuehrer.'

He laughed a little and went to the bar, cracking open another Bud. He considered her momentarily and then poured her a coke.

'I hope you're paying for those,' Jess said.

'I'll settle up with your granddad tomorrow.'

He brought the drinks over and she sipped thoughtfully.

Russ picked up his papers, squared them and put them inside a manila folder. 'Am I allowed to ask what you need to speak to Rory about?' he asked. 'He's not supposed to be talking to you.'

'I know he isn't.' She twisted a lock of hair absently around her index finger and stared into the empty room. Russ mused at how she could look twenty one minute and twelve the next. He drank deeply, his Adam's apple bobbing as he swallowed.

'He told me that he'd come to see you,' he said. 'He's very intuitive.'

Jess felt a touch of guilt as she remembered him following her home, trying to make her understand that he could help her if she would just let him.

The door opened and Jess, lost in thought, almost let out a scream. Human hands didn't usually open doors around here at such a late hour. Rory paused after closing and locking the door, looking at her with interest. She thought that he was trying not to grin.

'Shish donner mix on a fresh naan, no sauce or salad,' he said as he strode over, fishing a small parcel wrapped in white paper from a blue carrier bag. Russ took it, made room on the table by dropping the manila folder onto the floor and unwrapped the kebab.

'If I'd known you were awake I'd have asked if you wanted anything,' Rory

159

said. 'I suppose we can share. Long as you don't mind garlic mayo.'

He sat beside her as if they'd been friends for the last hundred years and tore the paper away from his kebab. 'This yours?' he asked as he picked up her coke. She nodded and watched as he swallowed half of it. 'Thanks,' he said as he put the glass back on the table. 'I'll get you another when I've finished this.'

He began to pick up shredded meat that was thick with garlic mayonnaise and stuff it into his mouth. 'Tuck in.' He motioned towards the kebab and she took a piece of donner meat, rolled it up and put it in her mouth.

'So, why are you up so late?' Rory asked, the dim lights glinting off his grease glossed lips.

'I couldn't sleep,' she replied.

'I thought we weren't talking to each other?'

He tore off a piece of fat saturated naan and dipped it into a puddle of mayo before munching on it happily. Jess glanced at Russ who was tearing up his naan and making small donner sandwiches.

'I changed my mind,' she said, throwing a chunk of mayo slicked shish into her mouth. He nodded and took another drink from her glass. She expected him to laugh or cry out triumphantly. Instead he ate, occasionally wiping his hands on his jeans.

'What made you change your mind?' Russ asked.

'You don't have to answer that,' Rory advised, sounding like a bored lawyer. She didn't.

Russ went back to his food, washing it down with Bud until there were only a few scraps of meat left. He screwed up the greasy paper and took it to the bin. Rory looked over at Jess and smiled. It was a strong, sincere smile that said he didn't care why she'd changed her mind, he was only glad that she had.

'Get me a Bud,' Rory said. 'You'd better get Jessie another coke as well.'

Russ brought the drinks over, picked up his folder and tucked it under an arm. 'I'll take this upstairs,' he said. 'Nice to have met you, Jess.'

'You too.'

They both watched him go behind the bar and open the door to the living quarters. As the door closed behind him they looked at each other tentatively, neither knowing how to proceed.

Rory pulled a pack of cigarettes from his breast pocket, lit one and blew smoke into the air above the table. Jess shook her head when he offered her the pack.

'Are you here because you want to talk or because you want to apologise for treating me so badly when I was only trying to help you?' he asked.

She looked at him with something that she hoped would pass for irritation, but her features softened when she saw the small smile he was offering. 'A bit of both,' she replied.

'Well I'm happy to talk, but I'm not sure I can accept your apology.'

'Are you winding me up on purpose?'

He nodded and she couldn't help but smile.

'I'm glad you changed your mind,' he said.

'I'm not sure where to start,' she replied.

He wrapped his long fingers around her hand and squeezed it gently. 'What was it that you saw?'

'I didn't see anything,' she said. 'If you're hoping to hear a ghost story, I'm sorry. It's not like that.'

He rested back in his chair. 'Why don't you just tell me what it is about and we'll go from there.'

She glanced at the door behind the bar, fully expecting to see Jean standing there even though she never came downstairs after hours.

'I want to talk to you, Rory,' she said. 'But at the same time I never want to talk about it ever again. Does that make sense?'

'It scared you?'

'It still does.'

161

He sat forward now and put out his half smoked cigarette. 'Okay, just relax for a minute,' he said. 'There's no rush. We can take as much time as you like. Do you understand?'

She nodded and ran a finger around the rim of her glass. A heavy weight landed in his stomach as she looked at him. Those old eyes didn't belong inside the head of a fifteen year old girl.

'I know things.' Her eyes fell to the floor. She was telling him something bad, something secret. 'I know things that are going to happen. I know people I've never met.'

'How can you know people you've never met?'

'You tell me,' she said. 'Sometimes I'll meet someone for the first time and I'll know who they are and stuff that's going to happen to them. I know people who exist but I've never met them.'

'If you've never met them how can you know that they exist?'

'I don't know, I just do.'

'Can you give me an example?'

She nodded and spoke quickly. 'I was at the doctors with my mum once and this boy walked in and I just knew his name. I knew our neighbour was going to get cancer. I knew Princess Diana was going to die last summer. I knew when and how and where and . . .'

'Woah,' Rory raised his hands. 'Slow down.' He drained his bottle and went to the bar. 'Do you want another?'

'I'll have what you're having.'

He raised an eyebrow, decided that one wouldn't hurt, and took two bottles of Bud from the fridge. 'Pork scratchings?'

'I'm not hungry.'

'You wont be, you ate my kebab.'

'I did not, I only…' she smiled. 'You're winding me up again aren't you?'

He grinned, returning to the table with a bottle in each hand and a bag of pork scratchings clamped between his teeth.

'Jessie, this isn't a police interview. Calm down, have a drink. Let's try to relax shall we?'

She took a deep breath, exhaled slowly and then took a long drink.

'I know all sorts of stuff,' she said. 'I've always known. I could sit here right now and write down the lyrics to songs that haven't been released yet. I know that my dad's going to have an accident and damage his spine when I'm eighteen and it'll be my fault because Scott . . .'

Her face blanched. Her ancient eyes stared out at nothing. Her hands curled into fists.

'Jessie?' He touched her arm gently. 'Jessie, are you okay?'

She nodded and blinked hard. 'I'm sorry,' she said.

'Do you feel okay?'

'I'm fine. I just, I haven't thought about Scott in a long time.'

'Who's Scott?' He relit his cigarette and blew smoke rings into the air.

'My boyfriend,' she replied and then shook her head. 'Joanne's boyfriend. I wont really know him until I'm seventeen.'

'Who's Joanne?'

'She's a bitch,' Jess replied with venom. 'I hate her, she hates me.' She took a long, slow drink from her bottle. 'I haven't actually met her yet.'

Rory's head ached. 'So how do you know that either she or Scott exist?'

'Dad's mentioned Joanne to me,' Jess replied. 'And Scott? Well, I don't know, Rory, but I'm absolutely one hundred percent sure that he does. And one day he's going to ask me to marry him.'

'You've never met him but you know that you're going to marry him?'

A tear slid mournfully down her cheek. 'No,' she said quietly. 'I don't marry him. I turn him down.'

'I'm still in with a chance then,' Rory joked. She managed only a weak, troubled smile as she swiped at her face with her sleeve.

'I'm sorry. I really appreciate you listening to me, Rory. It's just,' she paused, looking thoughtfully at her bottle. 'It's just hard to talk about.'

Rory took a final drag before he crushed out the cigarette. Jess sniffed and he rubbed her shoulder supportively. 'You're doing really well,' he soothed.

She tried to smile but couldn't.

'If I were to ask what was going to be on the front page of The Sun tomorrow would you be able to tell me?' he asked as he started on the pork scratchings.

She shook her head. 'It doesn't work like that. I don't know everything. It doesn't make any sense to me so I don't expect it to make sense to you. All I can tell you is the stuff I do know is always right.' Her face paled again and she stiffened. 'No.' She shook her head violently. 'I got it wrong once. That's how I ended up here.'

'Do you want to tell me what happened?'

'It was my mum.' Tears spilled freely down her cheeks now and he put an arm around her, pulling her close. Her head fell against his shoulder 'She wasn't supposed to die. I had dreams since, since as long as I can remember. My mum was supposed to die when I was ten, not when I was four. Something went wrong. I did something and it made her die.' She pulled away from him and drank deeply. 'From when I was really little I knew that my mum was going to die in a car accident.' She spoke with the tone of a person discussing an average meal they'd had last week. 'I don't know how I knew but I did and I knew that I'd be ten when it happened. But she died just before I turned five. I don't really know what happened to her, they all did their best to keep it from me. All I know is that there was an accident when me and dad were out and she died.'

'And why do you think that it's your fault?'

She looked at him with wet eyes. 'I don't think it was an accident.' Her voice was barely a whisper. 'She was scared of me, Rory. She was scared of the things I said. I don't think she could bear to be around me anymore because of what I knew.'

'You don't know that, Jessie.' He reached out for her again but she turned away from him. 'You can't blame yourself.'

'You're not my therapist, Rory, and you don't know what happened, so don't tell me what I do and do not know.'

He sat silently back in his chair, munched on pork scratchings, sipped at his beer and lit another cigarette.

'In my dreams I used to see my dad lying in a hospital bed,' she said. Her face was still turned away from him. 'And there was a woman sitting beside him, waiting for him to die. When I was little I wondered who she was but as I get older I look in the mirror and I can see that I'm growing into her. And one day I'm going to wake up and look in the mirror and I'll look how she does when she's sitting by that bed and then . . .' She put her head in her hands and started to cry quietly. She was waiting right now. She was looking in the mirror and thinking *not today* every single day.

'How long has it been since you talked to someone about this?' Rory asked.

She looked over her shoulder at him, her eyes dark and haunted. 'Not since mum died.'

He shook his head. 'Did they just expect it all to go away if they ignored it?' he asked angrily.

'It wasn't like that,' she replied. 'I was the one that hoped it would go away.'

He dropped his cigarette into the ashtray. 'They don't know that it's still happening, do they?'

She turned and looked at him earnestly. 'And I don't want them to.'

'I'm not telling anyone anything.'

'If they think that it's gone then as soon as I'm ready I can go back to my

165

dad,' she explained. 'The thing is that all the people I know about live where dad does. I'm scared of what's going to happen if I go back and I can't put my dad through all that again.'

'You don't know the people here?'

'Not like I know the people there.'

He folded his arms over his chest and sat back. 'Do you know me?'

She looked at the floor and then back up at him. A frown creased her pale brow. 'It's really strange but I feel like I do. It's like I've seen you somewhere before but I don't know anything about you.'

'Phew!' he smiled.

She nudged him with her shoulder and finally managed to smile back.

'Let's get down to business then,' Rory said, rubbing his hands together. 'Lottery numbers? Grand National winners?'

'That isn't how it works,' she said. 'I don't know things like that.'

'Shame,' he said without a trace of disappointment.

'I do know every Christmas number one for the next ten years or so though,' she offered.

'Good enough,' he grinned.

'Can you help me?'

His smile faded and he dropped his hands into his lap. He saw the hope fade from her eyes like a doused fire.

'You can't, can you?'

'I can't tell you what you want to hear,' he admitted. 'I can't tell you that I know exactly what this is or that I can make it go away, but I hope that you understand now that just because you're different that doesn't make you a freak and it doesn't make you a bad person.'

'I need more from you than reassurances,' she said solemnly and his heart sank at the disappointment in her voice.

'Jessie, I will help you,' he said. 'But I need to think about this first. The

166

stuff you've told me wasn't what I was expecting.'

'I understand that.' She took a final drink and rubbed her eyes.

'Please stop looking at this as a negative,' Rory said. 'Look at it as a positive, Jessie. Think about all the good things you could do with this.'

'Like what?'

He pondered this for a moment and then admitted that he didn't know right at this second, but he'd work it out.

She stood up and stretched. 'I'm going to go to bed,' she said. 'I'm sorry if I didn't give you what you wanted, but thanks for listening to me.'

He waved his hand dismissively. 'You gave me what I wanted, Jessie. I'm just not sure what to do with it now that I have it.'

Jess collected up the empty bottles and took them to the bar. 'I don't know if you're working tomorrow night,' she glanced at the clock. It was almost three. 'Well, tonight, but I've been invited to a party if you fancy coming with me?'

He stood up and buried his hands in his pockets. 'What kind of party?'

'My friends parents are away for a week so her and her older brother are having some friends round,' she said. 'It'll probably be your typical teenage get together that ends up getting out of control because everyone's too stoned or drunk to look after themselves.'

'Why would I want to go to a party full of fifteen year olds?' Rory asked.

'Her brother and his mates'll be there,' Jess replied. 'They're your age. Just thought it'd be a change to staring at this place twenty four hours a day.'

He brought the glasses over and stood opposite her with the bar between them. 'Do you want me to come?'

She smiled warmly. Rory was good company. He made her smile, he made her think, and he didn't treat her like she was a child who needed to be constantly protected from the world. 'Yes,' she replied.

'What time should I pick you up, madam?' he asked.

'I'll meet you at the end of Station Road,' she said. 'We can get the bus.'

'I'll get my dad to drive us.'

'Okay, I'll meet you there at seven.'

He nodded. 'I'll tidy the rest of our stuff up. See you tomorrow.'

She opened the door and wished him goodnight before climbing carefully up the stairs.

10

Lights blazed from all of the front windows although it wasn't anywhere near dark yet. Rory looked the house over, suspecting that the party had started without them, as Jess thanked Russ for the lift.

'I was never here,' he said. 'For god's sake don't let your gran know Rory was either.'

'Cross my heart,' she replied as both she and Rory got out of the car, thanking Russ again for the ride.

She went to the door and knocked. It was opened almost immediately by a stocky blonde boy holding a three litre bottle of White Lightning.

'Hi, Jess,' he cried enthusiastically.

'Hi, Neil,' she replied. 'This is my friend, Rory.' Neil nodded briefly at Rory and led them both into the living room. Emily and Anna were sitting beside a large stereo system, through which Billie Piper was currently telling everyone why she always played that song so loud. Two bottles of Hooch stood on the table in front of them as they looked through a pile of CD's.

'Jess,' Anna said as she looked up. Both girls looked at Rory before their faces split into grins. Emily blushed.

'This is Rory,' Jess said. 'Rory, this is Anna and Emily.'

'Nice to meet you, Rory,' Anna said. 'Do you want to help me pick out some music?'

'I think I'm going to get a drink first.'

'Okay.' Anna practically threw the CD's at Emily and went to the kitchen. 'We've got cider, lager, hooch or vodka.'

'I'll take a can of lager please.'

Anna passed him a can with a sweet smile. 'Jess?'

'I'll have the same.' They took their drinks back to the living room where Anna sat beside Emily and patted the space next to her. 'Come on, Rory, help

169

me pick what music to put on.'

'Please don't make me do this,' Rory whispered into Jess's ear.

She laughed. 'We're going to sit outside for a bit, Anna,' she said. 'It's really warm in here.'

As they wandered through the crowded kitchen a group of girls pushed past them, each holding bottles of strong lager. Rory watched them file through to the living room with disapproval.

Jess stepped out into the garden and he followed, closing the back door behind them. She sat at a wooden picnic table on the patio and he took the seat opposite her, resting his head on his fists. 'Thank you,' he said.

'No problem,' Jess replied with a smile. 'She is a bit full on.'

'And a little bit young to be drinking that stuff,' Rory replied.

'What did you expect?' Jess asked. 'Lemonade and cheese footballs?'

Another group of teenagers approached the back door, laughing loudly and passing a bottle of cider between them. One of them stumbled and fell over a low hedge on the other side of the garden, sending them all into a fresh fit of hysterics. Rory shook his head. 'By the time these people are twenty five they'll all be lying in hospital dying of alcoholic liver disease and wondering why.'

Jess suddenly clutched at his hand, her knuckles turning white, her eyes large and glassy.

'Jessie, are you alright?' he asked with concern. She nodded but her eyes rolled up into her head. Rushing around to her side of the table before she could pass out and crack her head open on the patio, he grabbed at her. Her body slumped limply into his arms and somehow, straddling the bench uncomfortably, he held onto her. If he hadn't been able to hear her rapid, shallow breaths, he would have believed that she was dead.

'I need an ambulance,' he called. The kid that had fallen over the hedge had picked himself up and was following his friends inside. They all seemed

170

oblivious to them.

'Rory, unless my heart stops, you do not call for an ambulance,' she said in a low voice. Her eyes were still closed.

'What?' he asked, his voice reedy with panic.

'Please.' She squeezed his bicep tightly. 'Unless my heart stops beating you do not call an ambulance.'

'You can't ask me to do that.'

Her eyes opened and he could see nothing but white. Recoiling, he almost let her go, clutching at her vest and pulling her back to him before she could slide to the floor. 'Please, Rory,' she begged. 'I know what I'm talking about and I promise I'll be fine, just get me away from here. I don't want people to…'

Her eyes closed again and he felt the grip on his arm loosen. He checked her pulse. It was fast, but he didn't think it was dangerous. Her breathing was normal.

'If anything happens to you, Jessie, I'll never forgive myself.'

He laid her down gently in the recovery position, checking her pulse again before taking off his shirt and placing it under her head. He ran topless into the house, almost tripping over the same group of kids that had been outside a minute ago as he entered the living room.

Anna was sitting in the lap of a boy on the far side of the room, apparently trying to eat his face. Emily looked up as he entered the room and he was relieved to see that she looked half sober. Her eyes ran hungrily over his naked torso.

'I need you,' he said to her. She stared blankly back at him. 'Come on,' he urged, pulling her off the sofa when she didn't move. He dragged her past another group of arriving guests into the back garden.

'Listen to me, Emily,' he said as they reached the patio. 'Jessie's not very well. I need to get her away from here and I need your help.'

171

'Is, is she alright?' Emily asked as Rory bent over Jess and held a finger under her nose. She seemed hesitant to get too close, as if whatever was wrong with Jess might be contagious.

'I think so,' he said hopefully. 'Emily, I need to take her away from here, somewhere quiet, but I don't know where to go.'

'Why can't you take her home?' Emily asked.

'That's a really long, really boring story,' he replied. 'Please tell me you can think of somewhere.'

'We could just take her upstairs.'

'Okay, yes,' Rory stood again. 'Stay with her a second.'

He ran back through the house, taking the stairs two at a time. It took only a few seconds to establish that all of the upstairs rooms were occupied. Flushed, he ran back to the garden.

'No good,' he panted.

'Why don't you call an ambulance?'

'Because she asked me not to,' he replied irritably. 'Come on, Emily, think.'

Emily sat on the edge of the bench and put her head in her hands. Rory sat beside Jess, constantly checking that she was breathing.

'Have you tried to wake her?' Emily asked.

'I don't think I'm supposed to,' he replied. 'She didn't panic and she told me not to call an ambulance.' He was still haunted by her milky eyes but she had been in control, unafraid. Hadn't she?

'I live three streets away if you want to take her to mine,' Emily suggested. Rory nodded. 'I'll just need to ring my dad and check it's okay.'

She went into the house and pushed her way through the clusters of bodies to the phone in the hall. It rang four times before her dad answered.

'Dad, it's me.' She willed her heart to stop beating so quickly. 'Jessica Morgan's not very well and because our house is closer than the pub I wondered if she'd be okay to stay over at ours tonight?'

'Emily?' Jon Sharpe put his fork down and chewed quickly at a mouthful of chop suey. 'I thought you were at a party?'

'I am, dad.' She plugged her ear with her finger so that she could hear him better. 'Jessica isn't feeling very well and I wondered if she could stay with us tonight?'

He swallowed and pushed food around the plate with his knife. 'She isn't going to chuck up all over the place, is she?'

'No, she hasn't been sick or anything, she's just got a really bad headache and says it's too loud here.'

'Okay.' He picked up his fork and speared a piece of chicken. 'Do you need me to pick you up? I can be there in about twenty minutes, I'm just having my tea.'

'We'll walk,' Emily said. 'We can be there in two minutes.'

'Okay, Em, I'll see you soon.'

Emily hung up and went back outside. 'We can go to my house but he can't pick us up for twenty minutes, which in my dads language means about an hour, so we'll have to walk. Is that okay?'

Rory stood up and kissed her cheek. 'You've done really well,' he said. 'You tell me where I'm going and I'll carry her.' He bent and lifted Jess. She moaned from somewhere a million miles away and her head lolled over his arm. 'I'm going to end up breaking her fucking neck,' he said to himself.

Emily led him around the side of the house. A couple were kissing between the house and the wooden fence next door. 'What's wrong with her?' the boy asked as Rory barged past.

'None of your business,' he growled back.

He followed Emily to the end of the street and they turned right. 'Slow down,' he said breathlessly. She was running ahead of him and he was struggling to keep up. Jess seemed to have gained a lot of weight since they had left the house and every time he tried to speed up his legs protested. He'd tripped twice, his heart catching in his throat as he clutched at his strange cargo, waiting to overbalance and spill her to the floor. Dead weight. That was the phrase that kept coming to his mind. She's a dead weight. Dead.

People looked at them suspiciously as they passed but nobody stopped them. He felt a sinister gratitude for these people who, through disbelief that anything malicious could possibly happen in their town, right before their own eyes, walked straight past them.

Emily turned and waited for him to catch up before starting to walk again, this time a little slower. 'My dad isn't going to let you stay with her,' she said. 'He wont let boys stay over at my house.'

Rory heaved Jess back up into his arms. She kept sliding away from his grasp. His arms were close to numb. 'I'll worry about your dad,' he replied. 'You just get us there.'

She did that in just under four minutes and called for her dad as Rory followed her through the door. 'In here,' Jon called from the living room. She went in with Rory behind her. His face was a deep, desperate red. He was holding Jess tight against his bare chest, his arms shaking with tension.

'You said that she had a headache,' Jon said as he crossed the room quickly, took Jess from Rory's arms and laid her down on the sofa. Rory knelt beside her and looked into her expressionless face.

'She said she felt faint,' Emily lied quickly. 'Then she just passed out, so Rory carried her.'

Jon looked at Jess, then at her half naked companion. Rory's back shone with sweat in the artificial light of the room as he bent over her. 'We should ring Jean,' he said.

'No,' Rory said, turning quickly from Jess to Jon and standing up. His legs threatened to give way and he begged for them to just give him another minute. 'You can't do that.'

Jon's eyes narrowed. 'Why not?' he asked, placing his hands on his hips.

'Because if Jean knows she's been drinking she'll be in big trouble,' Rory replied. 'If we can just stay until tomorrow she'll never know. I know it's a lot to ask but I don't know what else to do.'

Jon turned to Emily. 'Who's he?' he asked.

'This is Rory,' Emily said. 'He's a friend of Jess's.'

'You're responsible for this young lady?' Jon had turned back to Rory, his stance very similar to the one Rory's dad chose to take when he was going to talk to Rory like an adult only to remind him that he was still acting like a child. Rory nodded despondently. 'How did she get into this state?' He went to Jess and checked her pulse for himself now, wondering whether she required medical attention.

'She doesn't normally drink,' Rory said. 'But I was talking to someone and the next thing I know she's disappeared. I found her in another room drinking shots with some boys. I think she just needs to sleep it off. She'll be so embarrassed in the morning.'

Jon turned to his daughter. 'Is that what happened?'

Emily nodded. 'I think she was trying to look clever in front of some older boys.'

'Can you wake her?' he asked Rory.

'I haven't tried,' he replied, scared that he wouldn't be able to and then Jon would insist on an ambulance. Maybe that was exactly what they needed to do.

But she had begged him.

'I'll get the kettle on,' Jon said. 'She probably just needs a strong cup of coffee. You try waking her up.'

Rory could have hugged the small man. He wasn't going to the phone to call an ambulance or, worse, Jean. As Jon went to the kitchen, Rory and Emily looked at each other.

'Is she really okay?' Emily asked in a low voice. Rory nudged Jess. She moaned and rolled over onto her side, pulling her legs up to her body. 'Do you think she just fell asleep?'

'I don't know,' Rory said. He was getting sick of being asked questions he didn't have the answers to. 'But that's what we're going to tell your dad. We tell him that I woke her up, she told me to leave her alone and went back to sleep.'

'Do you think he's going to believe us?'

He ran a hand through his hair instead of slapping her with it. 'We're screwed if he doesn't.'

'Just wake her up.'

He looked at her coldly and felt a prick of guilt when she seemed to recoil. 'Emily, I'll be honest with you,' he said. 'If she looks like she did before she fell asleep or passed out or whatever, we're safer if she doesn't wake up while your dad's around.'

Emily looked more scared than hurt now. 'What happened?' she asked.

'That's not important,' Rory snapped. 'You need to go into the kitchen and tell your dad that we woke her and she just wants to go to bed.'

Emily looked at him helplessly. She wished he hadn't picked her to help him. She wanted to be back at the party. Ten more minutes and she was sure that Simon Clarke would have kissed her. 'He wont believe me,' she said resignedly.

Rory put his hands on her shoulders and rubbed them in a rough gesture of comfort. 'You've done so well, Emily,' he said softly. 'Just one more lie and we're done.' Emily nodded, knowing that if she didn't do it this awful situation was only going to get worse. She went slowly to the kitchen, closing the door behind her. Rory checked Jess's pulse again before stooping to pick her up.

'Acolic liver disea,' she mumbled.

'Jessie?' he asked with quiet hope. She didn't respond. He stood with her in his arms, waiting for Emily to come back. It was only now that he remembered his shirt, lying on the patio behind Anna's house. He'd only bought it a month

176

ago.

The kitchen door opened and Emily came out with Jon. 'We'll put her in the back bedroom,' Jon said. 'Do you want me to carry her?'

'I'm okay,' Rory said, although he could feel his aching limbs throb and threaten to buckle as he followed Jon to the stairs. He struggled upwards, thankful when he saw the bed and was able to lay her down. He took off her shoes and Emily pulled the covers over her.

'Would you like a coffee?' Jon asked.

Rory shook his head. 'I'll just stay with her until she wakes up.'

'I don't think so,' Jon said. 'You can stay on the sofa, Rory. I wasn't born yesterday.'

'I'm not leaving her,' Rory said.

'You don't have a choice,' Jon replied defiantly as he folded his arms over his chubby chest. 'Look, you might be her boyfriend and your parents might approve of you sharing a bedroom with a fifteen year old girl but it wont happen while you're under my roof.'

Rory stood up, pleading again with his aching legs. 'First,' he counted on his fingers. 'I'm not her boyfriend. Second, she's my responsibility and I've already messed up once tonight. And third, no, my parents wouldn't approve of me sharing a bedroom with a fifteen year old girl. So if you'd rather she slept in the living room so I could stay with her, then that's fine with me.'

Jon's shoulders twitched backwards as if Rory had pushed them.

'Dad,' Emily's voice was small. 'You can trust him. I promise.'

Jon looked Rory over, trying to measure him up. He didn't look like he wanted to get into Jess's underwear as soon as his back was turned. He looked scared and tired. 'I can only drag a chair in and give you a blanket,' he said finally.

'Thanks,' Rory replied gratefully as his body slumped and he finally yielded to the screaming muscles in his legs.

11

Jon fetched the chair from his bedroom and Emily took a blanket from the airing cupboard while Rory watched over Jess. He declined Jon's second offer of a coffee at nine but took him up on the offer of a sandwich and a beer at ten thirty. Jon had been sneaking up the stairs and coming into the room at regular intervals. Checking up on him, Rory knew. Emily looked in on them on her way to bed at half past twelve but Jess still hadn't woken up.

'I'm starting to wonder if we should have called an ambulance,' Rory said sadly. 'She looks like she's just sleeping, but isn't that what people look like when they're in a coma?'

'Do you want me to ask dad to get one to come?'

Unless my heart stops beating you do not call an ambulance.

'No,' Rory replied uncertainly. 'We'll wait a bit longer.'

'If you need anything I'm just next door.'

'Thanks,' he smiled at her, trying to convey thankfulness as well as an apology for the way he'd spoken to her earlier.

Between half past one and two twenty he dozed. When he awoke he stood up and stretched, cursing himself for falling asleep at his post. He needed a drink but didn't dare leave her alone. He checked her pulse. It had slowed down. Maybe she had just fallen asleep. He went downstairs and poured himself a glass of water, drained it, poured another, and went back to the room where Jess lay silent and still as a corpse.

He put the glass down on the floor and moved the chair closer to the bed. He held her hand, checked her pulse, held a finger under her nose to make sure she was still breathing, held her hand again.

He woke again at ten past three. He had dozed for another quarter of an hour. His back and neck ached. The bed that Jess lay in looked unbelievably

178

comfortable from his current position. He could lie down just for a while. If he fell asleep while he was lying beside her, she would wake him if she moved. And if Jon walked in he would have a fit. But if he lay on top of the covers? They were both dressed. Surely he'd understand that Rory needed some rest?

His stomach growled. Before the sandwich his last meal had been a tuna salad and a Kit Kat at two yesterday afternoon. His eyelids were heavy.

'I need food and I need sleep,' he told the empty room. The digital display of the clock in the windowsill said that it was a quarter past three. He felt as if he'd been awake for a week.

He stood, yawned monstrously and then lay down beside her. He put one hand under his head and stroked a stray lock of hair from her face with the other. She lay facing him, one hand was tucked under the pillow, the other lay across her stomach. Her knees were pulled up to her chest and her toes pointed towards the bottom of the bed.

'I didn't call the ambulance,' he whispered. 'But I'm starting to wish that I had. Please wake up, Jessie.'

He pushed her shoulder lightly and she stirred. Her hand slid out from beneath the pillow and crossed over her chest. She was sleeping, he was sure of it. If he wanted to he could wake her, and he did want to. He just couldn't bring himself to do it. She looked peaceful, as if all the hurt she carried with her couldn't touch her where she was now. He couldn't take that serenity away from her.

'Sleep well, princess,' he said as he closed his eyes.

She woke him half an hour later, shaking him violently. 'Dad? Dad, wake up.'

Rory opened his eyes slowly. His head felt heavy and for an insane moment he was going to tell her to go back to sleep. 'Jessie?' his voice was hoarse. He cleared his throat. Her eyes were open and she was staring straight at him. His skin prickled with goose bumps. She wasn't staring at him, she was looking straight through him.

'Dad, I need you to get Rory,' she said quickly. Rory was afraid that she would wake Jon. 'I need to speak to Rory.'

'Jessie,' he stroked her cheek and she leaned into his touch. 'Jessie, it's Rory. I'm here.'

She looked puzzled. 'Dad?'

'No,' Rory replied quietly. 'It's Rory.'

'Rory?' She sounded like she didn't believe him. He held her face and moved it closer to his own, looking into her eyes. 'Jessie, I'm here, I am Rory.'

She blinked hard and her eyes ran over his face, trying to take in what she was seeing before she flung her arms around him and pulled him to her. 'Rory,' she breathed into his neck.

He held her tight. 'I was so worried about you.' His eyes stung with tears of relief.

She pulled away from him and sat up, looking around. 'Where are we?' she asked.

'You said you needed to get away from the party,' Rory explained. 'So we brought you here. We're at Emily's house.'

'The party,' she said distantly. Then her eyes widened and she put a hand to her mouth. 'Oh god, did I make a complete idiot of myself?'

Manic laughter bubbled inside him. He'd been sitting here, waiting, wondering if she would wake up, and this was what she was worried about when she finally did? He shook his head. 'No,' he said. 'Me and Emily brought you here. Nobody knows what happened apart from us and her dad.' *And I'm not sure any of us really know what happened.*

'What time is it?'

'Almost four.' Rory pushed himself up on the bed and sat with his back against the old padded headboard, crossing his long legs out in front of him.

'Does gran know I'm here?'

'Emily phoned her and told her that you both came here after the party and asked if you could stay the night.'

Her shoulders slumped and her breathing slowed. Despite the sleep she looked exhausted.

'What happened, Jessie?'

She pushed hair away from her face. 'Thank you for not calling an ambulance,' she said.

'I almost did a few times,' he admitted. 'It was pretty scary.'

She smiled apologetically. 'I was trying to tell you,' she said. 'It happened once before. It was like everything made sense. Then it, I don't know, it overwhelmed me and I blacked out and when I woke up I couldn't remember what had happened. That's what happened at Anna's. That's how I knew I didn't need an ambulance.'

'I wish you'd told me that before,' Rory said. 'I was worried sick.'

Jess apologised and shuffled closer to him, drawing her knees up to her chest. 'It was like hundreds of images flashing through my mind, the way people say that your life flashes before your eyes just before you die. Then I felt really sleepy. I dreamed, no, I didn't dream. I wasn't dreaming. I was remembering.'

Rory, still fighting fatigue, felt slow and disoriented. 'Remembering what happened when you blacked out last time?'

She shook her head solemnly. 'Before that.'

'Jessie,' he sighed. 'It might be because I haven't had much sleep, but you're not making a lot of sense.'

'You helped me, Rory,' she said excitedly. 'You said you'd help me and you did.'

He rubbed his eyes with the heels of his hands. 'How?'

'Alcoholic liver disease,' she said as if it was glaringly obvious. 'That's what killed my dad.'

'Jessie,' he said slowly, 'your dad's still alive.'

'I know that.'

He ran a hand over his face. 'Okay, you've lost me,' he surrendered.

'The things I know,' she explained. 'They're not premonitions. In fact their the opposite. They're memories. I know what's happening in Filton and not what's happening here because I didn't live here last time.'

'Last time?' he asked.

'I died, Rory,' she looked at him shamefacedly. 'And I did it to myself, but she sent me back.'

'Tonight?'

'No, not tonight. It was, it was after my dad died. I don't remember when.'

Rory rubbed his eyes, trying to wake himself up so that he could understand what she was saying.

'I made the wrong choices,' Jess continued. 'Something like that. That's why she sent me back. So I could start again, right from the beginning.'

He listened as she explained what had happened. It was sketchy and full of holes. She remembered that she had killed herself but not how or when and it chilled him that she spoke of her own suicide as if she was recalling a minor accident she'd had as a child. It was just something that had happened to her a long time ago.

'Why would you do something like that?' he asked. 'How could things get so bad that you couldn't see a way out?'

'That was my way out,' she replied sadly. 'You don't understand.'

'Well, I'm not going anywhere, so why don't you explain it to me?'

She looked at him gratefully. 'Why do you care?' she asked.

He put an arm around her shoulders and offered her a supportive smile. 'I promised that if you talked to me I'd help you.'

She took a deep breath before she began. 'Me and dad lived on our own for a long time,' she said. 'We never really went out, we just kept ourselves to

182

ourselves and,' she sighed heavily, 'and thinking about it now it seems
pathetic, but it wasn't. We were happy like that.'

'Until he dies and leaves you on your own,' Rory finished for her.

'I didn't know what to do and the only person I could go to was Scott.'

'Is this the same Scott that asked you to marry him?'

She nodded. 'When dad died he was married to Joanne.'

'Okay, now I'm confused,' he said. 'Did he ask you to marry him before or
after your dad died?'

'Before.'

He took a swallow of water and offered her the glass but she shook her head.
'Scott helped for a while,' she continued. 'But then things got out of hand.' She
tugged uncomfortably at the bottom of her vest. Rory saw that she looked
horrified when she realised what she was doing and wrapped her arms around
her knees. 'He told me he was going to leave her, that he loved me and wanted
to be with me. It's my own fault for being so gullible, I suppose, but Joanne
made him choose, her or me. He chose her.' Rory squeezed her shoulder,
unsure of what to say. 'And that was it. I had nothing. There was nowhere for
me to go, nothing I could do. It was the end.'

'What a bastard,' Rory commented.

'That's not what matters.'

Rory thought that she sounded more defensive that she should.

'What do I do now? That's what matters. I made the wrong choice or
choices and that's why I got sent back. How do I fix it? How am I supposed to
know what I did wrong?'

Rory kissed the top of her head. 'Jessie, I could help you to become sensitive
to spirit. I could show you how to open and close doors so that you didn't start
getting messages at inopportune times.' He thought of the time a woman, long
dead, had suddenly appeared at his side while he'd been standing, dick in hand,
in front of a pub urinal. 'But the meaning of life? I'm as stumped on that one as

everyone else, I'm afraid.'

Jess got up and went to the window. It was light outside and the birds were singing their dawn overture. 'What am I going to do?' she asked.

'Look on the bright side,' Rory said as he sat on the edge of the bed. 'You know what it is and why it's happening now. You have an advantage over everyone else. You know what's coming.'

'Not here I don't.' She slumped onto the chair in front of Rory.

He sighed and leaned forward, planting his hands on her thighs. 'But you're not supposed to be here, are you?' he said sadly.

Jess thought about Filton. All those familiar faces doing all those familiar things. She had wanted so much to sort this out so that she could go back to live with her dad. But now? She looked up at Rory. It had been so hard for her to finally trust someone with her secret and now that it was out, a macabre gift given only to him, she wanted to keep him close. Could she really handle Filton without him? Could she handle it at all? Did she actually have a choice?

Her voice cracked with arid misery as she said, 'I have to go back.'

12

Jon dropped them off at the corner of Station Road, only a few feet from where Russ had been waiting for them the night before, and they began to walk towards The Unicorn. Jess was dragging her feet. She hadn't talked much since breakfast. Rory had told Jon that she had a monster of a hangover and she just wanted to get home.

As the long driveway came into view she stopped. 'I don't want to go back yet.'

Rory looked down the driveway. The hairs on Jess's forearms had bristled and her shoulders were studded with goose bumps. 'You're going to catch pneumonia if you stay out here,' he said.

'Please, Rory.' She looked at him hopefully. 'I don't want to have to sit on my own in my room with this. You're the only person I can talk to.'

'You said your dad was coming to see you.'

'He wont be here until this afternoon.' She rubbed her arms absently. 'I need to think about this before he gets here.'

'Are you going to tell him?'

'How am I supposed to do that?' she asked.

'You told me.'

'My dad wouldn't understand like you do.'

Rory wrapped his arms around himself, feeling the sharp morning cold even as the sun slowly began to wake and warm the air. 'I'm not sure that I understand it, Jess.'

'But you don't treat me like I'm a leper or something,' she argued. 'It's bad enough now without me telling him any of this.'

'I'm sure he doesn't do it on purpose.'

'But he does,' she insisted. 'It's as if he has to consider everything he's thinking of saying to me before he says it, and he watches me when I talk to him. Like he's analysing what I'm saying or what I'm doing with my hands or my eyes.'

Jon had loaned Rory a tee shirt but it was no defence against the chill. He wasn't even sure if it was coming from the air or from her. 'Wait here,' he said. 'I'll go and get the car and we can talk about this in the warm.'

She watched as he jogged away from her and then sat on the low stone wall beside the road to wait for him. Her head felt as if a rat were inside it, gnawing relentlessly at the soft tissue of her brain. She couldn't think properly. When she tried to make sense of what was happening, her train of thought would derail and leave her thinking about something unrelated and meaningless. She tried to remember how she had died. How had she done it? Pink flowers bloomed in her mind and she gave up.

What was she going to say to her dad? *Guess what, I feel a lot better now and I want to come home?* The way her dad's mind worked around her, he'd know something had happened, or at least suspect it. And did she really want to go back? Did she want to leave this haven where things were new and people were strangers to her? No. She wanted to hide here. Filton was a different place now. The happy times she had shared with her dad, with Scott, they were a dim future past that no longer existed except in her own memory.

'Any idea where we can go?' Rory asked as he pulled up and she climbed inside the car.

'There's a place where people have picnics and stuff,' she said. 'We can go and sit in the car park there if you like.'

And make love in the rain.

She shivered.

'Okay, just let me know where I'm going.'

The journey began in contemplative silence for both of them. Jess only spoke to direct him through the winding roads of the countryside. As they turned onto a wider residential road a man walking two Alsatians strolled across a zebra crossing in front of them. 'There's a turning on the right just past that crossing,' Jess said. 'You need to go down there.'

Rory followed her directions and she pointed him down a long gravel path that came out at a small picnic area.

'If you go through the trees you come out at the river,' Jess said. 'A lot of people go for walks down there.'

The engine died as he slowed to a halt beneath the arching branches of trees that surrounded the picnic area. A breeze ruffled their leaves as Jess and Rory took off their seatbelts. They were the only people here. Five picnic tables stood in the grass and birds landed on them, pecking at the scraps that yesterday's picnickers had discarded and then left.

'I told my dad that it had stopped.' Jess pulled her knees up to her chest and stared blindly at the picnic area. 'I've got nothing to gain by telling him the truth. He'll be worse than he is with me now. He'll want to wrap me up in cotton wool and keep me locked away from anything that might take us back to how it was before. He'll know that I've been lying to him. He might not even let me go back at all.'

Rory turned in his chair, pulling one leg up onto the seat. 'And what's the alternative?' he asked.

'I just carry on like I have for the last eleven years.'

He lit a Marlborough and rolled down his window, allowing cool air to drift into the car. 'Jessie, this is a pretty big thing,' he warned. 'How are you going to get through it all by yourself? I mean, it's okay while you're here and you don't know everyone and the stuff you know is kept at arms length. But being right back in the thick of it? Do you really think you can deal with that on your own?'

'I wont know until I try.' She sounded truly miserable. 'But if this is about the choices I made, then aren't I supposed to do it by myself?' She put her hands over her face and shook her head. 'Why did this have to happen to me?'

187

Her voice was muffled, but the despair was easily recognisable nonetheless.

'Maybe you're supposed to do something useful,' he suggested. 'Did you ever watch that programme about the doctor or scientist or whatever he was, travelling through time, putting right what once went wrong?'

He was pleased to see her lips curve in the direction of a smile as she turned in the seat, folding her legs beneath her. 'You mean Quantum Leap,' she said. 'My dad loves that programme.'

'Maybe that's what this is but you're supposed to make your own life better.'

'How?'

He flicked ash out of the window and took a deep drag on the small stump that was left of his cigarette. 'You'll have to give me time to think about that one,' he admitted. 'I mean, I don't know what happened last time.'

'Not much,' she said. He thought he heard a touch of regret but didn't mention it.

'Maybe you're just supposed to live a fuller life,' he suggested. 'You know all those Christmas number one's. Get your money on them and make yourself rich. Or better, write the songs yourself and sell them.'

She laughed a little. 'I don't think that's how this is supposed to work.'

'Well you weren't given any rules or instructions were you?' he asked. 'If I were you I'd play the game to my full advantage.'

'I know you would,' she said with a wry smile. 'But she said something about making more informed decisions. I assume that means that I'm supposed to change something that happened the first time around, not use what I know to make myself rich.'

'Although that wouldn't be a bad side project.' He took a last long drag on the cigarette and threw it out of the window.

'Or maybe it's not about me at all,' Jess suggested. 'Not really.'

'What do you mean?'

'That this is probably more Terminator than Quantum Leap.' She had wrapped her arms around her knees again and pulled her thighs tight against her chest.

'I'm not sure that I follow,' Rory said as he rolled up the window.

'The Terminator was sent back in time to kill Sarah Connor.'

'Yeah, I've seen the film,' he said.

'But not because of Sarah Connor. Because of John Connor.' Rory looked at her blankly. 'I can only remember making one big decision in my life,' she explained. 'I chose to stay with my dad instead of marrying Scott. Maybe I made the wrong choice. Maybe me and Scott are supposed to have our own John Connor. A kid that finds a cure for cancer or something.'

'But if you and Scott do get together you run the risk of someone sending Arnold Schwarzenegger after you,' Rory said seriously. 'Tough choice.' Jess smiled. 'When are you going to leave?' he asked more quietly.

'As soon as possible,' she answered without looking at him. 'I'm not making any progress here.' She thought again of the ghosts waiting for her in Filton and shuddered.

'Do me a favour,' Rory said. 'Stop taking this so seriously.'

'It is serious.'

'Kids your age can't wait to grow up.' He touched her knee and she rested her cheek against his hand. 'They don't appreciate being kids until it's too late. Whatever mistakes you make, don't make that one. Are you ready to go back to the pub?'

She shook her head. 'Not yet.'

Rory turned on the radio to fill the uncomfortable silence that followed. Elton John blared out at them, making Jess jump. 'Didn't have you down as much of an Elton John fan,' she said.

'My dad's been messing around with the radio again.' Rory started to turn the dial slowly, filling the car with loud crackles and whines. 'I'm more of a

189

Bon Jovi man myself.'

Jess nodded. 'My dad likes Bon Jovi.' She smiled to herself and then snorted laughter.

'What's funny?' Rory asked.

She took a deep breath, exhaling as she watched a sparrow land, snatch up a crumb of discarded bread and flutter away. 'There's a song they did,' she said. 'It's My Life, that's what it's called.'

'You sure it's Bon Jovi?' Rory asked. 'I've never heard of it.'

She looked at him with a strange smile playing at her lips. 'It hasn't been released yet,' she said.

Rory fought the urge to look away from those old, tormented eyes.

'The words of the chorus,' Jess said, 'they seem pretty meaningful now.'

She spoke, her eyes on the picnic tables again, and the words, just a couple of lines from a song that was yet to be written, gave Rory a feeling of hope for her. She would be okay. She wouldn't waste what she'd been given. She didn't need him.

When she had finished she looked at him hopefully. 'Will you keep in touch?'

He withdrew his hand and looked down at his lap. 'We should probably get back,' he said. 'Your gran's going to be wondering where you are.' He started the car and reversed, spinning it around and kicking up gravel as he went back down the narrow pathway.

'Did I say something wrong?'

Don't do this to me, Jessie, he thought. *Because whatever I say is going to sound bad, like I'm abandoning you.* 'I don't think staying in touch is a good idea,' he murmured.

'But you're my friend,' Jess replied. 'Or am I just a job to you?'

'No,' he said. 'Please don't think that.' He paused to check the road before pulling out and speeding over the zebra crossing.

190

'You're just going to abandon me?'

Told you.

'No,' he said again. 'You're right, Jessie. The choices you make have to be your own. You can't be ringing me all the time asking for help.'

'That's not why I want to stay in touch.'

'I'm not having this conversation with you,' he said a little too firmly. 'You can't stay here because this isn't where you're meant to be and I don't belong where you're going. I wasn't part of your life before, so I shouldn't be part of it now.'

'But you are,' she insisted.

'The only reason I'm anything to do with this is because you needed help remembering what had happened.'

'What if that's not true?'

'Stop it, Jessie.' He shot her a look that was somewhere between anger and sadness. 'The what if's are for you to work out. Leave me out of it.'

They were both silent. Rory stared straight ahead and Jess kept her eyes on the floor until Rory pulled up inside the garage.

'I don't want to spend however long it is that we have left arguing with you,' Jess said. Rory could hear bitter defeat in her voice. 'You've been a really good friend to me, Rory. Even when I didn't want you to be.' They both smiled. 'I've got stuff to sort out and my dad's got to make sure he can get me back into school. We've got time.'

He took off his seatbelt and held her. 'I'm going to miss you,' he said. 'I think we would have been friends for a very long time.'

She nodded against him and then gazed up at him curiously. 'So am I fifteen or not?' she asked.

'Of course you are,' he replied. 'It's just your memories that are older.'

'I feel older,' she said.

'That's psychological.'

191

'See, this is why I need you around.'

'Please don't,' he said. And she didn't.

13

Paul turned the ring over between his fingertips, smiling sadly at the tarnished silver. The band was inlaid with three small hearts, a tiny zircon set in the centre of each. It had been a gift to his wife over fifteen years ago. She'd still been in the hospital with their newborn baby and he'd been wandering around town, lost without her at home, when he'd spotted it in the window of a cheap jewellery shop.

Me and my two girls.

Sheila had been decidedly grumpy since giving birth. Hormones, pain, sleepless nights, breast feeding; she'd already grown tired of it all. Paul had wanted to cheer her up.

It looked a little tacky, but he hadn't been out for twenty four carat gold; wouldn't have been able to afford it if he had. He'd been looking for anything that would put a smile on his wife's face that wasn't chocolates or flowers. Too predictable.

'You're such a softie,' she'd said, her eyes sparkling and her face beautiful as she slid it onto her finger and held her hand out at arms length to admire it.

'I saw it and I thought of us,' he'd replied, taking her hand and pointing at the hearts. 'One heart for you, one heart for me and one heart for Jessica.'

Sheila had stared at the ring, at the three hearts and what they symbolised. To Paul it had been their family. To Sheila it had been sharing, and she hadn't wanted to share Paul. The kid meant he had to stay, that was all. For her, the ring had been an end, not a beginning. The more she'd had to share her husband with their daughter, the more she'd looked for attention in other places.

As he looked at the ring he only saw the beginning of their family. Him, a husband and now a father. Him and his beautiful, beautiful girls. He'd felt like the luckiest man alive.

But it had been short lived.

It hadn't taken long to realise that Jessica was a special child. A prodigy, he'd thought. She had been walking as soon as her legs would support her weight, talking in sentences when her peers had still been learning to crawl.

And then *poof!* Just like magic, it was all gone.

The phone rang suddenly, making him drop the ring. He cursed and picked it up quickly from the carpet, thrusting it into his pocket as he went to the hall.

'Hello?'

'Hi, Dad. It's me.'

'Jess,' he said brightly. 'How are you, sweetheart?'

'I'm fine,' she replied. 'Actually, I'm really good and I want to ask you something.'

'I've told you before,' he smiled, savouring the sound of her voice. 'No tattoos until you're fifty and no boyfriends until you're sixty.'

She laughed and he laughed because she did.

He frowned at the silence that followed, wondering if she was still on the line. 'You still there?' he asked.

She sighed and the sound crackled across two counties to Paul's expectant ear.

'I want to come home, dad.'

Tears fell unnoticed over his cheeks and he leaned his forehead against the cool wall.

'Dad?'

'I heard you, sweetheart.'

'Do you want me to come home?' she asked tentatively.

'Of course I do,' he replied. 'Have you spoken to your gran about it?'

'Not yet.'

He touched the ring in his pocket and stood up straight. His heart told him to hang up, get into his car and fetch her immediately; but his head urged caution.

194

'Why now, Jess?' he asked.

'You don't think I should come back, do you?' Jess sounded disappointed.

'I want you to, sweetheart,' he said. 'I do. More than anything. I just want you to be safe.'

'I wouldn't be asking to come back if I didn't think I was okay.'

'What about . . .'

'How many times, dad?' She sounded annoyed. 'It's gone. All of it. I'm sick of everyone treating me like a nutcase. I want to come home and live with my dad, what's wrong with that?'

'Nothing,' he replied. 'Nothing at all. I'm sorry, Jess, I just worry.'

'I know you do, dad,' she replied softly.

'I'll come up at the weekend and we can talk to your gran and granddad.'

'Thanks dad,' she said. 'I love you.'

'Love you too, sweetheart.'

After he hung up he stood, looking at the phone as if he knew he should be doing something but unsure what. He rang Karen.

If Paul had been nervous, Karen was terrified. But he'd made up his mind. Jess wasn't four anymore, she was almost an adult and she knew her own mind. He was scared too, but how do you tell your own daughter that she can't come home?

After a long conversation Karen lit a cigarette and sat next to her sister in the living room.

Joanne had had a bad day. Scott Jordan was ignoring her and then she'd seen him walking through the park with Dawn Embassy after school.

'Jess Morgan's coming home,' Karen said. Of course Joanne knew all about Jess. About her mum, the dreams, the drawings. Karen had talked to her about it several times after she had asked why Paul visited so frequently.

Joanne's fingers paused between two pages of Smash Hits magazine. 'What?' They were releasing her and allowing her to mingle with the normal

195

people? Had the lunatics finally taken over the asylum? 'Does she still have those weirdo dreams?'

Karen shook her head. 'Paul wondered if you'd look after her the first few days at school.' She already knew what the answer would be.

'No way!' Joanne cried.

'Stop it,' Karen said. 'Look, I don't like it any more than you do but I do feel a bit sorry for her. She's scared about coming back.'

'She should stay there then.'

'She wants to be with her dad, Joanne.'

Joanne went into the kitchen and came back with a chocolate digestive. She munched at it thoughtfully. 'Is she still a freak?'

'Joanne!'

'You know what I mean.'

Karen blew smoke into the room and Joanne flapped a hand at it. 'I could get cancer because of you,' she said spitefully.

Karen ignored her. 'She's fine.'

'I can't believe they might actually let her come to normal school.'

'Joanne, she is normal.' She tapped her hand against her knee nervously. 'Please just look after her for a couple of days,' she said. 'She doesn't know anyone. How would you feel if you were in her shoes?'

'Like I should start walking back to my grandparents.'

Karen didn't smile. 'Please. Just introduce her to some kids and help her make some friends. Just please do me a favour.'

Joanne began to chew nervously at her nails. 'I can't,' she moaned. 'I can't be seen in public with her.'

'Don't be such a bitch,' Karen scowled at her. 'If you don't want to do it then you can tell Paul, or come up with a better idea.'

'Not my problem,' Joanne said finally as she stood up and stormed out of the room.

Karen took another drag and shook her head. Well, she'd tried.

14

Russ was nearing the climax of a John Grisham paperback and scowled as the make believe world he had sunken so gladly into was ruptured by a knock at the door. His working hours started at eight. Four am to eight pm was his time. He ignored it. Whoever it was could come back later.

The knock came again. He sighed dramatically, even though there was nobody in the room to hear it or see the deep frown that creased his brow, and sat up.

'Come in,' he said, laying the book face down on the crumpled sheets.

Jess poked her head around the door. 'Did I wake you?' she asked.

He shook his head. 'Just having some me time,' he said. 'What can I do for you?'

'I was looking for Rory.'

Of course she was. Rory had told him that she was going home today and had slunk out to the garage about half an hour ago. 'What do I say if she comes looking for you?' Russ had asked.

'Tell her you haven't seen me.'

Russ opened his mouth to tell her that he didn't know where Rory was but motioned for her to come in instead. She stepped inside, glancing back over her shoulder before she did, and closed the door. 'When's your dad picking you up?' he asked.

'Two,' she replied. 'I wanted to see Rory before he got here.' Russ looked at the clock above the door. It was a quarter past one. 'I tried the bar, the kitchen, I thought he might have gone into York but the car's still in the garage. I even checked the cellar but I couldn't find him. This was my last option. I know he's normally only in here when he's sleeping.'

The garage? He was in the garage. Russ knew for a fact that he was in the garage. Was he that childish that he would hide from her?

'Have you seen him?'

Tell her you haven't seen me.

'He's in the garage.'

'I checked the garage.'

'He's in the garage,' Russ repeated, wanting to get back to his book. 'He told me he was going there half an hour ago. If he wasn't there when you checked, then he was hiding.'

'Hiding?' Jess rubbed her forehead with the heel of her hand and looked at the ceiling with frustration.

'He's just sulking,' Russ said.

She took a sealed white envelope from the back pocket of her jeans. 'If I don't find him before dad gets here, would you give this to him for me?'

Russ took it and nodded. 'He's in the garage,' he said again.

'Thanks.'

She was having a bad enough time as it was without Rory doing a vanishing act. Jean had been decidedly icy with her since she'd told them she was going home. Jess obviously didn't appreciate a thing they'd done for her, at least not enough to even think about discussing it with them before making a decision. It wouldn't hurt to check the garage once more. If he wasn't there, or if he wouldn't speak to her, that was fine. At least she'd know that she'd tried.

'You've been wandering around for the last hour,' Geoff said as she came out from behind the bar. 'What have you lost?'

'Nothing,' she replied. 'I suppose I'm just nervous. Trying to make sure I've got everything, giving the place a last look over.'

He asked if she'd like to join him for a last drink but she was already halfway to the door and didn't hear him. He shrugged and handed his empty glass to Don.

'Rory?' she called as she swung open one of the heavy garage doors. 'Rory?' If he was in here he'd been sitting alone in the dark. At first glance there was nobody inside the garage and nobody sitting in the car. 'Rory?' She walked over to the car and peered inside. He was lying across the backseat, looking at the floor of his hiding place. She tapped on the glass with a knuckle and he looked over at her sheepishly.

'Are you going to let me in?' she asked.

He sat up slowly, as if it required considerable effort, and climbed out of the car. He closed the door softly and leaned against it, putting his hands deep inside his pockets as he looked at the floor.

'My dad's going to be here soon,' she said.

'I know.'

'Were you just going to stay in here until I'd gone?'

He shuffled uncomfortably, like a child being scolded for staying out past his bedtime.

'I wanted to say thank you,' she said.

He raised his head slightly and looked at her. In the dimness of the building and with his hair hanging over his face, she could barely see his eyes.

'How'd you know I was here?' he asked.

'Your dad told me,' she replied.

He looked back at the floor. 'Nice to know who's on my side.'

'I'm on your side, Rory.' When he didn't respond she went on, if only to fill the gloomy silence. 'I would have thought that you of all people would understand the importance of having your chance to say goodbye properly.'

'You're not dying, Jessie.'

They stood in silent stalemate, him listening to her breathing and looking at a floor he could barely see; her trying not to cry, understanding now how he had felt when he had tried to get her to talk to him and she had only put up her barriers.

'I'd take you with me if I could,' she tried, wanting this to end better than it had begun. He looked up again and she held his eyes with her own, desperately

200

trying to think of something to say before he looked down and she lost him again; unaware that he had done exactly the same thing the day he had met her by the willow. 'I'm going to miss you, Rory.'

'I'm not going to give you my phone number,' he said.

'Oh, come on, Rory.' She pushed playfully at his shoulder. 'Stop playing hard to get.'

He took her hand as she withdrew it, squeezing her fingers gently. 'Going to miss you too,' he said. He let go of her hand and she let it fall to her side. 'You're still not having my number,' he said. 'You can't be ringing me all the time asking me for answers that I don't have.'

'That's not why I want your number,' she argued. 'I just want to be able to speak to you every now and again, see how you are, what you're up to.'

He shook his head. 'That's not how it would work,' he said. 'That might be your intention now but sooner or later there's going to be a choice you have to make that you're struggling with and you'll want me to help you. That can't happen.' He reached out, sliding his fingers through the belt loops of her jeans and pulling her towards him by the hips. She felt a rush like a low voltage skipping over her stomach as they collided softly and he leaned his forehead against her own. 'I'm sorry I hid,' he said. 'I just,' he sighed. 'It was like if I didn't say goodbye then you couldn't leave.'

She put her arms around him and laid her head against his chest. 'I have to go,' she replied sombrely. 'I'm not supposed to be here, I'm supposed to be in Filton.'

They both looked towards the door as they heard approaching footsteps crunching over the gravel, not daring to breathe in case they were heard. Rory reached carefully behind him and pulled on the door handle. The door opened with a small creak and he pushed her inside. They both clambered into the back seat. Jess lay, curling herself into the smallest shape she could manage as Rory slid inside, crouching behind the passenger seat and peering over it at the sliver of light that fell through the crack between the double doors.

As one of the doors was pushed open the shaft of light grew bigger and sunlight fell over the car.

'Anybody in here?' Jean called.

Jess gasped, brightly aware of how much worse it would be if she were to be discovered in the back seat of a car, alone in the dark with Rory, instead of just standing outside talking to him. Rory slid across the front of the seat, lying on his side in front of Jess. He could feel her warm breath on the back of his neck.

'Hello?'

They both lay, listening as the door creaked, neither of them sure whether it was being opened or closed until darkness surrounded them. As Jean's footsteps faded to nothing they lay, breathing heavily, not daring to say a word.

Slowly, Rory poked his head over the passenger seat again. He couldn't see anything; the garage had been plunged into thick darkness as soon as Jean had closed the door. Jess let out a long breath of relief as they sat beside each other in the back seat.

Rory began to laugh uneasily. 'Can you imagine what would have happened if she'd caught you in the back seat of my car?'

His laughter was smooth and contagious and Jess giggled. 'It'll be worse if my dad finds us in here,' she said.

'Better make it worth our while then, hadn't we?' Rory slid an arm around her shoulders and they both laughed again. She leaned in against him, smiling, and closed her eyes.

'This could be the last time I ever see you,' she said, the smile fading.

He didn't reply.

'When someone dies,' her voice slid into the darkness like the slow deliberate stroke of a poker between glowing coals, 'the people left behind mourn. The only thing they do more than mourning is regretting.' Rory considered speaking then but she sounded as if she was talking to herself rather than to him. 'They regret not taking that trip to Florida, putting it off until next year for a decade until it's too late. They regret not telling people that they loved them as much as they should have. They regret not getting them the gift they really wanted for their last birthday because of the price. They regret not saying goodbye properly or not patching things up after the argument they'd had that morning. People regret all kinds of things and they all wish they could have that last day or week back again so they could say their goodbyes or make their peace. I don't have the last day or the last week. I have years to enjoy my dad's company, to see him smile and hear him laugh and feel his arms around me when I need a hug. That's the gift, Rory, that I get that part back. The curse is everything that comes with it.'

She lifted her feet onto the seat and laid her head in his lap. His arm crossed over her chest and she placed both hands on it, stroking his bare forearm absently as she looked up at him. Her eyes were wet despite the lack of emotion in her voice.

'I don't want to see the future. Once I go back there, nothing's a surprise. I know what's going to happen to everyone that's close to me. Nothing's new. Except somewhere along the line I have to do something differently. I don't know when, I don't know why. All I know is that after I make that choice some things will change. But even then, will things change for the better or not? Do I *want* to change anything I did last time?'

He thumbed a tear away from where it had pooled below her eye. 'Stop thinking so hard,' he said softly. 'Just go with the flow and see where it takes you.'

She said nothing. She only looked up at his face which was over laced with shadows. His eyes gleamed back at her like dark stones and she felt that low voltage again, deep in the pit of her stomach, as her eyes flitted between them and his soft, full lips. Rory's eyes locked on hers and he began to stroke her hair as she sat up against his leg. He kissed her shoulder softly, his eyes

203

remaining on hers and her fingers traced a ticklish line along the length of his arm, resting at the nape of his neck. He laid one hand against the small of her back, caressing the dent of her spine with his thumb, feeling his heart begin to pound as his free hand found her waist and she tugged lightly at the back of his neck as her lips parted.

They didn't see the door swing open for a second time and only knew that it had happened when bright sunlight flooded the car, making them first squint and then cover their eyes. They came apart before they had come together and both looked at the figure in the doorway as it moved towards them like a shadow come to life.

'Rory?' They both exhaled breath they hadn't been aware they were holding as Russ's voice echoed through the garage. Jess opened the door and they climbed out of the car. 'Your gran's looking for you,' he panted. 'Your dad's here.'

Jess looked at Rory, who looked at the floor. 'He's early,' she said.

'Well, he's here and they're looking for you.' Russ stopped at the bonnet of the small car, planting both hands on it and leaning over to catch his breath. 'You need to get back up there before they find you in here.'

'Just give us a second, dad,' Rory said despondently.

Russ looked from his son to Jess and nodded. 'Just hurry up,' he said as he walked slowly back out of the garage and closed the door.

Rory hugged Jess tightly. 'I don't want you to go,' he said. Her head fell against him and she began to cry. 'You can't cry, Jessie. If you go up there and you're crying they're going to know something's been going on.' He rocked her gently in his arms and she sniffed.

'Thank you,' she said, tilting her head to look at him. 'For everything.'

He broke the embrace and held her out in front of him, his hands resting on the slight swell of her hips. 'You don't have to thank me,' he replied.

'Yeah I do,' she insisted. 'You're like my own personal guardian angel,

204

Rory.'

'I'm not giving you my number,' he said with a smile.

She slapped at his arm and pushed him away gently. 'You can't blame a girl for trying.'

He pulled her back, meaning to kiss her, but the moment had passed and instead he only held her again. 'Take good care of yourself, Jessie,' he said.

She kissed his cheek softly. 'You too, Rory.'

They stood, observing each other silently for a long moment, neither of them wanting to say the last goodbye. Finally, she took his hands, squeezed them briefly and smiled sadly as she turned to leave. She opened the door and stepped out into the light with her head down.

Paul was standing in the cool bar with Don when Jess pushed open the door. They were chatting about the new carpets Don wanted to get for the restaurant. 'They'll cost a fortune,' Don was saying. 'Because they have to be fire resistant and all that. And as if that isn't enough . . .'

They both looked up as the door closed behind her. She forced a cheerful smile to her lips and Paul turned. He grinned back at her.

'Hello, sweetheart.'

They hugged and released, went through their usual greeting ritual, then it was time to go. Jess wheeled the heavy suitcase out from behind the bar. Both Don and Jean hugged her fiercely before she went out into the car park with Paul, making her promise that she would come back and see them.

'Are you sure you're ready?' Paul asked as they sat in the car together. Jess nodded. She was thinking about Rory and how it had felt to sit alone with him in the dark. Paul keyed the ignition and started down the long drive as she looked over at the garage but Rory wasn't there. She dropped her head and looked at nothing, her minds eye creeping over how close she had come to kissing him, wondering how he would have tasted.

Rory watched the car disappear from view as it turned right at the end of the long road and then went back to The Unicorn. It didn't look the same somehow. He went up to his room and sat on the bed, glancing only briefly at Russ, who was now only three pages from the end of his book.

'She left this for you.' Russ stretched out an arm and handed the envelope to Rory without looking away from the page. Rory tore it open and pulled out two sheets of lined paper which had been folded at strange angles, as if in a rush.

Rory

I don't know if I'm going to find you or not before I go but if I don't I want you to know that I hate you for being a big kid and not coming to say goodbye to me (only joking).

I wish you hadn't taken this so personally. I'm not leaving here to get away from you I'm going because I have to be in Filton. I'd take you with me if I could, I promise. You're my best friend and I wouldn't leave you if I didn't have to.

I know that you're probably not going to give me your number but I'd like us to stay in touch if possible. I've written my address and phone number on the back of this so if you ever want to talk just give me a ring or write me a letter. I'd really love to hear from you.

If you choose not to, for your own reasons, just know that I'm grateful for what you did for me and I'll always be thankful that I got to meet you and be your friend for a while.

Jess

He frowned and then turned the letter over, looking at her address with a small smile before he refolded it, dropped it onto his chest and looked at the second sheet of paper. He frowned at the crude grid but as he read the information for a second time he realised what it was and began to laugh.

Russ looked over at him, raising an eyebrow. 'What's funny?' he asked.

'The list,' Rory said. 'She left me the list.' He laughed again.

'What list?'

'Every Christmas number one for the next ten years,' he said. 'Ha ha, she left me the list!'

As Russ went back to his book, Rory smiled. She wasn't lost. He could ring her, he could even drive over to her house if he wanted to. He knew that he never would. That was against the rules. She had to do this by herself. But he could if he wanted to. The choice was there. Yes, he agreed, when you lose someone you do mourn them, but most of all you regret the things you never did. He regretted not spending the whole day with her, sulking like a five year old instead. If he could go back…

He shivered. All too easy to wish for something like that.

Part Four

1

She expected to feel differently as soon as they arrived in Filton, but there was nothing until they pulled up outside the house. Paul took off his seatbelt and looked at her.

'Welcome home, sweetheart,' he said.

They went to the house together and memories stirred as Paul opened the front door. As the smell of the house invaded her head she felt an urge to sit down on the doorstep. She had come here with Scott after… that wasn't important. Not now. She stepped into the house, fearing that the spectres of past, present and future were crouching around every corner, ready to attack as she approached. Paul followed her into the living room, wheeling her case behind him. The house hadn't changed much. The sofa and chair were different to the ones that had been here when she'd left, but they were the same as before.

'No need to stand on ceremony,' Paul said from behind her. 'Sit yourself down and I'll make us a cuppa.'

She sat on the sofa automatically. Nobody sat in dad's chair except dad. She looked at the pictures that hung on the wall opposite her. A picture of her mum and dad standing outside Filton Church, just married. Her mother looked beautiful, she'd never noticed how beautiful before. Her dad looked proud. Her school pictures hung in a neat row in the order they had been taken.

'Tea or coffee?' Paul called. She told him she wanted coffee. *Nothing like a hot mug of cats piss to get the day started.*

What?

She got up. She didn't want to be in here on her own anymore. 'I told you to sit down,' Paul said.

'I'm not a guest,' Jess said. 'I live here.' She went to the fridge and took out the milk. As she closed the door she caught sight of a bottle of pain killers standing next to the iron on top of the fridge. She shuddered and then stood, motionless, staring at them. Was that it? Had she overdosed? She'd had a headache. Cider and pain killers. *Maybe I'd take all of them and wash them down with bleach. Who cares?*

'Jess?' Paul held out his hand for the milk and she passed it to him, turning away from the fridge. They took their drinks into the living room and sat down. Jess on the sofa, Paul in his chair. He rolled a cigarette and lit it as Jess continued to look around the room, taking in all the familiar knick knacks and furniture. All that was different was that her stuff wasn't scattered around. Her slippers should be on the floor beside the television but they weren't because she hadn't been here. This wasn't like last time. It was like arriving late to watch a film, trying to find your place, work out what had happened before you got there.

'They're talking about changing the shifts at work,' Paul said. 'Including a week of nights as well as days and afternoons. Would you be alright on your own if I'm working all night?'

'I'm fifteen, dad, not five,' she said. 'I'll be fine.'

'You're sure?'

'I'm sure.'

Was she supposed to be here? Should she have come back? Or was part of the plan to take her away from Filton? She felt out of place, as if she'd just woken up and things had changed while she'd slept.

Paul watched her as she looked thoughtfully around the room. 'I cleaned up as best I could,' he said and she smiled again.

'You got a new sofa,' she said.

'The old one was, well, it was old,' he said. 'This one's second hand but there's nothing wrong with it.'

Sharp nostalgia stabbed at her again. He'd had the sofa for two years. Someone at work had bought a new one because his wife had wanted it. 'More money than sense,' her dad had said as they had pushed it through the hall.

'It's nice,' Jess said. 'Some people have got more money than sense.'

It was Paul's turn to smile. 'You still take after your dad.'

'Yeah,' she agreed.

'Do you want to get yourself unpacked before your clothes crease too much?' he asked. He hated ironing. He'd have twice as much to do now and he wanted to avoid that particular task wherever possible.

They took the case upstairs. Everything was as she remembered it. The same carpet, the same wallpaper. Not from when she'd lived here with both of her parents. From when. From before.

She put a hand to her mouth as he opened the door to her room. This was different. He'd prepared for her coming home the best way he could. It was different because he'd picked the colour of the walls, the bed linen. A white plastic bin stood in one corner of the room, a round sticker with 99p printed in black was still attached to it's curved body. The old wallpaper had been stripped from the walls and he had painted them a creamy yellow. The curtains were pale blue and matched her bedclothes.

'You don't like it,' Paul said.

'It's really nice, dad,' she contradicted. 'I didn't expect this.'

He nodded, pleased with his work, and lifted the case onto the bed. 'It's a new bed,' he said.

'Thanks,' she replied.

He left her to unpack alone. She filled the wardrobe with her clothes, put her few photographs along the windowsill and on the bedside table beside the squat lamp her dad had also bought for her return. She picked up her slippers and took them downstairs, putting them in their place next to the television.

'All done?' Paul asked. She nodded and drank her cold coffee, noticing the open can of lager on the table in front of him. *Alcoholic liver disease.* She looked at him, wondering if he'd noticed the change in her face. He didn't look

213

as though he had. 'I spoke to Karen yesterday,' he said. 'Been doing my research.'

'Research?' she asked as she sat down.

'Long time since I was fifteen,' he replied. 'And I wasn't a girl, believe it or not.'

'Debatable,' she said. He scowled at her, but the smile below it gave away good humour.

'I just don't know what girl's your age do.'

'I can look after myself, dad.'

'Well, maybe you can and maybe you can't,' he said nervously. 'I just don't want to mess up.'

She went to him and hugged him, needing to feel him close to her. His scent, the one that belonged only to him, filled her head as he hugged her back clumsily, his fingertips digging into her ribs. She was home.

2

There's no feeling quite like that of being the new kid. People stare at you like you're from another planet, they ask about where you've come from and why. What you offer them in response will either make or break you. Jess had forgotten what that was like.

She walked slowly behind Mr Ward, following him to her tutor base. Her dad would call it a home room. She stopped outside room F4, waiting for him to open the door, but he walked on. Confused, she followed him down the clean corridor to F7.

'I know this must be daunting,' Mr Ward said. 'But I'm sure you'll fit in just fine.'

She doubted it but smiled back at him anyway.

He opened the door and they both stepped inside. The room buzzed with conversation as Jess looked around. This wasn't her tutor group. She had thought that Mr Ward was only showing her where she needed to go but as he went to the desk at the front of the room and put down his heavy bag she realised he was now her tutor. She'd arrived late and had just been slotted in wherever there was room. Jess wanted to tell him that he'd made a mistake, that she should be in F4 with Mrs Hughes, not here. Mr Ward wasn't her tutor he was...

She looked around the room, scanning the faces quickly. And there he was, sitting at a table with three other boys. His face was young and had not yet battled with a razor blade. His hair was not yet greying around the temples as it would begin to when he was in his mid twenties. His body was thin and childish, as yet only poised to broaden as he grew older.

Mr Ward was Scott's tutor.

He only glanced up when Mr Ward introduced Jess to the class. His eyes scanned her quickly before he went back to his conversation.

As the boisterous talk of the classroom died down she moved quickly past Scott to the only other person in the room that she knew. Dean Meakin couldn't believe his luck. Of the three empty chairs she could have picked, she'd picked the one next to him. She didn't speak though; she sat silently beside him and stared menacingly at Scott Jordan.

'I'm Dean,' he ventured.

She offered him a quick smile and then her eyes went back to Scott. She knew that there was no way he could remember her, but she had still felt offended by his cursory glance. She was nothing to him. He could sit there and chat with his friends and have no idea that he'd had anything to do with her death. Well, maybe that was just fine; she didn't want anything to do with him anyway. She could hear him from where she sat, talking and laughing and enjoying being fifteen and in another room down the corridor, Joanne Howard would be doing exactly the same thing; unaware that she would marry Scott Jordan or that he would cheat on her.

But Jess knew.

Jess knew all of it.

She couldn't laugh and enjoy being fifteen because she knew what came next. You realised that at fifteen years old you hadn't actually known everything. Relationships were far more complicated than believing that you were meant to be together because your fortune teller troll with the flashing red and green eyes and gravity defying pink hair told you so. Not being allowed to stay out past ten o' clock wasn't the end of the world. And Sugar magazine did not have all the answers.

She spent the morning listening hard to her teachers. She'd made up her mind that if she was going to have to do this all over again then she was going to do it properly. She was going to get her head down and study hard while education was free and then decide what she wanted to do with the rest of her life. But the more time she spent sitting beside Dean Meakin, trying to help him, trying to be friendly and realising that he might not be too bright but he was actually okay to hang around with, she knew that it wasn't going to be that easy.

Local Man Charged With Son's Murder.

She remembered the headline as if she'd read it only yesterday.

It had been a single blow to the head, but a single blow with a hammer to the head of a sixteen year old boy had been enough. Dean probably hadn't even known about it before he'd hit the floor, his skull caved in and his heart still in his chest.

As she tried to explain algebra to him, seeing from the vacant expression on his face that she'd already lost him, she knew that she couldn't stand back, study hard and just let him die.

She agreed to spend lunchtime with him and they ate together in the noisy hall. The sounds of clattering plates and cutlery were secondary to the gossip and giggles of hundreds of students. When they'd eaten she followed him out to the playing fields where groups of kids sat in the grass, enjoying the waning warmth of early autumn.

She spotted Joanne and Scott standing together near the tennis courts and led Dean on a deliberate detour in order to walk by them. She was curious to know what mini Joanne and Scott had to talk about. Nothing interesting by the sound of it. Scott mumbled and Joanne giggled, tossing her long blonde hair over her shoulder and looking at him like he was the most interesting person in the world. She looked up as Jess passed and their eyes met. Joanne hit Scott on the shoulder with the back of her hand, pointing at Jess and then cupping her mouth with both hands, leaning against him and whispering in his ear. She heard Scott tell her that she was in his tutor group. Joanne whispered something else and he told her not to worry, he'd steer well clear of her if she really was that mental.

Dean stopped as Jess turned, flexing her fingers before curling them into her

217

palm as she strode back towards Scott and Joanne. Dean called her name but only Scott turned, seeing Jess pull back her fist and drive it towards him only when it was too late. She hit him square in the mouth and he stumbled backwards a couple of steps before he fell.

'I told you! I told you!' Joanne screamed.

'What the hell's your problem?' Scott yelled.

Jess didn't say a word and Dean could only look at her, mystified and a little fearful, as she walked back to him, grinning from ear to ear.

'What did you do that for?' Dean asked.

'Doesn't matter,' she replied, still smiling.

She hated him. Hated how it was at least partly his fault that this was happening to her and he was happily oblivious to it all. Hated that he'd chosen Joanne over her. Hated that she was suffering because of what he'd done and he was holding *her* hand and enjoying being fifteen when he should have been begging for Jess's forgiveness.

Dean didn't dare to ask any more questions and led her to the far end of the playing fields. As soon as the small crowd came into view she froze, the smile gone.

Trip Jameson.

When Dean realised that Jess wasn't walking by his side anymore he looked around quickly, worried that one punch hadn't been enough and she was heading back to finish whatever business it was that she had with Scott Jordan. But she was standing still behind him, her eyes blazing with anger. Dean was beginning to think that her choice of seat this morning hadn't been so lucky for him after all.

Connie Long had been the kind of girl who people joked would get asked for ID until she was thirty. A spray of freckles had spattered her nose and cheeks and at fifteen she had still been wearing clothes made for ten year olds. Jess should have been here. The old lady in the white building had said that she

218

should remember but she hadn't. And because she hadn't remembered she'd been waiting tables at The Unicorn instead of keeping Connie safe.

As Jess stared at Trip, her stomach rolled. Tall and broad with thick dark hair, he stood up and sauntered over to them as they approached. Jess found it hard to even look at him and was sure that there was distaste etched all over her face. His eyes slid over her as they met. She tried to smile.

'Hi, Trip,' Dean said. 'This is Jess. Jess, this is Trip.'

Trip tipped Jess a greeting nod which she didn't return and Dean led her to a group of people who were sitting on the grass in the corner of the field. Jess recognised some of them; others were strangers to her. Connie wasn't among them. Connie was gone. All of them looked at her suspiciously as she approached with Dean. As they sat down in the grass Trip took a cigarette from an almost empty deck and offered it to her filter first. 'This one's on me.'

She declined.

'Ever tried it?' he asked.

'Once.'

Trip smiled. 'Everyone hates it the first time.'

The whole group was looking at her. She hated being a teenager. Peer pressure seemed to live and breathe as an entity created by all those pairs of staring eyes.

'Wanna share?' Dean asked.

'You can have it.'

She passed him the cigarette gratefully and he snatched it from her fingers, planting a clumsy kiss on her cheek. 'Thank you, darling.'

Jess didn't notice the kiss. She was thinking about Connie. They had been friends for eighteen months before a heroin overdose had cut her life short. Jess should have been here. She could have done something. She could have saved her.

'Are you new?' Trip asked.

219

Jess looked at him distractedly. 'Yes. Long story. Don't ask.'

'Trip has parties all the time,' Dean said. 'You should come to one.'

'Maybe.'

Jess looked at the other girls in the group. Two were sharing a joint. One was rolling a joint. The other was staring into space and humming to herself. A yellow bruise was fading in the crook of her elbow.

'What's the matter with her?' Jess asked.

'She hit the hard stuff bad,' Dean lowered his voice.

'Drugs did that?'

He looked away from her as if he didn't want to discuss it. The girl who was humming to herself was too pale and too thin. She wouldn't have looked out of place in a Nazi concentration camp. Her clothes were a good three sizes too big for her and her dark hair was tied up in a matted clump at the back of her head.

'If I ever needed a reason not to do drugs, she'd be it.'

Trip tore up a handful of grass from the field and stuffed it down the back of the tee shirt of the girl who had now finished rolling her joint. She jumped up, flapping the bottom of her tee shirt until most of it had fallen out and then kicked out at Trip. She missed and stumbled in a semi circle before sitting back down.

'Shithead,' she shouted at him.

Trip laughed.

'He's such a laugh,' Dean said.

'Dean,' Trip called. 'You got what you owe me?'

'Oh shit, Trip, I forgot all about it,' Dean replied. 'Tomorrow, yeah?'

'You better.' Trip pointed the first two fingers of his left hand at Dean and cocked his thumb. 'You know what happens if you don't repay your debts.'

Dean nodded. 'Tomorrow, Trip, I swear.' He offered Jess what remained of the cigarette but she shook her head. He shrugged, took two quick puffs and flicked the butt away into the grass.

'Well then, guys and gals,' Trip said as he buried his hands in his pockets. 'I'm gonna have to love you and leave you. Miranda?'

He held out a hand to the pale, humming girl and she took it without looking up. He pulled her to her feet and led her away. The other three girls stood up, brushed the grass from their jeans, and wandered slowly back towards school.

'We'd better get back,' Dean said as he stood up, helping Jess to her feet as clumsily as he had kissed her.

As they walked back Jess remembered the knock at the door. It had been Jay, Connie's older brother. He hadn't even known his sister had been taking drugs. Jess hadn't dared to tell him that she had. Tears had been falling over his red face and he'd only managed to tell her between sobs. How had Jess forgotten that?

They joined the back of a larger group of students as they filed back inside. Nope, just getting on with her education was not going to happen. Day one at school and she'd already lost a friend and accumulated one lost soul to save.

3

The pungent aroma of slowly cremating food struck Jess like a soft blow as she opened the living room door. She heard intense sizzling in the kitchen and could see small wisps of smoke coming in through the kitchen door.

'I'm home, dad,' she called.

His head appeared, face strained, hair sticking up in unruly tufts. 'Good day?' he called above the noise of eggs shallow frying behind him.

'Not bad.'

She threw her bag onto the sofa and went into the kitchen to see what she could salvage from what looked like a battleground. Eggshells lay dead on the counter, bleeding slimy albumen. A raw sausage had fallen onto the floor and been stamped flat in Paul's rush to try and get everything ready at the same time. A puddle of vegetable oil lay beside an overturned bottle by the sink and bacon rind hung over the lip of the bin like the pale corpses of flatworms.

'Want some help?'

'Nearly done,' Paul said as he stuck a spatula under the egg in the pan and all but threw it onto a plate. Hot oil splashed back at him and he hissed as it burned the back of his hand. 'Go and sit down.'

In the time it would have taken to persuade him that he should be the one to sit down so she could finish tea it would have been ruined, so she went back to the living room and flopped onto the sofa. The grill pan was set down on the worktop with a clang.

'Aaaggghh!' Paul cried. 'Bastard sausage.'

After more noise and a couple of choice swear words aimed at his egg, Paul put a plate in front of Jess and handed her a knife and fork. 'Dig into that, sweetheart,' he said serenely, as if he'd been completely in control of what was happening in the kitchen. 'Your tastebuds'll love you for the rest of your life.'

Jess thought she actually heard them screaming in protest but took the knife and fork and began to eat. Apart from the sausages looking like rods of charcoal and having a bitter, gritty taste to them, tea was good. Paul put on Fifteen to One and mumbled mainly wrong answers though his food, exclaiming 'Oh, I should have got that one', 'Of course it was', and 'Oh shit, I knew that', when his answers were a million miles off the mark. When it was over, Jess hoped that they would be able to just sit together and watch Countdown. She'd missed playing against her dad. She'd played against Don a couple of times but it hadn't been the same. Don didn't look for rude words like her dad did and he wasn't as fast at the number rounds. But Paul didn't seem interested in Countdown today. He cleared away the plates, fetched himself another can of Carling from the fridge and eased into his chair.

'Good first day?' he asked. She could tell by the way he'd asked that this wasn't going to be a conversation. It was an inquisition.

'Not bad,' she replied.

He rolled a cigarette and lit it. Her eyes settled on the orange glow at the tip and she shivered.

'Your teachers okay?' he asked. 'Subjects not too hard?'

'Much the same as they've always been.'

'Did you make any new friends?'

Which one do you want to hear about first, daddy? she thought. *There's the drug dealer or the addict that's going to get beaten to death by his own dad pretty soon.*

'A couple.'

'And?' Paul sucked at his roll up, his eyes never moving from hers, and blew a cloud of thin smoke towards the ceiling.

'And what?'

'What are they like?'

Jess shrugged. 'Okay.'

223

'You should invite them round for tea one night.'

'The way you cook?' Jess scoffed. 'I don't think so'

He threw a look of mock astonishment at her and she saw him relax. 'Long as you're okay, sweetheart.'

'I'm fine, dad.' She rolled her eyes. 'Stop worrying.'

'I'm your dad, it's my job to worry.'

'I've got homework to do,' she said, picking up her bag. 'See you later.' Before he could reply she planted a quick dry kiss on his cheek and went to her room.

She dropped the bag onto the floor and lay down on her bed. Her mind was restless. Connie had died and she hadn't done a thing about it. And what was she going to do about Dean?

As she drifted off into a sleep brought on by pure mental exhaustion she added these to the list of questions she didn't know how to even begin to answer.

4

'Dean.'

His own name filled his ears like the cold claw of a monster falling upon his shoulder. His hand froze halfway to the glass of coke, although he now needed the drink even more than he had a moment ago. The saliva in his mouth had dried up, leaving behind a sickly taste like sour milk. His heart thudded heavily in his chest and for a second he considered slipping silently out of the front door and tearing away to – to where? – to anywhere that wasn't here. Any place where he wouldn't hear him calling his name.

'Dean.'

Sharper now. He picked up the glass with both hands, fearful that the trembling fingers of one hand might not be enough. He had intended to drain the glass. Instead he managed only a single swallow before his twisting stomach threatened to send it straight back up again. If he didn't go now the next sound he would hear would be Carl Meakin's heavy feet on the stairs before he was dragged by his hair to the bathroom. And then it would happen anyway.

As he rose from the old settee he pleaded with whatever god watched over scrawny faithless children for his mother's key to jangle in the lock. This hadn't happened when she'd been here. If she came back maybe it would stop. But his mother was with That Prick Hargreaves. That bitch had left her only child in the care of the beast from whose loins he had sprung so that she could be with That Prick Hargreaves. Sometimes Dean didn't know who he hated the most. His father for what he did or his mother for what she'd done. Mostly he hated himself for what he was.

He heard his father thumping across the landing and hurried to the stairs. He'd made a climb of three risers before Carl's face appeared at the top, dark and angry.

'Get up here.' Years of smoking forty a day had scuffed his voice and to Dean he always sounded as if he was growling.

Dean went to him obediently and followed him into the bathroom where Carl locked the door behind them. Dean didn't understand why his father felt the need to do this. Nobody else would ever open that door, no matter how hard Dean prayed to the god of scrawny faithless children.

Carl stood in front of the sink beside the bath as he always did and Dean had to fight the urge to throw up again as his father's underwear landed in a pool around his ankles. This was the routine. Since the first time no words had passed between them after the bathroom door was locked. They both knew why they were here.

'You see,' Carl had said on that first occasion after he'd locked the door. A twelve year old Dean Meakin had been sitting on the corner of the bath, listening to his poor father whose woman had just left him for That Prick Hargreaves. 'Mummies will kiss you and you'll kiss them and hug them back. That's how you show that you love each other. But men don't do all that hugging stuff, Dean. If you want to show daddy that you really love him, and now that mummy's gone, who else is going to love me?'

That thick feeling of guilt, that maybe he himself had been responsible for his mother leaving them, had overwhelmed Dean and he had felt sad and sorry for his father.

At this point Carl had pushed his trousers to the floor and stepped out of them, moving towards the boy. 'If you love me, Dean, you'll put this in your mouth until I tell you to take it out again.'

The hard crack of Carl's spade like hand connecting with his ear brought Dean back to the moment. He looked up at his father's face with eyes that pleaded not to make him do this. Carl returned this look with a stare of cold contempt and Dean sank to his knees.

226

He looked up and to the left at the clock his mother had bought before she'd left. A blue and white fish with a clock face where it's guts should be. The hands remained at 7.57.

Before the clock had stopped, never to be started again, that had been Dean's escape. Watching the second hand, trapped, forever revolving, had been almost hypnotic and he'd focused on this rather than the awful thing he was doing. His father could tell him that it was the best way to show a father you loved them as much as he wanted but Dean knew that what he was doing was wrong.

At school one of the other boys had stolen a porno from his dad's stash and shown it to a group of them in his bedroom. Some blonde slut with doe eyes and tits as big as watermelons had taken this guys foot long cock in her mouth and gobbled him as if her life depended on it. That had been when the heavy feeling in Dean's stomach had turned to the sick feeling he got every time his father growled his name. It was sex. This wasn't how a son showed his father than he loved him. This was what women did to men when they were horny.

It had been that night that Dean had come home with angry tears boiling over his face. The one and only time he had dared to threaten his father.

'Good day at school?' Carl had asked without looking up from the TV.

'Not really,' Dean had sniffed. 'I know what you're doing to me dad and I'm going to tell.'

He had expected his dad to start shouting, to hit him, maybe even take his belt to him like he had the time Dean had taken five pounds from his wallet while he slept.

'No you wont,' Carl had replied calmly. The relaxed tone of his voice had unnerved Dean even more.

'I'll tell the teachers at school and they'll send the police to come and get you.'

'No they wont.' Carl had turned off the TV and turned to his son, his face a picture of serenity. 'They'll take you away, Dean. They'll put you in a home

227

with kids who are bad. And the adults that look after kids like that are even worse. They'll do things to you that you don't even want to think about.'

Dean had swiped at his eyes with his sleeve, trying his best to stop those hot tears from falling over his flushed cheeks. 'There's a number I can call. It's called Childline and it's especially for kids and the people you talk to are really nice and they send nice people to come and rescue you and the police to take away bad people. Bad people like you, dad.' He'd pointed a trembling, accusatory finger at Carl and burst into fresh tears.

Carl had lost his patience. His face had contorted, his features becoming those of a horror movie monster. Strangely, this had put Dean at ease. This was what he was accustomed to. This was what he understood.

'The second you dial a number I get a bill,' Carl had spat through gritted teeth. 'Every phone call that's made from this house, every number that's dialled, I get a bill. Now do you think that those nice people are going to get here before I get that bill?'

Dean didn't know. He could barely spell the word telephone, let alone understand how bills worked.

'As soon as I get that bill I'll take you away, Dean. Then it'll be just you and me. No friends, no school, nothing and no one but me and you. And I'll make you suffer, you little shit.'

Dean's bottom lip had started to tremble at this and he had gone to his room with a cry of 'I hate you,' before he'd started to sob. He hadn't wanted his dad to hear him crying like that.

As if to close the subject forever, Dean had been called to the bathroom an hour later and, after considering trying to bite it off, he'd knelt and opened his mouth like a good boy. The clock had still worked back then and he had watched the second hand spin the time slowly away. Each time he had been called here since he had tried to get out faster, watching the clock and trying to beat his previous time.

Then the clock had stopped and in this room it would always be 7.57 and Dean Meakin would always be on his knees.

5

It wasn't that Jess was dreading the end of school, but she could think of better things to do with the rest of the afternoon. Sticking pins in her eyes for instance. She looked over at Scott who was busy working from a tatty copy of Tricolor. The cut on his lip was a deep, angry red. She was pleased. She hoped it hurt.

French lessons usually seemed to go on for twice as long as any other subject but today it had gone too quickly. Mrs Wren called for them to start packing away and began collecting the battered text books from their desks. Dean scribbled quickly to finish what he had started and then stuffed his book and pencil case back into his bag.

The classroom emptied, leaving Mrs Wren to wipe down the whiteboard. Jess and Dean left together. They walked over the sports field and took a shortcut through an alleyway onto Carrington Lane. Trip had a ground floor flat in the block at the end of the road. She had been there only once before. With Connie. It hadn't been particularly dirty but there had been cigarette burns in the furniture and kids had scratched their names into the low coffee table in the living room the way they did to the wooden science tables at school. It had been the people that had gotten to her. Kids younger than her and Connie had been passing joints around, snorting powders that Jess couldn't name. Older kids had been there too but most of the twelve people that had been in the flat that day had been under seventeen years old.

'We're not staying long, right?' Jess asked. 'You're coming to mine for tea?'

Dean nodded enthusiastically as he ran up to the door of the building and pushed the button for Trip's flat. A buzz sounded a second afterwards.

'Who is it?' Trip's voice coming from the small metal speaker on the wall.

'It's Dean.'

''Kay, I'll buzz you in.'

There was a long buzz and Dean pulled open the door. The cool hall smelled of disinfectant. White doors dotted the walls, looking idiotically close together for saying there was supposed to be a living room, kitchen, bedroom and bathroom behind all of them. Somewhere a baby began to cry. Dean went over to a door with a gold number three hanging below the peephole and knocked. Trip opened it and offered them a friendly smile. It was easy to see how the kids got taken in by him.

'Dean,' he said. 'Come in.' Dean did as he said and Jess followed. 'You brought your new friend.' Trip offered Jess his hand and she shook it reluctantly. 'It's Jess, isn't it? Well come on in, Jess. Make yourself at home. I'm sure Dean'll show you around.' He closed the door and turned to Dean, who nodded. 'And if you want me for anything you just come and find me. I'm never far away.' He winked at her and then disappeared into his bedroom.

Dean sat in an armchair in the corner of the living room. He lit a cigarette that he'd taken from his dad's pack. Even here he sat alone. She went with him and perched on the edge of the chair. 'Want some?' he asked, lifting the cigarette up to her.

'No thanks.'

He shrugged, tried to slide an arm around her waist and had his hand batted away like a tiresome fly.

'Just trying to be friendly,' he said. 'What are you here for anyway?'

'I came because you did.'

'You don't need any gear?' Jess didn't know what gear was. She shook her head. 'Want to share mine?' Dean pulled a small bag of white powder from the pocket of his trousers.

'You know that could kill you?' Jess asked.

He stuffed the bag back into his pocket. 'You've never tried it, have you?'

'I don't even know what that stuff is,' she replied honestly.

231

'It's magic,' he said almost lovingly.

'It's bad stuff, Dean.'

'There's a lot worse in the world than white powder,' he replied soberly.

'Dean?' Trip poked his head around the door and Dean looked up at him. 'Can I borrow you for a minute?' His head disappeared as soon as Dean got up.

'Wont be long,' he said as he followed Trip back to the bedroom. Jess followed but the door was closed as soon as Dean was inside. She should have knocked. But she didn't. Instead she stood alone in the tiny hall, listening to the sounds of the small flat. She could hear UB40's Rat In The Kitchen. *Actually, it's in the bedroom*, Jess thought as she went back to the living room.

It was too smoky in here. A sweet burning smell hung in the air and she was conscious that it would get into her clothes for her dad to smell. Three boys and a girl shared the old sofa, passing a joint between them. One of the boys was dozing and the girl had to nudge him awake when it was his turn to smoke. She looked around uncomfortably. Connie's death didn't seem to have warned any of them of the risks of what they were doing. But they were all kids, all invincible. Jess waited another ten minutes and when Dean still hadn't returned she went to Trip's bedroom.

'We need to go now if you're coming to mine,' she said as she opened the door.

Trip jumped up from the mattress on the floor, clamping one hand on the door and the other on the wall, stopping her from going any further. 'New girl doesn't know how to knock,' he said with a shark's grin.

'Sorry.' Jess took a step backwards.

'Well, Dean's staying here a bit longer,' Trip said. 'So you just run along home and he'll see you tomorrow.'

'Is that right, Dean?' Jess called, trying to look past him into the room.

Trip forced himself through the small gap he had made in the doorway and closed the door behind him. 'He's staying here,' he snarled.

232

'Fine,' Jess replied, feeling very uncomfortable being alone with him in the dark hallway. 'If he wants to stay, that's fine, but I'd like him to tell me himself.'

'I'm telling you.' Trip moved towards her, forcing her against the wall.

'I know what you're doing,' she said, trying not to look intimidated. 'Dean might swallow all your bullshit but I'm not buying it.'

He slammed the palms of his hands into the wall on either side of her head and she gasped. 'You know nothing,' he said.

'Well why don't I let the police decide?' she asked. 'See if they think what you're feeding all those kids is legit? See if what you gave Connie Long was legit?'

He took hold of her throat with one hand and she yelped. 'For someone with such a pretty face, that's a very ugly threat to make.'

'You don't scare me,' she replied shakily.

He pulled a pocket knife from his jeans, flipped it open and held it an inch away from her eyes. 'It'd be a shame to see such a pretty face get all messed up,' he said. 'You leave. Now. On your own.'

She nodded, willing Dean to open the door and see what was happening.

Trip dropped the knife back into his pocket. 'You're not welcome here anymore,' he said. 'And any pigs knock on my door I'll know exactly who I need to pay a visit, wont I?'

She left without saying anymore. Her legs began to shake as soon as she was outside the flat and she had to lean against a graffiti covered wall to keep her balance. As soon as she felt she was okay to move she started to walk home, the events of the last ten minutes running over and over in her head.

She stopped halfway down Redwood Avenue, sitting down on the low brick wall that surrounded the park and putting her head in her hands. She needed to get a grip before her dad saw her. She started to sob quietly, wanting it all out of her system right now; the anger, the fear, the despair.

'Are you okay?'

She looked up, laughing when she saw Scott standing at what he considered to be a safe distance from her.

'Fine,' she sniffed.

'I saw you coming out of Trips building,' he said.

'So you decided to follow me?' She crossed her legs and folded her arms over her chest.

'You looked upset.'

'I'm fine,' she said without conviction. 'So you can leave me alone.'

He looked around uncomfortably as if leaving her alone was exactly what he wanted to do. 'You know Trip's a drug dealer, don't you?' he asked. 'Everyone at school knows.' When she didn't reply he pulled nervously at the bottom of the white shirt he'd untucked as soon as he was out of the school gates and she watched him do it, smiling to herself. 'I'm sorry I called you mental,' he said quietly.

She shrugged and looked down the street. A group of kids with a football were approaching the park.

'You're not sorry you hit me?'

No, she wasn't. But she hadn't hit him because he'd called her mental and mini Scott Jordan hadn't actually done anything wrong.

'Sorry,' she mumbled.

'Trip's bad news,' he replied as if the apology meant that they were now friends. 'Even if you are going out with Dean Meakin, you should stay away from Trip.'

'I'm not going out with Dean,' she replied angrily.

'Okay.' He held up his hands defensively. 'Are you doing drugs with him?'

'What I'm doing or not doing with Dean isn't anything to do with you.'

'That's a yes,' he said.

'It's a fuck off and mind your own business,' she hissed.

Scott sat beside her on the wall and she edged away from him. 'Until his mum left he was okay, then he started causing trouble, getting into fights. Trip picks on people like that. He gives them somewhere to go, a smile and a smoke. Then he reels them in. Don't think Trip looks at you any differently because he doesn't.'

She thought about Dean. A scrawny, scruffy boy that would always look like he needed a wash no matter how hard he tried. 'I know exactly what Trip is,' she said.

'So why are you hanging around with him?'

'Why do you care?' she asked. 'You don't know me, you think I'm mental anyway . . .'

'I said I was sorry for . . .'

'So why don't you just let me do whatever I want and go back to your girlfriend?'

He looked at her with desperation. 'You've got no idea what he's like,' he insisted. 'There are so many stories about him.'

'Like what?' she asked.

'Like he sells to kids as young as eleven,' he replied. 'Like a girl overdosed a few months back and he was there when it happened. Like there was this lad that owed him money for stuff he'd never paid for and after a while Trip gets sick of it and the next thing this kid gets kicked to death. Kicked to *death*, Jess. And do you know how much they reckon he owed? Forty five quid. Kicked to death for forty five quid.'

'They're just stories,' Jess said, although she knew that stories like that didn't just appear out of nowhere. She thought about the knife he had waved in her face. She thought about Connie.

'Have you met Miranda?' Scott asked.

Jess nodded without looking up. The kids passed them, vaulting the wall and arguing about who was going to play in nets.

235

'How old do you reckon she is?'

Jess shrugged.

'Seventeen.'

She looked at him with wide eyes. She would have guessed at late twenties. He nodded gravely. 'Been using since she was twelve. Doesn't even know where she is half the time. She had a boyfriend about a year ago and he tried to stop Trip from giving her stuff. I don't know what Trip said to him but he soon backed off and stopped going out with her. Do you know who Miranda is, Jess?'

She shook her head. Scott looked around, as if Trip could appear from anywhere at any second, and then he looked back at her. 'That's Trip's little sister,' he said. 'And if he can do that to his sister he can do it to anyone.'

She hadn't even know that Trip had a sister. But last time she hadn't spent much time around him. Connie was usually either with Trip or with Jess. Jess had always hated being around him.

Scott looked at her with genuine concern. He knew more about Trip than she did. A couple of boys he'd been friends with at primary school had been suckered in by him. One was Dean Meakin. They'd stayed friends for about six months after he'd started using and Scott had seen him lose his grip on reality, worshipping Trip like a god and constantly asking if Scott wanted to share. At first it had just been weed and poppers and that hadn't bothered Scott too much. It was when the powders and pills showed up in Dean's pockets that Scott had decided to jump ship. Of course, he had tried to talk him out of it, but Dean hadn't needed anything from Scott, had he?

Scott rolled up his shirtsleeve. A twisting white scar ran down his arm from elbow to wrist. If they'd met in two years time he would have told her that he'd gotten it falling off his bike.

'That was my warning,' he said. 'Some idiot in a Bart Simpson mask grabbed me on my way home from school last year. He had a knife, Jess.' He rolled his sleeve down and buttoned it at the cuff.

'I promise I'm not getting involved with Trip or drugs,' she found herself saying, although she hadn't got a clue why. It was none of Scott's business, just like his story about Dean and Miranda was none of hers. She wasn't thinking. Her mouth was moving while her mind continued to see his scar, white and twisting through his forearm. She had touched that scar. She had felt it against her naked body when he held her. Her finger had traced its line while she lay against his chest, waiting for the rain to stop . . .

She shut her eyes tight and pressed her fingertips against them. 'I need to go home,' she said suddenly, needing only to be as far away from him as possible. 'My dad'll wonder where I am.' She slung her schoolbag over her shoulder as he stood to leave too. 'And I am sorry,' she said, unsure exactly what it was that she was apologising for.

6

'Are you alright?' Paul asked as Jess threw her bag into the corner of the room and sat down heavily, putting her head in her hands. Coming back had been a bad idea. She should have stayed at The Unicorn where she could keep the ghosts at arms length, where she could have carried on as if nothing had changed because her friends and her home were new, and where she had Rory to help her feel less alone.

Paul picked up the remote from the arm of his chair and turned off the TV. Something was really wrong. 'Sweetheart?' he said hesitantly.

She lifted her head from her hands and looked at him.

You, she thought. *This is all because of you.*

As quickly as the silent accusation had bubbled up from the pit of her stomach she regretted it.

'I've just had a really shit day,' she replied.

Paul sighed, bracing himself for the conversation to follow. 'What's his name?' he asked.

It had been one of Karen's tips. *If she ever comes home pissed off, nine times out of ten it'll be about a boy. Or a girl if, well, you know.* He was waiting to hear it. Waiting for her to say his name for the first time since she was four years old.

'Trip Jameson.'

Paul felt momentary relief until his daughter began to cry. He hopped over to the sofa and put an arm around her shoulders. She fell against him and his protective arms enveloped her, a big hand touched her hair, soothing her as best he could.

'Do you want to tell me about it?' he asked, releasing her slowly.

She shook her head. 'It'll work itself out.' Far too complicated to have a conversation with her dad about this.

'What?' he asked desperately. 'You're crying your bloody heart out, Jess. Talk to me.'

She shook her head. 'It's not as bad as it looks,' she said. 'It's just a bit of everything, I suppose. New school, new friends.'

Paul looked at her with concern and she tried to offer him a reassuring smile. 'I don't regret coming back,' she said as she put her arms around him. 'I hated being without you. I love you, dad. I don't want to be anywhere else in the whole world but here.'

Paul made beans on toast for tea and Jess watched TV with him until it was time for bed. Then she lay alone, listening to cars as they passed the house, looking up at the ceiling for hours as sleep refused to come.

Connie.

Already lost. Jess could curse the old woman in purple as much as she wanted for not doing her job properly and leaving her in limbo for fifteen years but she couldn't change it. Connie was gone and she wasn't coming back. Jess wondered how Jay was doing. When this had happened before, him and his mum had moved to the other side of Filton after Connie's death and Jess had lost touch with them. She didn't know if never meeting any of them in the first place was better or worse.

Dean.

One hammer blow to the head. Dead at sixteen by the hand of his own father. How was she going to stop it?

Dad.

The most important lost soul of them all. Alcoholic liver disease. It hadn't registered before, how much he drank. He'd always had a drink in front of him and she'd always fetched it from the Co Op for him. But it had just been part of their life. It had been normal. Now she noticed every refill, every empty can and bottle in the bin. She'd have to talk to him.

Scott Jordan.

No. No way. She was not going to lie in bed and think about him. She'd already done that. For weeks, maybe even months after they split up. Lying here, she'd convinced herself more than once that she could go round to see him and things would go back to how they'd been before he'd proposed. But in the morning, when sunlight brought reality into sharp focus, she wouldn't dare. She'd stay at home and wait for him to make the first move. And as time passed she had stopped waiting, stopped thinking about him. Almost.

When sleep came it was light and uneasy. She awoke several times, knowing that her dreams had been dark and haunted. She was damp with sweat, shaking, scared of her own mind. It wasn't supposed to be like this. The chance to live her whole life all over again should be an opportunity for her to add to what she'd had before, erase mistakes, take life by the scruff of the neck and demand better for herself. But it wasn't like that.

Yes, doing better at school would be easy. Yes, she knew to stay away from Scott Jordan and Joanne Howard. But what about the rest? She couldn't just ignore Dean and her dad and focus on what she wanted. And if she did manage to change things, what then? Would the changes be for the better or would they actually make things worse? Would staying away from Scott make her whole life better? She hadn't got a clue. She only had the answers to one set of problems. She was as blind as anyone else to any other path she might choose to take.

A world full of lost souls. Her own as much as anybody else's.

7

The buzzer sounded the end of another school day and Jess accepted Dean's offer to go to his. Maybe he would be able to fill in a few gaps for her. Trying to remember when it was that Dean had his date with his dad's hammer was proving problematic. Maybe his house would jog some of those faded memories.

She followed him through the door and put her bag down behind it. Three empty beer cans stood on the floor in front of the sofa, their sides crushed inwards. A pint glass with half a centimetre of flat lager in the bottom stood beside them. An ashtray that looked as if it hadn't been emptied in a week stood beside the glass.

Dean picked up her bag and handed it back to her. 'Bring it upstairs with you,' he said. 'Or my dad'll start going through it when he gets in.'

'It'll be a waste of time,' she replied. 'There's nothing in there that he'd want.'

'You'd be surprised,' he said as he went to the stairs. His dad had been known to steal pens and calculators from his friends bags before. Of course, that had been when he'd had friends.

He tossed his bag over the bed as they went to his room and it fell heavily beneath the window.

'What do you want to do?' he asked. 'I've got some smokes if you want one.'

She shook her head and looked around, hoping that something would trigger her memory and she'd remember when it was that Dean was supposed to die. She knew it was in the two weeks between them breaking up from school and the start of their exams and had a feeling it had happened sometime in the second week, but she couldn't be sure. She had fourteen days to choose from.

'I was talking to Scott about you the other day,' she said.

241

'Why?' he asked suspiciously.

'He said you'd been friends since primary school.'

'Yeah, until he turned into a snob.' He sat on the bed and took off his battered trainers. 'I don't bite,' he said as he motioned for her to sit with him. 'Not unless you want me to.' He grinned as if he'd just cracked the world's funniest joke and she couldn't help but smile back as she sat beside him.

'Scott isn't a snob,' she replied.

'Yes, he is,' Dean argued. 'He never liked Trip because he lived in that block of flats at the end of the estate. He wouldn't go there with me because he didn't want to be seen there.'

'He didn't like Trip because he knew he was selling you drugs,' she replied.

Dean shook his head violently. 'He used to smoke with me sometimes,' he said. 'He just wouldn't go with me to Trip's to get the weed.'

Scott had smoked weed? She bet that his mother didn't know about that.

'What I saw in your pocket at Trip's wasn't weed.'

'I never tried to make Scott take that stuff,' he said. 'But he tried to talk me out of taking it. He was just going on what the teachers had said about stuff like that, but teachers don't know everything, do they?'

She didn't know how much good it would do to tell him they knew a lot more than he did. Probably not much. Her mind kept going back to the twisted white scar on Scott's arm.

'I asked Trip if what Scott was telling me was right and Trip told me Scott was wrong. Trip just gives me stuff to calm my temper down, he wouldn't give me anything that'd hurt me.'

Of course he wouldn't. Good ole Doc Trip wouldn't ever hurt anyone, would he?

'Have you seen the state Miranda's in?' she asked.

Dean nodded as violently as he had shaken his head earlier. 'She's really poorly,' he said. 'Trip told me all about what happened.'

242

'Did he?'

'Yeah. Miranda got taken in by this bloke she fancied. I think his name was, erm, oh, I don't remember what his name was. But anyway, he got her smoking weed.'

'Like Trip got you smoking weed?'

How could this not be obvious? How could Dean not see what was happening?

'No,' he said. 'This is completely different. Trip gave me weed because it calmed me down. I smoked it when I started to feel angry. This boyfriend, oh, what was his name? Well, anyway, he got Miranda taking it for fun, when she didn't need it. I mean, you don't take painkillers if you haven't got a headache, do you?'

She didn't answer. She remembered something Connie had said to her once, something about her stress levels coming down after she took her medicine. When she'd asked what medicine, Connie had changed the subject.

'He ended up getting her hooked on some really nasty stuff and then he just dumped her with Trip and now he has to look after her.'

It was different to Scott's version of events but she knew that Trip had a way of telling people whatever he wanted them to hear.

'Isn't she still using?' Jess asked.

'She has to,' Dean replied sadly. 'I was there once when she hadn't had her fix and she had this fit. It was horrible. She was scratching her own face and trying to climb the walls and she couldn't sit still. Trip had to take her into another room and give her something.'

He hadn't finished what he'd been saying about Scott and she was interested to know what Dean thought about him having his arm slashed open as a warning from Trip.

'When did you and Scott stop talking to each other?' she asked.

'After I got the pills,' Dean said. 'A couple of days after I spoke to Trip

243

about what Scott had said. I came into school and Scott was sitting with Sean. He told me he didn't want to sit with me anymore. Sean's from Scott's road, his dad works in a bank. He said he didn't want us to be friends anymore.' He lay back on the bed and put his hands under his head. 'I think his parents didn't like him hanging around with me because they didn't think I was as good as them.'

It wasn't her place to defend Scott. If he'd wanted Dean to know what had happened he would have told him at the time. She looked at his face. Chocolate from the Boost he'd eaten at afternoon break still stained the corners of his mouth. His eyes were on her as if he was studying her, trying to answer a question he knew only she could and her mind began to race. *Dirty Dick Dean.* As she tried frantically to think of something to stop this, he said it.

'You haven't got a boyfriend, have you?'

'No.' The word fell into the room before she could stop it.

'I don't have a girlfriend either.'

She had to open her mouth to breathe properly. Her fists were clenched painfully in her lap, her nails punching small crescents into the palms of her hands.

'Have you ever,' he paused, trying to choose the right words to end his question, 'done it?'

Yes and no, she thought. 'No,' she replied.

'Me neither.' He sat up and shuffled over to her until their hips touched. 'Ever wanted to?'

The last time this had happened she'd wanted to scream and run all the way home. *Sex?* You're talking to me about *sex?*

'Sometimes.' She had meant to say no. She didn't want to have sex with Dean. Dean was the dirty scruffy kid that sat at the back of the class and drew pictures of comically large breasts inside his exercise books.

'Me too,' he replied. 'A girl put my joystick in her mouth once.'

244

'Joystick?'

'That's what Trip calls a dick.'

Joystick? The crudeness of it made her skin crawl but it did little to cool the warmth than she was starting to feel The same feeling lots of girls her age got when sex was discussed among friends or thought about in private. It was the feeling of being ready and not being ready at the same time. Of wanting it and being afraid of it simultaneously.

And how long's it been, Jess? Her hormones asked greedily.

'Really?'

'She said she enjoyed doing stuff like that.' He hoped that she wouldn't know he was lying. He'd never had anyone anywhere near his naked body but it sounded better if he said he had. He knew it would probably taste horrible because . . . he couldn't tell her about that either.

'Do you think you'd enjoy it?' he asked.

Would she? Had she? Did she?

'I don't know,' she said quietly.

'Do you want to try?'

'Not a lot in it for me, Dean.' Her mouth was working without her brain's consent and she cringed at the look that suddenly appeared on his face. She hadn't said no. She was willing to negotiate. In fact, that was as good as a yes. The only problem with negotiating was that he didn't know where to negotiate to.

He licked his lips. 'What do you want to do?'

Her brain screamed at her that this was absolutely not what she was supposed to change, but this was none of her brain's business. This was between her and her hormones. This was what had taken over in the back seat of Rory's car and if Russ hadn't barged in, how far would she have gone? Not far. Rory wouldn't have taken it any further than a kiss. She was fifteen for god's sake. But she would never have told him to stop.

She took Dean's hand and placed it over her right breast. He squeezed gently, staring at his hand with wonder.

Is that really a girl's tit under there? Under my hand?

He stroked it, gripped it lightly, feeling the nipple harden to his touch. He withdrew his hand, watching her chest rise and fall with each breath. Then he put both of his hands to her chest, feeling her small breasts in his palms, hypnotised by them. Only her blouse and a thin bra separated them from his fingers. Was she going to let him see them? Actually look at them? Would she let him touch her bare tits? Would she let him kiss them?

He fumbled with the top button of her blouse, expecting her to swat his hand away at any second, but she didn't. She sat, looking down as he undid the first three buttons. He could see her bra now, only the first glimpse of white cotton but it was enough to make his hands begin to shake. His trousers began to feel tight and uncomfortable as heat rose in his groin.

'Dean?'

He withdrew his hand quickly. 'Shit,' he said. 'My dad's home.'

Jess began to button up her blouse as he pulled her schoolbag open and took out a couple of books. 'I'm up here,' he called back.

Carl had had a particularly awful day. He'd been caught trying to steal plasterboard and given a major bollocking and a final warning by Mr Jessop. Now he'd have to phone Steve and tell him he hadn't got all the stuff he'd promised to get him for his loft conversion. Steve would want some of the money back he'd given to Carl in advance and Carl simply didn't have it.

He stomped upstairs and pushed open the door to his son's small bedroom, opening his mouth to order him to the bathroom, closing it when he saw the girl sitting beside Dean on the bed. They both looked flustered. A text book was open in Dean's lap, hiding the biggest clue to what had been happening in here before Carl had come home.

'Hi, dad,' Dean said innocently.

'I want to talk to you,' Carl said. He was talking to his son but his eyes were on Jess.

'We're just doing some homework,' Dean replied. 'We'll be done soon.'

'Now,' Carl said.

Dean put the book aside and stood up. The sight of his father in such an obvious rage had calmed his childish passion. The image of Jess's breasts pushing gently against his palm was the furthest thing from his mind. He followed Carl into the room he had once shared with his mother.

'Get rid of her, Dean,' Carl said as he sat down on the bed and pulled off his heavy work boots.

'We're only doing homework,' Dean insisted.

'You think I was born yesterday, Dean?' Carl began to growl. 'What were you really doing in there? Swapping smokes for handjobs?'

Dean blushed and looked at the floor. 'No.'

'Get rid of her, Dean,' Carl repeated. 'We've got things to do.'

A lump rose in Dean's throat.

'Either you get her out of here or send her in the bathroom.'

Dean gasped. 'You wouldn't,' he challenged.

Carl stood, towering over his son, and took off his belt. 'Have her in there in two minutes,' he said.

'No,' Dean said, a sickly vision of Jess kneeling before his father brought tears to his eyes. 'I'll get rid of her, I promise.'

Carl smirked as Dean hurried back to his room. He must have fertilised the stupidest egg that ever rolled off that bitch's reproduction line. Reproduction line. Pretty funny. He'd have to remember that one.

'You've got to go,' Dean said.

Jess frowned. 'Why?'

'Just go. I'll talk to you tomorrow.'

What's he going to do to you, Dean? She daren't ask. She had to admit that

247

despite the reputation Carl Meakin had as a bully, she could only remember Dean coming to school with bruises once. He'd said he'd fallen down the stairs. 'You could come to my house,' she suggested.

He shook his head, stuffing her books back into her bag. He handed it back to her and she slung it over her shoulder. As she left the room, she passed Carl on his way to the bathroom. He didn't speak to her.

'Sorry,' Dean said as they went to the door together.

'It's okay,' she said. 'I'll see you tomorrow.'

As Dean went back upstairs as slowly as he could, Jess headed home through a light rain, feeling disgusted. Dean Meakin? Why had she let him touch her? She wasn't interested in him.

Felt good though, didn't it? Weren't you ready for it? Haven't you been ready for the last eighteen months?

She had noticed her hormones beginning to play havoc over the last year or so. Last time she hadn't really understood it and it had been one of the few subjects she'd never discussed with her dad. When she'd allowed James Barker to take her into his bed it had been a messy, awkward ten minutes. But it had gotten better. And for the three months they had been together she had enjoyed it. Feeling his body against hers, feeling like an adult because that was what adults did, not fumbling teenagers. She'd seen James around at school but he wasn't in any of her classes anymore. He probably didn't even know she existed.

'Jess.'

She looked up. 'Scott,' she said flatly.

He approached her, the smile on his face melting into a frown. 'Something wrong?' After what he'd just left behind he'd been pleased to see her. Now he wasn't so sure. Her face was stormy.

'I don't know,' she said. The rain was beginning to fall harder now and she pulled up the hood of her coat. 'I've just been to Dean's and,' And what? Was

248

she really going to tell him what had happened? 'Have you ever met Dean's dad?'

'Lot's of times.'

'Don't you think he's a bit creepy?'

Scott nodded. 'I didn't go round much after his mum left.'

She considered Carl Meakin for another moment and then forced him away. She'd have plenty of time to think about him and Dean later, when she lay alone in bed before sleep took her for a few restless hours.

Scott's face said that she wasn't the only one that was troubled. 'So what's up with you?' she asked as his hair began to drip onto his coat.

'Had an argument with Joanne,' he said.

'Get used to it,' she replied with a wink.

'Karen says it's her,' he blushed and pulled at the bottom of his coat, 'her time of the month. Reckons she takes after her mum. You can't say anything without her biting your head off.'

'I don't think I'd notice the difference,' Jess smiled.

'She's okay,' Scott defended. 'And she's really pretty.'

Ah, the complexities of adolescent romance. *Who gives a shit if she's a bitch? Have you seen how jealous my mates are that she's on my arm?*

'I'd better go home,' he said, pointing at the sky.

'I'll walk with you,' she offered.

They started to walk together. *I loved you Scott Jordan,* she thought. *And you loved me back.* Looking at him, remembering how she'd felt with him, she didn't see the car. Scott did and he quickly pulled her to the ground behind a parked Land Rover.

'What the hell?' Jess asked.

'It's Karen,' Scott whispered, as if he might be heard. 'Just wait until she's gone.'

Jess crouched on the pavement and they both watched the road until Karen's car had passed and was out of sight. Scott stood up, sighing relief, and offered her his hands. As rain began to pound the pavement her heart rose in her throat. He looked so much as he had at the lake. Younger, but with the same bright eyes and easy smile. Fat droplets of rain ran down his cheeks as she took his hands and he pulled her to her feet. Without thought she put her arms around him and pressed her lips firmly against his. His hands pressed against her back. He tasted as he always had.

He has a girlfriend. He has a girlfriend and he's kissing you.

Well surely that meant that he wanted her more?

Just like it did when he had a wife, right?

She stepped away from him quickly.

'Jess, what . . .'

'Don't,' she said. 'I'm so sorry I did that.'

'Thanks,' he scoffed, feeling annoyance and embarrassment in equal measure.

She covered her face with her hands and then dropped them to her sides, unable to think of any words that could possibly excuse what she had just done.

'I'm going home,' Jess said. 'I'll see you tomorrow.'

'You're just as mental as your mum,' he cried with indignant embarrassment as she started to walk away.

She turned, her eyes ablaze. 'What?'

'You heard.'

She went back to him slowly, giving him a chance to run, but he stood his ground. 'What kind of lies has Joanne been feeding you?' she asked.

'It wasn't Joanne,' he replied menacingly. 'It was Karen. I heard her talking to her mum just before you came back. I know all about it. I know how quiet you and your dad have tried to keep it, but I know about her cutting her throat, Jess. And exactly how mental do you have to be to do that to yourself?'

She half turned and then fell back against the front of a house. If it hadn't been there she would have fallen straight to the ground. She slid down the wall, her chin resting on her knees, her hands over her face, and began to cry hard.

'Jess?' He bent and touched her arm but she flailed it at him and he backed off.

'Suicide,' Jess said to herself, shaking her head as if that would undo the past.

Scott felt sick. She hadn't known. 'Jess, I'm sorry. It might not be right,' he tried.

'Nice try,' came out from behind her hands.

'I'm so sorry.'

She looked up at him, her face red and tearstained and he crouched beside her on the pavement. When he put his arm around her she fell against him, sobbing into his coat. Her mum had cut her own throat? Jess saw all the frightened glances her mum had thrown her way, remembered her dad telling her that her mum was scared. It was her fault. Her mum had chosen to do that rather than have to listen to her daughter for one more day. She let Scott walk her home and he apologised again before he left.

Jess went to her room and cried into her pillow. She couldn't ever discuss this with her dad and she was only pleased that he didn't despise her for what she had done to her mother.

8

She sat down and looked across the grass at the river. She put the bottle of orange juice she had brought with her down by her side and crossed her legs, silently contemplating the water. She had expected fear or anger or sadness; but she didn't feel any of these things. A light breeze caused the long grass to dance and her hair blew gently away from her face. It was quiet here. Here she could think and know that she wouldn't be disturbed. And she had a lot to think about.

The day after she had kissed Scott she hadn't wanted to go to school. She'd wanted to bury her head beneath the covers of her bed and never come out. Instead she had gone to school as normal, ignored Scott in registration as normal and sat with Dean as normal, laughing only on the inside that this was as normal as it was going to get.

Dean had apologised for the night before and she had told him that it should never have happened, that they were friends and nothing more. He'd been disappointed and she'd been angry with herself for hurting him but they had gone to lunch together the same as they did every day, sitting at a table gossiping about who was doing what with whom, when the stranger approached.

'My mate fancies you.'

The boy was short and had a chin full of red pimples. He crouched by the side of the table and grinned up at her. She cast her eyes skyward. She hated being fifteen.

'Really,' she said without interest. 'And who would your mate be?'

'Scott Jordan.'

She dropped her fork onto the plate of chips and gravy and glanced at Dean. He was pretending to be busy with his chocolate sponge.

'I thought he was going out with Joanne Howard?' she asked as she leaned

252

back in the chair and stretched her arms out across the table.

Pimple boy shrugged. 'Think he's waiting for you to make him a better offer.'

She picked up her fork and pointed it at him. 'Well, you tell him I'm not interested,' she said.

The boy's grin widened. 'Playing hard to get?'

She resumed eating without giving him an answer and he stood up.

'You sure?' he asked.

She wasn't. God damn her fifteen year old heart but it had lurched at his name. 'I'm sure.'

In seven months, Scott had never sent pimple boy back. To begin with she had been relieved, pleased that things could just go back to normal - however normal a relationship with Joanne Howard could be. But then she'd been annoyed. Hadn't it meant anything to him? She sat, day after day, staring at him in class and wondering if they should be together, wanting to know that he wanted them to be together even if it was only so that she could turn him down. Would she do that? If Scott told her that he'd been thinking about her as much as she'd been thinking about him would she tell him to forget about it? Or would she make the same blind mistakes that she had made last time?

He still spoke to her; she still caught him looking at her sometimes at school. And her heartbeat accelerated every single time. It was getting harder and harder to not just give in to her feelings and tell him that she'd made a mistake, that she did want him after all. From the way he looked at her she thought that he might know that already.

She rubbed her eyes with her fingertips and took a drink of juice. She needed to focus on Dean. There was plenty of time to work out what to do about Scott. They weren't even supposed to start going out until they were seventeen.

At Christmas, after Jess had talked her dad into putting a substantial bet on what would be the Christmas number one single as per the information in

Smash Hits – like he was going to know any better – they had both travelled up to The Unicorn to spend the day with Jean and Don. It had been the best day she'd had since her return to Filton. Every second with her dad was precious and to see him happy, laughing with her grandparents, hugging her the way only he could as he thanked her for her presents, it had made her feel lucky. Because of what she knew she didn't take one moment of it for granted. She savoured every smile, every bad joke he told at the dinner table, every look he threw in her direction. He was her dad and she loved him so much.

Jean had talked about Rory. How he and Jean had ever become friends Jess didn't know, but he came back every now and again, just to give the place a glance over and see how she and Don were. As word had spread about the work he and Russ had done there, customers at The Unicorn had approached him for private readings and to see if he could visit their houses and work out why things were being moved around when nobody was home.

'He's doing really well for himself,' Jean had said. 'Last I heard he was rubbing shoulders with Gerald Wheatley.' She'd had to explain that Gerald Wheatley was a very highly regarded psychic medium, neither Jess nor Paul had ever heard of him.

Jess had been pleased to hear that Rory was doing well but had been disappointed that he'd never contacted her.

At school she had been aware more than ever before that time was running out for Dean. She had only narrowed the time of death down to a timescale of two weeks and that was nowhere near precise enough. She couldn't just take Dean and lock him away for a fortnight. She'd needed a date.

She picked up the bottle of orange juice again and drank, looking at the water and thinking hard. It had kept her awake at night, trying so hard to remember how she'd found out what had happened, where she'd been and who with, and when. And then today, finally, she had remembered.

They had broken up from school three days ago and she had been out of her

254

mind with worry. All she could remember was that it had happened between four and six in the evening. The way her mind had clung to some pieces of information but flippantly discarded others was infuriating. So she met him every day at three and stayed with him until seven. So far this strategy seemed to be working. She even thought that she might have succeeded and that the day could have been and gone without her even realising. But then today she had gone to the Co-Op to fetch some milk and Carl had been in there, chatting up the girl behind the cigarette counter, and she had known immediately. It had happened last time. She remembered saying to her dad after it had happened that she'd only seen Dean's dad in the shop yesterday.

Dean had twenty four hours left.

She got up and walked back to the road, wondering if she could really stop this from happening. It was a quarter to three, time to go and meet Dean, even if she knew that today he was safe. He was sitting on a bench in the park, smoking one of his dad's cigarettes while he waited for her. He waved as she approached and she sat next to him, watching the little kids play while their mothers chattered and warned them to be careful and not to run so fast.

'What you been up to?' she asked.

He shrugged. 'Nothing.'

'Want to come to mine and watch a video?'

'Okay.'

He flicked the cigarette butt into the grass as they got up and headed towards her house. He shuffled along, the cuffs of his jeans already frayed and torn after constantly being dragged across the ground by his short legs.

A video, Jess? Is that the best you can come up with? He might have one day left and you want him to come round and watch a video? Well, it wasn't like she could jet him off to Vegas or anything.

'We can do something else if you want,' she suggested, but he shrugged. He didn't care what they did as long as he didn't have to go home. Yesterday things had gotten better and worse all at the same time. He'd refused to go to the bathroom with his dad. Carl had been angry but Dean had stood his ground and finally realised that his dad could threaten him and frighten him but he couldn't force him to do it. And Carl had realised that as well. The feeling of triumph over his abuser hadn't lasted long though. When Carl had worked out that it didn't matter what he said, his son was not going to do what he wanted, he'd changed tactics, and oh, sweet Jesus, it had felt almost as good. Hearing Dean begging him to stop, feeling his fists driving into his boys kidneys, seeing him lying there, helpless and hurt, he'd felt that same bittersweet feeling of release.

Dean's ribs and hips hurt where he had been struck with fists and boots and grabbing, pinching hands, but he felt good too. It might have hurt but it had been a victory. He'd managed to say no. And he could say no whenever he liked, as long as he didn't mind feeling like he'd suffered ten rounds with Mike Tyson afterwards.

He didn't really watch the film. He wondered if all dad's were like his. Did Jess's dad hurt her when they were alone? Had she had to choose between one evil and another? Or was it just his dad that thought it was okay to do what he did?

'Do you fancy coming round tomorrow?' Jess asked after they'd watched a second film. It was almost eight and he knew his dad would be waiting for him when he got in. Hopefully he'd be able to just slink off to his room, unnoticed.

'Okay,' he replied.

'Meet me here at two?'

Although daylight was fading and a chill spiked the air, she wanted to get out of the house. She left with Dean and as he turned towards home with his head down and his hands in his pockets, she headed back towards the river. Kids walked the streets in groups, chattering loudly and laughing. She smiled to herself. They were her age but she still saw them as kids. Her stupid adult

256

brain was trapped inside the body of a hormonal teenager like some dark version of Freaky Friday. Except in this version there was nobody else who understood how it felt. Before, when she'd been caring for her dad, she'd thought about it a hundred times, going back to when she was younger and life was easier, but without the naivety it was pointless. She wasn't interested in the same things as everyone else, she didn't know how to communicate with her peers anymore. Even her language was different and it was so hard trying not to sound like one of their parents.

She looked at her watch and it seemed to stare back, taunting her. Less than twenty four hours; that was all he had left if she couldn't save him. It would help to have more information, but she couldn't ask him and she couldn't work it out for herself no matter how hard she tried. Why would Carl beat his own son to death? How could any parent do that to a child? She thought about her dad. He'd never hit her. Not even once. Not now, not before, never. Dean had never looked like he was being abused and he'd never said anything. But then why would he? And maybe it had been a one off; they'd gotten into a fight or something and Carl had hit him in the wrong place. And maybe . . .

'Careful.'

Her shoulder hit him even though he'd tried to step out of her way. She looked up quickly as if she'd been dragged out of a dream. Scott. What a surprise. 'Sorry,' she mumbled, still walking.

'You okay?' he asked.

She looked at him over her shoulder and stopped. No, she wasn't okay. She wasn't ever okay. She shook her head.

'Where you going?'

'Just walking.'

Would he have left Joanne? If she'd waited until after the funeral, would he have done it? She wondered how he would have felt, finding out that she had left his house and walked into the Swanmore River.

257

'You've been hanging around with Dean a lot.'

She nodded. Dean was okay, he was just a sixteen year old boy who was struggling to deal with his mum not being around to deal with his dad's temper.

Almost over, she thought. *One way or another, my babysitting duties with Dean are almost over.*

'Are you seeing him?' Scott asked.

She shook her head again.

'Everyone thinks you are,' he said. 'Everyone reckons you're both off your heads on crack and that you do, well, stuff for Trip 'cause you can't afford to buy it.'

She smiled derisively and nodded. The high school grapevine. How much she hadn't missed it. 'What do you think?' she asked.

He shrugged.

'You think I'd do that?' she asked. 'Any of that?'

'You don't look right,' he replied. 'You look like Dean did when he started hanging around with Trip.'

She couldn't argue with that. She was pale, guarded, constantly exhausted, always distracted. Teachers, on numerous occasions, had had to call her name two or three times in class before she'd even heard them because she had been so deep in thought.

'I've had a lot on my mind.'

'My mum reckons a problem shared's a problem halved,' he offered. He was pulling at the bottom of his jacket. She smiled. 'I was going to go to Sean's but if you want to talk . . .' he trailed off, leaving the offer to hang between them.

She nodded, then shook her head. She wasn't thinking about talking. She was thinking about getting him back. Stupid adolescent hormones. 'I don't think so,' she said regretfully. 'But thanks for the offer.'

'Okay.'

She watched as he turned and started to walk away. How many times had she watched him do that? The time they'd fallen out because of Joanne, the countless times they'd fallen out because of her dad. She'd watched his back as he walked away too many times to remember. At least this time she hadn't done anything wrong.

'Scott,' she called.

He turned, barely a shadow in the fading light.

'Okay,' she said. 'You can walk me home if you like.'

He smiled and they walked together towards her house.

'So what's going on with Dean?'

She nudged him playfully with her shoulder. 'Nothing's going on,' she replied. 'We're just mates.'

'So what's up?'

'Lots of stuff.'

'Like what?'

She looked across at him as they walked, as if, just for a minute, she could pretend they were together again. That they were walking as a couple, going back to her house to sit together, snuggle up on the sofa and watch TV like every other couple.

'I've been thinking about you.' It was hard to say.

'What about me?'

She looked at the pavement. 'You don't want to know.'

'Me and Joanne aren't together, you know,' he said.

She stopped and turned her face up to his. 'Now why would you tell me a thing like that?'

He shrugged. 'Just something to say.'

'Why did she finish with you?'

'I finished with her,' he replied indignantly.

She raised an eyebrow. Wow, at some point Scott Jordan had possessed a pair of balls. 'Why?'

259

He shrugged again but wouldn't look at her.

'Okay,' she said. 'None of my business. So you're a free man.'

'I really like you, Jess,' he blurted before his brain could tell him it wasn't a good idea.

Jess bit her bottom lip. It was so good to hear him say it. It wasn't *I love you* but it was good enough. 'You don't even know me, Scott,' she replied guardedly. She couldn't let this get out of hand, not now, not when she needed to be focusing her energy on keeping Dean safe tomorrow.

'I've seen you looking at me at school,' he persisted. 'You could just let me take you out to youth club or something.'

'How romantic,' she replied with a smile. 'Scott, you don't know the first thing about me. For all you know I am on drugs and I am doing gross stuff with Trip.'

'You're not though.'

His eyes pleaded with her to just agree to one date and she felt her heart begin to pound. Who was she trying to kid? She stopped walking and pulled him against her, kissing him softly. She felt like laughing and crying and screaming all at the same time. Half of her mind pleaded with her to stop while the other urged her to go with her heart.

Kissing him didn't feel like it had before. This wasn't a beginning, it was a rerun. They wouldn't learn about each other together; she already knew more about him that he did. But the kiss still felt good. And he was hers, wasn't he? Didn't he belong to her? Weren't they supposed to be together? Right or not, she wanted to be with Scott and who was going to stop her?

9

'Dad, I need to talk to you.'

He looked up the stairs as she descended and hung his coat on the banister. 'You're not pregnant, are you?'

Jess rolled her eyes. Every time she wanted to have a serious chat with him he asked the same question. 'Yes, dad,' she replied. 'With twins. And their dad's already married to someone else.'

'Long as you're happy, dear.'

She went into the living room while Paul filled a pint glass with cider and they sat down together.

'There's a boy I like,' she said.

He paused, the glass halfway to his mouth. He drank and then put it down on the coffee table. Out of every conversation they could possibly have, this was the one he'd been dreading the most. Was he supposed to tell her to make sure they carried condoms or forbid her from having sex altogether? But that only led to the unthinkable thought – that maybe his little girl was having sex already.

'And he likes me.'

'Okay,' he said slowly. 'You don't normally speak to me about boys.'

'But this is different, dad,' she said. 'This is serious.'

'How serious?'

She was beginning to feel uncomfortable already. 'I think I love him.'

Paul opened his mouth to speak but she continued quickly. 'I know that I'm only sixteen and as far as you're concerned I couldn't possibly even know what love is at my age, blah blah blah, but he is special.'

Paul closed his mouth and considered this. He was trying to interpret 'special'. 'How long have you been with this boy?' he asked.

'Not long,' she replied. What had it been? Twelve hours? 'But I know how I feel.'

He nodded, feeling reassured. Nothing more than an adolescent crush.

'I really like him and I just thought that I should let you know.'

'I appreciate that,' he said sincerely. 'Is it anyone I know? Please don't tell me it's that scruffy lad.'

'No, it's not Dean.'

'Do I know him?'

'It's Scott Jordan.'

At this point Jess had expected her dad to explode with rage and forbid her from ever seeing him again.

'I thought he was seeing Joanne?' he said quietly.

'They broke up.'

He cleared his throat and looked at her seriously, remembering how she'd told him time and time again that Scott had been nice and then he'd been mean.

'I don't think he's right for you, Jess,' he said.

'I think it's for me to make that decision.'

'Sweetheart,' he said as he ran a hand over his face. 'Jess, do you remember when you were little? When your mum was alive?'

'Not really.'

'But you remember that you used to tell us things?'

She knew where he was going, the dark road he was leading her down. The look on his face was enough to scare her and she was fearful of what he would mention that she really might have forgotten.

'I don't really remember much at all,' she said. 'I was four.'

He nodded. 'But it did happen, Jess. You remember that much, don't you?'

'Of course I do.'

His eyes were red rimmed and she could only imagine how much she had damaged him all those years ago. 'You used to wake up screaming in the night,' he said. 'You had terrible nightmares. And you mentioned Scott

262

sometimes when you had them.'

'That's impossible,' she said. 'I didn't know him then.'

'It probably wouldn't have been so disturbing if you had, sweetheart,' he replied gently. 'You said that he was nice to you and then he wasn't. And it had something to do with Joanne.'

She remembered. She remembered drawing the picture of them by the lake. And she knew that she was just as scared as her dad of things turning out the way they had before.

'I don't remember,' she said.

'I don't expect you to, sweetheart, you were just a little girl. But the stuff you said, it had a way of being right.'

She nodded. 'I'm glad you told me.'

'So you're not going to see him anymore?' he asked hopefully.

'I'm still going to see him,' she said. 'I'll just be careful.'

Paul's mood changed visibly. His face was dark, his hands clenched to fists in his lap. 'He'll hurt you, Jess.'

'Dad, I've got to make my own mistakes,' Jess argued. 'I wont learn by just doing whatever you tell me to.'

'We agree that this is a mistake then?' Paul said spitefully.

She didn't reply.

'Jess, I hate having to put my foot down with you but I'm going on what you said.'

'I was four,' she said. 'I don't even remember most of it. You can't hold it against me for the rest of my life.'

'But it was right,' he said with despair. 'You've got no idea what it was like, Jess, but everything you said was right.'

'Nothing's set in stone,' she said, thinking about her mother. Her mother who had killed herself. She would never discuss that with her dad. She couldn't begin to imagine how it must have felt to find your wife, the woman you loved,

263

the mother of your child, dead, and know that she had done that to herself.

'Well, it's obviously pointless me even talking to you,' he said. 'You do what you like but when it all ends in tears, which I assure you it will, don't you dare come crying to me.'

She went to him and ruffled his soft hair. 'You don't mean that,' she said.

He looked at her with annoyance. 'No, I don't,' he admitted. 'But I'd still be a lot happier if you didn't bother. That scruffy kid seems nice.'

10

He wasn't answering the phone.

It was almost two thirty and he wasn't answering the phone.

What if she'd gotten the time wrong?

She left home and ran to his house, stopping at the low wooden fence that separated the small front garden from the street. Carl Meakin was just putting his key in the lock.

'Mr Meakin?' she asked, keeping her distance. The man turned, looking her up and down slowly. 'Is Dean in?'

'Only just got here,' the man replied as he stepped inside the house. 'I'll see if he's about.'

Jess stayed outside, listening as Carl called for his son. 'That Jess girl's here for you,' he shouted up the stairs. Seconds later he came back to the door and shrugged with a knowing smile. 'Must be out.'

'Okay,' she replied, not liking that smile one bit. 'Thanks.'

Carl closed the door as she turned, looking up and down the street as if for clues. What if he'd gone to hers while she was here? She went back to her house. Dean wasn't there.

She tried the park without success. The only other place he could be was Trip's. She couldn't go there. She went home again and sat beside the phone, waiting for it to ring, waiting for a knock at the door, anything. After twenty minutes she called Dean's again and Carl answered on the fourth ring.

'Hi, it's Jess Morgan,' she said hurriedly. 'I called for Dean earlier. I don't suppose he's in yet is he?'

'No,' he replied flatly.

'When he gets in can you please ask him to ring me? It's really important.'

'What do you want Dean for?' Carl asked.

'I, I was supposed to meet him earlier and he never turned up,' she explained.

'Well he wouldn't, would he?' Carl laughed as if that much was obvious. 'I saw you last night, you know. Kissing that boy in the street.'

'What?'

'You've been leading Dean on for months,' Carl said. 'I thought he should know.'

Jess felt faint. She leaned against the wall and closed her eyes. 'You told him about Scott?'

'You was just using our Dean to make that other lad jealous,' Carl taunted. 'I can see straight through girls like you.'

'Mr Meakin, I never . . .'

'Goodbye, Jess.'

He hung up and she went to the living room, slamming the door behind her and falling onto the sofa as the tears came. They burned as they fell, boiling down her cheeks. Her vision blurred and breath came only in gasps. What the hell was she going to do? She looked at the clock. Almost half past three. *Tick tock, Jess.*

She went back to New Road and waited by the post box on the corner where she had a clear view of Dean's house. When he came back she'd stop him from going inside. She could still win. She could still save him.

Four came and went. As five o' clock approached she wondered if there was any way he could have gotten inside without her noticing. Had she taken her eyes off the house at any point? She knew that she hadn't. As long as he wasn't inside that house, he was safe.

At half past five she heard sirens.

No.

Nothing to do with her. Nothing to do with Dean. Couldn't be.

The ambulance tore down New Road and for a horrible moment she

266

expected it to stop outside Dean's house but it didn't. It sped past her and turned right at the end of the street. She watched until it disappeared around another corner and then the sirens stopped. They hadn't faded, they'd stopped.

She looked at Dean's house again. Five minutes there and back. Just to check. Three if she ran. Then she could bang on the door and make sure he hadn't returned home while she'd been away. She ran as fast as she could. The ambulance had stopped opposite the turning onto Dukes Court. She froze.

It was parked by the fence. Over the fence were the fields. And then there was the river.

A crowd of people stood in the street, looking at the ambulance. She walked cautiously towards it. Looking over the fence she could see two paramedics near to the river. She heard more sirens and a police car rushed past her in a blur, pulling up in front of the ambulance. Before the police were out of the car she climbed over the fence and ran to where the paramedics were bent over a very still body. The trainers were old and dirty and the jeans were frayed at the cuffs.

'Dean,' she managed.

One of the paramedics turned, waving his arm at her and telling her to go back to the road. When she didn't move he called to the police and they came across the field quickly, removing her when her feet refused to move. Back at the road she continued to stare down at the green suited paramedics as more police arrived.

'Is he dead?' Jess asked the female officer who had hold of her arm. She didn't answer. 'Is he dead?' she asked again. 'He's my friend.'

The woman looked at her and then at her colleague, a tall male with stony features and dark eyes. 'You know him?' she asked.

Jess nodded. 'His name's Dean Meakin. He lives with his dad on New Road, just around the corner.'

The two officers exchanged glances again and the woman led Jess to their car, opening the back door. 'Would you mind taking a seat for me just for a moment?' she asked. 'I'm going to need to ask you some questions.'

Jess sat. They went away to talk to the other officers who were cordoning off the area and then the woman returned, crouching in front of Jess. 'What's your name, love?' she asked.

'Jessica Morgan,' she replied, trying to see what the paramedics were doing to her friend.

'I'm Officer Raynor,' the woman said, offering a small smile. 'Was it you that called the emergency services?'

Jess shook her head. 'No.'

'Okay. You said that you know where the victim lives.'

Victim. How had this happened?

Jess nodded. 'Number twenty three New Road.' She pointed down the street. 'First left.'

Officer Raynor scribbled the address down in a small black book. 'And you said that his name's Dean?'

'Dean Meakin. His dad's name's Carl.'

Raynor scribbled away as Jess put her head in her hands. She'd failed. They didn't have to tell her, she knew that Dean was dead down there. She wondered if it was a cruel warning; putting him there by the river, in a spot she had probably crossed on her way to the water. If she ever got to see that ancient crone in the white building again she was going to beat the hell out of her.

'Can you think of anyone who might want to hurt Dean?' Raynor asked.

'I don't know,' Jess replied. 'I think his dad might have been hitting him, but I'm not sure.'

'What makes you think that?'

Nothing that would make any sense. 'Everyone knows that Carl's got a temper,' she said. 'He used to hit Dean's mum. Then she got sick of it and left but she didn't take Dean with her. I don't know where she lives.'

'Is there anything else you can tell us that you think might help?'

She started to shake her head and then stopped abruptly. 'He spends a lot of time with Trip Jameson,' she said. 'Some people reckon Trip sells drugs to the kids at school, so if this is drug related you might want to start there.'

Raynor nodded as her pencil moved quickly across the tiny pages of her notebook. 'And do you have an address?'

Jess gave her the address and, after taking her contact details, Raynor told her that she should go home. She took her advice. Walking away from the scene she heard a woman talking to Raynor's colleague.

'He had a mask,' the woman said. 'It was one of those yellow people off the telly, you know, the ones in the cartoon.'

Trip. Trip or someone working on his behalf. She paused for a moment, wondering if there was anything that she could do, and then, defeated, she went home.

She lay on the sofa with one thought filling her mind. *I failed.* There wouldn't be another chance. She'd had one opportunity to get it right and she'd failed. And now Dean was dead. How? Not important. Why? Because it wasn't up to her who lived and who died. When their time was up it was up and she couldn't do a thing about it.

The phone rang and she dragged herself to her feet to answer it, thinking that it might be Raynor. It was Scott.

'There's a load of police and an ambulance down the end of the street,' he said. 'I'm not sure what's gone off but two or three people have mentioned Dean Meakin.' He sounded scared. 'My mum went down to have a nosy. She doesn't know what's happened but they're saying he's dead, Jess.'

'Yeah,' she said as she sat on the chair by the phone. 'I was there.'

'You saw it happen?' Now he sounded terrified.

'No,' she replied, wondering how many phone calls the same as this one were being made all over the estate by now. 'I got there just after the paramedics. I spoke to the police already.'

'Are you okay?'

'No.'

'Do you want me to come round?'

She said that she did and hung up.

She felt unnervingly calm. It was over. She hadn't been able to change it and there was no point worrying about it anymore. Looking at it from this side, with Dean now on his way to the morgue, she felt only an emotional numbness. She was hungry for the first time since yesterday. She made a sandwich, grating cheese directly onto the bread, staring out of the window and wondering if Dean would have an audience with the old woman in purple.

Tossing the knife into the sink to wash later, she chewed thoughtfully. Should she have warned Dean? She'd considered it a hundred times but it was a ridiculous idea. She would have had to explain herself and then Dean might not have believed her and then after his dad telling him about Scott he would have told her secret to anyone who would listen just to get back at her.

She went, sandwich in hand, spilling cheese onto the living room carpet, to answer the knock at the door.

'Are you okay?' Scott asked, breathless and wide eyed.

She nodded. She was no longer hungry. 'Come in,' she said as she went to the kitchen and threw away what was left of the sandwich.

'I can't believe it,' Scott said. 'I only saw him the other day. They reckon he was beaten to death.'

Beaten to death? Same death, different location.

'Do they know who it was?' she asked.

'From what I've heard, the woman who rang the police reckons she saw four lads running away across the fields.'

He put his arm around her and she sank willingly into his embrace. 'He can't be dead,' Scott said.

'He didn't look like he was getting up to me,' Jess replied.

'Maybe he was just knocked out.'

'I don't think so, Scott. He definitely looked like he was dead.'

'And how many dead people have you seen?'

Scott was frightened. Jess held his hands. Their fingers entwined automatically and she could feel him shaking.

'Who would do something like that?' Scott asked. 'How could someone do that?'

She wanted to cry for him. She wanted to tell him that everything was okay. But everything wasn't okay, was it? Things were very fucking far from okay. People were dying. And she couldn't stop it.

'I don't know,' she said. She had visions of whatever power it was that was in charge of this sort of thing sending its own demons or ghouls to beat Dean to death just to make sure that he kept his appointment.

She thought about Carl Meakin. He wouldn't go to prison for killing his son. Maybe nobody else would either. Something had changed. Something was different. And it was because of her. She'd prevented a child killer from being locked away because in this twisted version of the world, Carl wasn't a child killer. And she had nobody to blame for that but herself.

11

She pinned the banner up above the fireplace and looked around at her handiwork. Balloons littered the floor and were pinned to the walls in the cock and balls formation her dad always found hilarious. He hadn't been asked to decorate at any of her birthday parties since she'd been seven years old after mum had noticed. Well, he wouldn't have been asked, if things had gone the same way.

Dean Meakin wouldn't have any more birthdays. It had been three months and Carl was still roaming free around the estate. There had been no arrests for Dean's murder. Not this time.

It was all wrong. Her mum, her dad, Dean, Scott. All of it.

Especially Scott.

Since she had refused his marriage proposal a lifetime ago, Jess feared that she had reinvented Scott Jordan. She had turned him into her own ideal; remembering selectively, creatively, editing his personality until she was left only with what she wanted him to be.

That was what she had done after her dad had died. When Scott had been so nice to her, so caring, she had clung to that, forgetting how selfish he could be sometimes, how unwilling to compromise he was.

She saw the ring in her minds eye. A sparkling solitaire diamond set in white gold.

'Marry me, Jess.'

She smiled, then grinned, then laughed and he laughed with her. 'Yes,' she said excitedly. 'Yes, yes, yes.'

He quickly removed the ring from it's plush black velvet box and slid it onto her finger. He grabbed her, holding her tight, kissing her cheek, her mouth, her chin.

'I love you, Jess.'

272

'I love you too, babe.'

He grinned as she splayed her fingers and stared at the ring. 'I was so nervous that you might say no,' he confessed. 'I've been thinking about this for so long.'

He kissed her hand and embraced her again. 'I've planned it all,' he said excitedly and laughed. 'The wedding, the kids. Once mum and dad go to Spain we can live here and we can decorate it together and we'll have our own family.'

'It'll be perfect,' she giggled, his laughter contagious.

'Mrs Jordan,' he mused. 'Mrs Jessica Jordan. I like it.'

'I love it,' she grinned. 'And we'll be local so I'll still be able to sort dad's meals out and then have tea ready for you when you come home and ...' She trailed off. Scott had stopped laughing. 'What?' she asked.

'Your dad's an adult,' Scott said. 'He can cook his own meals.'

This again? Really? How many times did she have to do this?

'He can't,' she replied. 'He can't stand up for long. Sometimes he can hardly stand at all.'

'But *we'll* be a family.'

'And my dad wont be a part of that?'

'You'll have the kids to look after,' Scott said with a tight frown.

'I can take them with me,' she argued. 'I assume my dad's going to be allowed to see his grandchildren?'

'He'll manage, Jess.'

'Manage.' Her voice was low with barely restrained fury. 'It's my fault he fell down those stairs, Scott. And even if it wasn't, he's my dad, he's *my* family. I'm always going to be there for him.'

'So you're just going to neglect our children and ...'

'Oh my god, Scott.' She ran her hands through her hair and shook her head with disbelief. 'You can't throw our imaginary children at us when my dad's

273

real and the problem with his back is real. Why is he always such a big issue?'

He lunged at her, taking her roughly by the shoulders. 'Why aren't I enough for you?' he yelled at her. 'Why does he always have to come first?'

She pulled herself from his grasp and looked at him. Pain was etched all over her face. He glared back at her.

'I love you, Scott,' she whispered.

'But you love him more.'

'I love him differently.'

'We'll never get rid of him, will we?'

Get rid of him? 'He's. My. Dad.' She glared right back at him and could feel her hands beginning to shake.

'He's a leech,' Scott spat, his face red and his eyes dark with rage.

She brought her hand up to her eyes and looked sadly at the ring before removing it from her finger and offering it to him. He looked at it dumbly.

'If he ever spoke about you like that,' she said softly, 'I'd hate him for it.'

'We both know that's exactly what he does do.'

She shook her head. 'He might be frightened that you're going to take me away from him and you might not see eye to eye, but he's never talked about you like that.' She took a step towards him, holding the ring out to him. 'Take it,' she said.

He put his hands in the pockets of his jeans. 'I don't want to.'

'Me neither,' she said, her voice breaking as tears welled in her eyes. 'I want to marry you, Scott. I want us to be together forever. But he's always going to be a part of my life and a ring isn't going to change that.'

He looked at the ring and then quickly snatched it from her fingers. 'I see,' he said. 'We might as well call it a day then, hadn't we?'

She couldn't believe what she was hearing. 'Did you ask me to marry you because you love me or because you thought you'd be able to take me away from him?'

'Because I love you,' he replied. 'But I want it to be me and you, Jess. I don't want him hanging around our necks for the rest of our lives.'

Jess looked down at her hands and picked absently at her thumbnail. 'Then this conversation's over.' She didn't look up as she went to the door.

'If you walk out that door, don't you ever think you can come back,' Scott warned.

She looked over her shoulder at him and then opened the door. 'You know where I am if you want to talk,' she said. 'Once you've calmed down.'

'Forget it,' he shouted as she stepped outside. 'You go back to him. You go back there like a good girl and you forget all about us.'

And that was exactly what she had done. She had cried her way through the streets and avoided her dad until the next day. When she had finally told him what had happened, giving him only a diluted version of events because she couldn't bear to tell him exactly what Scott had said, he'd told her that if Scott made her happy then she should go back and apologise.

But she hadn't.

Should she have gone back? Was she doing the right thing now? But if she was supposed to accept his proposal, if they were meant to be together, then why was their relationship making her feel so hopelessly miserable?

As she heard her dad coming downstairs she shook Scott from her head and ran to the kitchen. She'd forgotten about the food. She heard him laugh when he saw the balloons.

'Happy birthday to you,' she sang, clapping joyfully as she came in from the kitchen. He laughed again and gave her a hug, his fingers pinching into her ribs.

'What's all this for?' he asked.

'It's the first birthday I've been with you since I went away,' she smiled. 'I wanted it to be special.'

He released her, smiling at her smile. An elaborately wrapped gift sat on the coffee table, surrounded by yet more balloons.

'I'll get you a coffee.' She danced away into the kitchen and he sat down. His newspaper was sitting on the arm of the chair, folded as he folded it so that he could do the crossword. His yellow pencil was laid on top of it, sharpened and ready to go.

She brought the coffee out to him, still grinning, and told him that breakfast would only be a couple of minutes. No distressing sizzles or pops came from the kitchen like they did when he cooked. She definitely took after her mother when it came to cooking. She swiped balloons off the table and they bounced idly as she put down knives, forks, salt, ketchup and HP sauce before going back to fetch bread and butter. He looked in awe as she presented him with a plate of sausage, bacon, eggs, beans, mushrooms and fried bread.

'Wow,' he said. He put the newspaper beside his plate and mulled over the clues, reading them out loud when he needed her help, filling a couple in while he chewed on his bacon.

After they'd eaten she took the plates away and pushed the small parcel towards him. 'Open it,' she said.

Smiling, he took the flat package and pulled off the ribbon. 'What is it?' he asked.

She rolled her eyes. 'Open it and you'll find out,' she replied impatiently.

The smile faded when he saw her gift and his eyes filmed with tears. She'd expected no less. 'Do you like it?' she asked. The frame hadn't cost much, but she hadn't wanted anything fancy. The focus was the photograph, not the frame.

It had been taken on the day they'd gone to the beach together. Paul had asked an old couple if they wouldn't mind taking the picture for two reasons; First, they were a couple and therefore statistically more trustworthy. Second, they were old. If they tried to steal his camera he'd catch them pretty quickly. Jess sat on his shoulders. She was holding pink candy floss in one hand and she

276

was laughing. Sheila's arm was around her husbands waist and her head rested against Jess's knee. They were both laughing too. Behind them was the burger stand they'd bought hot dogs from.

'Where did you find it?' he asked. 'I spent ages looking for this.'

'I took it with me to gran's,' she said. 'I meant to put it up when I got back but I forgot. I thought you'd like it.'

'I love it,' he wept. She knelt in front of him and they held each other tightly.

As Jess took the wrapping paper to the bin Paul immediately hung her gift above the neat row of her school photos. Front and centre, pride of place.

He hugged her again and kissed her cheek. 'Thank you, sweetheart.'

'And I'm going to buy Chinese for tea,' Jess said, trying to lighten the mood. 'Do you want another coffee?'

'It's my birthday,' he said as he went back to his chair. 'Let's have a beer.'

The smile withered on her lips. 'It's only nine o clock,' she said.

'It's my birthday,' he repeated. 'I can have a drink on my birthday can't I?'

'Not at nine in the morning.'

'Okay,' he said. 'I'll have a coffee then please.'

She refilled his mug and turned on the TV.

'I've got an idea,' Paul said. He pulled a ten pound note from his pocket. 'Why don't you nip down the Co-Op and grab us one of them cheesecakes you like. We can have it with some sandwiches or something for dinner.'

She took the money and stuffed it into her pocket. 'And grab us an half ounce of Old Holborn while you're there,' he added.

She went obediently, hardly noticing the sun on her face as she walked through the warm June morning. Drinking at nine in the morning? That was bad. She didn't think she'd have to worry until he started losing the weight. That was the thing that stood out in her mind; how thin he'd been. But he still looked healthy and bright eyed.

But he wants a drink at nine in the morning.

She had to start now.

The Co-Op was cool and bright. She walked the aisles in a daze, wondering how she was going to do it. Knowing was one thing, trying to stop it was another, and other peoples free will and determination to do whatever the hell they wanted to was something else altogether.

Birthday cakes in colourful boxes sat on shelves beside the crumpets and Soreen. She picked a plain white iced sponge with delicate blue flourishes and decided they'd have that instead of cheesecake. She fetched a pack of small blue candles and checked her pockets to make sure she had enough money on her. She did. She paid Pam for her purchases, Elaine not having been employed yet, and went back home with her dads surprise.

Paul was still hunched over the crossword and he'd turned the TV off. She hurried into the kitchen so he wouldn't see the cake and took it out of the box.

'Did you get my backy?' he asked.

She took it into the living room and stopped, her hand held out to him, her eyes on the table. A bottle of cider stood beside a half empty pint glass.

Never seen an apple, all chemicals and alcohol.

'It's my birthday,' Paul said as he followed her gaze.

'Is that why you sent me out?' she asked. 'So you could have a drink without me moaning at you?'

He paused before saying no. The pause said more than the word.

'Dad, you can't be drinking at this time in the morning.'

'But it's . . .'

'Your birthday,' she finished for him. 'I know. And if you want to have lots more you can't start drinking at nine in the morning.'

'I was only having one pint.'

'That's why you brought the bottle in?'

'I'm an adult,' Paul argued. 'And if I want to have a drink on my birthday, I

278

will.'

'Dad, please.' She sat down, putting the pouch of tobacco on the table. 'If you came down and saw me drinking at nine in the morning, what would you say?'

'That you were a chip off the old block.'

'Seriously.'

'It's one pint, sweetheart.'

'No, it isn't,' she protested. 'It's at least two of those bottles every day.'

'You never say no to a glass.'

She sighed. 'Every now and again, dad,' she said. 'There's a big difference between that and four litres a day.'

She knew he wouldn't back down. He was an adult and if he wanted to drink, birthday or not, then he would. Even if she confessed her secret to him she knew what he'd say. He'd tell her that she'd said her mum would die when she was ten and that hadn't happened. Checkmate. She could argue if she wanted and god knew he'd argue back, and at the end of it all nothing would have changed. There'd be an atmosphere for a while and nobody was as good as her dad for dishing out the silent treatment. She'd be the one to give in, and then she'd have to start all over again.

'You know it can seriously damage your liver,' she persisted.

'Jess,' he said as he kicked absently at a balloon. 'I smoke a bit and I drink a bit.'

'A bit?'

'I look after us, don't I?' he asked. 'I always make sure the bills are paid and we've got food in the fridge. What did I tell you when you started working for your gran? If you're old enough to earn it, you're old enough to spend it. On whatever you want.'

'God, dad, you're not twelve,' she replied with frustration. 'You're hurting yourself.'

279

'I feel fine.'

'Now, dad. Now you feel fine.'

'Jess, it's my birthday.' He saw her roll her eyes as he tried the same line again. 'Let's just enjoy today and we can talk about this tomorrow.'

She knew exactly what that meant. He didn't have a decent argument. He wasn't asking so he could enjoy his birthday, he was asking so that she'd give him twenty four hours to work out how to get her off his back. Fine. Let him have a day. He could throw whatever he wanted at her, she wasn't going to let it drop. She went to the kitchen to put the candles on his birthday cake.

12

The curtains were out of focus. That was good. Jess blinked slowly and turned her head to look at the ceiling. Her arms felt heavy. She untwined her fingers and allowed them to slide off her belly onto the bed. She tried to make herself sit up, but her weighty arms didn't seem to want to help. She pushed clumsily with her feet, sliding her head, her neck, her back, up the headboard until she sat, her limp arms by her sides. Breathing heavily, exhausted by the act of simply sitting up, she clamped a hand around the neck of the bottle and slid it off the bedside table, almost spilling the contents onto the bed as she tried to coordinate what, an hour ago, had been the simplest hand to mouth action. She drank clumsily, her hand wasn't steady and vodka escaped from the sides of her mouth and ran over her chin. She swiped it dry with another heavy arm.

Sleep would come soon, she could feel it. Her eyelids felt as heavy as the rest of her body. It wouldn't take her for long, but not long was better than no sleep at all. As long as the dreams didn't come. The dreams trapped her in a bloody abyss that was as hellish as being awake. Sleep should be a sanctuary. It should be where she could go, just for a little while, to be away from what had happened. To forget. To pretend that all was well.

Maybe this was hell. Maybe the woman with the purple robe and the attitude problem had sent her to hell for taking her own life and she would have to live those terrible moments from her past over and over again. Connie and Dean would always die. She would never be able to save them. Because this was hell and she was being punished for what she did.

Just after Dean had died, when the nightmares had been so bad and the feeling of being imprisoned in this life where everything was just a series of triggers meant to drive her insane had overwhelmed her, she had taken the bottle of NeuroHelp from the top of the fridge and sat, alone in the darkness of the living room at two in the morning, just staring at it. She had been shaking.

She'd turned it over with her trembling fingers, wanting to take them but not daring to.

Because what if this wasn't hell? What if she took her own life again and had to go back to that woman without her dad's help? How pissed off would she be? What would she do? Would she send her back again with a teacher's Must Try Harder telling off? Oh god, no. She couldn't do this again. She could live this life a hundred times and all that would change would be her level of sanity.

Turning the bottle over in her hand, enjoying the inviting sound of the many pills rattling around inside it, she had thought of a different plan. A plan nobody else could interfere with.

It had come to her as she thought of her dad. Because if things didn't go as planned, then he was next.

But what if she could outdrink him?

That was her way out. If she drank hard enough she would never have to see her dad die. She would get to the finish line first. He hadn't been sent back. She would be able to die, to go to that big building and do whatever the people in the silver pyjamas did. And he would know how it felt. He would understand the hurt and the anger and the loneliness and the sense of responsibility. And it would serve him right. It would serve him fucking right because all of this was happening because of him. Him and that stupid old bitch that he'd blabbed to. What gave them the right to do this to her? Why hadn't they let her decide? If she'd wanted her stupid crappy life she wouldn't have walked into the river in the first place, would she?

She took another long drink from the bottle. Her stomach turned and she clenched her teeth together, holding her breath and tensing her throat. She didn't want to vomit; didn't think she could actually make it to the bathroom in time. She put the bottle on the floor. No way could she lift it back onto the table.

She hated them. Every single one of them. Her dad for his drinking, Scott for choosing Joanne a lifetime ago. She hated Connie for not waiting for her to come back and at least give her a chance to save her. She hated Trip. She hated Dean. She hated Joanne and Karen. It was okay for them, wasn't it? They got to go about their business, oblivious to where the path's they wandered would lead.

And she hated herself most of all. For not saving Connie, for not saving Dean. For analysing every word that passed between Scott and Joanne and watching Scott's reactions every time Joanne got a new boyfriend. Once Joanne had calmed down she'd decided that Jess was her new best friend. Jess knew exactly what Joanne was doing. She didn't like Jess, she was only trying to reclaim Scott. And Jess was waiting. Waiting for Scott to cheat, waiting for her dad to die. Waiting for some kind of sign to point her in the right direction and show her what she was supposed to be doing. Until then she'd do whatever the hell she wanted to do. And now she wanted to sleep. She wanted to drink hard and she wanted to sleep.

Closing her eyes, feeling as if she was on a boat moved by the motion of the waves beneath it, she slid beneath the covers and lay on her back. Tears leaked from the corners of her eyes and ran into her ears.

Connie and Dean were gone now. She could do no more for them. She needed to focus on herself. And her dad. And Scott.

What was she doing with Scott? Was she with him because she just thought that she should be or because she loved him? Could she even make a distinction between what she wanted and what she thought was right? Did she even care?

And what could she really do for her dad? Trying to stop his drinking had only resulted in arguments. For a while he'd said that he'd stopped but she'd seen him sneaking bottles of cider upstairs, hiding them in his room. She'd given up. What if he was going to die at the same time anyway just like Dean

283

had? Did she want to spend what time they had arguing? No. She'd rather he drank himself to death and they had the same relationship as last time than him sneak around and hide things from her.

Did she want to torture herself by trying, and most probably failing, to save him? Or could she outmanoeuvre him and die first? That was the easy option. But even now, as self pity forced tears to her eyes, she knew that she'd never be able to do it. Thinking of him sitting beside *her* in the hospital, holding *her* hand, watching *her* die, she knew she would never do it. Even as she began to slip into a damp, vodka induced slumber, she knew she could never put him through that.

She wanted her life back. Not this one, the last one. The one where she could mourn those that died without feeling more guilt than loss, the one where she could truly enjoy spending time with her dad without wondering how often he was lying to her. The life where she wasn't a prisoner in her own mind, lost in an endless battle between what would happen and what could happen, depending on the decisions she made. She couldn't think of one right decision she'd made. Every turn seemed to take her in the wrong direction.

Part Five

1

He took another sip of champagne, wishing it was beer, and forced a smile as he entered the huge and very tastefully decorated hall. Elegant women in casual clothes that he bet had cost more than his car seemed to float around, their eyes and diamonds sparkling in the sunlight thrown in through the open French doors and floor to ceiling windows. He strode confidently into the room, sweeping his shaggy hair back from his face, and looked for someone that he knew. Mrs Dellinger saw him wandering and called him over.

'I wasn't sure if you'd come,' she said.

'I never let a lady down,' he replied.

She smiled at him bashfully. 'You're such a charmer. Felicity,' she called. 'Felicity, there's someone I'd like you to meet.'

A woman in her mid twenties glided towards them, her pale pink dress long at the bottom and low at the top. Her breasts bounced prettily as she came over and smiled politely.

'Felicity,' Mrs Dellinger said. 'This is Rory Hamilton, a very dear friend of mine. And Rory, this is Felicity Thornton, another dear friend of mine.'

'Pleased to meet you.' Felicity offered her hand and Rory shook it gently.

'Oh, believe me,' he said. 'The pleasure is all mine.'

'Mr Hamilton was recommended to me by my niece,' Mrs Dellinger said. 'After my dear mother passed on. His words were such a comfort to me.'

'Ah,' Felicity smiled. 'You're the medium.'

'At your service.'

'I'm not sure that I require any of your services, Mr Hamilton.'

'Rory,' he said. 'And don't be too sure about that.' He tipped her a wink.

The women giggled and Felicity blushed. 'Don't let her husband hear that,' Mrs Dellinger said.

Rory took another sip of champagne. He was only here because Mrs

Dellinger had asked him to come and she was such a sweet lady. It was someone or others wedding anniversary. How many years? He didn't know. The name of the happy couple? Absolutely no idea. But the champagne was free.

'Rory's just about to begin his second tour with Gerald Wheatley,' Mrs Dellinger said. 'He's very good.'

Rory smiled modestly.

'Maybe I'll have to try you out, Mr Hamilton,' Felicity said.

'Anytime.'

'Mrs Dellinger,' a male voice called across the hall. 'The archery's about to start.'

Mrs Dellinger rolled her eyes. 'I'll be there in a minute, Larry. Tell them to start without me.' She turned back to Rory. 'Little men pretending to be hunter gatherers,' she said. 'Give them a bow and arrow and suddenly they're all Robin Hood.'

Rory laughed.

'Well, I'd better go and show my face,' she said. 'Anyone would think this was my party.'

'Archery?' Rory said as he watched Mrs Dellinger leave the room in a haze of silk and expensive perfume. 'What kind of weirdo's have archery contests at an anniversary party and no beer?'

'My parents,' Felicity replied curtly.

Rory slapped his forehead. 'Okay,' he said with a touch of embarrassment. He looked through the large French doors that opened onto the garden. A crowd had gathered to watch the archery and the grounds buzzed with conversation.

'How long have they been married?' Rory asked.

She looked at him with amazement. 'How did you ever get into this party?' she asked. 'You don't know them at all do you?'

288

'Ah, but I am friends with the lady of the house,' he replied. 'She invited me. Said I looked like I could do with a party. I think her idea of a party and my idea of a party are very different things.'

Felicity nodded knowingly. She took a sip of her champagne and turned her back on the garden, the click of her spike heels echoing as she walked across the room.

'Don't get me wrong,' she said. 'I like the big house in the country thing. It's just the people. Most of them are just pretending that they're something they're not.'

'And what does your husband think of all this?'

She turned to look at him with a cynical smile. 'He's lapping it up,' she said. 'He works hard, he does everything the right way. This is what he strives for. He's a good man. A good father. He's a provider.'

'How long have you been with him?' Rory asked.

'We've been married for three years,' she replied. 'We met at uni. He was studying law and I was doing a degree in fine art. Ian's a very successful barrister.'

'And what is it that you do?'

She looked slightly embarrassed. 'I look after our children,' she replied.

Rory raised an eyebrow. 'You went to university so you could be a housewife?' he asked.

'I believe that a mother should care for her children,' she replied. 'I wasn't going to put them with a nanny so that I could go to work.'

'That's a lovely sentiment,' Rory said. 'But you look like you're bored out of your mind.'

She looked around the room instead of at him. 'I'm fine,' she replied. 'It's not exactly what I expected from my life, but I'm content.'

Rory looked outside again, smiling to himself. Content was just another word for bored in his book. He looked at his watch. Ten past two. He bet he could have her dress off by three.

'Don't you wish you'd done more?' he asked. 'Seen more?'

'It must be difficult for you to understand,' she said after finishing what remained of her drink. 'You get to travel the country and meet lots of different people. You perform in front of audiences who adore you.' He loved it when they did his job for him. 'I suppose I look pretty boring compared to you.'

He shook his head and went to her. 'Pretty,' he said. 'But not boring.' She smiled again and he returned it. 'I'm sorry,' he said. 'I suppose we should go out and see how the boy's are doing.'

'I've got a better idea,' Felicity replied. 'Come on, I know where they hide the really good stuff.'

He followed her out of the hall and watched as she took off her shoes, dangling them from manicured fingers as she went down an old stone staircase into a dark cellar.

Rory saw the light switch at the top of the stairs and flipped it. He didn't want to be caught down here, especially not with a woman who had fallen and broken her neck. When he got to the bottom Felicity was already pulling bottles from the racks that lined the walls and reading the labels.

'Can you see the word Budweiser written on any of those?' he asked.

'No,' she grinned back at him. 'But I've found a really nice red if you fancy sharing it?'

She had found a corkscrew somewhere in the dimness of the room and opened the bottle expertly. Rory guessed that opening bottles of wine was something that she did a lot.

'Not really,' he said.

'Well there's no way I can drink the whole thing by myself,' she said. Rory disagreed but said nothing.

'Can't you just put the cork back in and put it back?' he asked.

'Of course I can't.'

'We could just throw it away.'

'Have you got any idea what this wine is worth?'

Rory shrugged. 'I think I'm out of idea's.'

He sat on the bottom step, the stone cold against him, She poured wine into her champagne flute and drank deeply. 'Just a small one?' she asked, waving the bottle at him. He drained his glass and raised it in acceptance of her offer. She shivered as she poured. The wine cellar was much cooler than the sun soaked rooms above ground.

'Cold?' he asked. She nodded and continued to sip at her wine. They couldn't go out to watch the archery with the stolen bottle and they both knew it. Rory smiled to himself. 'There's a room upstairs we can go to,' he suggested. 'It looks out over the back so we'll be able to see when they're coming back from their bows and arrows. We can go up there, have a drink and I'll put the evidence in my car when we're done.'

She smiled gratefully as he took the corkscrew from her, twisting the cork from its helter-skelter spike and slipping it into his pocket. 'Don't forget your shoes,' he reminded her. She picked them up as he collected the glasses and she allowed him to lead her upstairs. The room he had chosen was large, light and airy. Rory peeked outside from behind a heavy curtain and smiled. 'They still look pretty busy,' he said.

'Oh, they will be,' Felicity replied. 'I think after archery they're playing bowls. If they had horses no doubt they'd be jousting.'

'Bowls?' Rory asked. 'This has to be the most mind numbing party in the history of civilisation.'

Felicity topped up his glass. 'The masses seem to say otherwise,' she said. 'We're the only people who aren't enjoying ourselves.'

'I can think of much better ways to enjoy myself than playing giant darts.'

He'd thought that a bedroom would be too obvious. This room was . . . well, he didn't know what the hell it was. A table with a small radio on it and two

291

chairs sat almost ornamentally in one corner and an old cot stood against the far wall. Apart from that the room was bare. Mrs Dellinger had probably forgotten that it was even here.

They could hear the noise from the crowd outside. Muted cheers and chatter drifted up to them without intruding on the peaceful atmosphere of the simple room.

'How did you know about this room?' Felicity asked as she sat at the table. 'You must have been here quite a few times before.'

'I found it by chance the first time I was here,' he replied. 'I was looking for the toilet.'

'So you do come here a lot?'

'I was recommended to Mrs Dellinger by her niece,' he said. 'After my first visit she asked if I'd be interested in coming here one evening a month. She wanted to get a group of friends together, make a night of it. She said it was something different for them to do instead of their normal bridge nights. She's invited me to charity events and all kinds of stuff.'

'Do you make a lot of money?'

'Not at charity events,' he replied. 'But between us and the contacts we have I think we must have raised a hell of a lot of money for different charities.'

Felicity drank deeply and refilled her glass. 'Mrs Dellinger does do a lot for charity,' she said. 'Ian and I have been to events before. Never seen you though.'

'Unless you were interested in the kind of services that I offer then you wouldn't have.'

She shrugged. 'I suppose so.'

'See, while everyone else is enjoying the food and the wine, I'm shut away in a little room just doing my thing until it's time to go.'

'They just shut you away?'

'I need the quiet,' he replied.

'Where are you going after you've been here?' she asked. 'Are you staying for a while?'

'No,' he said. 'I'm going back up to Leeds tomorrow morning.' *So if you want it this is your one and only chance. And I know that you want it.*

'Oh,' she sounded disappointed.

'Are you okay?' Rory asked.

'Yeah,' she replied despondently. 'I just thought that if you were around for a few day's you could come and keep me company for a while. Sometimes the day's are so long.'

'I don't think your husband would approve of that.'

She rolled her eyes and took another long drink from the glass, topping it up and swallowing half of it again. 'He wouldn't notice if I stood naked on our roof and sang Rule Brittania.'

'I think you should slow down on the wine,' Rory said.

She looked at him with sad eyes. 'Mr Hamilton, you're right,' she said sadly. 'I should have done more with my life. Look at me, I'm twenty four years old, married with two children, and all I did before I met my husband was go to school. I've got no interesting stories to tell my grandchildren in years to come. My parents have been married for thirty years and they still adore each other. Me and Ian? It's only been three years and I just feel miserable.' She got up and went to the window, looking out at the smiling crowd below. 'I'm sorry,' she said, her back to her drinking partner. 'It's not your problem.'

Rory went to her and put his hands gently on her shoulders. 'First,' he said, 'it's Rory, not Mr Hamilton. And second, I don't want you to be miserable. You seem like a lovely girl, Felicity. You're intelligent, you're beautiful.'

She turned, almost colliding with him. 'You think I'm pretty?' she asked.

'Beautiful,' he replied.

She smiled warmly. 'I can see why Mrs Dellinger likes to have you around.'

He drank, remaining by the window as she went back to her seat. The

293

archery contest or whatever they called it was still ongoing. Some of the men out there were actually a pretty good shot. He turned his head as music filled the room. Felicity had turned on the radio and was attempting to tune it, trying to find a song she liked or could at least hear properly. Bryan Adams filled the room and Rory laughed quietly to himself at the irony; the song from the Robin Hood film playing while he screwed the wife of a man who was shooting arrows outside unawares.

Felicity sauntered over to him and put her hands against his chest. 'I love this song,' she said.

She ran her hand over his flat stomach, stopping at his belt, and withdrew it. She glanced out of the window and then back at Rory. 'They're going to be hours,' she said.

'Felicity, you've had a lot to drink,' he said. 'I'm not going to take advantage of you.'

She leaned in close to him as if the room was filled with people and whispered into his ear. 'Maybe *I* want to take advantage of *you,* Mr Hamilton.'

He smiled, finished his wine and went to the table, putting his glass down beside the radio and glancing at his watch. Not even half past two. He cleared his throat. Even if she was throwing herself at him after only twenty minutes, she had to know the rules before she played the game. 'Felicity, I'm very,' he ran his eyes over her, taking in every line, every curve, 'very attracted to you. But you have a husband and, and well, even if you didn't, I have to leave tomorrow. I want you, I really do, but I'm not going to mislead you. This is only going to happen once and then I'm gone.'

'You're killing the mood,' Felicity replied.

'I just don't want to hurt you,' he insisted. 'I'm not going to make out that I'll change your life just so I can get that dress off.'

She smiled. 'You're a good man, Rory,' she said. 'I wish I'd met you a few years ago.'

'No you don't,' he replied honestly.

She kissed him softly and his arms enveloped her. Her breasts pushed against him as another cheer rose from the crowd below. 'You'll make someone a good husband one day, Rory,' she whispered as he nuzzled against her neck, inhaling her perfume, kissing her throat gently.

'No I wont,' he replied absently.

Felicity pulled him to the floor, feeling the plush mauve carpet beneath her as he unhooked the delicate buttons of her dress with well practised fingers.

'Do you do this a lot, Rory?' she asked.

He didn't like to lie to anyone. 'No,' he said. It wasn't for him, it was for her. If he told her that yes, actually he did this sort of thing all the time, she would feel cheap and used. He didn't want her to feel like that. 'Do you?'

She smiled. 'I don't think that's any of your business,' she replied, pulling him to her and kissing him again.

As she pulled at his clothes, peeling off his jacket and popping the buttons of his shirt with an expert hand, she hummed along to the song that had replaced Bryan Adams on the radio as if she were inside her own little world and he was nothing more than something to pass the time. Rory didn't think that he was in any position to judge her motives. He kissed her throat again, almost losing himself in the subtle musk of her perfume, feeling the gentle vibrations of her trachea against his lips as she began to sing softly, turning soft rock into a sweet ballad.

His lips paused, hovering above her exposed throat. The words she was singing belonged to someone else. 'What did you say?' he asked.

She opened her eyes. 'I'm sorry, Rory,' she said. 'Am I distracting you?'

He shook his head and sat up, ears pricked, listening intently.

'Rory?' Felicity asked. 'Is something wrong?'

'Quiet,' he replied irritably. And there they were again. He knew those words, they meant something to him. 'What's this song?' he asked.

She looked hurt and confused. He rubbed her shoulders and tried to smile. 'I'm sorry,' he said.

'What's the matter, Rory?'

'Nothing.' The smiled felt artificial and it was clear from her expression that it looked that way too.

'It's Bon Jovi,' she said. 'It's My Life. Do you know it?'

'I know it,' he replied. 'Well, not really, but I know those words.'

As the chorus began for the third time the answer, previously floating beyond his reach, was caught. His eyes widened and Felicity began to look scared.

'Rory, can we . . .'

'I'm sorry, Felicity,' he said. 'I can't do this now.'

She looked down at her exposed breasts and pulled her dress together quickly. 'What do you mean?' she asked. 'What did I do?'

'Nothing,' he replied. 'You didn't do anything, Felicity. It's me.'

'But I . . .'

'I can't,' he said.

She looked around self consciously as she buttoned up her dress. Rory stood up, buttoning his shirt as he went to the table. 'I'm sorry, Felicity.'

She shook her head without looking at him and stood up. 'I'll let you get rid of the wine,' she mumbled sulkily.

'Okay,' he replied. He watched her slip on her shoes and walk to the door, pulling at the dress to make sure that it didn't look dishevelled as he sat by the radio. As her hand closed around the door handle she turned back to him. Her face was stony and set in an expression of controlled superiority. She looked as if she couldn't remember why she'd ever come here with him in the first place.

'You're going to regret turning me down for the rest of your life,' she said simply.

Rory doubted it but didn't say anything. A woman scorned and all that. He was silent until she closed the door behind her, then he released a sigh of relief and ran a hand over his face. He turned off the radio. How long had it been since he'd thought about Jess? Probably not as long as he thought it had been. He'd scribbled the words she'd recited that day in the car at the bottom of her note, only meaning to keep them as an experiment, just to see if the song ever would really materialise. He usually dug out her note in early November to place his bet; never a huge amount of money and always with a different bookie. Then the note went back to its place inside the old tobacco tin his granddad had passed on to him before he had died. He'd read those words every time he'd taken the note out and now they made him smile. He smiled because he could remember following her home from school. He smiled because he could remember her hunting high and low for him, desperate not to leave without saying goodbye to him. He smiled because once upon a time he had made her smile too.

He poured himself another glass of wine and raised a lonely toast to old friends.

2

Jess sat silently on the sofa and stared at the candle she had lit, the only light in the dark room. She poured a small measure of vodka into a tumbler and topped it up with coke before raising it to the candle in a toast.

'I'm sorry, Connie,' she said to the empty house.

It would have been her birthday. She would have been eighteen. Instead she was nothing but another body reduced to ash and scattered in the grounds of a crematorium.

This was worse. It was so much worse than last time. Last time she had been an innocent witness to all of this horror. However painful it had been to mourn before, the thought that she could have possibly saved her had only been a niggling regret at the back of her mind. Connie had chosen Trip, she would never have let Jess take her away from him. She even remembered wondering at the time that, if she'd known how it was going to end, would she have made more of an effort? Would she have told Jay about the drugs and not had to comfort him until he left, talking to Jess less and less because she only reminded him of his dead sister? Her innocent, fifteen year old brain had answered yes, but at the same time she had convinced herself that making more of an effort wouldn't have changed it. Connie would never have chosen her over Trip, and Jess had mused that hindsight was always a wonderful thing.

She swallowed half of the drink and put the glass down on to the table, thinking about her friend's smile, hating what had changed as much as what had not. Connie's death had remained the same. Her mothers had not. And what had any of the changes actually meant in the long run? Absolutely nothing. She was right back at square one without any idea of what she was supposed to be doing.

It was supposed to be different this time. The old bitch in the purple robe had told her as much. But even if she did manage to change things, for how long would her life be different? Both Connie and Dean had kept their appointments, would it be the same for her? Did she only have until the same time of that same day to just do what she could? If she left her dad and married Scott, would she still die then anyway? Well, if she did, if Scott was completely head over heels in love with her and they got married and then she died and it devastated him, that would serve him right. It would be payback.

But what if she didn't? If she changed things enough could she outlive herself? She remembered the day she had left The Unicorn, sitting in her room, smiling over the list that she had been writing out for Rory. The smile had faded as her pen hovered over the page. That was when she had remembered. She didn't know the next Christmas number one, couldn't remember the one after that either. Her focus had narrowed to the months between the last song she could remember and the first that she couldn't. The pen had fallen from her fingers and she had cried. She knew. She knew when.

If she chose not to walk into the Swanmore River would she live to be old and grey or would she somehow drown anyway? Keep her engagement in the same way that Dean had? But wasn't that half of the problem? She'd come back to Filton and instead of trying to sort her own life out she'd spent her time trying to save Dean. Should she have left him alone? Could she have left him alone? No. No way. She felt wretched but it would have been so much worse knowing that she had never even tried. If she'd been back in time she would have done exactly the same with Connie.

And Connie was going to be a vet. She had deserved to be saved.

Her head jerked up and she stared at the flame of the candle. Connie was going to be a vet. Going to be. That had been before Trip. If Jess had, by some miracle, managed to save her friends life, did she honestly believe that Connie would have just given up the drugs, given up Trip and gone back to being good old wannabe vet Connie? The flame danced in her glassy eyes. Her cheeks burned. She knew Connie better than anyone and she knew Connie would never have given up on Trip. She would have always have been blinkered, convincing herself that he would change, that she just had to be patient. Would wannabe vet Connie have been just one more bad statistic, a disappointment to her family for the rest of her life? Jess couldn't see how not.

Suddenly the flame seemed to be watching her, listening to her thoughts, judging her. Would trying to save Connie have been a waste of her time, regardless of whether she had lived or died?

Scott. It always came back to Scott.

Was she making the same mistake with him? Was she trying to save something that couldn't be saved? Her dad or her fiancé? Had that choice ever mattered?

She finished her drink in a large, gulping swallow and considered pouring another, larger shot of vodka into the glass. She resisted, taking the glass into the kitchen and filling it with water before she went back to the sofa.

Okay, so instead of staying with her dad, she marries Scott. What changes? She considered the question for a moment, closing her eyes, taking a drink, staring around the room as if the answer might be scrawled on one of the walls. It wasn't. She didn't know. Had she imagined that decision to be so important simply because of what had happened after her dad had died? Maybe.

So, she's living with Scott, maybe they had a couple of kids, everything's peachy. And then one day her dad gets really ill. He needs urgent medical assistance. What happens? How does he get it? If he'd been capable of phoning for an ambulance himself he would have done it before she'd arrived home with the shopping.

So he's ill, really ill, and she's halfway across the estate watching Spongebob with her kids, living happily ever after with Scott.

'I wouldn't have been there,' she told the silent room. But the result would have been the same. Whether she'd been there or not her dad would have died. But how would she have know that?

If she'd married Scott and her dad had died, alone on the living room floor, the blood that had spewed from his mouth at the time of his second heart attack dry on his face and sticking him to the carpet, could she ever have forgiven herself for not being there? Would Scott's support have been enough? She had an awful feeling that the answer to both of these questions was no.

And then she would have regretted leaving her dad to marry Scott. She would have regretted it for the rest of her life.

Suddenly the decision that she had previously assumed had defined her seemed decidedly unimportant. The result would be the same. Her dad would die and she would be inconsolable. With or without Scott she would be alone.

And where did she really want to be? Was she in love with Scott? She didn't know. Sometimes she adored him. Other times she didn't. Was the idea that she was supposed to be with him influencing how she felt? Shouldn't she only be with him if she was certain that she loved him and not because she felt like that was what she should be changing?

Her head hurt. She wished that this could have happened to Connie. If Connie had been given a second chance then surely she would have avoided Trip and made something of herself.

Jess closed her eyes, trying to focus her mind on the here and now rather than the past and the what if's. She needed to stop thinking about other people. It didn't matter why someone else hadn't gotten this chance, it mattered that she had. This was happening to her. Not to her dad or Scott or Connie. Her. Jess. And that was exactly who she needed to be thinking about. Instead of constantly feeling sorry for herself she needed to make the most of the opportunity.

She went to the front door, opening it, allowing the world in, challenging it to do its' worst. How would she feel if, when it came to her time to die again, the only thing she had done with her life was chase her own tail? She stared the world in the face, defiant and determined.

An old woman walked by the house, heavy with shopping, bent and slow. Compared to her, Jess was vibrant. Compared to every other person in the world, Jess was gifted. She knew where her life would lead her if she took a certain path. Things had to change. She had already wasted enough time.

3

'Good morning, birthday girl,' Paul called cheerily as he poked his head around Jess's bedroom door.

She opened one eye and aimed it at him. 'Time is it?' she asked.

'Almost eight.'

She groaned and rolled over, pulling the cover over her head. Paul went to the bed and sat down. 'You can't go back to sleep, I'm halfway through cooking breakfast.'

She didn't reply.

'Jess?' He shook her gently. 'Jess, wake up.'

'Tired,' she protested.

'You've got cards and presents to open and your friends will be here soon.'

Jess rolled onto her back and pushed the cover down to her chin. 'You're not going to give up are you?' she asked. Paul shook his head. 'I'll be down in five minutes,' she submitted.

Paul grinned and kissed her forehead. 'Happy birthday, sweetheart.' Then he left her to wake up. She turned on the bedside lamp and looked at the clock. Seven thirty. She scowled.

She forced herself out of bed and glanced at her reflection in the mirror. Her hair stuck out at the gravity defying angles only sleep could create. What she would give for a pair of GHD's. She stretched, yawned and looked back at the bed. Just another half an hour? She knew that it wasn't a real choice. If she wasn't downstairs in five minutes he'd be back up. She went to the bathroom and cleaned her teeth on autopilot. The water spotted mirror over the sink told her to go back to bed. Her eyes were still half closed. She tried to flatten down her hair with her free hand but ended up making it look like she had just perched a squashed birds' nest on top of her head. She wandered back to her room, still massaging her gums with the toothbrush, and tried to drag a brush

303

through her hair. Nope. She was going to need two hands. Paul called up the stairs and she mumbled through a mouthful of toothpaste that she was up. She spat and rinsed and then spent a few minutes getting her hair back to something that resembled its normal shape before she went downstairs.

'Happy birthday, sweetheart,' Paul said again as he gave her a hug.

She giggled and rubbed her still sleepy eyes. 'Thanks, dad.'

Her cards were on the table. Two white envelopes and one that was pale blue. Paul had already made coffee and hers sat in front of a small box that looked as if it had half a roll of sellotape wrapped around it. She could see her face strangely reflected in the metallic silver wrapping paper.

'Open your cards,' Paul said excitedly as he brought a plate of bacon and sausage through and put it next to a plate of buttered bread. 'Sausage and bacon sarnies,' he announced, just in case she couldn't make out what the blackened food was. Jess covered her bacon in brown sauce and started to eat.

'Open your cards,' Paul said again.

'Anyone would think it was your birthday,' Jess smiled.

'You haven't noticed have you?' Paul swallowed and pointed at the envelopes. 'There's three.'

She looked at the cards and then took another bite of her sandwich. 'So?' she shrugged.

'So, how many birthday cards should you have gotten through the post?'

'I don't know.'

'Yes you do,' Paul looked at her like she was stupid and she frowned back at him. 'One,' he said. 'From gran and granddad Baker.' He fingered the two white envelopes. 'That one's from me and that one's in your gran's handwriting.'

Jess wiped her hands on her pyjama bottoms. 'So?'

'So who's the other one from?'

She shrugged. 'Go on.'

'Well, I don't know, do I?' Paul looked at her eagerly. 'Open it.'

'I think I'll wait until Scott gets here before I open them,' she teased.

'Open it now, open it now.' Paul wiped away a stray dribble of brown sauce from his chin and sucked it from his finger.

She picked up the envelope and looked at it. She didn't recognise the handwriting. She finished her sandwich and opened the card from her dad. It was something predictably sentimental about what a wonderful daughter she was. She kissed him and stood the card up on the table. Gran and granddad Baker's was the same, although they told her what a wonderful granddaughter she was and had slipped a twenty inside.

'Don't forget to ring and thank them,' Paul said.

'I wont.' Jess picked up the blue envelope and waved it at him. 'Time to find out what's behind door number three.'

She turned the envelope over and tore it open. 'Happy birthday to a very special friend,' she read before opening the card. Instead of a tacky verse the inside of the card was filled with large, rushed strokes of slanted handwriting. She didn't read any of it, she only wanted a name. 'Your friend,' She put a hand to her mouth, which was slowly curving into a bright smile. 'Oh my god.'

'Who?' Paul asked urgently.

She looked up at him. This was a conversation she didn't really want to have. But then what harm could it do now? She scanned the card. There was no phone number, no return address. 'It's from Rory.'

Paul's shoulder's slumped. He'd been waiting to find out who the card was from and now he hadn't got a clue who it was anyway. 'Who's Rory?' he asked.

'Just someone I knew when I lived at gran's.'

'You never mentioned a Rory to me,' Paul replied, sounding a little put out. 'I knew who all your friends were.'

'You made it your business to know who all my friends were,' she corrected.

'Right,' Paul pointed at the card. 'And there was no mention of any Rory. What was he? A boyfriend you were hiding from me?'

'No.'

'What does Rory have to say for himself?' he asked.

Jess looked through what he'd written as quickly as she could to make sure there was nothing that would lead to an even harder conversation with her dad. She should have known better. Rory had covered himself well. Her dad would read it completely differently to how she would read it. She smiled again.

'Jessie,' she read. 'I hope you're well. I'm sorry that I didn't contact you sooner but you know I had to stay away. I just wanted you to know that I haven't forgotten about you or the times we talked. You're a very special person, Jessie, don't waste what you've got.'

'Rory,' Paul said to himself. 'Did I know him?'

'You knew of him,' she replied cryptically.

'Did he go to school with you?'

'Why don't you just ask me who he was instead of trying to guess?'

Paul quickly rolled a cigarette and lit it. 'Go on then.'

'If you start shouting at me I'm going back to bed.'

His eyes narrowed. 'That means you're expecting me to shout at you.'

'Promise you wont?' she asked.

'I promise I'll try not to.'

She sighed. 'Rory came to The Unicorn with his dad,' she explained. 'You remember when people kept saying they saw ghosts and stuff?'

'The psychic?' Paul cried with outrage. 'You went behind my back, Jess?'

'I'm not going to sit here and justify my actions to you,' she shot back. 'I can't change what happened and I'm not going to sit here and argue about it when there's no point.'

'What did happen?' Paul's voice was quieter now, apprehensive.

Jess actually felt a little sorry for him. Here he was trying to protect his daughter and she had defied him at every turn. Worse than that, she had lied to him. Was still lying to him every day.

'Nothing,' she replied. 'Well, nothing for you to worry about.' She made another sandwich and took a large bite out of one side. The bacon was beginning to cool.

'I'll decide what I should be worrying about, Jessica.'

She took a swallow of coffee. 'He helped me with my homework,' she said. 'I was really struggling in English. He did me a favour.'

'Did you give him this address?'

She nodded. 'We were friends, dad,' she said.

'Just friends?' he asked, his eyes asking what he really wanted to know. Jess remembered being so close to him in the back of the car, waiting for him to kiss her across the darkness. She nodded.

'What else does he say?'

'I hope you have a great birthday. I'll have a drink for you. If you're going to have a drink just make sure you don't end up having another night like that party we went to at Anna's. Miss you, Jessie, keep smiling. Your friend, Rory Hamilton.'

Paul raised an eyebrow at the mention of Anna's party.

'Haven't we all had one too many at some point in our lives?' Jess asked sardonically.

'Are you going to thank him?' Paul asked apprehensively.

'Don't worry, dad,' she replied. 'No return address, no phone number.'

'You look sad,' Paul observed.

Jess looked again at Rory's card and put it with the others on the table. 'It would have been nice to speak to him,' she said.

Paul looked at the card with mixed emotion. He was sad because his daughter was sad. And he'd seen the look on her face when she'd seen the name on the card. She'd looked so happy. The kind of happy he knew she

307

reserved for friends and not her old dad. He had felt jealous that anyone could light up her eyes that way and was glad that Rory hadn't given her any contact information. He was having enough problems with Snot. Stupid Snot who he knew would one day take his daughter away from here to a place where she would have daughters of her own.

His baby girl was eighteen years old. Despite her protests he had managed to convince her that she shouldn't leave school after her GCSE's and soon she would have three A Levels to her name. Little Jessica was all grown up with a bright future ahead of her, turning into a woman before his eyes. She looked so much like her mother.

His thoughts were broken by a knock at the door and he remembered the sausages that he'd left in the oven to keep warm. 'That'll be your friends,' he said as he got up, clearing away what remained of their private breakfast. 'I'll go and get the sausages, you get the door.'

Karen gave her a tight squeeze on the way in, followed by Joanne and Scott. 'Happy birthday, Jess.'

This was it. This was her friends. Scott was her boyfriend so he didn't really count. Karen was more her dad's friend than hers, and Joanne was only here because Scott was. Jessica Morgan didn't have any friends. Yes, she could have done with a nice long chat with Rory about the way things had turned out.

'Morning, Paul,' Karen said as she went into the kitchen. 'Do you want some help?'

'You can butter me some more bread if you don't mind.'

'Happy birthday, babe,' Scott kissed Jess briefly and Joanne scowled. 'Did you get anything good?'

'Twenty quid off my gran.'

'What's that?' Joanne asked as she looked at the unopened gift on the table.

Jess smiled. It was the best birthday present her dad had ever given to her and she wanted to open it with only him by her side. 'I'll open it later,' she said. It was a ring. Tarnished silver inlaid with three hearts.

Scott and Joanne sat down with her and handed over their cards and gifts. She opened Joanne's card first. She had left the price tag on.

'Thank you,' Jess said politely.

Paul brought a fresh plate of sausages through and put them down on the table. Karen followed with more bread and butter.

Joanne sat back on the sofa, unimpressed. 'I'm vegetarian,' she said.

Paul hurried back to the kitchen and reappeared a minute later with a smaller plate which he put it in front of Joanne. Jess put her hand over her mouth to prevent herself from laughing. A huge lettuce leaf sat on the plate with a cherry tomato on top.

Joanne looked first at the plate and then at Paul. 'I had cereal before I came out,' she said, handing it back to him.

Jess and her dad exchanged amused glances as Paul shrugged and took the food back into the kitchen.

Jess opened Scott's card next. It was beautifully sentimental, splashed with tiny red hearts. Paul screwed up his nose and looked out of the window. No doubt he'd written something suitably slushy inside which would make Jess smile and earn him a kiss of appreciation.

'Oh, Scott, that's lovely,' Jess said as she leaned over and planted a kiss on his cheek. Paul rolled his eyes. As she took his gift he went back to the kitchen. He had noticed that she hadn't opened his yet. The silver package sat forgotten on the table. She didn't need her dad now, she had her friends – and Snot.

The sharp intake of breath from his daughter made his head turn and he went back quickly to peer over the sofa.

A ring?!

Scott smiled. 'Before you start thinking it's an engagement ring, it isn't,' he said quickly. 'It's an eternity ring.'

Jess took it out of the box and slid it onto her finger. 'It's beautiful, Scott.'

309

'You're beautiful,' he replied.

Karen looked through Jess's cards as the couple embraced. Paul felt sick jealousy wrapping itself around his heart.

'Who's Rory?' Karen asked.

Paul could have kissed her. The look on Snot's face was a picture. He took a ringside seat in his old chair.

'He's someone I knew when I lived at gran's,' Jess replied innocently.

Karen smiled as she read the card. 'Well, he likes you, doesn't he?'

Scott stood up and peered over Karen's shoulder at Rory's message. 'You never told me about him,' he said.

'I never told you about any of my other friend's either.'

'Were you two an item?' Joanne asked.

'No.'

'Just a fling then?'

'It was nothing like that.'

Joanne grinned. 'Yeah, right. You're only saying that because Scott's here.'

'I'm going to get dressed.' Jess stalked out of the room and up the stairs. As soon as she had left the room Joanne started to laugh.

'Shut up, Joanne,' Karen said.

Joanne looked up at her with innocent eyes. 'I didn't do anything.'

'They were just friends,' Paul defended, knowing that the damage was already done. Scott was flushed and quiet.

'A boy and a girl?' Joanne asked. 'How can a boy and a girl just be friends?'

Paul looked at her and then switched his gaze to Scott. 'Something I should know?' he asked.

Joanne looked at Scott, embarrassed. 'We used to go out,' she said. 'That's different.'

'Really?' Paul shook his head at her and went to check on Jess as Joanne took the card from her sister and read it.

310

'Rory Hamilton?' she asked, looking at Karen with big eyes. 'As in *the* Rory Hamilton?'

Karen shrugged. 'Who's *the* Rory Hamilton?'

Joanne looked at the card again and then at Scott. He was frowning at her.

'Oh my god,' Joanne said. 'Don't any of you read the papers?'

Karen was frowning as well now. Paul came back to his chair and lit a cigarette.

'Paul, do you know who this Rory Hamilton is?' Karen asked.

'Yeah,' he said with mild annoyance. 'It's one of them psychics we told to stay away from Jess when she lived with Jean.'

Joanne laughed excitedly. 'No way that's a coincidence,' she grinned.

Scott looked concerned now but he said nothing. He liked to say as little as possible whenever he was anywhere near Paul.

'If it's the same psychic Rory Hamilton that's been in the papers, I want his phone number,' Joanne said.

'What?' Paul asked. 'Why's he been in the papers?' He picked up his Telegraph and started to rifle through it. He couldn't see anything with Rory's name on it.

'He's been on tour with another psychic,' Joanne explained, 'and loads of girls have been in the paper saying he took them back to his hotel room afterwards. I mean, he's gorgeous, you wouldn't say no, but he's got a bit of a bad reputation. It's in today's paper,' she said as if they should all know exactly what she was talking about. She began to rifle through her bag for this mornings Sun.

Scott snatched the card from Joanne, reading it again. *You're very special. I haven't forgotten about you or the times we talked.*

Paul didn't like what he was hearing, but the look on Scott's red face was priceless. He smiled to himself as Jess came back downstairs and helped herself to a sausage, nibbling obliviously as she sat beside Scott. He put the

311

card back onto the table with artificial nonchalance.

'Is this the Rory you know?' Joanne asked as she spread the newspaper over Jess's lap. Jess chewed as she stared down at the pictures. One was a publicity shot of Rory dressed in a black suit and tie and a long black wool coat. He was standing in a darkened street with yellow lamplight over his left shoulder and mist swirling around his feet. The second was a picture of him with the girl who had contacted the newspaper to tell them all about her sex life. The photograph had apparently been taken by a friend only three hours before she was 'seduced' by the psychic. She was a pretty girl. Long dark hair fell over her shoulders and her blue eyes sparkled with excitement. It was the kind of picture you saw of a groupie meeting their favourite rock star. The third was older. It was the Rory that Jess saw in her head when she thought about him. His smile was full of boyish charm and youthful optimism. Taken just before his first tour according to the newspaper.

Scott hated the smile that touched her lips.

'Is it him?' Karen asked.

Jess nodded. She was looking at the centre picture now, another shot of the girl, Donna Reed, wearing a skirt that showed off her long legs. She scanned the parts of the story that stood out in bold black print.

Donna tells how:

Psychic lied about message he had received for her from 'the other side'.

Hamilton took her for meal to 'apologise' for losing psychic connection before passing message on.

Seduced her with champagne and ghost stories before taking her back to his hotel.

Further down:

'I didn't think he would be the type to just throw me out in the morning.'

'I felt used and stupid for believing what he'd said to me the night before.'

Paul was standing behind the sofa now, reading over his daughter's shoulder.

'Donna is the latest in a string of girls who have told us how Hamilton tricked them into bed using the same story each time,' he read aloud. 'Something that ironically seems to have made him even more popular with the ladies.'

Jess started to chew at her fingernails as she tried to understand how this Rory could be the same person she had met at The Unicorn.

'I suppose the most pathetic thing is that if I could go back and do it again, I would,' confesses busty Donna from Hertfordshire.

'You know as well as I do that these papers only print what they feel like,' she said, unsure who she was trying to convince.

'Looks pretty bad from where I'm standing,' Paul replied. 'His parents must be so proud.'

She flashed a tired scowl at his sarcasm. She bet that Russ Hamilton wasn't proud at all. Russ Hamilton would probably be sitting in his own living room, shaking his head as he read all about what his son and Busty Donna From Hertfordshire had been up to. Then he'd probably pick up the phone and ask his son what the hell he thought he was playing at.

'Have you read this?' Paul asked, poking at the page. 'Most of the conversation was one sided, says Donna. He talked about his tour, his charity work, his childhood and a pub in Yorkshire he worked at that was reportedly haunted by more than five ghosts.' He looked at Jess. 'That's got to be The Unicorn, hasn't it?' he asked before going back to the paper. 'This tale of a haunted pub appears to be a favourite of Mr Hamilton's. Six of the girls that have contacted us mention the same story.'

Joanne pointed at the bottom corner of the page. 'Read this,' she said to Jess. 'He's on tour at the moment. He's got tickets left for the last night on the twenty third. It's local. If I phone the box office as soon as they open I reckon we can still get tickets.'

313

Jess was his friend. Jess could get her access to Rory Hamilton. Joanne was close to pleading with her to say that she would to go.

Jess's head was spinning. Rory Hamilton? She closed her eyes, trying so hard to remember.

'Book the tickets, Joanne,' she said, handing her the twenty from her grandparents. 'Just make sure I get my change.'

'The twenty third?' Scott asked.

As Joanne squealed excitedly something caught in Jess's mind. Rory Hamilton? The twenty third? Had that really been the gig she'd wanted to go to? She tried to remember exactly who it was that had invited her to go out that night.

Carla Hargreaves. A girl she had studied A Level biology with. And Susan something or other. Susan . . . oh for god's sake, why couldn't she remember?

Her mum had seen Gerald Wheatley before.

Jess put her hands over her eyes. Hadn't her gran mentioned Gerald Wheatley? Jess had been intrigued but had turned down Carla's offer of a ticket. Why?

Because they were going to see Gerald on the twenty third.

Because of Scott.

They'd only been going out for a few weeks. Scott had been going to Spain with his parents for a long weekend to look at a house they were interested in buying. Carla had asked if Jess wanted to go to see Gerald Wheatley but she'd turned it down because it would be the last night she'd get to spend with Scott before he left. But they had argued. Jess couldn't remember why but she was sure that it had been something to do with her dad. Well, it usually was.

She hadn't gone to see Gerald and Rory because she had wanted to stay with Scott. The argument had happened on the twenty second. She remembered it so clearly because . . .

Scott, Scott, Scott, she thought as she glanced at him. He looked annoyed.

314

He didn't want her anywhere near Rory. He believed what the papers were saying.

Would that same argument happen this time?

When she'd gone home that night she had intended to call Carla in the morning and find out if they could get an extra ticket. She had carelessly kicked off her shoes as she stomped upstairs to bed and her dad hadn't noticed them when he'd jogged downstairs in the morning. Then the days had been filled with hospitals and tests and bad news about his back. Everything else had been forgotten.

She hadn't been friends with Carla and Susan this time. This time she had sat beside Scott Jordan in all of her A Level classes and had never even thought about them. This time it was Joanne that had asked if she wanted to go to see Gerald Wheatley.

To see Rory Hamilton.

It wasn't about seeing Gerald this time, they were going because of Rory.

It could just be a coincidence.

Maybe she should have said no.

4

The foyer buzzed with pre-show chatter as people fanned through large black programmes and waited for the auditorium doors to open. Jess thought the programmes were strange, as if they had come to see Medium: The Musical, or something. Others stood around the bar, talking and occasionally glancing at their watches.

'Hi,' she smiled sweetly as she approached the man at the security desk. 'My name's Jessica Morgan. I'm not sure if it's you I need to talk to, but I'm a friend of Rory Hamilton's and I wondered if you could let him know I'm here?'

The man raised his eyebrows. 'I'm sorry,' he said. 'Nobody gets through that door,' he pointed at a heavy grey door beside the stairs that led upstairs to the auditorium, 'unless their name's on my list. And your name is not on my list. In fact, I don't have a list, so today nobody gets through that door.'

She smiled again. 'If you just ask him, he'll tell you.'

He lifted up papers and the telephone from the desk, looked beneath them and then put them back down again. 'Nope,' he said as he shook his head, 'no list. You remember what that means?'

Prick. Her smile disappeared.

'Look, he's been here for four nights and for four nights I've had girls trying to get through that door.' He smiled derisively at her. 'And my orders are that unless I've been told, in advance, that someone should be allowed to see him, nobody goes through that door.'

'Excuse me,' a petite blonde leaned on the desk and held an envelope out to the security guard. 'Could you please see that Rory Hamilton gets this?'

He took the envelope and smiled at her. 'Of course I can,' he said amiably. The girl thanked him and went to the bar. As soon as her back was turned the smile fell from his face and he tossed the envelope into a small metal bin beneath the desk. Jess looked at him with outrage. He shrugged.

'I have to see him,' she said desperately.

'There'll be none of this when Death of a Salesman opens here next week,' he said to himself as he rolled his eyes.

'I swear he'll know who I am.'

'No.' He sounded bored.

'If you just ask him,' she persisted.

The phone rang and he looked at her as if to say that he was very sorry that he couldn't continue this conversation with her before answering it quickly.

She turned, beaten, and went to the bar.

'Wouldn't he let you through?' Karen asked.

She shook her head and sighed.

'Let's go and get our seats,' Karen said.

They all went into the auditorium and Karen sat between Joanne and Jess. The three of them hardly spoke for the twenty minutes before the house lights went down. Jess was sulking, trying to work out how she could get to see Rory without calling out to him when he came out on stage.

When the lights did go down, heavy red curtains swept back, revealing Rory, dressed in a black suit with an equally black shirt, open at the throat, standing tall and proud. He looked good on the stage; as comfortable and confident as ever. The audience erupted into cheers and applause filled the room. Jess couldn't help but smile. She felt like a proud parent. All that noise, all for him.

'What would you do if he spoke to your mum?' Joanne whispered across at Jess.

Karen's heart froze in her chest. What the hell would she do if that happened? But surely Rory wasn't in a position to start accusing her of driving a woman to suicide?

'No idea,' Jess replied after considering the question for a moment. Although that would give her a chance to talk to him. Was that what this was about, if it was about anything? Closure on her mum's death?

'Thank you,' Rory said, hushing the crowd. 'You're very kind.'

He paced the stage as he talked, sometimes looking out at his audience, sometimes looking at the floor. His hands remained in the pockets of his black trousers as he spoke. 'Okay, how many of you have seen me before?'

Arms rose all around the room and he looked out at them, squinting in the bright stage lights. 'Welcome back,' he nodded. 'For those of you who haven't seen me before but may have seen Mr Wheatley, you should know that I work a little differently to him. I don't sugar coat what comes through. I'm not stupid, I wont say anything to embarrass you too badly and I'll try my best not to upset anyone, but I'm not going to tell you that whoever says they love you just because I think that's what you want to hear. I had a grandfather who couldn't complete a sentence without swearing and if someone told me that they had him on the psychic hotline and never swore once, I'd call them a liar. I am merely a messenger. It's not for me to decide how and when messages should be edited.'

He stopped pacing momentarily, took his hands out of his pockets, cocked his head to the side for a moment as if he was listening to something nobody else could hear, and then began to pace again.

'If you believe that I'm talking to you, please raise your hand and we'll get a mic over to you as quick as we can. Once I start to receive information it tends to come through quite quickly, so you might get bombarded with questions. Don't feel intimidated, answer me honestly and tell me to slow down if you need me to. I don't want information from you, so yes and no answers are fine in most cases.'

Jess didn't think he'd paused for breath and only now realised that she was still smiling like a proud parent.

'Okay,' Rory said. 'So let's kick off.'

Jess watched, as hypnotised by him as everyone else. He commanded the

318

stage like a showman but spoke to everyone like they were old friends. It was easy to see why those girls had gone back to his dressing room. And once they were there, with all of his attention focused on them and them alone, how could they ever have said no?

She blinked hard, reminding herself that it was her friend up there that she was practically slobbering over. As she looked back at him he finished talking to an old man with tears coursing over his gaunt face as he passed a microphone back to a girl in a black tee shirt. Around Jess, the audience began to applaud.

5

Flopping down heavily into the high backed leather armchair, Rory lit a cigarette and smiled. This was what he looked forward to at the end of the working day; the leather chair that sat in every dressing room at every venue. It had belonged to his father for eighteen years before Rory had inherited it. He smoked indulgently, sitting quietly in the chair which had once stood in their living room, almost comically out of place among the battered third hand leather sofa and mismatched chairs of varying ages and stages of disrepair.

Rory had only been small when it had arrived at the house. Six or seven maybe. His parents had argued in the kitchen where they thought that he couldn't hear and he'd sat on the living room floor, staring up at the new chair in its polythene shroud.

'Three hundred pounds on a chair?' His mother was close to tears. 'We could have got a new sofa for that.'

'It spoke to me, Lou,' Russ reasoned quietly.

'Well, now I'm speaking to you. You take it back.'

Nothing for a moment. Russ knew that she was right. Of course she was right. And he hated to see her cry.

'Louise, please,' he said, almost begging. 'Do you think I'd spend this amount of money on something just because I felt like it?'

'That's exactly what you *have* done.' A strangled screech as she battled the heat at the back of her throat.

Rory went to the chair, a new toy for him to play with. He reached underneath the polythene, pulling it up far enough for him to climb into its' monstrous leather lap. He slid comfortably into the cool dent made by over a hundred years of use and his head suddenly became full of disembodied whispers, too many to understand. His heart seemed to stop as fear began to course through him.

320

His slid quickly from beneath the polythene, escaping from the dead conversation and stood, staring open mouthed at the chair for a second or two before his mouth widened and he began to cry loudly for his mother.

As his cries reached her ears she sighed. 'I'm not talking about it anymore.' She swept her hair away from her forehead as Rory would when he was older. 'You take it back tomorrow and that's the end of it.'

They both went to the living room, glancing at each other fearfully when they saw their son. Rory stood with his back pressed tight up against the wall opposite the new chair. He was staring at it with wide, watery eyes and sobbing hard.

His mother crossed the room and swept him up in her arms, turning his face away from the chair and looking uncertainly at it herself. 'Shh,' she soothed as she stroked his soft hair. 'What's the matter, baby?'

He was sobbing too hard to answer and made only loud vowel sounds as he tried to explain. 'Air, air,' he wept.

Both parents frowned at each other. Russ could see his wife was struggling not to cry herself and stepped in, taking the boy from her arms and crossing to the new chair to sit down with Rory in his lap. He was getting too heavy to carry around. As he bent to sit, the boy let out a long scream, squirming to release himself from his father's arms.

His mother saw what was happening and raised an eyebrow. 'Even he knows you shouldn't have bought the damn thing,' she said before she turned and left the room.

'What's the matter, Rory?' his father asked, settling for the sofa.

Rory glanced at the chair and then turned his face up to his father's, trying to control his snatched breathing.

'Chair spoke to me.' He almost whispered, as if he didn't want the chair spirits to overhear. Cold fingers tickled Russ's spine.

'What?' he asked.

321

'People talking in the chair.' Rory risked another quick glance at the polythene shrouded monster. 'No faces, just voices in my ear.'

Rory crushed out his cigarette in a small glass ashtray in front of the dressing room mirror. That had been the day he had found out that his father could hear the dead, and that this macabre talent had apparently been passed on to him. That had ensured that the chair stayed, outliving every other piece of furniture before Rory had asked if he could take it on tour with him. His father had agreed. The chair had stayed because of Rory and really it belonged to him.

It was because of his dad that he was where he was today. And Gerald. Don't forget Gerald. And tonight had been another triumph. Everything was perfect and now he could just relax and revel in another moment of unequivocal success.

Except he couldn't.

Not really.

He enjoyed it too much. Enjoyed the thunderous applause and deafening cheers. After the show was over he was always left with excess adrenaline.

'Rory?' Adam's voice from outside the dressing room.

'Come in,' Rory called.

Adam entered the dressing room head first, peeking around the door as if to check that the coast was clear before bringing in the rest of his overweight body. 'Are you going out for autographs tonight?' he asked. 'We've got ourselves quite a crowd by the stage door.'

'Any of them my type, Adam?'

Adam rolled his eyes. That meant no autographs. Again. 'Same as usual. A few trying to get in without us knowing about it. Couple who say they know you personally and just want to talk about old times. Most of them aren't old enough to know what old times are.' He shook his head. 'What do you want me to do, boss?'

Rory smiled crookedly and brushed his hair away from his forehead. 'Same

322

as Friday,' he said. 'Need to get rid of some of this tension, man.'

He lit another cigarette and offered one to Adam, who shook his head. 'Give me five minutes to get this make up off my face then go fetch this dog a bone.'

He snatching a cleansing wipe from the table and went to the small adjoining shower room, swiping unsuccessfully at his face. 'You'd better make that ten,' he said. 'That girl ought to hire me an industrial sander to get this crap off.'

Adam smirked and left the room. Strolling down the corridor to the stage door, he sighed. He had a good job and he knew it. But he hated this part. Most would be disappointed but just go away. Some might shout about how they'd paid their money and wanted to see him. He'd only been spat at once. By a middle aged woman in a boob tube. He shuddered at the memory.

He wished he was at home with his boyfriend, listening to him talk about his day. He'd be disgusted if he knew that taking girls to Rory was part of Adam's job. He spent his days counselling the bereaved, helping them to move on after the death of loved ones. Adam spent his time using the death of loved ones to lure young women into his friend's dressing room.

'Is he coming out tonight?' Gerald asked as he stepped out into the corridor. A white towel hung over his meaty shoulders.

'You're the psychic,' Adam teased. 'You tell me.' He didn't care very much for Gerald.

Gerald nodded. 'Very clever.'

'He's feeling tired,' Adam lied. 'Wants to rest a while.'

'Like he did on Friday? The noise I heard when I went past there I doubt very much that anyone was resting.'

'Haven't got a clue what you're talking about, Gerald,' Adam replied innocently.

'After everything the papers have already got hold of, hasn't he learned his lesson?'

'Like I said, Gerald, I haven't got a clue what you're talking about.'

323

Gerald wiped his face with the towel, shaking his head as Adam walked on.

'Stupid old fart,' he muttered to himself as he approached the door that separated him from the crowd. He could almost smell them. Maybe they could smell him too; his fear, his distaste.

He opened the door, stepped out into the crowd, and pulled it shut, listening for the click that promised it was locked behind him. He quickly scanned the people before him. Nobody immediately looked like trouble, but you could never be too careful. There was always someone prepared to shoot the messenger.

Behind the crowd was the bar. Three girls sat together at a table close to the toilets. *Bingo Bongo,* Adam thought. *We have a winner.* The key to this unenviable task was to locate and approach the intended target as quickly as possible. This meant identification of a willing subject that fit Rory's preferences with the speed of a tranquiliser dart. Sometimes this was much easier said than done but on this occasion he seemed to have luck on his side.

'I'm terribly sorry to keep you waiting,' he started. The crowd, mainly women, most below average looking, stopped their excited chatter and turned to stare at him. 'But Mr Hamilton isn't feeling well.' The whole thing sounded flat and rehearsed. 'I'm afraid he wont be out to see anyone tonight.' The news was met with the usual groans and mumbles of disappointment. 'However, any requests or questions can be submitted to Rory via our website and they will be responded to by Mr Hamilton personally.'

The crowd stood, stupid and slack-mouthed, for a few moments before it began to break up. It always made Adam smile. Nobody ever asked if Rory was okay, they didn't care.

Adam watched his target as she rose from the table, looking over and seeming disappointed that Rory hadn't materialised. Bonus. He almost tripped on an overturned stool as he went to her table. Her two companions looked at him with interest.

324

'I'm sorry to disturb you,' he said politely. 'My name is Adam and I've been sent by Mr Hamilton. He believes that he has a message for you but thought it would be best to speak to you about it in private.' The whole thing sounded as flat as the groan speech he had given to the crowd. 'I do have identification if you have any concerns.'

Jess beamed and shook her head. Rory did remember her. That stupid man had spoken to him earlier and Rory had sent this Adam out to find her.

'How long will you be?' Karen asked, terrified that Sheila was ready to tell her secret. 'We've got to get the bus in half an hour.'

Jess picked up her coat. 'If I'm not back, you two go without me.'

'No room for a couple of her best friends?' Joanne aimed directly at Adam, who shook his head. Jess bit her lips against a grin.

'If you'll follow me, please.'

Jess followed Adam back towards the door. 'What's your name?' he asked as he unlocked the door and led her into the dimly lit corridor that led to Rory's dressing room.

'Jess,' she replied.

He looked at her. Another lamb to the slaughter. He felt bad that he was party to this, but knew how Rory worked. All of the girls Adam brought to his dressing room were 'briefed before they were debriefed' as Rory liked to put it. They all knew that it was no strings sex, pure and simple. They all had the opportunity to say no. But that never happened.

'Well, here we are, Jess.' He opened a door on the right hand side of the corridor and showed her into the dressing room. 'If you need anything just give me a shout. I'll only be outside.'

She thanked him and took a seat, checking her reflection in the mirror as other girls in other locations had before her.

'Help yourself to a drink.' Rory's voice floated in from the small bathroom to her left. 'I'll be out in a minute.'

'Thanks,' she called back as she took a bottle of Bud from an ice bucket and flipped the cap. 'How are you?'

'Fine,' he replied over running water. 'Have you enjoyed the evening?'

'Very interesting.' She gulped down half of her drink. 'What's all this about a message that you've got for me?'

'I can't guarantee anything, but I saw you during the show and got a strange feeling that I thought I should act on.' He turned off the tap and groped for a towel, checking his reflection in the mirror above the sink to make sure his face wasn't still smeared with make up. He put on his best thigh loosening smile and stepped into the dressing room. The smile faltered immediately as he saw Jess sitting opposite his dad's old chair, bottle halfway to her mouth. Her face creased into a look of confusion.

'Jesus,' he exclaimed before he could stop himself. 'Jessie?'

She put the glass down. Did she really look so terrible? Had the past couple of years taken their toll so badly? But as Rory looked sheepishly at the floor and busied himself with the towel her eyes grew big with realisation.

'Oh my god,' she said quietly. 'You didn't even know I was here, did you?'

The stories she had read exploded like flares inside her head.

A private reading.

A message that he didn't think should be discussed in public.

A lie.

For endless moments they looked at each other, both embarrassed, neither sure of what to say.

It was Jess who finally broke the silence. 'Still fancy your chances?' she asked with a smile.

6

Rory released a short, uneasy laugh and went to her, holding her to him, feeling her hands rest gently on his back. 'I missed you.'

She wanted to pull herself away from him and demand that he explain himself, but she liked having his arms around her. 'Missed you too,' she said.

Rory kissed her forehead and got himself a drink.

'You'd better explain yourself, Rory,' she said. 'You didn't know it was me he was bringing here, did you? You know I've stuck up for you over those stories and now I feel . . .' *Cheap? Pleased to see you?* 'Weird.'

He sat in his chair and ran his hands lovingly over the scuffed arms. 'Thank you,' he said. 'For sticking up for me. Because it wasn't how they said.'

'And yet here I am.' She put the bottle down beside her bag with a deep sigh and the sound made him feel like the worlds biggest arse. He had to tell her something. Any minute now there would be the knock at the door. Good old Adam following orders. But if that knock came before he had time to explain, she might just leave him to finish his drink alone.

Painful embarrassment prevented him from even raising his eyes to look at her. He opened his mouth and spilled in the rest of his drink. Got up, got another, sat down, took a drink. Forever buying time to think.

'Does Adam always fetch your girls for you?' she asked.

He closed his eyes, wishing that he could just rewind or fast forward to anywhere but this moment in time. And soon the knock would come.

'You make it sound a lot worse than it is.' A poor defence and he knew it. 'And don't pick on Adam, he's a good lad. He's going to be a doctor, you know. Lives near here, that's why this was the final gig.' He spoke rapidly, hoping she wouldn't notice his quick change of conversational direction. 'Going to do a residential at Medway hospital. Do you know it?'

'Medway?' She was temporarily distracted but quickly pushed images of dead dad and Sandra Thompson from her head. 'Don't change the subject, Rory.'

'You only know what you read.'

'It all seems pretty accurate so far.'

'I told every single one of those girls that it was just ...' he trailed off, feeling exposed.

'Adam just goes out, picks a girl and brings her back for you,' Jess said. 'Then you do whatever it is that you want to do to them and dump them at the stage door.'

He shook his head. 'It's not like that, Jessie.'

But it was. Fine, he buys them a meal and whatever it is that they want to drink, takes them to a beautiful hotel room. But it all came down to the same thing in the end. Adam brings him a girl, he does whatever he wants, and he dumps them.

'I get a car to take them home. I take them for a meal. I *ask* for god's sake. And they all know exactly what the deal is.'

He glanced at her through his hair and then looked back at his bottle of Bud. 'Since the last time I saw you I've wondered if we'd ever meet again and I've played it over in my head, what it would be like. I never saw this.'

'You're not the only one,' she replied, fetching herself another beer. 'So go on, what happens now?'

He blushed furiously, setting his bottle down in front of the mirror. He looked at the door. 'Adam's going to knock in a minute,' he said dismally, 'tell me my car's ready. I ask if you'd like to join me for something to eat, you say yes, I tell Adam to arrange for my table for one to be rearranged for a table for two and off we go.'

'Smooth,' she mocked. 'How do you know I'm going to say yes?'

'They all say yes to the free food,' he said. 'But you? I'd like you to say yes because I've missed you and I don't want you to leave.'

328

There was a knock at the door. 'Mr Hamilton, your car's ready.'

They both looked at each other awkwardly.

'Mr Hamilton?' Adam called again.

He offered her an apologetic smile. 'Would you like to join me?' he asked.

'My dad warned me about men like you,' she said.

'I bet he did,' Rory replied soberly. 'Look, I'm paying.'

She smiled. 'I'm in.'

He went to the door and Jess drank deeply as he spoke to Adam. He closed the door and sat back down. 'We've got a couple of minutes,' he said.

She didn't reply and he wracked his brains, desperately trying to think of something to say.

'Have you worked out the meaning of life yet?' he asked, trying to lift the mood.

'Of course I have,' she replied.

'Really?'

'No, not really,' she snapped. 'Actually things have been pretty shit. Can we go and eat please.'

Rory recoiled. 'Okay.'

He fetched his coat and led her silently to where the car was waiting. As it headed towards the hotel, Jess stared blankly out of the window.

'How's your dad?' Rory asked.

She looked at him and her eyes made the hairs on the back of his neck stand to attention. She looked scared and sad and angry all at the same time. They were the eyes of someone who had endured hour after hour of thumbscrews and racks and flogging and had resigned themselves to their fate; that more torture would tear away at them before merciful death would arrive.

'He's okay,' she replied simply before looking back out at the streets.

'Did you get the card I sent you?'

She nodded without looking back at him.

The car pulled up and they got out. 'We can skip the food if you like,' he replied. 'If you want to talk we can go to my room and I'll order us some room service.'

'Can I get a drink first?'

They ordered a bottle of wine and four bottles of Bud and took them to his room. He poured her a glass of wine as they sat at a small mahogany table by the window. She gulped down half of the glass and he brought over the room service menu, sitting down opposite her.

'What are you having?' he asked as she looked through the menu.

'If you're buying I'll have the steak baguette with a side of garlic mushrooms, an ice cream sundae and two helpings of cheesecake please.'

'You'll have a bread roll and you'll be thankful,' he teased. 'If you're good I might let you have butter.'

She laughed. 'I'll have a chicken sandwich please,' she said, handing him the menu. He went to the phone beside the bed and rang down their order. When he went back to the table her glass was empty.

'Thirsty?' he asked as he watched her pour another large measure.

'It's very good wine,' Jess replied.

'Surprised you could taste it how fast it disappeared.'

'Don't start being nasty just because you know you're not getting anything out of me tonight.' She waved the glass at him playfully but he could see the sadness in her eyes.

'I'm sorry I deserted you,' he said. 'I thought you should at least try to work things out on your own.'

'Yeah,' she said, throwing him an icy glare. 'That was fun.'

'I'm sorry,' he said.

She shook her head tiredly. 'You did the right thing.'

'No, I didn't,' he argued. 'You were fifteen years old and I just ditched you. How bad did it get?' he asked reluctantly.

330

'Bad,' she replied softly. 'A boy died,' she was staring vacantly into the room, 'and it was my fault.'

'That can't be true, Jessie, you wouldn't hurt anyone.'

She looked up at him sharply. 'I knew it was going to happen and I couldn't stop it.'

She told him about Dean and a lump rose in Rory's throat as her speech became more rapid and her eyes filmed with tears.

'And I'd forgotten all about Connie,' she said as a knock came at the door. Rory put the food in front of them but she didn't touch it. As she explained what had happened a tear slid down her cheek unnoticed.

She took a bite of her sandwich, chewed thoughtfully, and swallowed. 'She was found with a needle hanging out of her arm and her throat was full of her own vomit. The people who were with her at the time ran. Nobody tried to help her.'

Rory was cold and didn't fancy his cheese and pickle sandwich now. 'I can't even imagine what this has been like for you,' he said. 'I'm so sorry, Jessie, I should have been there for you.'

'You're here now,' she replied hopefully.

'Yes,' he said. He wanted to hold her as the silent tears ran down her face. 'And I'm not going anywhere.'

She swiped at her face with the heels of her hands. 'I'm sorry, Rory,' she said. 'I'm so happy to see you and all I'm doing is making us both miserable.'

He took her hands in his own. 'You've been through a lot, Jessie,' he said. 'I'm surprised you're not locked up in a nuthouse somewhere. I couldn't have dealt with what you've been through.'

She forced a small smile. 'Enough,' she said. 'I'm sick of feeling depressed.'

She drank some more wine and took another bite of her sandwich.

'I remember asking if you knew me,' Rory said. 'And you said that my face was familiar but you couldn't place it.'

'I remember that,' she nodded.

'Am I really that forgettable?'

She thought for a moment and then frowned. 'I'm sorry, am I missing something?'

'Well, didn't this happen the last time?' he asked.

She shook her head. 'Scott's going to Spain for four days tomorrow,' she said. 'Last time I was supposed to spend the night with him. I didn't know we were going to have an argument and break up the day before your gig. I'd been invited to come and see you, well, Gerald, but I'd said no. The only reason I booked to come here tonight was because I wanted to see you.'

'Scott?' Rory sounded surprised. 'I thought we didn't like Scott?'

'It's complicated,' she replied.

'You mean you fell in love with him all over again?'

'I mean it's complicated.'

'Did he still break up with you?'

She nodded. 'At least I remembered to put my shoes away this time,' she said. 'Dad's back is fine and dandy. For now.'

'You saved his back?'

She flashed a truly happy smile and nodded again. 'I just hope it stays that way. He was supposed to fall this morning and so far,' she crossed her fingers for luck, 'nothing.'

'So now you can go off and marry Scott without worrying about him,' Rory said. 'Is that the plan?'

'Scott'll ring me when he gets back,' she explained. 'Apologise, same as he did last time, and want us to make up.'

'And you'll live happily ever after?' Rory asked cynically.

Surprisingly, she shook her head. 'I don't love him,' she shrugged, dropping her sandwich back onto the plain white plate. 'I thought I did but I don't. And the only reason I've stayed with him as long as I have is because,' she swallowed hard and looked at him from beneath her heavy brow, 'I thought that maybe I was meant to be with him and I didn't want him to be with her. How childish is that?'

Rory drank without answering and watched as she gulped at her wine. She had almost finished her second glass.

'It's not fair to stay with him anymore,' she continued. 'I'm wasting his time as well as mine. I've been thinking that maybe I didn't really love him the first time, it was just because he was all there was after dad that I thought I was in love with him. I mean, if I'd been in love with him I wouldn't have just flat out refused his proposal, would I? I'd have tried to work something out.'

Rory had a feeling that whatever he said was going to be wrong and that if he remained silent that would be wrong too.

'But then what if I'm wrong?' she said before he could think of anything productive to say. 'What if I am supposed to marry him?'

'Jessie, you're not supposed to do anything but enjoy your life and live it the way you want to,' he urged. 'If that woman didn't give you an instruction manual then you stop thinking about what you reckon she wants you to do and start enjoying yourself.'

He ate one of his sandwiches, topped up Jessie's glass, leaned back in his chair and sighed. 'Does Scott know that you've done all this before?' he asked.

'No.'

'What about your dad?'

'No.'

'So you've had nobody to talk to about this?'

'No.'

'Has it been difficult keeping it from your friends?'

'What friends?' she smiled cynically. 'I put all my time into trying to take care of Dean. Then I just kind of stuck to Scott. He was safe, familiar. He wasn't going to go and die on me.'

333

Rory wasn't hungry anymore. 'I've got to take some of the blame for this,' he said. 'I just fucking abandoned you.'

She drank more wine. 'I don't blame you for any of this,' she replied.

'I've got a few days off,' Rory said, 'if you want me to stay around for a while?'

'You could come and stay with us,' Jess replied. 'If you don't mind the sofa. I'd really like you to stay.'

He nodded. 'Only one problem with staying at yours,' he said.

'What's that?'

'Your dad lives there.' Rory raised his eyebrows. 'Hater of all men who dare to speak to his daughter.'

'He'll be fine,' Jess said, rolling her eyes.

Rory didn't look convinced.

'Anyway,' she said. 'Enough about me, let's talk about you.'

Rory shrugged. 'Not much to tell,' he said.

'I think there's plenty,' she replied with a mischievous smile. 'So if we hadn't met at gran's and Adam had brought me to your room, how different would this conversation be?'

He leaned back in his chair, looking at his sandwich rather than at her.

'Come on, Rory, I want to hear your patter.'

He rubbed the back of his neck uncomfortably and then folded his arms. 'Don't be ridiculous.'

'You're not going all shy on me are you?' she taunted. His cheeks were a deep pink and his eyes remained on the table. He could hear her distaste. 'Okay, I'll start.'

'Don't,' he said.

'Well the food's very nice, Rory,' she said, ignoring him. 'Better than my dad's cooking. How's yours?' She giggled at herself, but it wasn't her usual giggle. It was tinged with malice and he knew she was only doing this because

334

she did blame him, in some part at least, for how bad things had been for her while he'd been enjoying himself.

'You've lost the plot,' he said.

'Not sure I ever had it,' she replied.

'I wouldn't want to hear about you or your dad,' Rory said seriously. 'I'm not interested in you.'

Her smile faltered. 'What?'

She wants the truth? Let her have it, Rory thought. 'I'd tell you about how it started, how my dad helped me, the work I did then and what I do now, how well I'm doing.'

She raised her eyebrows. 'Sounds like a lot of me and not so much what about you,' Jess observed.

'That's the point,' Rory explained. 'I don't want to know she's got a family waiting for her at home or what she does for a living. The less I know the better. I don't want to think about their feelings or that they have a life outside of this room.'

'You don't want to see them as people,' Jess concluded. Rory looked away from the look of disappointment on her face. 'They're just pieces of meat to you.'

'You asked,' he replied flippantly.

'Go on then,' she challenged. 'Tell me about your work, about how well you're doing.'

'You already know.'

'So do they.'

He couldn't help but be impressed by her tenacity. He was less impressed by how bad it made him feel though. 'There is one story that I like to tell,' he said with a small smile, not wanting to argue, wanting to have his friend back. 'The one about The Unicorn near York that me and dad worked at.'

'Yeah, I read that,' Jess replied.

'Feel better?' he asked. 'You'd ruin my evil plan as soon as I mentioned it.'

They both smiled and Jess drank thoughtfully. She was feeling tired. 'Have you got a tee shirt or something I can borrow?' she asked. 'I didn't think to bring my pyjamas.'

He went to the small wardrobe and pushed coat hangers along the rail before pulling one out. A old and tired looking Iron Maiden tee shirt hung from it. 'Thanks,' she took it from him and changed in the bathroom. It hung to her knees.

She climbed into bed as Rory lit a cigarette and went to the window. Looking out he saw the lights of the city spread out like stars. Jess was sitting up with a pillow at her back, the covers pulled up to her waist. Rory took an ashtray, his beer and her wine over to the bed and sat beside her, crossing his long legs out in front of him. He handed her the wine and she drank before putting the glass down beside the bed.

'You look tired,' he said. 'I'm going to be a gentleman and take the floor.'

Jess lay down, pulling the cover up to her chest. 'You don't have to,' she said. 'The bed's huge, I can shift over. Just keep your pants on.'

'Little bit weird,' Rory replied.

Jess rolled her eyes and went to the bathroom, bringing back two bath towels which she rolled up and laid down the middle of the mattress. 'Now we've got a bed each,' she said, lying down on her side. 'We're just sharing a duvet.'

He relented, sliding out of his trousers and taking off his shirt. He hung them on the back of one of the chairs and went back to the bed.

'I'm glad I got to see you again,' Jess whispered as Rory turned out the lights.

'Me too, Jessie,' he replied.

7

'Dad?' Jess called as she and Rory entered the house.

'In here.'

Rory followed her into the living room, wheeling his case through the narrow hall.

Jess gave her dad a quick hug. 'This is Rory,' she said.

Rory offered a hand which Paul shook only through obligation. The look in his eyes said that Rory had been right. If you stood up to pee, he didn't want you anywhere near his daughter.

'Thanks for letting me stay,' Rory said.

'You're on the sofa,' Paul replied.

'Bring your stuff upstairs,' Jess said. 'You can keep it in my room.'

Already thankful to leave the room Rory followed her upstairs and Jess helped him to hang his clothes in her wardrobe.

'Ignore him,' Jess said as if she could read his mind.

'I'd sooner he just said what he wanted and get it out of the way instead of looking at me like that'

'He will,' Jess said.

'Oh, joy.'

They went back downstairs and sat together on the sofa. For a while Paul said nothing and Rory thought he might escape any interrogation. He stared at the TV, hating the silence but unsure what to do, until Paul rolled a cigarette, lit it, and looked over at him thoughtfully.

'Am I being naïve letting you stay under the same roof as my daughter?' he asked.

'Shut up, dad,' Jess said wearily.

'You're being naïve if you're asking the question because of what you read,' Rory replied.

Jess looked from her dad to Rory and said nothing.

'Mind if I smoke?' Rory asked. Paul pushed the ashtray into the middle of the table so that they would both be able to reach it.

'Are you saying all those girls were lying?' Paul asked.

'No,' Rory replied as he lit a cigarette. 'I'm saying they're irrelevant.'

Paul looked at him with exaggerated curiosity. 'Irrelevant?' he asked.

'Would you think they were irrelevant if you were in my position?'

'Probably not,' Rory admitted.

'You went behind my back before,' Paul said.

'Dad, pack up,' Jess said. 'You're so embarrassing.'

'You were sneaking around behind our backs,' Paul continued as if he hadn't heard. 'After you'd specifically been asked to stay away from her.'

'Yeah,' the frustration was evident in Rory's voice. 'And I didn't fuck her then, either.'

Paul's eyes widened and Jess's closed as she prayed for this to end. Rory sighed, regretting his choice of words immediately. 'Paul, the only person in the world that cares more about Jessie than I do is you. And you can think what you want about me, but you know she's way out of my league.'

'Hello,' Jessie said as she waved her arms at them. 'I am still here you know.'

'And then there's the whole thing with Scott that I really don't want to get involved in,' Rory finished.

Paul looked at his daughter then back at Rory. 'Oh, she told you about Snot, did she? I bet you a tenner he doesn't like you.'

'Maybe it's just you, Paul,' Rory said. 'You don't have my charm, now, do you?'

Paul shook his head, almost smiling. 'You've certainly got something I haven't.'

338

'And calling him Snot probably doesn't help.'

Paul finally smiled. 'I don't call it him to his face,' he said. 'I know it makes Jess smile sometimes, even if she doesn't admit it.'

'Well I'll take your bet my friend, and later, your money.'

Rory held out his hand and Paul shook it. 'I've got to get ready for work,' he said. 'There's a pizza in the freezer and I got a few cans in for you.'

Jess watched him go and then turned to Rory. 'I tried to get him to stop drinking,' she said quickly as if she had to explain why her alcoholic father was allowed to have beer in the house. 'But it just caused rows. Instead of making him live longer it felt like I was just wasting the time we did have rowing with him.'

'I didn't say anything,' Rory said.

'I know what you're thinking though,' she said defensively. 'What kind of idiot would let their dad drink when she knew it'd kill him?'

'I wasn't thinking anything,' he protested.

'But I either enjoy what we have got or make him hate me. It was so uncomfortable sometimes and I don't want it to be like that.'

'Jessie, please, just shut the fuck up.' His words silenced her and she looked at him with surprise. 'Its not your place to play god, you already know that. You want you and your dad to be how you were before, I get it. If you need me to tell you that you're doing the right thing, I will. But if you feel better when he's drinking than you do when you're arguing about it, then you already know that.'

'You're right,' she replied, nodding sharply.

He shrugged. 'As usual.'

Jess made them both a coffee as her dad left for work. The phone rang as she set the mugs down on the table and she looked at the clock. 'Scott,' she said as she got up. 'To apologise.'

She answered the phone, smiling at Rory. 'Hi, Scott,' she said. Rory smiled back at her.

'I've been thinking about what happened,' Scott said. 'I'm sorry, babe, I didn't mean what I said.'

She leaned her back against the wall and crossed her ankles. 'We need to talk,' she said.

'I don't really want to finish with you,' he replied. 'I said it because I was angry.'

'I think you did the right thing,' she said as she twisted the curled wire between her fingers.

'What?'

'I don't want to do this over the phone, Scott,' she said. 'But I've done a lot of thinking and I'm not sure we should get back together.' The other end of the line was silent. 'Scott?'

'I'm sorry,' he insisted. 'I didn't mean any of it. I want to be with you.'

'I know,' she replied softly. 'I know, but I don't think I feel the same.'

She heard the crackled sound of a sigh before he spoke again. 'You slept with him, didn't you?'

She frowned and her mouth worked silently.

'Joanne told me you met up with that psychic.' Scott sounded as if he was trying not to shout at her.

'Yeah, but I didn't do anything.' Jess looked briefly at Rory. He was blowing smoke rings towards the ceiling. She turned her back on him and brought the mouthpiece close to her lips. 'Scott, it's got nothing to do with...' her mouth stopped, her breath caught within. 'You rang Joanne?'

'She rang me,' he corrected. 'To let me know that you were shacked up with him.'

'Shacked up?' she replied incredulously. 'I met up with my friend and that's it.'

'You stayed the night.'

How the hell did he know that? 'What?'

'Joanne called at your house this morning and your dad said you'd stayed out all night.'

'So?' She looked back over her shoulder at Rory. He was looking at her now. He looked concerned. She turned away again. 'If you really thought anything had happened you wouldn't be ringing me to make up, would you?'

'I didn't want to believe her,' he said. 'But you've just told me everything I need to know.'

'You're being . . .'

The line went dead.

She hung up and went back to the sofa, holding her head in her cold hands.

'You okay?' Rory asked.

'Yep,' she replied. She looked at the television although it was obvious she wasn't watching it. 'I'm going to put the pizza in.'

She went robotically to the kitchen and closed the door behind her. Rory heard the freezer door open and then shut hard. He looked over the back of the sofa at the door, wondering if he should have followed her. He decided to stay where he was and looked back at the TV. The oven door slammed next and he stood up, looking helplessly at the door. Then he heard muffled crying and went over, knocking before he entered the kitchen.

She was sitting on the floor with her back against the fridge. Her legs were pulled up to her chest, her arms wrapped around them and her head bowed. She looked up as he crouched in front of her and touched her arm. Her red face was streaked with tears.

'I'm okay,' she said before he could say anything to the contrary.

'Then I'd hate to see you when you're upset,' he replied. He stood up and gave her his hand, helping her to her feet.

341

'He knows I stayed with you last night.'

'Awesome,' Rory replied flatly. 'Why'd you tell him that?'

'I didn't,' she replied angrily. 'Joanne told him. Then I say I don't want to get back with him, he puts two and two together and comes up with about three hundred and now, well, I don't know.'

He caught her by the arm as she paced the kitchen irritably. 'So what?' he asked calmly.

'What do you mean, so what?'

He shrugged. 'So you don't want to get back with him anyway so who cares what he thinks?'

'I care.'

'Why?'

She didn't know. Her shoulders slumped as she realised how stupid she was being. Rory was right. It didn't matter. 'You're right,' she nodded. 'It's not important.'

'Not to you, maybe,' Rory said. 'But I'm pretty sure I owe your dad a tenner.'

Even this didn't raise a smile.

'Right, that's it,' Rory said. 'We're going out.'

'What?' Jess asked as if it was the most ridiculous idea she'd ever heard.

'I'm sick of you being miserable and down in the dumps all the time,' he replied. 'We're going to go out, have a few drinks and a good night. I'm going to make you smile if it kills me.' He looked at her sullen face and sighed. 'And it probably will.'

8

The White Swan was dimly lit. Booths covered in red plastic lined the walls of the huge room and tables were dotted between them and the bar, which was situated in the middle of the room; a large spot lit square manned by eight bar staff.

'You know if the wind changes, you're face is going to stay like that forever,' Rory said as they took their drinks to one of only three empty booths. The room was alive with chatter and small clouds of smoke hung over most of the tables.

She looked up at him, her eyes seeming to accuse him and study him at the same time. They sat opposite each other, him seeing only the length of the room, her looking out through large windows onto the darkening street.

'Scott's going to go crazy when he gets back and finds out you've been staying with us,' she said.

'Why?' Rory asked.

'Because I know how I'd feel if I came back off holiday and found out that he'd had some woman round to stay with him that I didn't know.'

'You talk like you just picked me up in a club one night,' Rory said.

'Because that's how he'll see it,' she insisted.

Rory didn't know what to say. He took a long drink from his pint of Pedigree and lit a cigarette.

'At the risk of getting my head bitten off,' he said cautiously. 'Can we forget about Scott and your dad and the millions of other things that make you worry and just have a good night?'

He looked ready for a torrent of 'what the hell?'

'Because,' she started and then laughed at the look on his face. 'Okay,' she submitted. 'Okay, fine.'

He relaxed. A little. 'Give me a smile then, princess.'

343

She grinned maniacally at him and they both laughed. Five men entered the pub and went to a stage on the other side of the room where drums and guitars stood, waiting to be played.

'Looks like we've got entertainment,' Jess said as she picked up a pile of menu's and started to look through them.

'Am I that boring?' Rory asked.

'I'm hungry,' she said. 'Aren't you hungry? Ooh, there's a cocktail menu.'

'Erm, hungry, yes. Cocktails, no.'

'Oh, come on,' Jess said. 'If you're going to make me smile all night you can at least share a pitcher of, er,' she ran her eyes over the brightly coloured cocktail menu, 'Excalibur with me. Excalibur, Rory. How cool does that sound?'

'Very cool,' he said without conviction.

'What do you want to eat?' She laid out the menu and he glanced over it.

They ordered a sharing platter and Rory looked at the glowing green jug of Excalibur with distaste. It was sweet but not as disgusting as he'd thought it would be. Behind him the band finished their sound check and went to change before they started. By the time they came back only a melting pile of pale green ice remained at the bottom of their pitcher.

'Another?' Jess asked.

Rory picked up the cocktail menu and looked it over. 'Mai Tai?' he asked.

Jess nodded enthusiastically and went to the bar. Rory watched her with interest. If she was faking having a good time she was doing a really good job. But he didn't think she was faking. This was how she should be, how she had probably been before. Eighteen and carefree, laughing and having a good time. And she was radiant when she was having a good time. She was fun and her smile lit up her eyes and, and . . .

Oh Jesus, Rory, get a grip.

He ran a hand over his face as she returned to the table and the band started with something by Take That.

'Are you okay?' Jess asked.

Before he replied she began to sing along absently.

'You're a Take That fan?' he asked.

She shook her head. 'Not yet.' She put the neon pink straw to her lips and drank from the pitcher. Then she smiled. 'I will be. When they reform. And then I get into all their old stuff and it doesn't matter that I just said that because you already know my deep dark secret.' She was pointing the straw at him now and smirking.

'Are you drunk?' he asked.

'Absolutely not,' she replied. 'I'm just, I suppose I'm actually enjoying myself.'

Rory picked up the empty pitcher, clinked it against the full one and raised it in a toast. 'Well, cheers to that,' he said. 'How's the Mai Tai?'

'I preferred Excalibur,' she replied. 'Trust you to pick one with a girly name.'

'What?'

'Excalibur,' Jess said in a deep, commanding voice. 'Mai Tai,' she squeaked.

Rory laughed and they talked while the band covered what seemed like every boy band that had graced the charts with their presence over the last twenty years. They emptied two more pitchers, laughed at a stag party dressed in drag and talked about everything and nothing. They were both somewhere close to drunk and had had enough of the sickly fluorescent cocktails. Rory fetched them both a Jack Daniels and coke and Jess glanced at her watch as she drank. 'Almost eleven,' she said. 'We should go soon.'

Rory shrugged. 'What's the rush?'

'No rush,' she said. 'It's getting late though.'

'Lightweight,' Rory teased.

345

'I'm just thinking that it's going to be hard to get a taxi at this time on a Saturday night.'

'Oh my god,' Rory laid his head on the table and threw his arms over it.

'What?' Jess asked.

Rory looked up at her and swept his hair back with a quick hand. 'Now you're worrying about taxi's?' he asked. 'Is there anything you don't worry about?'

'I don't worry about you,' she replied. 'You'll always be okay. Oh wow, they're playing Bon Jovi, Rory.'

The guitars carried Always over the room and Jess's head bobbed along. 'Come and dance with me, Rory.'

He shook his head quickly. 'No way.'

'But you love Bon Jovi,' she cried. 'They're your favourite, remember?'

'Yeah, but I don't dance to them.'

She looked at him seriously. 'If you don't dance with me I'm going to stop smiling,' she threatened. She looked at the table, the corners of her mouth drooped, and then she looked back up at him slowly. 'See,' she said. 'Smile disappearing. I'm going to start crying, Rory. I'm warning you.'

'I'm not dancing.'

She sighed dramatically. 'Any minute now,' she said. 'You're gonna make me cry.'

He laughed at her and she put a hand to her mouth so that he wouldn't see her trying to stop herself smiling. 'Come on then,' he said, offering her his hand over the table. She snatched it and dragged him onto the dance floor where other couples were rotating slowly.

'No funny stuff though, Rory,' she said as she put her hands on his shoulders. 'I'm watching you.'

He put his hands on her waist and they started to revolve. She was looking up at him, blinking slowly as she always did after too many drinks. 'I really

346

love this song,' she said.

He nodded agreement, looking back down at her. She was his. For now, for however long the song lasted, she would belong to him. Tomorrow Scott would probably talk her into getting back with him and later they would probably get married. But for now, they were his hands on her waist, his shoulders beneath her fingers. She laid her head against his chest and cradled her hands against the nape of his neck.

'Don't you go falling asleep on me,' he warned as the lyrics of the second verse resonated deep inside him and he was forced to speak to snap himself out it. She looked up at him again and smiled, then laid her head against his shoulder. His hands rested at the top of her hips and he could feel them swaying gently as she moved. He almost kissed the top of her head without thinking, catching himself at the last second and looking around the room to see if anyone had noticed. Everyone else was wrapped up in their own conversations and tiny circle dances. It was just them. Just the two of them. Just for now.

As the final chords played out he gathered himself, preparing to let her go. He found himself worrying about getting a taxi and smiled. Her pessimism was contagious. Thankfully there was a long line of them on the next street and Rory joked about how he'd been right – again.

Jess clambered in behind him and lay down on the cool imitation leather with her head on his thigh. Her eyes sparkled in the glow of the streetlights as she smiled up at him. He was taken back to that day again, feeling the close heat of the garage all around him. He put his hand on her shoulder, looking straight ahead, watching the red numbers on the meter rise steadily as they rode through the dark streets. She began to snore softly and he looked down at her, brushing her hair back from her cheek. Things he hadn't thought about in ages flooded back to him. Watching her sleep at Emily's house, wondering whether he should call an ambulance. He'd never been so worried in his life. Sitting up

347

with her while she explained what it was that he'd felt the first time he'd seen her. They had shared a kebab that night.

Her eyes opened, dancing over her surroundings as if she wasn't quite sure where she was. She smiled at him.

'Isn't this where you try to kiss me?' she asked.

He looked at her sadly. 'No, Jessie, it isn't.'

Her smile widened and he was sure that she was testing him. 'You're the best, Rory,' her words slurred into each other. 'You're the best friend in the whole wide world. I don't believe that you took advantage of those girls.'

She closed her eyes again and he didn't wake her until they arrived at the house. She let them in and stood in the hall, sliding out of her coat and shoes. Her face was bright again.

Rory hung up his coat as she looked at him curiously, bit her bottom lip and rubbed her shoulder slowly. 'Do you want to come up?' she asked.

Rory looked up the stairs and then at her. Her eyes were wide and expectant. 'Yeah, I want to,' he replied. 'But I can't.'

Her smile faded and she looked at the floor. 'Oh.'

'Jessie, you said it yourself. I'm your best friend in the whole wide world.'

She nodded.

'Well, I'd still like to be that in the morning,' he said. 'We've had a great night and a little bit too much to drink and you're not thinking properly.'

'I am,' she insisted.

He shook his head. 'You think you are, princess,' he replied softly. 'But in the morning you'll hate me.'

'I've had a really good night,' she said. 'I don't want it to end.'

'You said you wanted to come home.'

She looked shamefully at the floor.

'Oh,' he said. 'Right. Look, why don't I make us both a coffee and put the pizza in and we can stay up for as long as you want?'

Her smile returned and she nodded.

Rory went to the kitchen, feeling like he'd just made the worst decision of his whole life. But that wasn't his brain thinking, was it? Tomorrow she'd thank him. Because tomorrow she wouldn't be his anymore and she'd be thinking like a normal human being.

Jess went upstairs to put her pyjamas on. She didn't come back down. Rory ventured upstairs ten minutes later and found her fully clothed and sleeping on top of the bed.

9

'Coffee?' Rory asked.

'Yes please,' Paul replied without looking up from his newspaper.

Rory went into the kitchen and filled the kettle.

'Where did you end up last night?' Paul asked.

Rory went back into the living room instead of trying to shout over the rattle of the kettle. 'Where we started,' he said. 'We had some food then there was a band on so we stayed.'

'I heard you come in.'

'I'm sorry we woke you,' Rory apologised. 'We tried to be quiet.'

'You didn't wake me,' Paul corrected. 'I heard you talking. I heard what she said to you.'

Rory didn't think he'd ever felt so uncomfortable in his life.

'And I heard what you said to her as well.'

'Okay.' He couldn't think of anything else to say.

'You're alright,' Paul said. 'I gave you a hard time yesterday. Sorry.'

It was the best apology he was going to get and Rory nodded his acceptance. As they heard Jess coming downstairs Rory went back to the kitchen and Paul bowed over his newspaper.

'I hope you're making me one, Rory,' she called as she flopped onto the sofa and stretched.

'Like I'd dare not to,' he called back.

'Morning, sweetheart,' Paul said. 'Good night last night?'

Jess groaned. 'Had way too much to drink, but yes, it was a good night. I think.' She looked over the back of the sofa. 'Rory, did we have a good night last night?'

'Great,' he confirmed. 'You did half the band and I got the backing singer.'

Paul looked up at Jess with disapproval. 'It's just his sense of humour dad,' she said. 'If it wasn't me he was talking about, you'd find it funny.'

Paul went back to his puzzle without responding.

'Seriously though,' Rory called from the kitchen. 'I really enjoyed it. I think it was the cocktails that did you, Jessie.'

'Oh god, don't mention the cocktails.' She lay down as if being reminded of what she had drank the night before would worsen her hangover. 'Did we dance at some point?' she asked.

Did we dance? She couldn't remember. 'I tried to stop you but you weren't having any of it.' He hoped that she couldn't hear the disappointment in his voice.

'I said we, Rory, not me.'

'I'm fully aware that it was both of us,' he said as he brought coffee through for her and Paul.

He fetched his own drink and lifted Jess's legs up so he could sit down.

'Why didn't you stop me?'

'Believe me, Jessie, I tried,' he said.

'Can we discuss this in a couple of days when Scott's around?' Paul asked. 'I think he'd find it amusing.'

'I don't think he'll be coming round,' she said. 'He seemed pretty pissed off yesterday. And if he does, we don't tell him about any of this. He was angry enough that I even saw you, Rory, and now I've got to explain the fact that he goes away for a long weekend and when he get's back I've got a strange man sleeping in my house.'

'You think I'm strange?' Rory asked.

'I do,' Paul replied.

Rory offered him a crooked smile and then looked at Jess. 'I thought you didn't care what he thought anymore?' he asked.

'I don't,' she replied. 'But I don't want him to carry on making something out of this that doesn't exist.'

351

She wanted him back. Rory was sure of it. She didn't want to muddy the waters any more than she had to because that would make it more difficult to get him back.

Jess rubbed her head and sipped at her coffee. 'I can't really remember anything after the first pitcher of Mai Tai or whatever it was.'

'That was the second pitcher,' Rory said. 'The first one was something called Excalibur.'

Jess smiled. 'It was a really good night though, wasn't it?'

Rory nodded. 'It was.'

'Well,' Paul swallowed his coffee quickly. 'I'm nipping out to get some tobacco. Anyone need anything from the shop?'

'Orange juice,' Jess said. 'Lots of orange juice.'

Paul shook his head at her. 'You do get yourself into some states.' Then he left, leaving the room to fill with an unbearable silence. Jess put on the TV and stared blankly at the screen. Rory sipped at his coffee and lit a cigarette. He was trying to think of something to say when Jess started to laugh.

'What's funny?' Rory asked.

She put a hand to her mouth and shook her head. 'Nothing. I'm sorry.' She cleared her throat, staring back at the screen. 'Actually, yeah, I need to thank you for last night.'

'No need to thank me,' he replied. 'It was an excellent night, I had a great time.'

'Yeah, me too,' Jess nodded. 'But I'm not talking about that.'

Rory put his coffee down. 'Like I said,' he replied seriously. 'No need to thank me.'

'Yeah, there is.'

'I just didn't want you doing anything you'd regret.'

She smiled. 'Who said I'd have regretted it?'

Rory drew deeply on his cigarette and blew smoke out through his nose. It sounded like a sigh. 'Well I don't see you making any offers now you're sober.'

She opened her mouth, considering a response, and was interrupted by a knock at the door which she went to quickly.

'Scott,' she said with surprise. He looked tired and she felt like her hangover was getting worse. 'I thought you were in Spain?'

'I didn't go,' he said. 'I want to talk to you.'

She didn't think he'd want to talk once he got into the house and saw Rory. 'There isn't a lot more for me to say.'

'Can I please come in?'

Her head began to pound and she nodded painfully. Scott followed her to the living room and then stopped dead when he saw Rory sitting on the sofa. 'You're Rory Hamilton.'

'I am.' Rory offered Scott his hand but Scott's eyes went to Jess. 'What the hell's he doing here?'

'He's just staying with us for a couple of days,' Jess replied flippantly, hoping he'd understand that it was no big deal. He didn't.

'So now you've moved him in?' he seethed.

'Of course I haven't.'

Rory stood up and offered Scott his hand again. 'It's good to meet you, Scott,' he said as if the last thirty seconds hadn't happened. 'Jess's told me a lot about you. Most of it good.'

Scott looked at him, dumbfounded. 'I bet you couldn't believe your luck,' he said. 'Nice reunion with Jess, boyfriend out of the country.'

'Scott, there's no need for this,' Rory said.

'Ex boyfriend,' Jess said quietly.

'You what?' Scott asked.

'We split up, Scott,' she replied casually. 'You broke up with me. You can't do that and then come here throwing accusations around. He's my friend.'

353

'I know exactly what he is,' Scott said, staring at Rory.

'What he is is a guest in this house,' Paul said from the hall. The three of them were silent. 'I thought you were in Spain,' he called as he closed the door and came into the living room. His face was dark. Jess had seen that face before. Not very often. It was his angry face. He passed Jess a carton of orange juice and she sat on the sofa. Rory and Scott followed her lead, sitting on either side of her as Paul took his usual place behind the door.

'I heard you spent the night at Rory's hotel on Thursday.' Scott's eyes were cold and critical. He'd hoped that Paul wouldn't know but the man's silence said that this was old news. Rory didn't like this. He and Paul exchanged glances and Rory wondered which one of them would speak up first.

'Yes,' Jess replied simply. 'I was going to tell you but you had a nice long chat with Joanne before you even thought about speaking to me, didn't you?'

'Jess, I was just . . .'

'We shared a bed as well in case you didn't know,' Jess added.

Rory's smile disappeared. Paul's widened and for a moment Rory thought he was going to laugh out loud. Instead he looked back at his crossword. Rory could feel Scott's eyes on him and he looked up.

'You shared a bed?' Scott asked.

Rory gave him an innocent look. 'None of us were naked at any point during the night,' he said. 'I think it's important that you know that.'

Scott's eyes fell upon Jess. 'You shared a bed with him?' he asked. 'I'm not even out of the country yet and you're jumping into bed with another man?'

'He's a friend, Scott,' Jess replied calmly. 'Just like you and Joanne are friends.'

'Oh, I know who he is,' Scott grinned sourly. 'He's the psychic out of the papers that just uses every girl he comes into contact with.'

'Hang on,' Paul looked up as Rory spoke. 'Just a minute, Scott. You can't believe everything you read, you know.'

Jess put a hand on Rory's arm to silence him. It didn't go unnoticed by Scott or Paul. 'There's no need for this,' Jess said.

'And where's he staying while he's here?'

'On the sofa,' Paul replied. 'Look, Scott, I invited him into this house because it was cheaper than him staying in a hotel and I trust him not to lay a finger on my daughter for two reasons. Number one, out of respect for me and the rules of my house. And number two, out of respect for Jess. But that's not the point. Even if you don't trust him, you've got no reason not to trust Jessica.'

'This isn't about trust,' Jess said. 'Scott, we're not together anymore and if I want to see other people I will. And I'd tell you if you were that interested.'

'Knock knock,' Karen called as let herself in. Jess put her head in her hands. This was only going to get worse. 'Scott, you're back.'

'Never left,' he replied grumpily. 'Is Joanne in?'

'Yeah, why?'

'I'm going to go round and see her,' he said spitefully. He left without another word to anyone.

'What was all that about?' Karen asked.

'Oh, he's just doing it to piss me off,' Jess replied.

'Good to meet you, Rory,' Karen said purely to change the subject. 'I'm Karen.'

'Good to meet you too,' Rory said. 'You're Joanne's sister, aren't you?'

'Yeah. Jess, I heard Joanne had mentioned you staying with Rory to Scott. I'm sorry about her.'

'That's okay,' Jess replied tiredly.

'What do you think to the ex?' Paul asked.

Rory looked at Jess. 'I think I'm going to reserve judgement for the time being.'

'I wanted to tell him myself,' Jess explained. 'When it was just me and him.

It's not his fault Joanne told him.'

'Well, I can see why you didn't want him to know about last night,' Rory said grumpily. 'Talk about possessive.'

'Thanks for reserving judgement, Rory,' Jess replied.

'He does get very jealous though,' Paul said.

'Wait, wait, wait,' Karen said. 'What happened last night?'

Rory grinned at her. 'Wouldn't you like to know.'

Karen nodded slowly. 'Yes I would. That's why I asked.'

'Then you wonder why Scott thinks you're as bad as the papers make out,' Jess said with despair. 'We went over to The White Swan,' she explained. 'Had a little bit too much to drink.'

'She had a little bit too much to drink,' Rory corrected.

'I was very drunk,' Jess admitted. 'I don't even remember how we got home.'

Karen saw the muscles in Rory's face twitch. 'It was a black cab,' he said, taking another long pull on his cigarette. 'A very expensive black cab.' He thought again about Jess's hands on his shoulders, her head against his chest. 'Right, I'm going for a walk,' he said. 'I think I need some fresh air.'

'I'll come with you,' Karen said. 'I'm on my way home anyway.'

'Okay,' he agreed reluctantly. He waited as Karen put out her cigarette.

'Bad hangover?' Karen asked as they left the house.

'Not really,' Rory replied. 'I just need to clear my head.'

Karen nodded as if she understood perfectly. Rory ignored her. He wasn't in the mood for talking.

They turned right at the end of the road and he allowed Karen to lead him through the unfamiliar streets. She put her hands in the pockets of her jeans and looked at the floor as they walked. 'I came to see you the other night with Jess,' she said. 'You were really good.'

'You're a sceptic?' he asked, more at ease with this topic of conversation.

'I believe what I can see,' she said. 'I don't believe something just because someone tells me it's true. I have to see it for myself.'

'Fair enough.'

'I knew one of the people you spoke to,' she said. 'How you knew those things, it was amazing to see.'

'Thank you.'

'Jess used to see the future when she was a little girl.'

He stopped and looked at her, puzzled. 'Really?'

'You didn't know?'

Rory shook his head. 'No.'

'That's why her gran wanted to keep you away from her.'

He started to walk again, pleased that he had managed to fool her. Acting – just another talent possessed by the amazing Rory Hamilton. 'Well, that makes sense.'

'Jess never told you about it?'

'No.'

They turned onto Redwood Avenue and Rory left Karen's side, taking the lead and leaving it up to her whether she followed him or not. He went through a squeaky metal gate into the park and sat on a swing. He had started to rock gently back and forth when Karen came to his side. She looked back at the street. An old woman was walking slowly to the bus stop and a man in his twenties was walking a black bull mastiff on the other side of the road. Apart from them the street was quiet.

'Did anything happen last night?' she asked, wondering whether she actually wanted to know the answer.

'Absolutely not,' Rory looked at her with outrage. 'You think I'd take advantage of someone who'd had that much to drink?' Karen didn't answer and he scowled at her. 'I can tell you exactly what happened with those girls,' he said. A bus turned the corner and the old woman stuck out her hand. 'And Jess

357

means more to me than that,' Rory continued. 'She's my friend. She's …'

Karen laid a hand over Rory's to stop him talking. 'I don't need to hear it.'

He frowned. His hand began to tingle. He turned it over so that Karen's palm fell against his and cocked his head as if listening to something only he could hear. Karen watched him curiously, snatching her hand away as he looked up at her with horror.

'What?' she asked.

Did he tell her? He could only look at her, bewildered and shaken. He had to say something. His lips began to move but no sound escaped them. She continued to look at him, scared now. As the bus pulled away he ran a hand through his hair and got up to leave.

'What?' she asked again.

'Nothing,' he said quickly. 'Nothing. Look, I'm going to head back.'

'What's the matter, Rory?' she called as he strode away from the swings. He dug his hands into his pockets but didn't reply, didn't even look at her. She ran after him, taking him by the shoulder and turning him to face her. 'What did I do?'

He rubbed his lips, trying to find the right words. There were none.

'It's your fault she's dead,' he said. She could hear the anger in his voice. 'Jess and Paul have tortured themselves for years and it was nothing to do with either of them. It was because of you and her.'

Karen took a step backwards, staring at him with wide eyes. Her head began to shake from side to side. 'I don't know what you're on about.'

He shook his head, dismissing the lie. 'You know exactly what I'm on about. And you pretend to be his friend?'

'I am his friend.'

He took an aggressive step towards her and gritted his teeth. 'I hope that what you did tortures you until the day you die,' he said.

'I didn't know,' she protested. 'I hadn't got a clue that she'd do that.'

358

He shook his head again, his face creased with disgust, then he turned and started to walk back towards the house.

'Are you going to tell them?' she called after him.

'Like that would do anyone any good,' he called back. 'No, I'm not going to tell them. But I am going to give Paul the tenner I owe him.'

'Ten whole English pounds,' Rory said as he held out the note.

Paul sniffed, swiped at his eyes with a shirtsleeve and held his hand out for the money without looking up.

'You okay, mate?' Rory asked.

'Got something in my eye,' Paul replied thickly. 'Fetch us a can.'

Rory went to the kitchen and brought back a can of lager. Paul's eyes never moved from the crossword as he took it.

'Where's Jessie?' Rory asked.

'Went back to bed,' Paul replied. 'Still nursing her hangover.'

Rory sat on the sofa, looking at the can and then at Paul, whose cheeks were red and wet.

'You sure you're alright?' he asked with concern.

'She looks a lot like her, you know,' Paul said with a sad smile that Rory could only just see. 'The stuff she does as well. The way she touches her hair, how she walks, how she smiles. So much like her.'

Rory frowned as he lit a cigarette. *What the hell was he talking about?*
'Maybe you should have a coffee instead,' he suggested.

Paul looked up and Rory knew that his shock was evident. Paul's eyes were bloodshot and red rimmed. He'd been crying hard. And he'd been drinking.

'Coffee wont help,' Paul replied with a mournful shake of his head.

Rory was at a loss for something to say. This was an entirely different side to Paul, one he was willing to bet that his daughter didn't see very often. He was overwhelmed and vulnerable. He was lost.

'Paul, if you want to talk,' Rory offered cautiously, 'listening's kind of my job. I'm good at it. And I can promise it wouldn't go any further.'

'I don't need to talk,' came the gruff reply.

'Okay,' Rory nodded. 'Do you want a smoke?'

He nudged his pack over the table towards Paul, who took one and lit it, swiping again at his eyes with his free hand.

'She's so much like her mum, you know.' Paul smiled that sad smile again. 'It's so hard sometimes.'

He picked up the can and drank deeply. Rory's eyes widened. It was Sheila. She was why he drank. At least that was what it had been in the beginning. It didn't seem to be working much anymore.

'How many of those do you have to drink before it stops hurting?' he asked.

Snorting laughter escaped Paul and he sniffed hard. 'It's never enough.' A traitorous tear fell over his cheek and he wiped it away with the heel of the hand holding the cigarette. 'It used to be. It doesn't matter.' His voice was hard, as if he was trying to convince himself rather than Rory.

Rory sat, smoking silently, contemplating the can in Paul's hand.

'It's not your problem,' Paul said. 'Forget I said anything. I'm just having a tough day today.' He picked up the crossword, stared at it blindly for a few moments and then put it down again. 'It would have been twenty four years today,' he whimpered, 'since the day we got together. I took her for a meal. A curry.' A small laugh escaped his lips. 'She had a dodgy belly the whole day after. But she agreed to see me again.'

He flicked ash into the ashtray and took another drink from the can. 'I love her so much, Rory,' he said. 'I still love her so much.'

'Have you ever spoken to Jessie about it?' Rory asked quietly.

Paul nodded. 'I've told her about her mum,' he said. 'What she was like, the funny stuff she did sometimes. She could be so clumsy.'

Rory blew smoke at the ceiling and looked levelly at Paul. 'I mean have you told her that it still hurts sometimes?'

Paul returned Rory's gaze and shook his head. 'I want her to be happy, Rory,' he said. 'I don't want to depress her. And it's not normal, is it? Thinking like this so many years afterwards.'

'You'd be surprised,' Rory replied. He'd met many people who struggled to cope with loss. People who came to him to speak to those that they missed the most. People who clung to the hope that they could still have some kind of contact with the one's they loved so much.

'My friend Adam,' he said. 'His partner's a bereavement counsellor. If you don't want to talk to Jessie, maybe you should talk to him.'

Paul frowned. 'A counsellor?' he asked. 'Like a shrink?'

'This doesn't have to be a burden,' Rory replied. 'You talk, he listens, that's it. Just talking. Like how we're talking now.'

'Just talking,' Paul repeated.

'I'll give him a call,' Rory said before Paul could refuse. 'He'll see you. If you don't like it then you don't have to go again, but I think he's just what you need.'

Paul nodded. 'I'll give it a go.'

Rory smiled broadly. 'You're not such an ogre, after all, are you mate?'

Paul smiled back. 'I've got a little girl to protect,' he said knowingly.

'Yeah,' Rory put out his cigarette and rested back in the cushions of the sofa. 'And you're really good at it.'

Paul's eyes welled with genuine tears as he nodded proudly. 'She's my world, Rory.'

'I know that,' Rory agreed. 'And you're hers, believe me.'

'What do you want?'

Rory smiled politely. He'd already managed to make a start on Paul and was optimistic that he could make a difference here too. 'I'm very well, thank you,' he replied. 'How are you? You seemed a bit grouchy this morning.'

'What do you want?'

'I think we need to have a chat,' Rory said. 'I thought I should come and clear the air. We seem to have gotten off on the wrong foot.'

'I wonder why that is,' Scott replied with more than a hint of sarcasm.

'Me too,' Rory replied seriously, holding Scott's eyes with his own. 'Now, can I come in or do you want to do this out here?'

'We're not doing this at all,' Scott said firmly. 'Don't you come round here with all your mind reader bollocks and think you can win me over.'

Rory laughed heartily. 'Good one, Scott,' he said as he forced a smile. 'Very good.'

Scott tugged at the bottom of his tee shirt, wishing that his visitor would disappear.

'Jealousy's not an attractive quality,' Rory continued. 'And it's so unnecessary.'

'Go away.'

'Just tell me what I've done. Seriously, Scott, I'm not going anywhere until we've got this sorted out.'

Scott eyed him cautiously and then swung the door open to let him in. Rory went with him to the living room and sat in the armchair by the window. Scott stood by the fireplace, his arms folded over his chest. 'Well?'

'Scott, look,' Rory shrugged off his coat and settled back into the chair. 'I'm not sure what I've done to offend you, but I wanted to try and sort it out.'

'You don't know what you've done to offend me?' Scott asked sharply. He shook his head and tried to laugh but the sound was scratched and strangled. He cleared his throat.

'You know nothing's going on,' Rory replied, wondering if he should remind him for the hundredth time that Jess was his *ex*-girlfriend.

'The only reason I know that is because I know Jess wouldn't do that to me. But you?' He looked at Rory with contempt. 'You don't care. As long as you're getting what you want nothing else matters.'

'You don't know me anywhere near well enough to say that.' Rory's voice remained conversationally level as he imagined driving his fist into Scott's face, his nose exploding and blood raining down over the soft furnishings.

'All of those girls were lying then, were they?' Scott asked. 'Every single one of them?'

'You're clever enough to know that was exaggerated.'

'Save it.' Scott turned his back on his guest and went to the chair on the opposite side of the room, perching on the arm, his arms still folded. 'I've heard your side of the story and it doesn't change anything. Whether or not they knew you were going to have your way with them and then get rid isn't the point. You still used them, Rory. You say that they knew what they were getting into because that's the only way you can justify treating them how you do.'

Rory found himself at a loss for something to say. Even his usually easy wit seemed to have temporarily abandoned him.

'You can sit there and think that they used you as well,' Scott continued. 'Because your ego tells you they wanted it because you're the bloke on the stage, the name everyone knows. Who wouldn't want to sleep with the famous medium? But it's not the girls that use that, Rory, it's you. You know that they'll be flattered that the bloke on the stage wants to spend the night with them. Maybe you get rid of them in the morning before they have the chance to realise that they went to bed with the guy who can fill theatres and woke up with a nobody.'

Rory stood up, suppressing a smile as Scott flinched. 'You're talking bollocks,' Rory said, although he wasn't sure that he believed it.

'You take advantage.' Scott also stood, standing by the side of the chair, knowing that he was close enough to the door to make a quick escape if Rory lost it. 'You take what you want and you get rid. Now, if you were me would you want your girlfriend anywhere near someone like you?'

Rory looked at the floor. Disliking Scott didn't make what he said untrue. Rory thought he'd just never bothered looking at what he was doing from anyone else point of view. 'Probably not,' he replied honestly.

Scott opened his mouth, ready to shout down whatever defensive remark Rory made, and then closed it, smiling at his victory.

If Adam hadn't brought Jessie to him that night, Rory knew he would have gone through the same routine he'd gone through before. Chillingly, if he'd never met Jessie before and Adam had brought her to him, he would have gone through the same routine with her. *Come into my parlour, said the spider to the fly.*

'I'd never do anything to hurt Jessie.'

'Yeah, you would,' Scott said. 'You'd just convince yourself that you hadn't meant to hurt her or that it was her own fault like you did with all the others.'

'Give me a chance to prove you wrong,' Rory replied weakly. This wasn't at all how he'd imagined the conversation in his head. For such a young man Scott was remarkably astute. Bastard.

Scott shook his head. 'No way,' he replied. 'I want you to go away and leave us alone.'

'We're friends,' Rory protested. 'That's all.'

'You must have been so pleased when you found out we'd had an argument and I was going off to Spain.' Scott folded his arms back over his chest. 'Almost a whole week to talk her into bed.'

Rory felt fury building up inside him. 'You can say what you want about me but we both know Jessie's got higher standards.' Still trying to build bridges on her behalf. Just in case she actually did want to get back with this prick.

'If you want to talk about standards, we can.' Scott still refused to sit down. 'The fact of the matter is that you don't have any. You decide you want something and you do whatever you have to to get it. It's not her standards I'm worried about. It's your lack of them.'

'What?' Rory asked incredulously.

'If it's got a pussy and a pulse it's good enough for you,' Scott smirked. 'Everything else is incidental.'

'I turned her down,' Rory said, his eyes glittering maliciously.

'What?'

The look on his face was priceless and, consumed by his anger, Rory could have looked at it all day. 'You heard,' he replied, chewing his lower lip. He enjoyed the few seconds of quiet contemplation.

'You're lying,' Scott said eventually.

Rory shrugged. 'Think what you want.'

'When?'

'Last night,' Rory replied, savouring every second of Scott's discomfort. 'We went out, we even danced. And when we got back she,' he shrugged again.

'She what?' Scott asked. His face was stone but his voice was uncertain.

'She asked if I'd go upstairs with her,' Rory replied simply.

He thought that at that moment he visibly saw the man's heart break and was somewhat impressed when he said, 'You're saying this because you think it'll keep me away from her, aren't you?'

'Ask her,' Rory said, anger conquering respect. 'She wanted me, Scott, and I turned her down.'

He slid into his coat and went to the door. 'Well, you can't say I didn't try to patch things up,' he said with forced light heartedness as he stepped outside.

12

When he got back to the house he struggled to even make eye contact with Jess, as if she'd see the truth in them.

'What's wrong?' she asked.

'I'm going home,' he replied morosely. 'I've got stuff I need to do.'

'Oh.' He was pleased that she sounded disappointed. 'When?'

'Now.'

'Now?' she asked in amazement. 'As in right now this minute? Are you okay?'

He nodded. 'I'm fine. I'll come and see you again soon.'

'Why all of a sudden?' she asked.

Rory shook his head and went upstairs to fetch his things. He could hear her following him. 'Tell me, Rory.'

She closed her bedroom door behind them and leaned against it, blocking his escape.

'I went to see Scott,' he said. 'Try and talk to him.'

'And?'

'And it was a waste of time.' He sat on the bed and sighed. 'When I first met him I thought he was a lot like your dad, the way he wants you all to himself. But you know what? It isn't that at all. Him and your dad are the same but it's not about not wanting to share you, it's about protecting you. None of them want to see you hurt.'

She sat beside him and clamped her hands between her knees. 'What are you on about?'

'Your dad remembers you told him that Scott was going to hurt you,' Rory explained. 'That's why he doesn't want him anywhere near you.'

'Dad always hated Scott.'

368

'Last time I think he was just scared,' Rory said. 'He couldn't get out because of his back. He relied on you for so much and you were the only company he had.'

He started to gather his things together, throwing them into his suitcase as Jess watched helplessly.

'I don't know why you've got to go just because you and Scott don't see eye to eye,' she said. 'Let me talk to him. He's not a bad person, Rory.'

Rory tossed a can of Lynx into the case. 'I know that,' he said. 'And I'm not leaving because he doesn't like me. Just trust me, okay?'

'This doesn't make any sense.'

He bent, zipped up the case and stood up straight, dropping his hands into the pockets of his trousers. 'He's just trying to protect you, Jessie.'

'From what?' she asked. 'From dad?'

'From me.'

She laughed, the sound was similar to the one Scott had made earlier. A strained non laugh. 'You?' she cried. 'That's ridiculous. Look, I know he's convinced that those stories in the papers are right, same as dad.'

'That's because they are,' he almost shouted as his anger returned overwhelmingly. 'Yes, I told them that I wasn't in it for the long haul but it was just a game to me, Jessie. When Donna was in the paper I didn't even recognise her at first. None of them meant anything. I didn't give a shit about any of them. I didn't care if a wife had to go home knowing that she'd cheated on her husband. I didn't care if her husband found out and fucking left her. I got what I wanted and that was all that mattered.'

Jess blanched. 'What the hell did Scott say to you?'

'That given the chance I'd do exactly the same to you.' He was angry now. Angry with himself and angry that she wasn't listening to him.

'How dare he?' she sounded angry too. 'I hope you told him how stupid that sounded.'

369

The phone rang and Rory threw a couple of shirts into his case as she went to answer it. She came back a couple of minutes later, her face red.

'You couldn't wait, could you?' she spat. 'First chance you get you're round there telling him.'

'Local grapevine's still working at the speed of fucking light then,' Rory said more to himself than to her. 'That's why I didn't tell him earlier, is it?' he asked her.

'You only kept quiet because my dad was there.'

'Your dad was awake when we got in.' He was enjoying this almost as much as telling Scott that she'd offered it to him on a plate. 'He heard everything.' She closed her eyes, embarrassed and unsure of herself. 'So no, I didn't mean to tell him.'

'Why did you then?' she asked angrily.

'Because the jumped up little prick was trying to make out I'd drag you into bed just to piss him off.'

'Very mature, Rory,' she replied sarcastically. 'You know what? I'm glad you said no. Because you would have been right. Right about now I really would have been regretting it.'

'Whatever,' he scoffed. 'If I hadn't known you I'd have had you two nights ago. Because it's just a game to me, Jessie, and I always win.'

She looked as if he'd slapped her and that made his fury grow, black and hateful, taking over him. She stood silently in front of him, hating how he looked. Arrogance had curled his lip and it dared her to challenge him. She picked up his case, stalked out of the room and hurled it down the stairs.

'Get out,' she said. 'I don't know what's happened with Scott or what's happened with you and you know what? I don't care.'

They both stood at the top of the stairs with only the dim light that filtered through the frosted glass of the bathroom window betraying the angry tears in Jess's eyes.

'Go,' she ordered, but he stayed where he was.

'If my dad hadn't come into that garage when he did what do you reckon would have happened?'

He took her stunned silence for no more than what he wanted it to be and moved in on her, forcing her to back up against the wall. He leaned into her so close that she could feel his breath on her cheek. 'I could have had you then and I could have you now. You proved that last night.' He spoke directly into her ear and then lifted his head to look at her face. Although he tried to cling to his anger, the fear, the vulnerability and the confusion in her eyes somehow broke the black spell of his ferocity. She had done nothing wrong.

'Oh, for fucks sake,' he breathed. 'What am I doing?'

'Leaving,' Jess replied firmly.

He backed away from her, feeling like a fool. 'Jessie, I'm sorry,' he said. 'It's me I'm mad at, not you.'

'Get out, Rory.'

'I'm an idiot. I shouldn't have taken it out on you. I didn't mean it.'

She shoved him and he stumbled down the first couple of steps, grabbing hold of the banister to keep his balance. He jogged to the bottom of the stairs and then turned to convince her that his temper had just gotten the better of him, but she had already retreated to her room and slammed the door. He considered going back up but knew there was no point. He stood his suitcase up and sat on top of it with his head in his hands.

'I'm sorry,' he called, but there was no response. Paul would be home soon and he'd know something was wrong. She'd tell him what had happened and *Hey Presto!* Well done, Rory, you managed to prove everyone right – you're a useless prick who only cares about himself.

More to the point, Paul would be home soon. Rory definitely didn't want to be the one to have to answer the question *What's up with Jess?* He picked up his case, cast another look upstairs and, being unable to think of anything to say

371

that would make any difference, hauled it out to his car and drove away.

13

'Good morning, Trotters Independent Traders.'

'Hi, Paul, it's Rory again.'

'Rory, how are you?'

'Can I speak to Jessie please?'

Rory heard the crackle of Paul pressing the phone to his chest and a muffled shout upstairs.

'She says she's not in.'

Rory smiled sourly.

'What happened?' Paul asked. 'Why wont she talk to you anymore?'

'Can I please talk to her? It's important, Paul.'

'If she says she doesn't want to talk to you then she doesn't want to talk to you.'

'I really need to speak to her, Paul.'

'Will you please tell me what's happened because she's been walking round with a face like a slapped arse for the last week.'

Rory had worked out the first time Paul answered the phone that she hadn't told him. At the time he'd been pleased, concluding that if she hadn't told Paul what had happened it was because she didn't hate him quite as much as he thought she did. But she still wasn't talking to him.

'Just let her know that I rang,' Rory said. 'I'll try again tomorrow.'

He hung up before Paul could ask any more questions and Paul went back to his chair. He could hear Jess coming slowly down the stairs and she sat on the sofa without a word to him.

'If I have to look at that sour face of yours anymore, Jessica, I think I'm going to have to cut my wrists. Why don't you just ring him?'

'Who?'

'Don't be stupid,' Paul shook his head at her. 'You've been sulking ever since he left.'

'This isn't about Rory,' she argued.

He picked up the remote and turned off the TV. 'Do you want to tell me what it is about?'

'Not really.'

'Jess, I hate seeing you like this, sweetheart,' He went to the sofa and sat beside her. 'There must be something that someone can do to cheer you up.'

'I don't know.'

'I want to help you, Jess,' he said. 'But I can't if I don't know what the matter is.'

She tried to smile at him but she wasn't fooling anyone. Dark circles were beginning to appear beneath her eyes and she looked pale and sickly.

'Please,' he coaxed. 'I just want to try and help you.'

'I don't know if you can,' she replied.

'I can try.'

She sighed. 'I keep making the wrong decisions,' she started. 'Every time I have to make a choice I turn the wrong way and everything ends badly. I haven't got a clue what I'm supposed to be doing and I just don't feel like I can cope with it anymore.'

He put an arm around her shoulders and kissed the top of her head. 'That's what life's about, sweetheart,' he said. 'Nobody knows how things are going to end up. We all just have to do what we think is right and deal with the consequences.'

She smiled to herself resentfully

'What do you think you did wrong?' Paul asked.

'It would probably be quicker to tell you what I think I did right,' Jess replied without humour.

'Well you tell me what it is that you feel bad about and we'll see if we can think of a way to fix it.'

'Do you ever feel like you've wasted your life?' she asked, pulling her knees up to her chest as her mother used to. She was looking at him with huge, sad eyes, as if his answer might destroy her. He considered the question carefully as he took off his glasses and set them down on the table.

'I sometimes think I could have done more than this,' he said. 'You know, tried harder at school, got a job that I actually liked, that kind of thing. But then I might never have met your mum and we wouldn't have had you.'

Jess bit her bottom lip and looked up at the ceiling in the same way Paul did when he was considering a difficult clue.

'Do you feel like you've wasted your life, Jess?' he asked cautiously.

She looked back at him and offered nothing more than a small shrug.

'I think it can be only be a good thing if you do,' he suggested. 'To realise that you could be achieving more at such a young age is better than being my age and wishing you'd done it when you had the chance.'

She stared blankly back at him, as if he'd finished mid sentence. When he said no more she began to chew thoughtfully at her thumbnail.

'You're right, dad,' she nodded. 'I'm young enough to change things. I can make my life whatever I want it to be, can't I?'

He put his arms around her and she lay against his shoulder. 'You can do anything, Jess,' he said. 'Anything you want. But there's one thing you've got to do first, before you even think about doing anything else.'

She looked up at him, frowning. 'What's that?' she asked.

'Stop walking round with a face like you're sucking on a bloody lemon.'

375

14

She had slept well. Worrying about her dad had kept her awake until around two but then she had fallen into a deep and quiet slumber for six hours and now she felt refreshed.

Today was the first day of the rest of her life. She knew that her dad was still drinking, but now she could focus her absolute attention on him. Scott kept ringing and Rory kept ringing. If her dad was in he'd tell them she was out. If he wasn't, she just didn't answer the phone. Right now, she was enjoying her dad's company. It was like old times, just her and her dad against the world.

Today she was going to watch a bit of telly, go to the Co-Op and get something nice for tea, clean the house, then get tea ready for when her dad finished work. They could sit down and watch Fifteen to One together.

She brushed her teeth, dressed and went downstairs, putting on the TV to fill the silence of the house. She made coffee and a couple of slices of toast and sat on the sofa, her legs curled beneath her.

She was watching Trisha when there was a knock at the door. She got up and slid on her slippers. When she opened the door she immediately wished that she hadn't.

'Rory, what are you doing here?'

'You wouldn't take my calls,' he replied.

'That's because I don't want to talk to you.'

He slid inside the house and closed the door, standing with his back to it. 'Well, I want to talk to you and I think you'll want to hear what I've got to say.'

She folded her arms over her chest and walked back to the living room with him behind her. 'Whatever you've got to say, you'd better hurry up. I've got stuff to do.'

'It'll take as long as it takes,' Rory said as she sat down. He took the remote and turned off the television. 'And if you think we're falling out, you can forget it.'

He had her attention. She sat quietly and watched as he sat beside her. 'I really am sorry for the things I said.' He slipped out of his coat and rolled up the sleeves of his black jumper. 'But that's not important. I had, I don't know, like a revelation or something.'

She wanted to tell him that she didn't care but he sounded so excited that curiosity got the better of her. 'A revelation?' she asked.

'About the choices you've been making.'

'I'm not interested, Rory.'

His mouth hung open. 'You've been trying to work it out forever and now I think I've got some answers for you, you don't care?'

'I want to live this life, Rory,' she replied. 'I'm sick of worrying about the last one.'

'There's just no pleasing you, is there?' he mused.

She threw what was left of her toast into her mouth and shrugged. 'I was going to ring you,' she said. 'I just wanted you to stew for a bit.' He didn't look amused and she bit her bottom lip against a smile. 'You acted like a dick,' she continued. 'But the rest of the time you were here I felt better.'

'Better?' he asked. 'Just you wait.' He grinned and rubbed his hands together as if he were about to perform a magic trick. 'I'm going to ask you some questions and I need you to answer them honestly. You can't *think* you know the answer; you've got to *know* that you know the answer. Take all the time that you need but you have to be honest.'

She rolled her eyes impatiently. 'Go on, then. But not too many on sport, please.'

'I'm being serious, Jessie.'

And she could see that he was. 'Okay.'

377

'When you were here before you didn't stay with your grandparents the year I was there, did you?' he asked. 'Is that right?'

She nodded. 'They told me I'd be best to stay away that year because of you being there and everything that was going on. I was going to stay with them at half term in the autumn instead.'

'Okay. Good start.' He licked his lips.

'Would you like a drink?' she asked.

'Please.'

She went to the kitchen and brought back a bottle of coke and two glasses. She poured one and pushed it across the table to him. He drank quickly.

'And this time you *were* there and you needed my help. Even if you wouldn't ask for it,' he added with a crooked smile. 'Now, when you came to see the show, you came because you knew me and you wanted to see me. Am I right?'

'You know you are.'

'But you didn't come last time, you were suppose to be staying with Scott that night.'

'Correct.' She filled her glass and took the bottle back to the kitchen.

'Interesting,' Rory raised an eyebrow. 'Okay, so when you get to the show, hard as you try, nobody'll let you see me in case you're a lunatic.'

She nodded.

'You're absolutely sure that's right?' he asked.

'Yes, Rory, I'm absolutely sure. Is there a point to this?'

'Just bear with me please,' he said. 'It's important that we go over the whole thing and we get it right.'

She sat back down and folded her legs in front of her, looking at him intently. 'Okay. Next question.'

'When Adam came out, he picked you.' He said the last three words slowly. 'You didn't approach him, he came to you and he asked if you would come to my dressing room.'

'You know what, Rory, I should have seen this coming.' She stood up and began to pace the room with her hands on her hips. 'Everything has to be about you, doesn't it?'

'No,' he protested.

'Nothing that happens can mean anything unless it involves you.'

'Jessie,' he said softly. 'Please just go with me for a minute. I promise it'll make sense by the time we've finished.' She reluctantly sat back down. 'Did Adam pick you or did you approach him first?' he asked again.

'He came to me.' Jess chewed absently at her thumb.

'Now, here's where I want you to think,' he instructed. 'Because these questions aren't as simple.'

'Okay.'

'If you hadn't known me, if you hadn't met me at The Unicorn and Adam approached you that night with the same story, would you have come to my dressing room?'

'Yes.'

'I told you to think about it,' Rory said.

'I don't need to,' Jess replied irritably. 'I know what I'd have done.'

'Ok, fine.' He took another drink before he continued; 'Now, when I give you the old sorry I can't get anything line and invite you to eat with me, what do you say?'

'Yes,' she said quietly. 'I would have said yes. Rory, I don't want to play this game anymore.'

'It isn't a game and you need to look at it objectively, Jessie. Please just give me five more minutes.'

He moved closer to her, looking at her intently. Her heart thumped at her ribcage as if it were trying to escape. She didn't like this at all.

'Ok, so we go and have a lovely meal together. The conversation's good because conversation with you is always good, and the wine's nice . . .'

'Get on with it, Rory.'

She could tell that he didn't want to ask the next question any more than she wanted to answer it.

'And when we're done eating, I invite you back to my hotel room.' He took another drink and she did the same. 'Do you come back with me?'

'Yes.' She closed her eyes as she said it.

'Yeah?' Rory asked, the swagger back in his voice.

'I thought we were supposed to be looking at this objectively,' Jess said with a raised eyebrow.

He looked up at her and nodded but remained silent.

'So yes, I'd come back to your hotel room.'

'Okay.'

'Yes,' she said before he could ask. 'Yes, Rory, I would.' She looked at the floor, embarrassed. 'And it would have been for the same reason every other girl did. Because I wouldn't get another chance. Next question.'

Rory was looking at her with amusement. 'Well, that's really good to know, Jessie,' he said. 'But that wasn't what I was going to ask.'

'What?' she asked numbly. Her cheeks flushed and he laughed as she covered her eyes with a hand.

'There are two stories I always tell,' Rory said solemnly. 'At the restaurant I talk about my childhood; how I was different, how it was really difficult for me to fit in. No girl can resist a sob story.'

Jess looked decidedly unimpressed.

'Then at the hotel it's the story about The Unicorn,' he continued. 'My first big success, scary story, Rory the hero. And as soon as I mentioned that pub, you'd mention Jean and Don.'

'Yeah,' she replied. 'You said something about that last week. So what?'

'So Jean's a friend,' he explained. 'She's sent a lot of work my way. I still go up there sometimes just to check the place over, make sure she's alright. No way I'd dare treat her granddaughter badly. I have got a professional reputation to consider, you know.'

Jess shrugged. 'So you'd just send me home then, wouldn't you?'

He looked at her with annoyance. 'Despite what's been written, I'm actually an okay guy, you know.

'So what would you have done?' she challenged, folding her arms over her chest.

'I'd have talked about Jean and Don,' he said. 'I'd have got you another room. And I would have taken you home the next day. What about you?'

'What about me?'

'What would you have done?' he asked. 'What would you have talked about?'

She pondered for a moment. 'I'm not sure,' she replied. 'But I could tell you a lot of stories about nana and granddad Baker.'

'Me too,' Rory smiled.

'You think me and you would have ended up friends anyway, don't you?' she guessed. 'Even if I'd never met you at The Unicorn.'

He nodded. 'That's what I think.'

'It's a lot of guesswork,' she said.

He drained his glass. 'Do you remember when I helped you with your Shakespeare?' he asked. 'Sitting in that car, laughing, joking, just having a nice time before I ruined it? I think that's how it would have been if I'd met you for the first time last week. I didn't go to Anna's party because I wanted to spend the night with a house full of teenagers, Jessie. I went because you wanted me to.'

She could only look blankly back at him, remembering how she hadn't been able to stop staring at him while he talked her through thee's, thou's and thy's.

'I'm not done yet,' Rory said.

She narrowed her eyes at him. 'Go on.'

'How many arguments that you had with your dad or Scott or anyone else last time have you had this time?'

She frowned. 'I can't remember every argument I ever had.'

'Just think about it,' he urged.

She did as he said. She thought about the things she'd argued with her dad about; wanting to stay out late, what she was wearing to go out in, her music being on too loud. She'd only really ever argued with Scott about her dad, but this time she'd done her best to avoid those arguments.

'Very few,' she concluded.

'That's what I thought,' Rory said. 'So how come you still had the argument with Scott just before you came to see me?'

She shrugged. That was one argument she had remembered and one that she had done her best to avoid. And this time it hadn't been about dad, it had been about her going to see Rory and her commitment to their relationship. But it had happened at the same time on the same day.

'Another question for you,' Rory looked at her seriously. 'About this time around. Would you have invited me to come and stay with you if you and Scott hadn't broken up?'

'Not in a million years,' she answered quickly. 'You saw how he was anyway and that's after he broke up with me. I would have asked you to stay around but no way would I have asked you to stay at the house.' She looked at him thoughtfully. 'What would you have done?'

'Stayed at the hotel, I suppose,' he replied. 'Gone home before Scott came back. Given you my number and stayed in touch.'

'Why wouldn't you stay after Scott came back?'

'Girls boyfriend's seem to have a problem with me,' he said. 'Can't imagine why.'

Jess smiled cynically.

382

'But I wasn't supposed to be at the hotel, I was supposed to be here. In this house.'

Jess looked confused. 'Why?'

'Because I needed to see your dad.'

Jess frowned. 'My dad?'

'I can spot a man in mourning at a thousand paces,' he replied. 'It's kind of in my job description. Every single day he misses your mum. After so many years he still can't get his head around it, can't forgive himself for something that was never his fault.'

Jess looked hurt and guilty. How had she missed it? How could Rory spend five minutes with her dad and understand that when she had missed it?

'To cut a long story short,' Rory said. 'I put him in touch with a bereavement counsellor. Since your mum died he's really struggled. He struggles every single day.'

'It was the same last time,' Jess said, her hand falling into her lap. 'After mum died I hardly ever saw him with a drink that wasn't alcoholic. But that was when she died when I was ten. Oh my god, has he got six years less than he did have?'

Rory chose not to answer this question. He didn't know the answer and he didn't want her to distract him from where he'd been driving the conversation. 'So I think that was why we were supposed to meet,' he said. 'It's nothing to do with you and it's nothing to do with me. It's about your dad getting the help that he needs and not ending up in that hospital bed.'

An image of the hospital ran through her mind before she could stop it and she shivered.

'Are you okay?' Rory touched her elbow and she pulled away before she could stop herself. 'Jessie, what's wrong?'

'Nothing.'

'Jessie, what did I say?'

383

'Nothing.' Her face was white. The telephone rang and they both looked at it. Rory looked at Jess and went to answer it.

'Just leave it,' Jess said but Rory already had the receiver halfway to his ear.

'Hello?'

'What the hell are you doing there?'

'Oh, hi, Scott,' he replied cheerily. 'I just came over to see if Jessie was alright.'

'I know exactly why you're there.'

'Why ask then?'

'I can't believe that she let you in.'

'Yes you can,' he replied smugly. He smiled to himself as he imagined Scott getting more and more frustrated at the other end of the line. Jess was still deep in thought. She didn't appear to have heard any of the conversation so far.

'Can I speak to her?'

'Hang on a second, I'll see if she's dressed.'

'Rory, you're not funny. Just get Jessica for me.'

Rory put the phone down on the table and went over to Jess. 'Scott's on the phone for you,' he said.

She looked annoyed. 'I don't want to talk to him.'

'I don't think he's going to take that from me.'

'Tell him I'm in the shower or something. I can't talk to him now.'

'You know what, Jessie, I would love to tell him you're in the shower, but …'

'But nothing, Rory,' he eyes pleaded with him. 'Just please tell him that I can't come to the phone at the moment.'

He nodded and went back to the phone. 'Scott?'

'Oh, for god's sake, Rory, what now?'

'She's in the shower.'

Silence. Rory smiled.

'Very funny,' Scott said uncertainly.

'I swear I asked her to come to the phone and she said she was in the shower.'

'How long have you been there?'

'Long enough,' Rory replied slyly.

'You're disgusting.'

'You're in no position to judge me.'

Jess heard his raised voice and told him to hang up. 'Sorry, Scott, got to go.'

He relished hearing Scott shouting back at him as he hung up. Jess didn't seem to care.

'Did you bring your car?' she asked.

'No, I walked,' he replied with a sarcastic smile. Her face said that she wasn't in the mood. 'Yes, it's outside,' he said. 'Are we going somewhere?'

She grabbed her keys and they left together. 'Just drive,' she said. 'I'll tell you where to go.'

He drove to the edge of the estate and she told him to pull up beside a fence that separated the road from a steep grass verge that led out to fields. He followed her down towards the river, wondering why she had asked him to come here.

She sat in the long grass and he sat beside her. A trolley with only one wheel lay overturned to his left. She was shivering. He put an arm around her shoulders and she rested her head against him.

'Sure you don't want to sit in the car?' he asked. 'It's pretty cold.'

She shook her head.

'Are you okay?'

She nodded against his shoulder.

For saying how urgent this had sounded she seemed very reluctant to talk to him. She sat up, ran a hand over her face and stared out at the water. Rory pulled his coat around him tightly. The wind blew around them, sighing

385

through the grass that winter was approaching.

'So what's so special about this place?' he asked.

'This is where it happened.' The wind almost carried the words away before he heard them and he wished they were sitting in the car with the wind only whistling around them instead of through them.

'Where what happened?'

She hesitated, not really wanting to taste the words on her lips. 'This is where I died, Rory.'

Icy fear licked Rory's spine and he shivered. His forearms bristled but he knew that it had nothing to do with the wind. 'I,' he swallowed hard. The saliva in his mouth seemed to have completely evaporated. 'I didn't think you could remember?' he struggled.

She looked at him with something that resembled guilt and he searched frantically for something to say. He couldn't think of a single thing other than inappropriate questions. How do you sit in the place where you know you're going to die and not let it drive you insane?

'Is that what you want to talk about?' he asked carefully.

'Sort of,' she replied.

'How much do you remember?'

'All of it.' She swept her hair away from her face and turned her body to face him rather than the water. 'How, why, where and when.' She said the last word with a hint of sadness but not fear. 'When I first remembered I avoided coming here like the plague. It was like if I came here I'd be taken straight away.'

'Well, you seem to be over that now.'

She nodded slowly. 'I come here to think.'

Rory was beginning to consider the possibility that she was insane, that this last revelation had finally tipped her over the edge into cuckoo county where everyone wore pretty white coats that tied at the back.

'You obviously brought me down here for a reason,' he said. 'Talk to me, Jessie.'

'Rory, if you came across someone who was obviously distressed and really needed help but didn't ask you for it, what would you do?' She put up a hand. 'Actually, forget it, you don't need to answer that. I know exactly what you'd do because I watched you do it.'

Yep, Rory thought. *She's lost it.*

'Now if you had to help this person but you didn't know her and it was obvious that she was really distraught, what would you do?'

Rory thought hard. 'I'd try to find out what was up?' he guessed.

'Her dad just died.'

Rory felt as if his heart had stopped in his chest.

'And he left her all on her own. She's lost and she's scared and she misses him so much.'

'I'd take her to see my good friend the bereavement counsellor.' His voice sounded as if it was coming from a long way away, just blown through their conversation on the wind.

'Imagine that,' Jess produced a thin smile. 'The person you care most about in the whole world dies and you just happen to walk into a psychic medium and a bereavement counsellor. It sounds like the start of a bad joke.'

Rory looked puzzled. 'Are you saying that I was there when your dad died?'

'You were there when I went to collect the death certificate,' she explained. 'I came out of the hospital and broke down. You helped Scott get me to the car.'

'You're sure about this?'

'You carried me, Rory, and I felt so safe when you were holding me. I didn't want to let you go.' A single tear slid down her cheek. 'I don't know why I was supposed to meet you, Rory, and you know what? I like not knowing. I like that I can't see what's going to happen. But I can't see why Adam would have chosen me that night or why you'd be at the hospital that day. I mean, Adam doing his residential there. Maybe he'll be there for a long time, I don't know, but for you to be in the right place at exactly the right time?'

Her eyes were bright now. 'After I met you last week I've been coming here less and less,' she said. 'It's like I didn't need to. I came here to think about Scott and dad and Dean, to consider the day when I came here before. Since you came back I didn't want to think about all that stuff. Instead of thinking about my death all the time I felt like I wanted to enjoy my life.'

'That can only be a good thing.'

'You did that, Rory,' she said. 'I've always felt confused and isolated and cheated by the way things happened. You made me stop thinking about that and consider what it was that I wanted out of my life. Instead of worrying about other people and focusing all my attention on Scott, you made me think about me. You made me actually enjoy being me.'

He smiled. They looked at each other for a long moment. The wind was relentless. Rory took her cold hands and she gripped his tightly in return.

'I need to sort my head out,' she said. 'I need to get as far away from here as I can and I need to think.'

'There's a few miles between here and Leeds,' Rory suggested. 'I've got a spare room and it's yours for as long as you want it.'

15

It was a modest detached house with a small front lawn. As Rory approached the door Russ came out onto the porch.

'Hi, dad,' Rory called over the sound of the wind. It was really picking up. The sky was the colour of dull metal and rain had spattered the car sporadically throughout their journey.

Russ turned and smiled. 'You caught me,' he said. 'I needed your toolkit but I couldn't get into your shed.'

'No,' Rory said. 'I keep it locked so people like you can't steal my toolkit.'

Russ laughed. 'Fair play.'

'You remember Jessie?' Rory put a protective hand on her shoulder.

Russ nodded. 'How are you, love?'

'Okay, thanks,' Jess replied.

'Rory said you'd been having some problems.' She looked at the floor. 'I'll give you some advice,' Russ said, noticing her embarrassment. 'Don't regret a thing. You never know if it's the stuff you're regretting that actually led you to something better.'

Rory squeezed her shoulder gently. 'Oh wise and aged prophet,' he said comically.

'Less of the aged,' Russ called as they went inside and Rory fetched his toolkit from the shed at the back.

'Make yourself at home, Jess,' Rory said.

'Am I okay to have a quick shower?'

'Upstairs, first door you get to.'

She nodded and disappeared into the house.

'How is she?' Russ asked as they went to his car.

'She's been better,' Rory replied. 'But she's been a lot worse too.'

'What does her boyfriend think about her coming here?'

Rory looked over his shoulder, conscious that Jess could hear them easily, and went to the car with Russ. 'She didn't go back to him,' he said. 'Looks like they're over for good.'

'Give it time,' Russ advised.

'Give what time?' Rory asked as he put the toolkit in the boot.

'Her,' Russ nodded in the direction of the house.

Rory slammed the boot and stood with his hands on his hips, his face flushed. 'How many times do I have to tell you not to pull all that psychic shit on me?' he asked.

Russ opened the driver's side door. 'You don't have to be psychic, Rory,' he replied. 'You can spot it a mile off. No wonder her other half was worried about her spending time with you. Can I give you some advice?'

'Keep her away from sunlight and water and don't feed her after midnight, right?'

Russ ignored his son's grin. 'I know that what we do makes us emotionally sensitive, Rory,' Russ said. 'We wouldn't be able to do our job if we weren't. But I saw how messed up you were after Jess left The Unicorn. How you wouldn't put your number in that birthday card because you were scared she either wouldn't remember who you were or wouldn't ring you. It's not just her that'll get hurt if you do something daft.'

'Shut up, dad,' Rory said. 'I'll speak to you later.'

Russ submitted to his son's goodbye and Rory glanced at the sky again as he went back inside. The air felt thick and heavy and he wondered if there would be a storm.

He turned on the TV, seeing but not watching, thinking of nothing in particular until she came downstairs wrapped in a white towel. Her hair hung over her shoulders, beginning to wave as it dried. As she sat beside him his eyes were drawn to the vulnerable line of her neck as it curved into her shoulder. He lifted his arm to put it around her and then dropped it back into his lap. Beneath the towel she was naked. He couldn't touch her when she was almost naked, he wouldn't be able to think about anything else, was finding it hard enough as it was. He wished she'd dressed before she came down.

'Do you want a coffee or anything?' he asked.

She shook her head and stared at the television. 'What are you watching?'

He didn't know. Whatever it was had come on after the news that he hadn't been watching. He shrugged. 'Why don't you go and put your jim jams on and I'll make us some supper?' he suggested.

'Okay.' She stood up and pulled the towel tightly around her drying body. His eyes were sliding over her legs before he could stop himself. He looked away quickly as she glanced back at him over her shoulder. 'Thank you for letting me stay.'

He shook his head at her. 'You don't need to thank me,' he said. 'Now go and get some clothes on before you get a cold.'

He went to the kitchen and filled the kettle, putting three heaped teaspoons of chocolate powder into each mug as it came to the boil. In the fridge there were six teacakes in an unopened cellophane packet between a bottle of Sprite and the remains of a jam sponge that should have been thrown out a couple of days ago. He took the teacakes, which were thankfully still in date, and the sponge from the fridge.

As he tossed the sponge cake into the bin he heard Jess coming back down the stairs and cut the teacakes in half and put them under the grill.

'Need any help?' she asked as she came into the kitchen behind him.

He shook his head. 'Go and sit down. I'll bring it through.'

She went obediently through to the living room and curled up on the sofa, finger combing her hair before Rory joined her. Two steaming mugs of hot chocolate and a plate piled with the teacakes were laid on a large wooden tray. He set it down on the table.

'Are you cold?' he asked as she took a teacake from the tray. She shook her

391

head. 'How long are you going to stay for?'

She swallowed her food and wrapped her hands around her mug. 'Trying to get rid of me already?' she asked.

'No,' he replied. He liked having her all to himself. He just didn't know how long they could remain here, away from Filton and all that went with it, without him doing something stupid. 'You're welcome to stay as long as you like, you know that.'

He took half a teacake, eating thoughtfully as he stared out of the window. Jess took a sip of hot chocolate and took another teacake for herself.

They ate in silence, watching TV as night fell and the wind picked up, howling around the eaves of the house. Once the teacakes and the drinks were finished Rory piled everything back onto the tray and took it away. Jess felt full and warm and when Rory came back to sit with her she lay against him comfortably, her head on his thigh, her eyes on the white ceiling rose that framed a simple glass light fitting. It flashed blue as the light from the TV hit it. She allowed her heavy eyelids to close.

'If I fall asleep just wake me up if I start snoring,' she said as Rory automatically draped an arm over her middle.

'I'll warn you now, if you start dribbling on me you're going on the floor,' he replied. 'I only got these trousers last week.'

She opened her eyes as she laughed. Rory was looking at the TV, his face the same blue as the ceiling rose in the glare of the television. 'We've been here before,' she said softly.

Rory smiled. 'You've been everywhere before.'

'This is different.'

'Just me and you and the dark,' he said knowingly, not daring to look at her.

'Scott told my dad that I'd be here within a week,' Jess said. 'He'd convinced himself I was leaving him for you.'

'If that's what helps him sleep at night,' Rory said passively.

'But I am here.' She looked at him with dark eyes, studying him. 'And I do wish we'd had another thirty seconds in that car together.'

Something caught in his throat and an invisible, silent vacuum sucked all the moisture from his mouth. This was how he'd felt then, when they'd been in the car. He cleared his throat.

'Ten would have been enough,' he joked. 'Those stories you read were exaggerated.'

She laughed again and he bounced the leg beneath her head. 'Come on,' he said. 'Get yourself to bed before you fall asleep.'

She stretched as she sat up and Rory couldn't help but look as the tee shirt she was wearing rode up high, exposing her waist. What was she trying to do to him? He looked quickly back at the TV as her arms fell to her sides and she got up, the tee shirt falling back down to the waistband of her shorts.

'Goodnight, Rory,' she said.

'Night,' he replied as he watched her leave the room.

He waited twenty minutes before he turned off the TV and went to his room quietly, knowing that sleep would not come easily with her in the next room.

She heard him come up and lay on her side, one hand beneath the pillow, the duvet pulled up to her chin, staring at the wall that separated them until she fell asleep.

It was three o clock when a loud crack of thunder roused her. She gasped herself awake, her eyes wide, and turned over to look at the window. A flash of lightning glowed through the curtains and then it was gone. She could hear rain pouring over the house as she climbed out of the bed and peered outside. The streets were dark and empty and rain hammered the cars and dripped from the leaves of the trees that separated Rory's garden from his neighbours. Their branches waved and rocked in the wind.

Thunder rumbled ominously as she looked over the exposed street, feeling cosy here in her room, far enough away to be safe but close enough to touch it if she really wanted to.

And once upon a time she had touched the storm.

On the nineteenth of August next year a hard summer storm would send picnickers running back to their cars while she and Scott took shelter beneath the trees by the lake.

It was so strange, having that memory and knowing that it would never belong to Scott. Not any more. But that was okay because she knew that it wouldn't have been the same this time anyway. The spontaneity was gone, for her at least, and with it the magic had died as well. She liked the memory but she wasn't sad that that day would be completely different this time around.

Thunder cracked overhead and a moment later lightning filled the room like the flash of a camera. She wanted to be out there, touching the storm, feeling natures power hard against her, impartial to her freezing limbs. She quickly padded downstairs and opened the front door, looking out past the porch at the sodden grass. She stepped into the porch and held out her arm, feeling the rain cold against her skin, bouncing in her palm, dripping from her fingertips.

Rory sat up as he heard movement in the next room. His curtains were open and he'd been watching the momentum of the storm build since he'd come to bed. The sound of the rain comforted him. He liked to be inside, cosy and warm while he listened to the music of the storm outside. It had been a long and slow crescendo as the wind picked up, dragging music from the house, the trees and whatever else it clawed its way through. Rain now hammered hard against the window, thunder growled and lightning flashed, a symphony of the elements.

He heard her bedroom door open and looked stupidly at his own door handle. Did he seriously expect her to just wander into his room at three in the morning and climb into his bed? And what would he have done if she had? He didn't know and was grateful that the door handle remained still. She must have gone to fetch a glass of water or something.

He listened, straining against the sounds outside, as she went downstairs. He sat bolt upright as he heard the front door open. Was she leaving? Had she decided that this had been a bad idea and called a cab to come and fetch her in the middle of the night so that she could just sneak back home without having to explain why? He threw off the duvet and pulled on a pair of boxer shorts as he went to the landing. He could feel cold air floating up from downstairs. The front door was still open. He ran down the stairs, the skin on his arms and legs feeling tight and prickly as the cold hit them, snatching away their bed warmth.

He walked around the open door and his mouth fell open. She stood in the garden, framed by the archway of the porch, her dark grey tee shirt and shorts saturated and clinging to he body, her arms outstretched, her dripping hair pulled mercilessly by the wind. Her face was upturned, her eyes closed as she revolved slowly, catching the rain in her hands, smiling serenely as if she couldn't feel the cold. Rory smiled to himself and leaned against the wall. She looked beautiful.

'What the hell are you doing?' he asked.

Her chin dropped and her arms fell to her sides as she opened her eyes to look at him.

'It's like you can feel the electricity in the air,' she called over the noise.

Lightning flashed, illuminating Rory's face eerily as he looked at her.

'You've lost the plot,' he said. 'It's freezing.' As if in response the wind cried out noisily.

She laughed, crossing the garden and taking his hands, dragging him out onto the grass. He gasped as the rain began to pound his bare flesh like bullets and she laughed again, spinning him around, her wet hands sliding over his until they lost their grip and Rory stumbled, almost falling before he regained his balance. Jess doubled over, her laughter almost hysterical now as she watched his feet slide in the grass.

'Come inside,' he said, trying to sound serious but unable to suppress a

395

smile. She shook her head and took a step away from him as if she was challenging him to make her. Rain dripped from her chin, her eyes gleamed in the darkness and she waited, watching him intently. Thunder cracked loudly right overhead and as her eyes flew momentarily to the sky he ran at her. She saw him coming but it was too late. As she turned to run he grabbed her around her middle. She giggled as her feet left the floor and he carried her onto the porch, setting her down as soon as they were out of the rain but keeping hold of her in case she tried to run again. She turned quickly as if she might bolt and he stood up against her, pushing her back against the wall of the archway. And then he was kissing her, pulling her hips towards his as their wet mouths pressed together and lightning flashed unnoticed. His bare arms wrapped around her soaking tee shirt as her fingers tangled in his hair and her body pressed tight against his.

She looked at him apprehensively as his lips left hers, her head resting back against the wall. He kissed her tenderly and then took her hand in his. They went inside and he closed the door behind them, locking it against the storm.

She had started to shiver and her breath was sharp and shaking as he took her to his room, holding her again as soon as they were inside, kissing her lips, her cheeks, her throat, pulling her soaked tee shirt over her head and pressing his damp flesh against hers.

They could still hear the tempest outside as they stumbled over each other to the bed, peeling off their clothes and lying in a tangle of warming limbs and wet hair. Soon the thunder that rolled over the house began to sound distant and the flares of lightning blazed less frequently. The storm was beginning to wane and only the steady patter of the rain against the windows was constant.

16

She opened her eyes. The room was wrong. She didn't know where she was. Where the window should be there was a wall with a door at the far end.

Rory.

She smiled to herself as she remembered where she was and then turned her head to see Rory looking at her over the pillows.

'What are you looking at?' she asked with a sleepy smile.

'You,' he replied.

'Weirdo.'

She turned onto her side and his arm fell over her waist, pulling her against him as he planted a soft kiss on her lips. 'Never go back,' he said.

She held him, enjoying his warm body against hers, and stroked his spine with her fingertips.

'I love you, Jessie,' he said.

She ran a hand through his hair and then rested her palm beneath his jaw. 'I love you too,' she said.

'We don't have to mention it to you dad just yet though, do we?'

Jess giggled and he rolled over, pinning her to the bed, his face hanging over hers. 'I'm never letting you out of this bed,' he said. He kissed her slowly and they settled against each other. As her legs slid invitingly over his hips the doorbell rang and Rory moaned his discontent.

'We'll ignore it,' he said.

'What if it's important?' Jess asked.

'Define important.'

The mobile on the bedside table began to ring and Rory pulled the duvet over their heads, running his hands over her thighs as his lips brushed her shoulder.

'Rory?' A voice called through the letterbox. There was knocking at the door, his mobile continued to ring.

Rory lifted up his head, the duvet hanging over his ears, and groaned. 'It's Adam,' he said, grabbing at his mobile as he nuzzled against her. 'What?' he snapped into the phone. 'Oh, right, yeah, give me a sec I'll come down.'

He apologised, climbed out of the bed and slid into a pair of shorts. Jess found a clean tee shirt and a pair of jogging trousers in his wardrobe and pulled them on. 'I'll make us some breakfast,' she said.

'Grab the door, will you?' he asked as he pulled on a pair of socks. 'Sooner we let him in the sooner he'll piss off and leave us in peace.'

She pulled at the drawstring of the trousers as she went downstairs and opened the door. Adam's cheeks flushed the moment he saw her.

'Hi,' he said, obviously flustered. 'Erm, it's, erm . . .'

'Jess,' she finished for him.

'Yeah, yeah, of course. Good to see you again, Jess.'

'Good to see you too, Adam,' she replied, making a point of emphasising the fact that she could remember his name.

'Adam,' Rory said as he jogged downstairs.

Jess smirked as relief visibly washed over Adam.

'I brought your chair,' Adam said, throwing a thumb over his shoulder at the van parked by the kerb. The back doors stood open.

'Excellent.'

When Rory only stood in the doorway, a hand falling gently against Jess's back, Adam rolled his eyes. 'Don't worry, Rory, we'll bring it in for you.'

He jogged over to the van as Jess went back to the kitchen to make toast. Rory watched with amusement as Adam and his partner struggled to get the heavy chair out of the van and squeeze it through the narrow front doorway. 'Jess's just making breakfast,' he explained. 'You can have a slice of toast each if you want.'

Adam set the chair down heavily in the hall. 'Explain,' he ordered in a hissed whisper.

'What?' Rory asked.

'The girl,' Adam said. 'What's she doing here?'

Rory grinned. 'Oh yeah,' he said as if she'd completely slipped his mind. 'Seems I owe you a beer or two, buddy.'

'Why?' Adam asked.

'Because the girl, the girl in my kitchen, the girl you found for me, Adam, that's Jessica Morgan.'

'Jessica . . .' Adam's eyes widened as the name finally registered. 'What? That's her?' It took a quiet moment for this to sink in. It had been a while since Rory had mentioned her. 'She never said, and why the hell didn't you tell me?' He frowned and put his hands on his hips. 'Wow, Rory, what were the chances of that happening?'

Rory's grin widened. 'Chance?' he asked. 'Nothing to do with chance, my friend. It was always going to be her.'

Rory led the pair of them into the kitchen as Jess put slices of buttered toast onto a plate. They helped themselves while she found mugs and lined them up on the worktop. She turned to ask everyone what they wanted and a lump rose in her throat, making speech impossible.

Jay Long.

She could only stare at Connie's brother as he looked back at her curiously.

'Jessie?' Rory asked.

She blinked hard. 'I'm, I'm going to go and get dressed,' she said, leaving the kitchen and running to her room. She sat on the edge of the bed, numb with surprise. She hadn't met Rory at The Unicorn so she'd been invited to the gig. She hadn't gone to the gig so he'd been outside the hospital. And they were the events she knew about. How many times had Rory been there, waiting for her to come to him, waiting to save her dad or, when that was impossible, to save her?

399

Rory opened the door and sat beside her. 'What's up?' he asked.

'That's Adam's partner?' she asked. 'The bereavement counsellor?'

Rory nodded. 'The one who's going to help your dad.'

'It's Jay,' Jess said. 'That's Connie's brother, Rory.'

She suddenly flung her arms around him and kissed him deeply. When it had been too late to save her dad Rory hadn't just shown up to arrange counselling to help her through her grief, he'd been there to reunite her with an old friend, to provide a support network that meant she would never have to be alone, that she could leave Scott Jordan and the house she had shared with her dad behind her and still be okay.

Unwittingly, Rory had waited and waited for her the last time and when she had finally shown up she had let him go. She remembered wanting to call him back, feeling so safe in his arms, and she wanted to say that she was sorry for ignoring him last time, as if what had happened – her dad's death, her own suicide – had been her fault because she hadn't sought him out.

She couldn't be certain, nothing in life was ever that, apart from death and taxes, her dad would say. But she had to tell him.

She kissed him once more and then ran her hands through his shaggy hair. 'Rory,' she said with a broad smile. 'I think you might have saved our lives.'

Epilogue

Jess looked up at the house as Rory stopped the car. It looked different somehow. Usually just the sight of the house would make her smile. But today it looked different, darkly inviting, ready to eat her up as soon as she stepped inside. It seemed to be staring back at her, hypnotising her, beckoning her towards it with today's black secret.

She tore her eyes away from it, looking down at her lap. She didn't want to look at the house and she would have given anything not to have to go inside. Not today. She wanted to sleep today away and wake up tomorrow, when whatever was to come would be over and she would know.

'Jessie?'

She looked up, startled. 'Sorry.'

'You okay?' Rory asked.

'I'm fine,' she lied. 'Just tired.'

'You've been tired for weeks,' he replied. 'Probably because you're hardly sleeping at night.'

She looked back at her lap but didn't say anything.

'Come on then,' Rory took off his seatbelt. 'Let's go and see how he is.'

'No.' She took hold of his arm, her grip unnervingly strong for how drained she looked. 'I need to see him by myself.'

'Oh,' he replied. 'How long are you going to be?'

She looked at the clock on the dashboard. If it was going to happen, it would happen sometime between one thirty and two. 'A couple of hours.'

'Hours?' he asked. 'I can't just sit here and wait for you for two hours.'

'Go back home then,' she snapped.

'Jessie, please tell me what the matter is.'

She could hear the desperation in his voice and her eyes softened. 'Go and get yourself some dinner,' she said. 'I'll ring you.'

401

'What's going on, Jessie?'

She shook her head. 'Nothing,' she said. 'I'll meet you in a bit.'

'Why can't I come with you?'

'Please stop asking me questions, Rory,' she replied wearily. 'I just need a couple of hours with dad, that's all.'

He suddenly felt nauseous and goose bumps broke out over his arms. His mouth was dry and he had an awful feeling that he was going to throw up.

'It's today, isn't it?' She didn't reply. 'When should I come back?' he asked.

'I'll ring you,' she replied as she kissed his cheek. 'Thank you.'

He watched her go to the door and disappear inside the house, then he put the radio on and cranked up the volume as he headed out of the estate, his blood still coursing coldly through his body. She'd never told him how soon after her dad died that she'd made that final trip to the river, but he knew it was only a matter of days. He drove to the fish and chip shop around the corner from the school as if in a trance, ordered his food through numb lips, and turned to leave. He walked straight into the man behind him, overturning his tray of chips and gravy and spilling it down his front.

'I'm sorry,' he offered dumbly.

Scott looked down at his shirt and then glared at Rory. 'I'll get you some more chips,' Rory said.

'No,' Scott said loudly. 'Forget it, I'll get them myself.'

Rory followed him back to the counter as a young girl rushed at the mess with a dustpan and brush.

'I didn't mean to do it,' he insisted.

Scott looked at him again and Rory felt small and uncomfortable. 'Thought I'd seen the back of you a long time ago.'

'One fifty, please.'

Rory quickly passed her a five pound note as Scott looked at his food.

'Come on,' Rory said. 'Let me give you a lift home. You can't walk around looking like that.'

'I'm fine.'

'You look like a right idiot.'

'I said I'm fine.'

'Fine.'

Rory went back to his car and watched as Scott started to walk slowly towards home. He paused at the corner of the short street and turned back to look at Rory.

'How is she?' he asked.

'Let me give you a lift home and I'll tell you,' Rory called back.

Scott smiled. 'That means she's fine.'

Rory nodded. 'Yeah,' he agreed. 'She's fine. She's working with Jay Long, I don't know if you ever knew him, Connie Long's brother?'

'Yeah, Connie was in my year at school.'

Rory nodded. 'Jess's a bereavement counsellor. She helps people to deal with grief. She's really good at it.'

'I'm glad she's doing well.'

Scott turned to leave and Rory spoke quickly, hating the idea of sitting alone in the car until Jess called. It was like waiting for a jury to return with a verdict. *Death sentence or life sentence?* he thought grimly. 'Paul's not too good though.' He didn't know if that was right or not. He was hoping he was well off the mark and that Paul would be fine, meaning of course, that Jessie would be fine. Maybe.

'No?' Despite their turbulent relationship, Scott sounded genuinely concerned.

Rory shook his head. 'Don't really know what it is. Jessie's worried about him though.'

'Is she there now?' Scott was looking in the direction of her house.

'Yeah,' Rory replied. 'But she wants some time on her own with him. Let me take you home,' he offered again.

Scott walked back to Rory's car and they both got in. Scott immediately looked at the small photograph hanging from the rear view mirror. It had been taken in Paris last year. Jess was wearing the dress he had brought her for her birthday last year. Their arms were around each other. They were both smiling. Scott saw that Rory had caught him looking and quickly stuffed a plastic forkful of chips into his mouth.

'How's Joanne?' Rory asked.

'Okay,' Scott mumbled through his food. 'We got married last summer.'

'I heard. Never got my invite though.'

Scott looked up to see if Rory was being serious. He wasn't.

'You're happy?'

'Why?' Scott asked. 'Do you want to try stealing her away from me now?'

He started to eat again and Rory decided to stay quiet. He turned onto Dukes Court and stopped outside the house.

'Thanks,' Scott said.

'No problem.'

'I knew it was only a matter of time before she left me for you,' Scott said as he took off his seatbelt.

'You didn't know that.'

Scott looked at him sharply. 'Everyone knew that,' he replied.

Rory was quiet again.

'Her eyes lit up whenever she saw you,' Scott continued. 'And you were exactly the same. When she loved you she adored you and when she fell out with you still adored you.'

'When she fell out with me she hated me,' Rory argued but Scott shook his head.

'You couldn't see it,' he said. 'You couldn't see it because you weren't the one that was losing her.'

Rory was starting to feel sorry for him. He hadn't seen it. He hadn't been trying to steal Jessie away, not on purpose anyway. 'So you just settled for Joanne?' he asked.

'No,' Scott said. 'I do love Joanne. I love her to death. Just in a different way to how I loved Jess.'

Rory's mind went back to Jess. Jess and the clock that was ticking precious seconds away far too quickly. The full force of what was happening while he sat here and allowed that invaluable time to slide away hit him full force and he felt sick to the stomach.

'Rory?' Scott sounded concerned but his voice seemed to be coming from very far away. 'Rory, are you alright?'

Rory nodded. He was Rory Hamilton, of course he was alright.

'Are you sure?'

'Of course I'm sure,' he replied. 'Why?'

Scott offered a paper napkin that he had taken from the chip shop. 'You're crying, Rory.'

'It was just before I started school,' Jess said. 'You remember, don't you?'

Paul nodded and smiled. 'That was the last time I ever took your mum to the seaside.'

'Mum told you to shut up singing all the way,' Jess burst into hysterics. 'You didn't even know most of the songs, you were just making them up. You drove her insane.'

Paul started to laugh. 'I saw her smiling though,' he said. 'She thought some of the words I made up were funny.'

'And do you remember those shoes?' Jess asked. 'Oh my god, they killed my feet but I daren't tell you because I thought mum was going to shout.'

Paul stopped laughing and frowned. 'What shoes?'

'The ones we got from the shop on the front,' Jess said. 'The ones that ended up in the sea and I went in after them and you had to come and rescue me.'

Paul thought about it for a minute and then shook his head. 'I don't remember that.'

As she realised her mistake and tried desperately to think of something to say that would save her from the situation, he looked at her curiously.

'You said you didn't want the shoes,' he said. 'Because when you looked at them you felt like you were drowning.'

It was an elementary mistake. She'd been avoiding mistakes like this her whole life and now, when she probably only had days to go, she'd messed up. But that wasn't the scary part. The scary part was that she had forgotten this time. She had forgotten that she'd told him that she didn't want to shoes. She was forgetting things that had happened this time but could still remember last time? What was happening?

'That was when you used to have the dreams,' Paul continued. 'When you knew things that were going to happen.'

'I must have gotten it mixed up,' she tried.

'Mixed up with something that never happened?' he asked.

'I don't know,' she said. 'Maybe I dreamt it.'

'Tell me the truth, Jess.'

He sounded scared and that made her feel scared.

'Jessica?' his voice was stern, like it used to be when he was telling her off for not finishing her homework on time or staying out too late. Had that happened this time or last time? She didn't know anymore. She sighed and looked at him. He looked ill. Or was that just her mind playing tricks on her?

'It didn't go away,' she admitted.

Paul's eyes welled with tears that immediately spilled over his cheeks.

'Please don't cry,' she said, scared that it would set her off.

'Why didn't you tell me?' he asked.

'Because I can handle it,' she replied. 'It turned you into a nervous wreck and mum ...'

She trailed off and he looked up sharply. 'Don't you ever blame yourself for what happened to your mother,' he said.

'I'm sorry I lied to you, dad,' she said. 'But please, believe that I did it for the right reasons.'

'Did you,' he hesitated, swallowed hard, and went on cautiously, 'did you ever work out what it was?'

'Rory did,' she replied softly, knowing that he wouldn't like the answer. 'When I was at gran's.'

'After they told him to keep away from you.' Paul's temper began to rise.

'Dad, it was happening anyway.' She raised her voice in an effort to silence his rage for long enough to let her explain. 'I never stopped seeing that stuff but until I met Rory I hadn't got a clue what it was. I never knew what people were going to do at The Unicorn but I knew what was happening back here all of the time. Rory knew there was something going on and he said that he could help me.'

'I told them to keep him away from you,' he repeated.

'And they did,' she replied. 'We were sneaking around behind their backs and meeting up when they went out. They did everything they could.' She ran a shaking hand through her hair. 'Dad, that's not the point.' Her heart was beating too quickly and her breathing was shallow. 'Please, if you want to know, then just listen.'

He wiped his eyes and rested back in his chair. She took a deep breath and went on. 'We were talking about . . .'

Alcoholic liver disease.

'About something, and it triggered something inside me. Do you remember the day we went to the river?' she asked. 'The day that mum,' she looked at the floor, 'that mum died?'

Paul nodded. 'Of course I do.'

407

She looked up at him again. The red rims of his eyes looked like rings of blood set in his pale face. 'It was like that. I could feel myself losing control, like I was passing out. Rory got me to a safe place and he looked after me until I woke up.' A small smile played with the corners of her mouth and Paul saw the child she had been. The little girl with the old, haunted eyes. 'And I just remembered.'

'Remembered what?' he asked.

'Everything. I remembered everything.' She looked him in the eyes and bit her bottom lip before she confessed. 'I lived this life before.'

He looked puzzled and she knew that this was only the beginning. But time was running out and she didn't want to spend today talking about this. 'It's like I was reincarnated as myself, into exactly the same life I'd just left.'

'That doesn't make any sense,' Paul said.

She shrugged. 'That's what happened.'

'And Rory knows about this?'

She nodded. 'He was there when I remembered, I had to tell someone.'

'But you couldn't tell me?'

'Please don't take this personally, dad,' she said wearily. 'I wanted to be normal. I wanted to have a normal life. Nobody knew apart from Rory.'

She glanced at the clock and felt a sense of pending release begin to well up inside her. It was nearly all over. Whether they lived or died she was near the end of this nightmare.

'So the things you knew,' Paul said. 'It was because you'd done it all before?'

'Yes,' she replied quietly.

'Dean?'

'Yes.' Deep sadness overwhelmed her and she began to cry. 'I tried to stop it, dad, I promise. But I couldn't.'

'That's why you took it so hard.' He took her into his arms and rocked her gently back and forth. 'I can't even imagine what that must have been like.'

'It doesn't matter anymore,' she said.

Paul stopped rocking her and she sat up straight, looking at him sadly.

Daddy was dying in a hospital bed and a lady was sitting with him.

She was a lady now. Little Jess was all grown up and ready to face that recurring dream from her childhood.

'I assume there's a hospital bed waiting for me somewhere?' he asked. 'That's why you're here today, isn't it?'

'What?' she asked. He'd been doing well. She hadn't seen him with a drink in years. Maybe Rory had managed to save him.

And maybe when your time's up, your time's up.

She couldn't tell him. No way could she tell him the truth. 'No. No, I can't even believe that you remember that.'

'If not today then when?' He looked so frightened and she wondered if she was going to trigger a heart attack or something. How ironic that would be.

'That's years away,' she lied. 'And nothing's set in stone. Nothing can't be changed.'

'Like Dean?'

'Like mum,' she said. 'Mum wasn't supposed to die then and not like that.'

Paul held her again, feeling relief saturate him and she held him back. She cried against his chest and he held her, crying with her as the clock struck two.

'I love you, daddy,' she whispered.